Praise for #1 _New York_ [...]
Linda Lael Miller

"Miller is one of the finest American writers
in the genre."
—_RT Book Reviews_

"Only Linda Lael Miller can write the kind of
romance that melts your heart and makes you want
to shout Yippee ki-yay!"
—_Single Titles_ on _Creed's Honor_

"Miller tugs at the heartstrings as few authors can."
—_Publishers Weekly_

**Praise for bestselling author
Cathy McDavid**

"Here is a story that has not only a happy ending,
but also has entertaining characters, an engaging
plot and a romance that makes one smile."
—_The Romance Reader_ on _His Only Wife_

"The spiritual and emotional healing that evolves
naturally from McDavid's beautifully written story
touches on the fears and realities of homecoming
veterans and the families they leave behind, as it
neatly dovetails with a charming romance."
—_RT Book Reviews_ on _Her Cowboy's Christmas Wish_

LINDA LAEL MILLER

The daughter of a town marshal, Linda Lael Miller is a #1 *New York Times* and *USA TODAY* bestselling author of more than one hundred historical and contemporary novels, most of which reflect her love of the West. Raised in Northport, Washington, the self-confessed barn goddess now lives in Spokane, Washington. Linda recently hit a career high at #1 on the *New York Times* bestseller list with all three of her *Creed Cowboys* books, *A Creed in Stone Creek*, *Creed's Honor* and *The Creed Legacy*.

Linda has come a long way since leaving Washington to experience the world. "But growing up in that time and place has served me well," she allows. "And I'm happy to be back home." Dedicated to helping others, Linda personally finances her Linda Lael Miller Scholarships for Women, which she awards to those seeking to improve their lot in life through education. More information about Linda and her novels is available at www.lindalaelmiller.com. She also loves to hear from readers by mail at P.O. Box 19461, Spokane, WA 99219.

CATHY McDAVID

Cathy makes her home in Scottsdale, Arizona, near the breathtaking McDowell Mountains, where hawks fly overhead, javelina traipse across her front yard and mountain lions occasionally come calling. She embraced the country life at an early age, acquiring her first horse in eighth grade. Dozens of horses followed through the years, along with mules, an obscenely fat donkey, chickens, ducks, goats and a potbellied pig who had her own swimming pool. Nowadays, two spoiled dogs and two spoiled-er cats round out the McDavid pets. Cathy loves contemporary and historical ranch stories and often incorporates her own experiences into her books.

When not writing, Cathy and her family and friends spend as much time as they can at her cabin in the small town of Young. Of course, she takes her laptop with her on the chance inspiration strikes.

#1 *New York Times* Bestselling Author

LINDA LAEL
MILLER

Just Kate

H HARLEQUIN® BESTSELLING AUTHOR COLLECTION

ISBN-13: 978-0-373-18068-4

Recycling programs for this product may not exist in your area.

JUST KATE
Copyright © 2013 by Harlequin Books S.A.

The publisher acknowledges the copyright holders of the individual works as follows:

JUST KATE
Copyright © 1989 by Linda Lael Miller

HIS ONLY WIFE
Copyright © 2007 by Cathy McDavid

This edition published by arrangement with Harlequin Books S.A.

For questions and comments about the quality of this book please contact us at CustomerService@Harlequin.com.

® and TM are trademarks of Harlequin Enterprises Limited or its corporate affiliates. Trademarks indicated with ® are registered in the United States Patent and Trademark Office, the Canadian Trade Marks Office and in other countries.

Printed in U.S.A.

www.Harlequin.com

CONTENTS

Dear Friends,

It's wonderful to see the classic stories in these collections coming back to be enjoyed by new readers, as well as some who remember the book fondly and wish to revisit the characters and the setting.

Just Kate was inspired by a number of things—a trip to New Zealand and Australia, the movie *Crocodile Dundee*, and a particularly chunky metal purse I'd purchased somewhere. I kept thinking that purse could be used as a weapon of defense and—sure enough—Kate used it in the story to clock a presumed mugger on a dark Seattle street. The beyond-sexy Australian hero, Sean Harris—how I love that accent—will have to do a lot of convincing to get back on Kate's good side, after all that's happened.

So, if you've never read *Just Kate,* welcome. If you *have* read the story and want an encore, welcome back.

All best,

Linda Lael Miller

JUST KATE

#1 *New York Times* Bestselling Author

Linda Lael Miller

For Lisa Jackson and Nancy Bush, sisters in crime.
Remember the four-to-a-room trip to RWA?

Chapter 1

The exchange was so blatant, so audacious that Kate Blake couldn't believe she'd seen it. It was intermission and the lobby was crowded. People swirled past her, laughing and talking as they waited for the opera to resume. Kate stood frozen in their midst, fingers curved around her glass of orange juice, her indigo eyes wide, afraid even to blink.

She hadn't imagined it. Brad had handed another man a packet of white powder and taken money in return, right there in front of half the population of Seattle.

Perhaps, she thought desperately, it was all a mistake. Perhaps she had only imagined that the packet contained cocaine, and that Brad, the man she'd meant to marry in less than a month, had just accepted money for it.

In the next instant, Brad turned, tucking a folded bill into the pocket of his coat as he moved. His eyes met Kate's, and it was clear that he knew she'd seen. There was no apology in his gaze, however, only defiance. Then he was looking at his companion again, and Kate might not have existed at all.

She felt dizzy, and then claustrophobic, and she knew she had to get out into the fresh air fast. She set her cup aside and hurried toward the main door.

Outside, Kate gripped the stair railings in both hands and dragged in deep, clean breaths until the choking sensation passed. A glance back over one elegantly bared shoulder told her that Brad hadn't followed. He probably hadn't even noticed she was gone.

She looked up at the dark, star-speckled sky aglow with city lights, and her vision blurred as tears filled her eyes. She was torn. One part of her wanted to go back inside, grip Brad by the lapels and demand to know why he'd thrown everything away; another preferred to pretend that nothing had changed.

Kate inched down the stairs, still grasping the railing with both hands. Brad was the man she'd planned to marry. He was her father's campaign manager. And she'd just seen him break the law in the most brazen of ways.

A thousand thoughts whirled through her head. This wasn't new behavior for Brad; she was certain of that. And yet she hadn't known. She'd been engaged to him and *she hadn't known* what kind of man he was! How could that be?

There were no cabs lined up in front of the theater, since the opera would run another full hour. Kate looked back again, knowing she should go inside, call for a taxi and wait in the lobby until it arrived. But something within her demanded action. She needed to walk, hard and fast, with the cool, clean night wind blowing against her face. She started out in the general direction of her downtown condominium, chin held high, her grandmother's antique brass evening bag swinging at her side.

Hard-eyed street people watched her pass, but there was none of the usual panhandling. Kate supposed that in her present mood she didn't look approachable.

Moments later, as she passed a popular department store, her pace slackened. The breeze had dried her tears. Kate's reflection in the windows regarded her forlornly as she took in her own tall, slender body, the sleek designer gown that had cost the earth, the soft and loose arrangement of her dark hair.

"So who wanted to marry Bradley Wilshire anyway?" she demanded aloud. As she rounded the corner, Kate was careful not to look at her image in the glass, fearing it might answer, *You did.*

Kate pulled her silk shawl around her bare shoulders and shivered. In just a few minutes, she reminded herself, she would be home in her small, elegant condominium overlooking the harbor. She would turn on some classical music, pour herself a glass of low-cal Chablis and spend the rest of the evening soaking in a bubble bath.

Was it possible that Brad was a pusher?

Trying to forget what she'd seen would be useless, she knew, but the ramifications were more than she could deal with, too big to take in all at once.

She was nearly home when she noticed two men standing in front of the cash machine. Kate considered crossing to the other side of the street, but they seemed so engrossed in conversation that they probably wouldn't notice her, anyway.

The man facing Kate was tall and well built, familiar in a disturbing sort of way. In the dim light of the cash machine, she could see he was wearing a tuxedo, and his mouth was curved into an ingenuous smile. She sensed he was aware of her presence, though he gave no sign of it.

"Take it easy now, mate," he said in a thick Australian accent. "If it's money you want, you'll have it, but the machine will only give me so much in a twenty-four hour period."

An almost dizzying sensation of mingled despair and excitement filled Kate. The voice, the accent—it couldn't be!

It was then that Kate spotted the glint of a switchblade in the second man's hand.

She was filled with instant ire. Thanks to Brad, she'd seen her share of crime for the day, and she was fed up. Without considering possible results, she spun her grandmother's purse on its chain and threw it. When it struck the mugger in the side of the head, he dropped the knife. In the same instant, his knees folded and he sank to the sidewalk in an unlikely position of prayer.

The tall man collected the knife, recessed the blade with an unsettling expertise and tucked it into his pocket. "Nice work, Katie," he said, reclaiming a gold credit card from the slot on the cash machine, "but you shouldn't have taken a chance like that. The bleeder might have turned on you."

Kate sank against the rough concrete wall of the bank, not trusting her knees to support her. "Sean," she whispered.

His white teeth flashed in the night. The mugger started to rise from the sidewalk, but his would-be victim pushed him back down with a light, deft touch of one foot.

Kate thought she was going to be sick and put one hand to her mouth.

"Surprised to see me, are you?" Sean asked.

Kate lowered her hand. Holding her knees rigid and her backbone straight, she started to walk away. "I'll call the police," she said woodenly.

Sean stopped her by taking a light but inescapable hold on her elbow. "No need of that, love," he said in a gravelly tone that made sweet chills ripple over Kate's soul. "They're here already."

Kate glanced toward the street. Sure enough, a patrol car was pulling up to the curb. She considered having herself taken into protective custody until Sean Harris had gone back to Australia, where he undeniably belonged.

"What's going on here?" asked the older of two officers.

Sean explained, and the moaning mugger was hauled

unceremoniously to his feet. Kate listened numbly as his rights were read, her teeth sinking into her lower lip. Sean's grasp on her arm never slackened.

"You and the lady will need to come to the station and swear out a complaint," said the younger officer.

"And if we don't?" Sean asked, arching one dark eyebrow.

"They'll have to let him go," Kate answered.

"Can't have that," Sean replied lightly. "My car's just up the street—we'll follow you."

Both policemen touched the brims of their hats in a deferential fashion before hustling the prisoner into the back of the squad car. Sean fairly hurled Kate into the passenger seat of a late-model sports car parked half a block away.

"Well," he said, when they were following the police, "fancy meeting you here, Katie-did."

Kate folded her arms. First Brad's drug deal, then the mugging and now this. Boy, had her horoscope been off target this morning. "My parents would have appreciated a telephone call," she said stiffly, doing her best to ignore her former brother-in-law. "They worry about Gil, you know."

The reference to his young son did not visibly move Sean. At least Kate didn't catch him reacting, though she was watching him out of the corner of her eye.

"They know where we live," he replied, and this time his voice was as cold as a Blue Mountain snowfall.

Kate unfolded her arms and tried to relax. It was almost incomprehensibly bad luck that, of all the muggings she might have stumbled upon, it had to be Sean's.

She hadn't seen him since Abby's funeral, and she'd hoped that she would never lay eyes on him again.

She drew in a deep breath and let it out again slowly. "Did you bring Gil with you?" she asked.

"Now why would I drag the poor little nipper from one hemisphere to the other like that?" he countered.

Kate suppressed an urge to wind up her purse again and let Sean have it. "Maybe because his grandparents would like to see him," she said.

"Because they'd like to take him away, you mean," Sean answered, "and turn him into a proper little Yank."

"He's half-American," Kate pointed out, daring at last to turn in the car seat and look directly at Sean. His profile was rugged, like the outback he loved so much. "What's wrong with that?"

They had reached the police station, and Sean was spared having to answer—for the moment.

The next hour was consumed by the dubious process of pressing charges against the mugger. Kate seriously considered turning Brad in for pushing drugs while she was there, but she knew she couldn't do that without consulting her father. An unforeseen scandal might ruin his chances for reelection to the Senate; Kate had to give him time to prepare.

She went to the telephone when she was through issuing her statement and dialed the familiar number.

Her mother answered; it was late enough that the staff was off duty. "Blake residence."

Kate braced herself. "Mother, it's Kate. I'm at the police station and—"

"The police station!" The horror in Irene Blake's

voice was unmistakable. "Good heavens, what's happened? She's at the *police station*, dear!"

At this, the senator himself came on the line. Kate winced, just as if she'd been there to see him wrench the receiver out of her mother's hand. "What's this business about the police? So help me, Katherine, if you've been arrested, I'll fire you in an instant."

Kate made an effort to control her temper. "Of course I haven't been arrested, Daddy," she whispered into the phone, embarrassed. "I happened to witness a mugging, that's all."

"Are you all right?" the senator boomed. Now that he knew his career was safe, he could afford to be concerned about his daughter. Kate had never had any illusions about his priorities.

"I'm fine," she answered. "Daddy, the reason I'm calling is that—well—I ran into Sean."

"Sean who?" demanded the senator.

Kate felt a sweet, shivery sensation from head to foot, and looking to one side, she found that the handsome Australian was standing mere inches away. She reminded herself that he'd been Abby's husband, that he was a liar and a womanizer, but the tremulous, taut-bow feeling didn't subside. "Sean Harris," she finally managed to reply, her cheeks burning.

Sean's green eyes danced as he watched her color rise. Apparently he heard her father's question, for he took the receiver from Kate and spoke into it, his tone flippant and cool. "You know, Senator. That no-gooder from down under—the one that married your elder daughter."

Kate squeezed her eyes shut as she heard a burst of profanity explode on her father's end of the line. After a moment's recovery, she jerked the receiver out of Sean's hand and sputtered, "Daddy, remember your heart!"

The senator went right on swearing. He finally hung up with a crash, but not before blurting out a nonsensical sentence that ended in, "…bring that bastard here no matter what you have to do!"

Sean had heard that, too. He rocked back on his heels, his wonderful eyes full of laughter. "There's a welcome for you," he said.

Kate had a headache. She sighed and opened her purse, but there was no sign of the little metal box of aspirin she usually carried. All she found were her keys and a credit card. "He wants to talk to you about Gil," she said wearily. "That's all."

Sean didn't look at all convinced of that, but he offered Kate his arm and inclined his head to one side. "All right, Katie-did," he said, "I'll face the lion in his den. But I'm only doing it for you."

Kate assessed this man who had caused her family so much heartache and shook her head. He didn't look the least bit remorseful to her.

"Thanks a whole heap," she said.

The lights of Seattle glittered and danced in the rearview mirror of Sean's car as he and Kate drove toward the Blake mansion. Even in the dim glow from the dashboard, she could see he was no longer amused. His jaw was set in a hard, ungiving line.

The confrontation between Sean and the senator would not be a pleasant experience for anyone.

Unexpectedly, Sean reached out and caught hold of Kate's left hand. His thumb pressed against the large diamond in Brad's engagement ring. "Who's the lucky man?" he asked. His tone was gruff, as though he was trying to be congenial and finding it difficult.

Kate's heart ached as she remembered the scene in the lobby at the opera house. She opened the lid of her antique purse, slid the ring off her finger and dropped it inside. "There isn't one," she said sadly.

She felt rather than saw Sean's glance in her direction. "Funny. Abby always said you'd be the one to settle down and have a family."

He couldn't have known what pain that remark would foster—could he? Kate didn't know Sean Harris very well; it had been ten years since he'd married her sister in the garden behind the Blakes' house and five since Abby had driven her sports car off a cliff north of Sydney.

Kate's mother still believed Abby had died deliberately, unable to live with the unhappiness Sean caused her. Kate didn't know what to think.

She'd visited her sister in Australia several times, the last being when Gil was born seven years before. Although she'd watched Sean carefully, Kate hadn't seen any evidence of the emotional cruelty Abby had written home about. Oh, Sean might have been a little distant where Abby was concerned, but he'd been crazy about his infant son. Anyone could have seen that.

"Kate?"

The prompt from Sean brought her back to the present with a start. She pointed one finger. "Turn right on this next street."

Sean took a new hold on Kate's hand. "I remember," he said. "Katie, what happened?"

Kate lowered her eyes. "I thought I was in love," she confessed. "Tonight I saw Brad do something terrible."

He squeezed her hand. "You're better off out of it if you have any doubts at all," he said.

Kate had no doubt that was true, but she still wished she could go back in time and wave a wand and alter reality. In the new scenario Brad would only be making change for a twenty-dollar bill or giving someone his business card.

They had reached the foot of the Blakes' long brick-paved driveway, and the gates opened immediately. Of course, the senator had been watching for their arrival from inside the house, the gate controls in his hands.

"I don't know why I'm doing this," Sean muttered.

Kate sighed. "And my horoscope said I'd have a good day," she said as they passed through the gates.

"You don't believe in that rot, do you?" Sean asked, and he sounded short-tempered. He couldn't be blamed for dreading what was ahead, Kate supposed. She wasn't looking forward to it, either.

"Not anymore I don't," she answered.

Senator John Blake was standing on the front porch when they reached the house, his hands shoved into the pockets of his heavy terry cloth bathrobe. Even in slippers and pajamas, Kate marveled to herself, he looked imperious—every inch the powerful politician.

And he was powerful. Careers were made and broken on his say-so.

Sean shut off the headlights and the engine and got out of the car. He walked around to help Kate, but she'd pushed the door open before he reached her.

"Where is the boy?" the senator demanded. No hello. No "What brings you all the way to America?" It was clear enough that Sean wasn't welcome in his own right.

"He's in school in Sydney, where he belongs," Sean answered. He'd never been the slightest bit intimidated by the senator, and Kate suspected that was one of the reasons her father disliked him so intensely.

Senator Blake doubled one hand into a fist and pounded it into his palm. "Blast it all, Harris, that child belongs with his family!"

"I'm his family," Sean said quietly. Kate felt a certain admiration for his composure, even though she wanted her sister's son to visit the United States on a regular basis as much as her parents did.

Kate's mother, Irene, appeared in the massive double doorway behind the senator. "Let's not stand outside, making a public spectacle of ourselves," she scolded. "There may be reporters from those awful tabloids lurking in the shrubbery."

Despite everything, Kate had to smile at that. The tabloids didn't pick on dull men like her father. They fed on scandal.

Then her smile faded as she stepped into the light and warmth of her parents' house. Once word of Brad's profitable little sideline got out, there would be scandal aplenty.

"What are you doing here?" the senator demanded of Sean the moment they were all inside his study with the doors closed. He sounded for all the world as though he thought Sean should have had his permission before entering the country.

"I've been in Seattle for a week, if it's any of your business," Sean answered evenly. "My company is thinking of placing an order with Simmons Aircraft."

Kate saw the sudden interest in her father's face. Simmons Aircraft was one of the largest employers in the state, and the company was a pet concern of the senator's. "You're still with the airline, then?"

"You could say that," Sean replied. A forest of crystal decanters stood on the bar, and he helped himself to a snifter of brandy, lifting it once to the senator before raising it to his lips. "But you didn't have your daughter drag me up here so we could talk about Austra-Air, did you?"

Kate felt a flash of resentment. Sean made it sound as though her father orchestrated her every move.

"No," Senator Blake responded. "It's about my grandson."

Sean set the snifter aside, then brought a thin leather wallet from the inside pocket of his tuxedo jacket, opening it and extending it to his former father-in-law. Kate caught a glimpse of a handsome blond boy smiling up from a photograph.

It was no secret that Gil resembled his late mother, but surprise moved in the senator's aging face all the same—surprise and pain. "He's a fine-looking lad," the old man said in a strange, small voice. "Does he do well in school?"

"Mostly," Sean answered quietly. "He's got a weak spot when it comes to spelling and the like."

Mrs. Blake hovered close behind the senator's shoulder, peering hungrily at her grandson's picture. "Abby was the same way," she said.

The air in that large, gracious room suddenly seemed to be in short supply. Kate went to the window behind her father's desk and opened one side a little way.

"The boy has a right to know his mother's family," said the senator.

"A few years ago I might have agreed with that," Sean replied, pulling the photograph out from behind the plastic window in his wallet and extending it to Mrs. Blake.

"What changed your mind?" the senator wanted to know. It seemed to Kate that he was having trouble meeting Sean's gaze, but she was wrong, of course. Her father was virtually fearless.

"When a man's son is nearly kidnapped," Sean answered, "it tends to change his mind about a lot of things." He tucked his wallet back into his pocket and glanced at Kate once before telling his late wife's parents, "You're welcome to visit Gil anytime you want to, but I won't send him here. Not until he's old enough to take care of himself."

Kate was staring at Sean, hardly able to believe what she'd heard. Gil had nearly been kidnapped? That in itself was news to her, but it had actually seemed, for a moment there, as though Sean thought the senator might have been behind the attempt.

When Sean walked out of the study, Kate followed, partly because she didn't want to listen to another of her father's tirades and partly because she had to confront Sean. He couldn't go around accusing good people of a crime and then just turn and walk away!

Kate said a hasty goodbye to her mother and father and followed Sean outside.

"I assume you want a ride home," Sean said as he opened the car door on the driver's side. It was the first indication he'd given that he was aware of her presence.

Kate answered by getting into the car. "What the hell do you mean by implying that my father would abduct a child?" she demanded the moment Sean was behind the wheel.

He ground the key into the ignition, and the engine started with an angry roar. "He wouldn't try it personally, of course," he snapped. "He paid someone to steal my son off the playground."

"That's a lie!"

Sean stopped the car without warning and glared at Kate. "Is it?" he rasped. "The man the police picked up admitted everything—he said he was working for a powerful American politician, and I guessed the rest."

Kate felt the color drain from her face. "No," she whispered, stunned. Her father would never do a thing like that. He was honorable and good, the kind of man who belonged in a Norman Rockwell painting. "I don't believe you."

"Believe what you like, love," Sean sighed. "I don't really give a damn."

Kate stiffened in her seat. "If my father was guilty," she challenged, "why didn't you take your case to the press? That would have ruined his career."

Sean didn't look at her. He appeared to be concentrating on the road, and his strong hands were tense where they gripped the steering wheel. "I couldn't," he answered in a low voice. "I once loved a daughter of his, you see."

Kate sat back. This had been one hell of a day. "So now you're just going to fly back home and forget that Gil has a family here in the States?"

They had reached the bottom of the driveway. "Yes," he replied. "If you want to see him, you'll have to pay a visit to the land of Oz."

Kate remembered the nickname Australians had given their country from her sister's early emails. The later ones had been filled with anger and fear and a wild, keening kind of despair. "I might just do that," she said. It would be good to get away from what Brad had done, away from her father's campaign.

Sean gave her a quicksilver glance, one she nearly missed. "Really?"

"I'd need to get a visa," Kate told him. "But, with my father's connections, that shouldn't take long."

Kate couldn't tell whether Sean was pleased at the prospect of a visit from his former sister-in-law or not, since the car was too dark and he revealed nothing by his tone or his words. "Where do you live?"

She gave him the address of her building, and he nodded in recognition. It was near his hotel, he said.

"How long are you staying?" she asked as the expensive car slipped through the dark city streets.

He moved his powerful shoulders in a casual shrug. "Another few days, I suppose. I want to take the plane up at least once more before I make my recommendation."

Kate knew he was testing the airliner his company was considering buying from Simmons Aircraft. "Just how many planes are we talking about here?" she asked.

Sean favored her with a grin that might have been slightly contemptuous. She couldn't quite tell. "You're definitely your father's daughter," he said, and Kate felt as though she'd been roundly insulted. Her cheeks were throbbing with heat when Sean finally answered her question. "Roughly a dozen, give or take a plane. We're phasing out our old fleet."

A dozen airliners. A contract like that would mean prosperity for a good many of her father's constituents.

"What do you do, anyway?" Sean asked.

Again Kate felt vaguely indignant. "I work for the senator."

"I gathered that much," Sean retorted, bringing the car to a sleek stop in front of Kate's building. "Do you actually work, or do you just stand around agreeing with everything the old man says?"

Kate's color rose in anger, and she reached for the door handle, but Sean caught her hand in a swift grasp and held it prisoner. She trembled as he stroked the tender flesh on the inside of her wrist with the pad of his thumb.

"Cold?" he asked, knowing perfectly well she was practically boiling.

She gave a little cry when he tilted his head and melded his mouth to hers, but she made no move to resist him. The old attraction had returned to shame her.

Chapter 2

Kate's telephone was ringing when she let herself into the elegant condominium. She made no effort to lift the receiver, knowing the answering machine would pick up the call.

She listened to her own voice giving a recorded greeting as she carefully folded her silk shawl and set it aside, along with her grandmother's purse. There was a little dent, she noticed with a frown, where the solid brass bag had struck the mugger's head.

Brad's voice filled the room. At least there was one good thing about this whole incident, and that was the fact that Brad's job would be hers now. She was qualified, and she had more seniority than anyone else on the staff. "Kate, I'm at home. Call me immediately!"

"Go to hell," Kate muttered, her arms folded across

her chest. Even though the living room was warm, she suddenly felt chilled. She turned down the volume on the machine and, if Brad said anything more, she didn't hear him.

Her mind and senses were full of Sean. Her heart was still beating a little faster than usual, and her nipples felt taut beneath the thin fabric of her evening gown. She kept her arms folded over her breasts in an effort to hide her involuntary response, even though there was no one around to see.

Unlike her parents, Kate didn't keep pictures of Abby out in plain view, but she went to the shelf behind her couch and took down a thin leather-bound album. The names "Abby and Sean" were embossed on the cover in gold lettering, and Kate felt a lump thicken in her throat as she opened it to the first photograph.

It showed Abby sitting at her vanity table in her frilly room, her wedding gown a tumble of satin and lace and pearls. Kate saw herself, ten years younger and wearing a pink bridesmaid's dress. In the photograph she appeared to be pinning Abby's veil carefully into place, though in reality that task had fallen to a hairdresser.

With the tip of an index finger, Kate touched her sister's glowing, flawless face, her golden hair and wide brown eyes. *Abby.* The senator had called her his Christmas-tree angel.

Tears brimmed in Kate's eyes, and she closed the album and put it carefully back among the others. She couldn't think about Abby, not with Sean's kiss still burning on her mouth.

Kate kicked off her shoes and felt her feet sink deep

into the plush pearl-gray carpet on the floor. With a sigh, she wandered into her bedroom and slipped out of the dress, her panty hose and underthings. A long, hot shower soothed her a little, though the pounding massage of the water made her more aware of her body than she wanted to be.

Clad in a striped silk nightshirt, her shoulder-length brown hair blown dry, Kate climbed into the brass bed that had once graced one of her grandmother's guest rooms and pulled the covers up to her chin.

She wouldn't think about Sean. It was that simple. She had a good mind; she could direct it to other matters.

However, it would not be directed. Against Kate's will, she remembered the first time she'd seen Sean Harris.

She'd been nineteen at the time, and he'd come to the house with Abby. Attracted by his good looks, his sense of humor and his lilting accent, Kate had fallen in love. Although he had never said or done anything to encourage her, Sean had always been kind, and Kate had gone on adoring him long after he'd become her brother-in-law.

Then those emails had started arriving from Abby. Sean was a chauvinist, she'd claimed. He hated her, delighted in humiliating her.

"Why didn't you leave him?" Kate asked in the darkness of her room. She squeezed her eyes shut as memories of the funeral invaded her mind, unwanted and painful.

Sean had brought Abby home to be buried in the

family plot, though Gil, only two years old then, had remained behind in Australia. Sean's grief had loomed over him, like the dark shadow of something monstrous.

Even then she had loved him, though she wouldn't have admitted that to herself. The guilt, coupled with her bereavement, would have broken her.

For the past five years Kate had concentrated on putting Sean out of her mind. Until tonight she'd thought those treacherous, tearing emotions were behind her forever.

Now she just didn't know.

A furious pounding at the front door awakened Kate with a start. She squinted at the clock on her bedside table and saw that it was two-thirty in the morning.

Full of frightened bafflement, Kate scrambled out of bed and found her robe. Reaching the front door, she peered through the peephole and saw Brad.

"Let me in, damn it," he snapped, somehow knowing she was there.

Kate hesitated, then opened the door. Brad was capable of making a scene, and there was no sense in letting him awaken all the neighbors.

The tall blond man pushed past Kate. He'd exchanged his formal evening clothes for a pair of jeans, a lightweight blue sweater and the formidably expensive leather jacket Kate had given him for Christmas.

"Why the devil did you run off like that?" he rasped, his eyes snapping with barely suppressed fury.

Kate bit her lower lip and brushed her sleep-tangled hair back from her face. He was referring to her hasty exit from the opera, of course. "I saw you take money for cocaine," she said slowly and carefully. Even now she could hardly believe it.

She hoped for a raging denial, but Brad only stared at her in hostile puzzlement. "So?" he asked.

Kate felt fury flow through her like venom. "What do you mean, 'So?'" she cried, struggling to keep her voice down. "We're talking about a crime here—a felony!"

Brad shook his handsome head in apparent amazement. "I don't believe this," he said.

"Neither do I," Kate replied wearily. She found her antique purse, opened it and took out the ring. "Here," she said, extending it to Brad.

His eyes widened in his tanned face. "You're not serious."

"I can't marry you," Kate said. Tears filled her eyes as she mourned all her dreams—the suburban house, the children, the dog in the back of a minivan. All of it was gone. It wasn't fair.

Brad refused to take the ring. "Kate," he said reasonably as though speaking to a cranky child, "*everybody* does cocaine."

Kate shook her head. Her cheeks were wet now, and she dried them hastily on the sleeve of her nightshirt. "No," she argued. "That isn't true and you know it. Brad, you need help. If you'll check into a hospital—"

He held up both hands in a gesture so abrupt that it startled Kate into retreating another step. "Wait a second. A hospital? I haven't got that kind of problem,

Kate. And even if I did, I wouldn't just walk away from the senator's campaign."

Kate swallowed. "You'll have to resign as campaign manager, Brad. Right away."

He was staring at her as though she'd just told him she'd had supper with a Martian. "Resign? Are you kidding? This is the most important job of my career and you damn well know it!"

Kate did know that Brad had political ambitions of his own. He had left a prestigious law firm to take the job on her father's staff expressly to make contacts among the powerful. "Brad, if you don't resign, my father will fire you."

Brad paled beneath his tan. "Are you saying that you're going to tell him about tonight?"

"I have to," Kate said with miserable conviction. "It would be irresponsible not to."

Brad stood close, his hands cupping Kate's face. Although his touch was gentle, she sensed a certain restrained violence in him and she was afraid. "No. Listen to me. You can't do this—I've worked too long and too hard…"

Kate twisted out of his grasp and put the couch between them, her hands gripping its back. "Go home," she said quietly. "Think about this. We'll talk again tomorrow."

"We'll talk now!" Brad snapped. "If you tell your father about that cocaine, I'll be ruined!"

"Please leave," Kate said. She felt chilled from head to foot. She had almost married this man!

Brad didn't move at all. He only glared at her and

spit out, "You're naive as hell, Kate. This kind of thing goes on every day in every level of government. Why don't you stop being such a goody-goody and grow up?"

Kate could only gaze at him, feeling sick to her stomach. Dear God in heaven, how had he fooled her so completely?

After another long and frightening moment, Brad stormed out the door. Kate rushed to lock and bolt it behind him, leaning against it with her eyes closed while she waited for her heartbeat and her breathing to settle into normal patterns.

She'd been dating Brad Wilshire for a year. There must have been signs that he used and sold drugs, but she hadn't seen them. That fact in itself was terrifying; Kate wondered if she could trust her own instincts. Was she one of those self-destructive women she'd read about in pop psychology books?

After a few deep breaths and fifteen minutes spent pacing the darkened living room, Kate was tired enough to sleep. She crawled back into bed, closed her eyes and dreamed that she lived in a fine colonial house in the suburbs. Sean was her husband and Gil was her son and there were twelve gleaming airliners parked in the backyard.

The jangle of the telephone awakened Kate before her alarm clock could. She grappled for the receiver and pressed it to her ear, muttering a hoarse, "Hello?"

The senator's voice was like restrained thunder. "Brad has been arrested," he said.

Kate was wide awake. "When?" she asked, sitting up in bed.

"Early this morning. He's denying all the charges, of course."

Kate swallowed hard. "What charges?"

"You ought to know," her father responded coldly. "You're the one who turned him in, aren't you? How could you do this when you knew the effect a scandal would have on me?"

"I didn't turn him in," Kate protested quietly. "I would never have done that without consulting you."

"Be that as it may, the story will be all over the morning papers. We've got to decide whether to stand behind Wilshire or cut him loose."

"That shouldn't be too hard to work out," Kate said, flinging back the covers. "He's guilty—I saw him make the sale with my own eyes."

"But you didn't blow the whistle on him?"

"No," Kate insisted. "I should have, though."

"I take it the wedding is off?"

Kate shoved a hand through her hair. "I don't know how you can even ask that," she whispered furiously. "Of *course* it's off!"

The senator sighed. Kate knew he'd had dreams of his own where Brad was concerned. He'd meant to groom his prospective son-in-law to take his place one day. And John Blake wasn't a man who gave up easily. "I think I could persuade him to enter a treatment center."

"Give it up, Daddy," Kate sighed. "Brad will ruin

you if you keep him on as campaign manager, and we both know it."

Her father reluctantly agreed and ended the conversation. Kate showered, wound her dark hair into a tidy French braid and dressed in a businesslike black suit and tasteful silk blouse. As her father's press secretary, she was ready to meet the newspaper reporters.

It was a good thing, because they were waiting for her the moment she reached the elegant mansion on the hill, clustering around her car, shouting questions and shoving microphones and cameras into her face.

"Is it true you turned your lover in for pushing cocaine?" called one man.

Kate looked at him with distaste and hustled toward the front door. "The senator will have a comment for you later," she called over one shoulder.

Someone grabbed her by the arm, and Kate wrenched free, infuriated by the presumption of such a gesture.

Inside the house she found her father surrounded by aides. There was no sign of her mother. Although Irene was a seasoned campaigner, she tended to get headaches when the water got rough.

"Are you ready to issue a statement?" Kate asked, shouldering her way through to her father's desk.

He looked up as though surprised to see her. "Yes," he said. "Tell those vultures out there that even though we bailed Wilshire out of jail, we're washing our hands of him as of today. He's off my staff."

"When will you name a new campaign manager?" Kate asked. She fully expected her father to give the job to her, since she'd earned it. In fact, in many ways she was more qualified than Brad had been.

"Right now," the senator said decisively. "Tell the press that I've chosen Mike Wilson for the job." He glanced fondly at the young and inexperienced lawyer standing close by.

Kate turned to leave the room without a word.

"Where do you think you're going?" Kate's father called after her, his tone angry and imperious.

Kate froze at the study door, her hand on the brass knob. "I'm about to issue my last official statement as your press secretary," she replied clearly.

The senator's anger was palpable. It reached out and coiled around Kate like an invisible boa constrictor. "Not until you've told me what this is all about, you won't!"

Kate turned and faced him again. "You as much as promised that job to me. How many times have you said, 'If it weren't for Brad, you'd be my campaign manager'?"

"I was only joking, and you damn well know it. It takes a man to manage a campaign! Furthermore, I don't have time to indulge your temperament, Katherine. If you walk out that door, you can consider yourself fired."

Kate glared at the white-haired man seated behind the desk. His staff surrounded him on three sides, all of them looking at Kate as though she'd just lost her reason.

She offered a silent prayer that she wouldn't cry and

raised her chin. "That will save me the trouble of writing a letter of resignation," she said.

The senator swore, and Kate walked out of his study with her shoulders straight and her head high. Her mother was in the hallway, her perfect complexion gray with anxiety, her strawberry blond hair artfully coiffed. She gripped both of Kate's hands in hers, and her ice-blue eyes pleaded for understanding.

"I know your father is in a terrible mood," she said, "but it's sure to pass once the press backs off a little."

Kate could no longer hold back her tears. She shook her head and put one hand over her mouth.

"What's happened?" Irene Blake demanded.

Kate bit into her lower lip, struggling for composure. Her disappointment and sense of betrayal combined to overwhelm her. "He gave Brad's job to Mike Wilson," she finally managed to say.

Irene's gaze revealed honest bafflement. "And?"

Kate's patience was exhausted. "Mother, that job should have gone to me," she whispered angrily.

"But you're—"

"Don't you dare say 'But you're a woman,' Mother. If you do, I'll never forgive you."

Irene sighed. "Why don't you just go away for a few days, dear. Fly somewhere tropical and lounge in the sun until you feel better."

Kate sniffed and dried her cheeks with a tissue pulled from her purse. She still had to face the press. "That's a good idea, Mother. Tell Daddy I said, *adiós*, bye-bye and *ciao*." With that, she started toward the door.

"Don't be flippant, Katherine," her mother called after her. "It doesn't become you."

Kate rolled her eyes, opened the front door and stepped outside. Sean was just about to enter, and she couldn't have been happier to see him. He was like a barrier between her and the eager reporters. "Thank God you're here," she whispered.

Sean grinned, looking almost intolerably good in his jeans, cotton shirt and leather jacket. "Trust a Yank to do the unexpected," he said in a mischievous whisper that ruffled the loose tendrils of Kate's hair and sent a sweet shiver all through her system. "I was prepared to be thrown out on my ear."

Kate linked her arm with Sean's and smiled up at him. "Pretend we like each other," she said through her teeth.

"Don't we?" Sean countered, feigning an injured look.

Shouting questions about Brad, the covey of reporters closed around them as soon as they stepped off the porch. Kate held on to Sean and looked straight ahead, pretending not to see or hear the men and women vying for her attention. She wasn't her father's press secretary anymore; there was no reason for her to try to appease the media.

"What the hell's going on here?" Sean demanded good-naturedly, once they were safely inside his car and pulling away from the curb.

Kate pressed the tips of her index fingers to the skin under her eyes in the hope that she could keep herself from crying again. "I've just been fired from my father's staff."

"Given the sack, were you?" Sean didn't look at all sympathetic. "Best thing for you, love," he said cheerfully. "Now maybe you can be somebody besides your father's daughter."

Kate bristled. "What is that supposed to mean?"

"You've given the senator all your time and half your soul, Katie-did. When were you planning to live your life?"

Sean's words cut close to the bone, and Kate hugged herself in an unconscious gesture of self-defense. She wondered how he could have discerned something like that when they'd spent so little time together.

In that moment, Kate felt like a life-size paper doll. She had no real interests, beyond the senator's career, no hobbies and very few friends. She folded her arms, utterly demoralized.

"There now," Sean said soothingly. "It'll all come right in the end."

Kate turned her attention to him. It was better than thinking about herself. "What were you doing at my parents' house?" she asked.

Sean seemed to have a definite destination in mind, and it wasn't Kate's building. "Actually, I was looking for you. Good old Brad's arrest was all over the news this morning, and I thought you might need a sympathetic shoulder. When you didn't answer your telephone, I guessed that you were probably with your dear old dad."

Kate was beginning to rally a little. "Where are we

going?" she wanted to know. The car was speeding along the freeway now; they were leaving downtown Seattle far behind.

"Simmons Field," Sean answered. "I told you I wanted to take the plane up again."

"You're not expecting me to go, are you?"

Sean grinned fetchingly. "Sure. We can have lunch at thirty-seven thousand feet—that is, if you don't mind airline food."

"Me? I'll stay on the ground, thank you. I'm no test pilot."

"That's okay, love. We only need one of those, and I'm it."

Kate sighed. "I'm not dressed for this," she said, grasping at straws. She wasn't afraid to fly, but she didn't like the idea of going up in anything that had to be tested.

"It's a passenger jet, Katie-did—not a barnstormer. Come on, live a little."

Kate nodded grudgingly, and Sean's grin widened. He looked pretty pleased with himself.

They arrived at Simmons Field, and Sean parked the sports car in a space marked Reserved. His eyes moved appreciatively over Kate's trim figure when she got out of the vehicle and stood facing him.

"I could wait for you in the hangar," she offered.

Sean shook his head and drew her close. It felt natural and right to walk within the curve of his arm. "Don't be a coward, Katie-did. I'll take care of you."

My secret dream, Kate thought sadly, recalling how she'd thought Brad would take care of her. The truth was, there weren't any princes out here, though some of the frogs could do a pretty good imitation of one. "I can take care of myself," she said firmly.

Sean made no comment on that. Soon they were mounting the portable stairway that would take them into the gleaming jumbo jet he wanted to test. There was a flight attendant on board, along with a copilot and a navigator.

Kate followed the three men into the cockpit, where she buckled herself into a seat near the door. Sean winked at her before sitting down at the controls. She bent far to one side to watch as he put on a set of earphones and then reached up to flip a variety of switches. The craft roared to life, and Kate wondered if there was an ignition key, like in a car.

She gripped the armrests on either side of her as the plane began taxiing down the runway. She could hear Sean talking to the tower in a rhythmic, practiced voice, and she relaxed a little. Even her father would have conceded that Sean was an excellent pilot.

There she went again, measuring her opinions against her father's. She forced herself to relax, realized her eyes were squeezed shut and opened them to see Sean grinning at her around the side of his seat.

Kate made a gesture with the back of her hand, encouraging him to turn his attention back to the friendly skies, and he laughed as he complied.

The navigator smiled at her from his position close by. "Relax," the older man told her. "He probably won't stall it out with you aboard."

"Stall it out?" Kate squeaked. She didn't like the sound of that. "What does that mean?"

"Never mind," said the navigator.

Kate gripped the armrests again.

An hour later, Sean landed the airplane at Simmons Field, and Kate let out her breath.

A group of bald, smiling men wearing off-the-rack suits met them on the tarmac. "Well, Mr. Harris, what do you think of our baby there?" one of them asked, gesturing toward the sleek silver aircraft.

Sean's expression was strictly noncommittal. "The engines grab a little when you stall it out," he remarked.

Kate swallowed. She'd figured out what that phrase meant, and she wondered if she'd had a near-death experience and never even noticed.

One of the officials recognized Kate. "Aren't you Senator Blake's daughter?" he asked.

Kate winced. Maybe Sean was right; maybe she didn't have any other identity besides that one. She nodded, not knowing what else to say.

"I don't mind telling you," the man beamed, looking at Sean again, "that the senator has been a very good friend to Simmons Aircraft."

Sean's expression was bland. "No worries, mate," he said. "We might be able to deal in spite of that."

Kate bit back a grin.

Sean took her hand, said a polite goodbye to the contingent from the sales department and started off toward his car.

"There's a good day's work," he said happily, opening the door for Kate. "Now we can play." He glanced at his watch. "How about some lunch?"

Kate realized with some surprise that she was hungry. Due to the stresses of a political campaign and an engagement, she hadn't had an appetite in months. She nodded.

They went to a nearby steak house, and while Kate gravitated to the salad bar, Sean ordered something from the menu.

When his plate arrived, Kate stared at it in horror. It was a T-bone steak, and it was definitely rare. "Do you know what red meat does to your heart?" she asked.

Sean rolled his eyes. "Don't tell me you've turned into one of those curmudgeons who eats sprouts and drinks blue milk."

Kate speared a cherry tomato and popped it into her mouth. "It doesn't hurt to be health conscious," she said.

Sean cut into his slab of bloody meat, lifted a piece to his mouth and chewed appreciatively. His eyes slipped briefly to Kate's breasts and then rose to her lips, where they lingered for several unsettling moments. "No worries, love," he said. "I promise you, I'm healthy."

Even though Sean had not said anything out of line, Kate felt her cheeks color. Where this man was concerned, she was nineteen again, full of crazy needs and self-doubts. She dropped her gaze to her salad, but Sean's chuckle made her look back up at his face.

"What?" she demanded, nettled.

"I've missed you, Katie-did," he said.

Kate didn't know what that meant and was afraid to ask. She hadn't suspected that Sean ever thought about her, let alone missed her. "I guess you knew I had a major crush on you," she commented.

He reached out, placed an index finger under her chin and lifted it. "I was flattered," he told her.

She felt her cheeks heat up again. "You were my sister's husband," she reminded him, feeling the old guilt rise up within her.

"It's no sin to care about somebody," he reasoned, and for just a moment, shadows flickered in his eyes, sad and dark. Kate knew he was thinking about Abby, and she felt like an intruder.

"Did you love my sister?" she asked.

"Once," Sean answered, and there was no more talk of past loves after that. They finished their meal, and Sean drove Kate back to her building. He was parking the car, while she waited near the elevator, when Brad appeared.

He looked terrible. There were dark smudges under his eyes, his hair was mussed and he needed to shave. "How could you do it?" he rasped. "How could you sell me out like that?"

Kate automatically retreated when he took a step toward her. He lunged in a burst of rage, and Kate screamed when his hands closed painfully over her shoulders.

The next thing she knew, Brad was sailing backward, colliding with one of the concrete pillars that supported the floors above.

Sean had finished parking the car.

Chapter 3

Brad raised himself cautiously from the floor, one hand on his jaw. He was glaring at Sean, but he spoke to Kate. "It didn't take you long to replace me, did it?"

Kate was shaken. A brutal headache was taking shape behind her eyes. Beside her, Sean was silent, though she could feel his fury. "Please," she muttered, avoiding Brad's eyes. "Just go away."

She saw her former fiancé sway slightly on his feet and caught the scent of liquor. It was early afternoon and Brad was drunk.

"Thanks to you," he said, "I might be going away for a long time. Didn't I mean anything at all to you, Kate?"

Unconsciously, she moved a little closer to Sean, but she met Brad's gaze without flinching. "I didn't turn you in, Brad," she said. The elevator arrived then, and she stepped into it.

Sean followed, while Brad stared at her from outside. "I won't forget this, Kate," he vowed.

Kate covered her eyes with one hand and sank against the back wall of the elevator the moment the doors were closed. "Damn," she whispered. Her stomach began to churn as the headache intensified.

Without speaking, Sean put an arm around her. She leaned against him, too shaken to resist.

When they left the elevator at her floor, Sean held out his hand. "Let me have the key," he said softly.

Dazed, Kate found her key ring in the bottom of her purse and handed it to him. "It's the one with the number engraved at the top," she told him.

Sean opened the door, then surprised Kate by lifting her into his arms. "It's time somebody made a bit of a fuss over you, love," he said huskily, carrying her inside.

Kate didn't even think of resisting when he carried her to the bed and laid her carefully down on top of the comforter. He spoke soothingly as he took off her shoes and tossed them aside, then massaged her calves.

She wondered how Abby could ever have described this man as cruel.

He left her, and she heard the door of the medicine cabinet open and close in the bathroom. Soon he was back with a glass of water and a couple of aspirin.

Kate swallowed the pills gratefully and fell back to her pillows with a little moan. She rarely took aspirin because it always knocked her out.

When she awakened, the room was full of shadows, and Sean was stretched out, fully clothed except for his shoes, on the bed beside her. His hands were cupped behind his head, and he appeared to be asleep.

Kate gasped at the rush of sensations that washed over her, and lay down again. She was afraid to move or speak, in case Sean would awaken and leave her.

After a long time she became aware that he was already awake, despite the fact that his eyes were closed.

"Feeling better, Katie-did?" he asked in a low voice.

Kate licked her lips. She could feel the hard heat of his body to the marrow of her bones, and she was terrified of what she might betray when she spoke. "Much," she managed.

He opened his eyes and turned onto his side. Lightly he brushed her lips with his own, and rested his hand just beneath the fullness of her breast. "Good," he said.

Kate barely held back a whimper as he brushed his thumb over her nipple. "Sean," she whispered, and the word was a plea. She wanted him to touch her, and *not* to touch her.

He kissed her thoroughly, as he had the night before in his car, his lips mastering hers, his tongue foreshadowing an invasion of another kind. Kate eased her arms around his neck and responded with everything that was in her.

She did not want to think of how wrong she'd been before when she'd fallen in love with Brad Wilshire.

Presently Sean pushed aside her jacket and began opening the tiny pearl buttons on her blouse. She tensed, arching her back in a spasmodic surrender, when he pushed up her bra and cupped a naked breast in the warmth of his hand.

"Please," she whispered. *Please stop, please go on, please be the man I believe you to be.*

Sean slid downward and took her nipple into his mouth in a bold suckling kiss. Kate cried out, entangling her fingers in his hair to press him closer.

He reached beneath her skirt, grasping her through the thin material of her panty hose, forcing her to spread her thighs for him. He spoke quietly as he caressed her and, fevered, she put her hands behind his head and drew him back to her breast.

He chuckled as he nipped at the peak.

Kate, always cool and professional, was out of control. Between the stimulation of her breast and the masterful motions of his hand, she was losing her mind. She thrust her hips upward, and Sean immediately peeled her panty hose down to the middle of her thighs. She longed to part her legs, but she couldn't, and Sean took immediate advantage of her position.

Then, with the same finger, he invaded her. She sobbed his name and dug her heels into the bed so that she could lift herself to him. All the while suckling and plying her with his thumb, Sean worked her into a frenzy.

"Take me," she pleaded, clutching him. "Oh, Sean, please—please—take me!"

He left her breast to nibble and kiss the length of her neck. "Not this time, Katie-did," he said, just as Kate exploded and became a part of the sunset.

Her body jerked with sweet aftershocks for several moments, then she fell, exhausted, to the comforter. Sean withdrew his finger, caressed the pulsing bit of flesh where a lifetime of pleasure lay waiting to be shared, then raised himself on one elbow to look down at her. After studying her face, as if to memorize it, he kissed her and then sat up.

Sensing that he meant to leave her, Kate scrambled into a sitting position and laid her hands on his shoulders. "Sean, make love to me."

He shook his head once and then drew gently away from Kate to stand with his back to her. "Giving you pleasure is one thing," he said in a hoarse voice. "Taking it is another."

Kate was completely confused. She hadn't had a whole lot of experience with men, but she knew Sean wanted her as much as she wanted him. Her fingers were awkward as she tossed away her panty hose and tried to button her blouse. "I—I wanted to give myself to you."

At last he turned to face her. "I know you did, sweet," he said, "but you're not ready for that."

Kate gave up on her blouse and went to the closet, keeping her shoulders straight. "I'll be thirty years old in two weeks, Sean," she said, finding her pink terry cloth bathrobe. Turning, she tossed it onto the bed and began undressing. "Just how ready do I have to be?"

Sean looked at her the way a starving man looks at meat as she deliberately stripped away her jacket, her blouse, her tangled bra and skirt. She saw him swallow convulsively when she lowered her half-slip to stand before him naked.

"My God," he whispered. "Put your robe on."

Kate didn't move.

He shoved the splayed fingers of one hand through his hair. "Katie, if you don't do as I say, I'll walk out of here right now."

She reached for her robe and put it on. The motion of her hands was quick and angry.

Sean rose out of his chair. "In two days," he said gently, reasonably, "I'll be going back to Australia. I can't make love to you and then leave you behind."

There was a sob in Kate's voice as she shrugged and asked, "Why not? Don't guys do that every day?"

"Katie, don't," he pleaded hoarsely.

It had been another awful day, and sure as hell, Kate thought, her horoscope probably promised roses and moonbeams. "You don't have to feel guilty," she said as tears slipped down her cheeks. "After all, I came on to you—"

"Stop it!" Sean rasped, rounding the bed and grasping her by the shoulders. She winced, since Brad's hold had bruised her earlier, and saw her own pain reflected in Sean's eyes.

He pulled her close and held her. "Katie," he said, and that one word explained everything and nothing.

A few moments later Sean released her. "I'll go and get us something to eat," he said.

Kate didn't want food, she wanted Sean, but she knew he wouldn't violate his principles by making love to her. He probably still loved Abby very much, and that would make his guilt unbearable.

When she heard the door close, Kate went into the living room, opened the curtains to let in the sparkling night view of the city and put on some soft music. Her body was still reverberating with the savage pleasure Sean had introduced her to such a short time before.

About half an hour had passed when Sean returned with take-out hamburgers, sodas and french fries. By that time, Kate had lit the gas fireplace, brushed her hair and misted herself with her favorite perfume.

Sean looked at her and shook his head. "I was hoping you would have changed into a sweat suit by now," he said.

Kate smiled. "You're lucky I'm not naked," she told him.

He shook his head again. "I don't think lucky is the right word," he observed, and the paper bags rustled as he took out the fragrant food.

"This stuff is terrible for us," Kate said, just before she took a big bite of her hamburger. She was sitting near the hearth, and Sean joined her.

He glanced at the flickering fire, then the spectacle beyond the windows, then the sound system. "Are you trying to seduce me?" he asked forthrightly.

"Yes," Kate answered, chewing.

He laughed and brushed a crumb from her chin. "I ought to turn you over my knee," he said.

"Kinky," Kate replied, wriggling her eyebrows.

Sean reached out suddenly, yanked Kate across his lap, and gave her derriere a sound but painless swat. Laughing, she struggled to sit up, and in the process her robe opened and her breasts were bared. The firelight played over them with shadowy fingers, and Sean choked on a french fry.

Kate didn't move. She couldn't have, even if she'd

wanted to. It was as though the whole world, all of time and creation, was holding its breath.

Like a man bewildered, Sean reached out to touch her. She closed her eyes and let her head fall back as his fingers gently shaped her nipple. Within an instant, he drew back, and Kate trembled with humiliation, unable to meet his eyes when she felt him close her robe.

There were tears glistening along her lashes when she forced herself to look at him. "I'm sorry, Sean," she said brokenly.

He laid his hand to her cheek. "Don't be," he told her. Then he got to his feet and went to stand at the window, looking out. It had begun to rain, and the city lights were shifting, shimmering splotches of color against the glass.

Kate sniffled and rose from the floor. Carefully, almost primly, she retied the belt of her robe, as though to prevent what had already happened. She had to say something; she couldn't bear the accusing silence. "I'm really glad you were with me today when we ran into Brad."

Sean didn't look at her. "Does he have a key to this place, Katie-did?" he asked.

Kate supposed she deserved the kind of disrespect that question indicated, but she still had some pride. She lifted her chin. "What if he does?" she countered.

"If he does, I'm staying the night," Sean answered, glaring at her over one shoulder. "He might decide to come back here and avenge his honor or some such rot."

Recalling the way Brad had grabbed her, Kate shuddered. She'd seen a side of the man in the past twenty-four hours that she'd never suspected was there. "He might," she agreed.

Sean was examining the couch. "Does this thing fold out?" he wanted to know.

"Why?" Kate retorted. "Are you tired?"

He pointed a finger at her. "Yes," he answered. "And you stay away from me, sheila."

Kate wanted to scream and throw things. After all, *she* hadn't been the one to start all this.

She stormed across the room, picked up the newspaper that had been delivered earlier and turned to the horoscope page. She could expect everything to go her way that day, according to the prediction.

"Sure!" she yelled, wadding up the paper and flinging it down.

Sean's mind was not on the business of buying a fleet of airliners. He'd already read all the reports and blueprints and, most important of all, he'd taken the plane up several times. He was relieved when the last meeting with the Simmons Aircraft people ended and he was free to leave.

He was behind the wheel of his rented sports car, loosening his tie with one hand and turning the radio dial with the other, when the news story broke. Senator John Blake had suffered a heart attack en route to Washington. He was in critical condition in a Seattle hospital.

Even in the days when things were still good between him and Abby, Sean and the senator had not been friends. Abby's lies and the kidnapping attempt against

Gil had made things infinitely worse. For all of that, Sean was sorry to hear the news.

His first concern was Kate. She was a little fragile these days, given the falling-out with her father and the broken engagement. She was probably pacing in some waiting room, feeling guilty as hell.

He pulled out into traffic and headed in the general direction of the hospital mentioned on the newscast. When he arrived, there were news vans everywhere, along with a small contingent of reporters. He pushed his way through and strode up to the admissions desk.

"I'm Senator Blake's son-in-law," he told the clerk.

The young woman gave him a look of mingled appreciation and skepticism. "I'll just check that out, if you don't mind. Your name, sir?"

"Sean Harris," he answered, watching the woman press a sequence of numbers with a long manicured finger. That told him all he needed to know, but he waited politely while she relayed his name to someone on the other end of the line.

"That was Ms. Blake," the receptionist said. "She says it's all right for you to come up. It's suite 4102. We have to be very careful, you understand…"

Sean nodded impatiently and walked to the elevators.

Kate was waiting for him when he got off. She was dressed in jeans and a yellow cotton shirt, and her dark hair fell free around her shoulders. Her beautiful blue eyes were swollen from crying, and she kept running her palms down the legs of her jeans.

Wordlessly Sean held out his arms, and she flew into them.

"How is he?" Sean asked after a few moments, still holding her tightly.

She looked up at him and sniffled. "The doctors think he'll be okay," she said. "If only I hadn't—"

Sean laid a finger to her lips. "Don't say it, Kate. Don't even think it. The senator's heart attack wasn't your fault."

She drew back from him, but caught his hand in hers. "I wish I could be so sure of that," she said.

Sean wanted to take her home with him, to shelter and spoil her, to make love to her endlessly. She'd done what a long line of models, businesswomen and stewardesses hadn't been able to manage—she'd won his heart. A fraction of a moment before she'd swung her purse at that mugger's head, before Sean had realized who she was, he'd fallen in love.

He took Kate by the arm and ushered her to a plastic sofa, where they both sat down. Mrs. Blake was probably in the room with her husband, and no one else was around except for a couple of members of the senator's staff.

Kate was studying Sean's face. "You have to go back to Australia," she remembered with a note of resignation in her voice.

He nodded. Gil would be expecting him back, and the other members of Austra-Air's board of directors were anxious to hear his report on the new jet. He'd spent two nights on Kate's couch already, and he couldn't protect her forever, even though he wanted that more than anything.

"Did you have the locks changed?" he asked, worried about Brad Wilshire and his temper.

Despite everything, a grin formed on Kate's pale, fine-boned face. "I didn't need to," she confessed in a mischievous whisper. "Brad never had a key. I just wanted you to stay."

The knowledge made Sean happy, though he tried to hide it. It wasn't proper to jump up in the air and shout for joy when somebody was suffering from a heart attack just a few walls away. "Let's have a promise that you'll come and see us," he said softly, curving one finger under her chin.

She ran her tongue over her lips. "That'll depend on how Daddy is," she answered.

"He's made of iron, love," Sean assured her. "He'll be mean as ever in a few days."

Kate lowered her eyes, and Sean hoped devoutly that she wasn't retreating back into that one-dimensional identity she'd cultivated. "Maybe," she said.

Sean kissed her lightly on the forehead, and then they sat in companionable silence, holding hands and waiting.

An hour later a doctor came out and told them the senator was conscious and asking for his daughter. There was every reason to believe he'd recover.

With a small cry of relief, Kate flung her arms around Sean and squeezed. The embrace ended too soon, for she was anxious to see her father.

Sean glanced at his watch. If he hurried, he could still catch his plane. He would have to stop at Kate's to pick up the rest of his things, but that wouldn't take long since he'd never really unpacked.

"Goodbye, love," he said gently, touching her cheek.

"Your things—you'll need a key—" She rushed to find her purse and gave him her spare set.

A feeling of immense loneliness swept over Sean as he walked to the elevators. He made a point of not looking back; he knew she wouldn't be there.

Two weeks after the senator's heart attack, he was at home, preparing to return to Washington, where one of his aides had been voting as his proxy. Although things were better between Kate and her father, she still had no intention of going back to work on his staff. She didn't know exactly what she was going to do with the rest of her life but, for once, she planned to be the one who made the decisions.

Her passport and Australian tourist visa were in the mailbox when she arrived home from visiting her parents one afternoon. She was really going to do it. She was going to pack her bags, buy an airline ticket and fly to Australia to see Gil.

As for what had happened—or *almost* happened— between her and Sean, well, that had been nothing more than a momentary lapse. A reaction to her disappointment over the breaking of her engagement. Whenever she thought about that night, she was grateful that Sean had been too much of a gentleman to take advantage of her pain and confusion.

"Bring the boy back with you," her father instructed

her the next morning when she stopped by the house on her way to the airport.

Kate sighed. "I can't just grab him and throw him on an airplane," she pointed out. "I promise to take lots of pictures, though, and if Sean will let me, maybe I can bring Gil here for a visit."

"Just get him here. There's an election coming up in November, and I want to be seen as a family man."

Kate bent to kiss her father's wan forehead. "Don't get your hopes up," she warned. "Sean doesn't trust you, and he's not likely to do you any favors."

"He has a lot of gall, keeping a man from his own grandson. This wouldn't be happening if my Abby were still alive, that's for sure. She wouldn't stand for it."

The senator's words seemed to imply some lack in Kate. "Abby is dead," she reminded him gently.

She saw the old pain move in his keenly intelligent eyes. "Yes. And as far as I'm concerned, we have Sean Harris to blame for it."

Kate knew there would be no point in arguing in Sean's defense. To the senator, it would be like trying to vindicate the devil. "I'll see you when I get back. Don't overdo."

The senator was already reaching for the telephone. Kate gave him a fond half smile and left the room.

Her mother was waiting in the hallway.

"I know I told you you should get away," she began immediately, "but I really wasn't thinking of any place so far off!"

Kate squeezed her mother's perfectly manicured, lotion-scented hand. "I'll be fine, Mother."

"That's what Abby said," Irene fretted, "and look what happened to her."

Kate sighed. She had known her older sister better than anyone except, perhaps, for Sean. While Abby had certainly looked like an angel, she'd been spoiled and selfish, too, and her temper had been quick. Kate kissed her mother's cheek. "Goodbye, Mother," she said.

Irene caught at her arm when she started toward the door. "When will you be back?"

"I don't know," Kate answered honestly.

Hastily Irene embraced her daughter. She was not an effusive woman, and the gesture was decidedly awkward. "There'll be another man along soon, dear," she promised, completely misreading Kate's emotions as usual. "You mustn't let breaking up with Brad get you down."

Kate let the comment pass. "I'll see you soon, Mother," she said, and then she was outside and the warm June sun was on her face.

It was winter in Australia, but she didn't care. She would be far away from old entanglements there; she would be able to think clearly and decide what to do with the rest of her life.

The night breeze was cool and fragrant as Kate stood on the balcony outside her hotel room, watching the dark ocean reach out to the pale sand and then slowly fall away. She would spend just this one night in Honolulu before traveling on to Fiji, Auckland, New Zealand, and, finally, Sydney.

She thought about Gil. Judging by the picture Sean

had given her parents, the boy was a handsome blonde with his mother's wide brown eyes. She hoped he was more like Sean than Abby.

Below, the hotel pool sparkled like a huge aquamarine, and island music wafted up from the open doors of the lounge. On impulse, Kate decided to go for a swim. Quickly she changed out of her white cotton nightgown and into her sleek new one-piece swimsuit. Then, wearing a blue eyelet cover-up and carrying a towel, she took an elevator downstairs.

The sound of friendly laughter came from inside the lounge as Kate approached the shimmering pool. She looked up at the tropical moon, and for a single moment, her loneliness almost overwhelmed her. She plunged into the water to escape it, and when she surfaced, she felt more hopeful. After a short swim, she climbed out of the pool, dried off and ordered a mai tai to carry back to her room.

Four tractor salesmen from Iowa were in the elevator with Kate, and they invited her to their party. She declined politely and got off two floors below her own.

When she finally arrived in her room, the message light on her telephone was blinking. For a moment she was afraid. Suppose her father had had another heart attack? Suppose this time he'd died?

Kate forced herself to call the main desk. "This is Kate Blake in room 403," she said evenly. "Do you have a message for me?"

The operator asked her to wait for a moment, and Kate heard paper shuffling.

"Yes, Ms. Blake," came the answer. "You had a call

from Mr. Wilshire in room 708. He'd like you to contact him immediately."

Kate felt cold all over, as though she'd just plunged into the pool again. She managed a strangled thank-you and slammed down the receiver.

Brad was here, in this very hotel. Obviously he'd followed her, and he'd jumped bail to do it.

Kate peeled off her suit, showered and put on a sundress and sandals. When she'd combed her hair, she hurled the few things she'd unpacked back into her suitcase, called the desk and asked that her bill be prepared. She would spend the night at the airport.

When Kate opened the door to leave, however, Brad was standing in the hallway, smiling at her. "Maybe we can still have a honeymoon," he said.

Chapter 4

Kate resisted an urge to flee back into her room and slam the door. Brad would be delighted to see that he'd intimidated her. "I thought you weren't supposed to leave the state," she said evenly.

Brad was dressed for the tropics in white pants and a lightweight sport shirt to match. He folded his arms and smiled ingratiatingly. "The charges against me have been dropped because of insufficient evidence. The person who turned me in wasn't—" he paused, searching his mind for the right word "—reliable."

Kate's opinion of the judicial system plummeted. She indicated her suitcase and said, "Well, congratulations to you and apologies to society in general. I was just leaving. Sorry there's no time to talk."

Brad's gaze swept over her. "I'm not going to give

you another chance after this, Kate," he warned. "Either you marry me right away, or we're through."

"Don't look now," Kate answered, "but our relationship has been over since the night of the opera. So, if you'll excuse me—"

Brad shook his head, as though amazed that any woman could turn down a prize like him, and turned to walk away. Kate stepped back inside her room and bolted the door.

She slept fitfully that night, half expecting Brad to break into her room. Early in the morning she showered, dressed and set out for the airport. After breakfast in one of the coffee shops there, she boarded Flight 187, bound for Fiji, New Zealand and Australia.

The trip was incredibly long, with layovers at each stop, and Kate lost a full day of her life when they crossed the international dateline. By the time she arrived in Sydney, she was rumpled, cranky and exhausted.

She took a cab to the hotel where her travel agent had made reservations and, after checking in and taking a shower, she collapsed into bed. When she awakened, it was nighttime, and the bridge stretching across Sydney Harbour glowed in the rainy darkness. Seeing the dense traffic still filling the lanes, she guessed it was still evening.

She was wildly hungry. She called room service, then, sitting cross-legged on the bed, she dialed Sean's number.

A housekeeper answered. "Harris residence."

For a fraction of a moment, Kate didn't know what

to say. Should she introduce herself as Abby's sister, Gil's aunt or Sean's friend? "This is Kate Blake," she finally said. "Is Mr. Harris there, please?"

"I'm sorry, miss," the housekeeper replied, "but he's out with friends tonight."

Kate felt a pang of jealousy, imagining Sean on a date with some other woman, but she quickly suppressed that unworthy emotion. She wanted to see Gil; his father's social life had nothing to do with anything. "Will you tell him I called, please?" she asked.

The housekeeper promised that she would and rang off.

Kate's dinner arrived, and she sat on the edge of her bed to eat, feeling strange and far from home. She'd forgotten the keen sense of isolation Australia could give a person—especially when that person was traveling alone.

After wheeling the service cart out into the hall, Kate read for a while and then went back to sleep. A knock at her door awakened her early the next morning.

Never at her best at that hour, Kate scrambled awkwardly out of bed, stumbled over to the door and tried to focus one eye on the peephole. She couldn't see anyone, and was just about to turn around and stagger back to bed when another knock sounded and a young voice called, "Auntie Kate? Are you in there?"

Kate's heart hammered against her rib cage. She wrenched the door open and there stood seven-year-old Gil, looking up at her with Abby's eyes. He had his mother's hair, too, and Sean's infectious grin.

Until that moment Kate hadn't realized how badly

she wanted to see and hold this child. With a cry of joy, she enfolded the little boy in a hug, which he bore stoically, and then ruffled his golden hair. "Am I ever glad to see you," she said. "Where's your dad?"

Gil pointed one finger toward the elevators. "He's gone to get a newspaper," he said.

Kate appreciated Sean's attempt to give her a few minutes alone with his son. She just wished they'd called first, so she would have had time to dress.

Gil sat on the bed while she dashed into the bathroom to put on jeans and a turquoise pullover shirt. She was barefoot, both hands engaged in working her hair into a French braid, when she came out.

"You don't look anything like the pictures of Mom," Gil observed, watching Kate with quizzical eyes.

Of course, he would have been too little to remember Abby. A momentary sadness overtook Kate. "Your grandfather Blake used to call her his Christmas-tree angel," she said.

"What did he call you?" Gil asked with genuine interest, and Kate realized for the first time that her father had never given her an affectionate nickname. He called her Kate if he was pleased with her and Katherine if he wasn't.

"Just Kate," she said.

"Dad calls you Katie-did," Gil announced. This time Kate noticed that several teeth were missing from the endearing grin.

She searched her mind for something to say to a little boy. "Do you like to play baseball?"

Gil squinted, then shook his head. "Football," he said. "And cricket."

There was a light rap at the door, and Kate went to open it. When she saw Sean standing there, tall and handsome in his jeans, polo shirt and windbreaker, her heart skipped and her breath swelled in her throat.

"Hi," she finally managed to say.

His green eyes danced. "Hello, love," he responded. "May I come in?"

Kate remembered herself and stepped back. "Sure," she said, feeling like an adolescent.

"We woke her up," Gil commented, from his seat on the edge of Kate's crumpled bed.

Sean's gaze was as soft as a caress. "Sorry."

Kate bit her lower lip. "It's all right," she replied lamely.

Sean smiled at her nervousness. "Get your bags packed, Katie-did, and we'll take you out of here. Plenty of room at our place."

Kate hesitated. Seeing Sean again, she knew she hadn't really dealt with her feelings for him at all. It would be so easy to be wanton. "I...I wouldn't want to impose," she said quickly. "I mean, I can just as well stay here."

Gil looked so crestfallen that Kate went to sit beside him on the bed. She draped an arm around his shoulders. "What's this? A sad face when I've just come all the way from America to see you?"

"Let's take your aunt Kate out for some breakfast," Sean suggested quickly. He looked as disappointed as Gil.

Since it was drizzling, Kate took her raincoat. They left the hotel and walked through the clean, modern streets to a small coffee shop that Sean seemed to know.

A hearty breakfast made Kate feel better—and more adventurous. "Maybe I could stay with you for a little while," she said to Gil, "if you're sure I won't be intruding."

Gil's coffee-brown eyes were alight. "I'll show you my dog, Snidely," he exclaimed, beaming. "He can roll over and play dead."

"I'm very impressed," Kate told him. "What else can he do?"

Gil's expression turned sheepish. "Not much else, besides chew shoes and make messes in the garden."

Kate laughed. "He sounds like a regular dog to me."

"Except for Georgie Renfrew, he's my best mate," Gil said.

Sean winked at Kate from behind the rim of his coffee cup, and she was absurdly pleased, as though he'd made some grand gesture.

They left the coffee shop several minutes later, and Kate held Gil's hand as they walked back to her hotel. There, she packed her things and then checked out. She, Sean and Gil took a cab to Sean's house in an elegant section of Sydney.

It was as wonderful as Kate remembered, with a view of the harbor and the Opera House, and her room was a small suite, with its own bath and a real wood-burning fireplace. The carpets were a pale blue, the bedspread was a complementary floral print, and there was even a small balcony outside.

"It's beautiful," Kate told Sean softly, but she was already regretting her decision to stay in this house. The place had belonged to Abby first, just as the man had, and Kate felt like an intruder.

Sean touched the tip of her nose. "I see ghosts in your eyes. What's the problem, Katie-did?"

Kate bit her lower lip and turned away. In the distance she could hear a dog barking with unbounded glee. Evidently Snidely and Gil had been reunited. "I'm just a little tired, I guess," she lied.

Gently Sean turned her to face him. "And feeling just a little guilty, I think."

Kate nodded, not trusting herself to speak.

Before Sean could say anything more, Gil bounded in with a huge, hairy dog of some indeterminate breed.

"This is Snidely," he said, glowing with pride.

Snidely offered a yelp in greeting and then rolled over on his side to lie completely still. Kate supposed he was playing dead.

"Good dog," she said to please Gil.

"Take him outside before Mrs. Manchester sees him," Sean ordered.

Reluctantly Gil led the animal out of Kate's room.

Sean traced the outline of Kate's cheek with one index finger. "We'll talk later, love, when you're settled in and rested."

Kate nodded.

Sean bent his head and kissed her lightly on the lips, and Kate was almost knocked off her feet by the jolt that passed between them. In that moment she would have given her soul to lie beneath Sean, to share her body with him.

But he left her standing in the middle of that beautifully decorated room, listening to the patter of winter rain against the windows.

Kate was curled up in a chair, reading a paperback she'd brought with her on the plane, when the housekeeper rapped at the half-open door and stepped inside the room. Mrs. Manchester was a heavily built woman with friendly blue eyes and salt-and-pepper hair pulled back into a loose chignon. She smiled at Kate and went to the hearth to build a fire.

"Nothing like a cheery blaze on a wet day," she commented, dusting her hands together and looking back at Kate as the fire crackled to life. "Would you like some tea, miss?"

Kate shook her head. "No, thank you," she said, and an unexpected yawn escaped with the words.

"Seems to me you might want to lie down and take a nap," Mrs. Manchester observed. "Traveling so far takes such a lot out of a person."

The bed did look comfortable, and the dancing flames on the hearth gave Kate a cozy, protected feeling. "I think you're right," she said, and kicking off her shoes, she crossed the room to stretch out on the bed.

Mrs. Manchester kindly covered her with a beautiful knitted afghan and slipped out, closing the door behind her.

Kate drifted off to sleep and dreamed of a campfire under a sky ablaze with silver stars. There, in that imaginary world, Sean lay beside her, his hand on her breast. She whimpered and stretched, wanting more of his touch.

"Kate." His voice penetrated her dream, low and husky.

She stretched again, still asleep, still needing.

She felt his fingers at the buttons of her shirt. Cool air whispered over her skin as he took away her bra. The feel of his mouth on her hardened nipple brought her awake with a start.

Although Sean was in the room, he was standing by the fireplace, and Kate was still fully dressed. Her disappointment was keen.

"That must have been a pretty erotic dream," he said, throwing another log on the fire before approaching the bed.

Kate blushed in the relative darkness of the room, but her words were bold. "It was. You were making love to me beside a campfire."

"Rest assured, Katie-did," he said, bending to kiss her forehead, "I'm not about to make love to you."

Kate glared up at him. "Why not?" she asked, insulted.

"Because the guilt would eat you alive," Sean answered. "For you at least, there would be three of us in the room—you, me and Abby."

Kate closed her eyes. As much as she wanted to cry out that he was wrong, she knew he wasn't. She tossed back the afghan and sat up.

"Mrs. Manchester made tea," Sean said, indicating a wheeled cart sitting beside the fireplace.

Apparently they were going to pretend they hadn't

discussed sex. Kate smoothed her hair and disappeared into the bathroom for a few minutes. When she came out, she had recovered her dignity.

She sat down in one of the two wing chairs facing the hearth and poured tea from a small china pot into a matching cup. There were strawberry scones, too, and various cookies she knew Sean would refer to as biscuits. Kate took a raspberry scone, even though she normally didn't eat sugary foods.

Sean was leaning against the fireplace mantle, watching Kate as though she were a complex puzzle. "Why are you here?" he asked.

Kate took a sip of strong tea before answering, "I wanted to see Gil, of course."

"If that were all of it, you'd have been here a long time before now."

Avoiding his gaze, Kate reached for a cookie. The man made her nervous, and when she was nervous, she ate. She shrugged. "I guess you could say I'm looking for myself," she replied. Her indigo eyes rose of their own accord to his face. "You were the one who said I needed a life of my own."

Sean poured tea into the second cup, added generous doses of sugar and milk and sat down in the chair across from Kate's. "Are you serious about that?"

Kate nodded. "I turned thirty a few days back, Sean, and look at me. I've never been married, never borne a child, never even worked at a real job that I landed on my own."

"And now you're out for an adventure?"

Kate considered for a moment. "Something like that."

Sean set his teacup down in its saucer. Even in the firelight Kate could see the mischief dancing in his eyes. "I think I can provide you with one of those," he said.

Before Kate could think of a response, Gil burst into the room with Snidely loping at his heels. "Mrs. Manchester's gone out to see her sister," he explained, "so I brought Snidely inside straight away." He glanced at the scones and biscuits.

"Have one," Kate said, watching him with delight.

Gil hesitated, looking to his father for permission. Sean must have given it silently, for the boy closed one grubby hand around a scone. After saying thank you and breaking off a small piece for Snidely, he ate hungrily.

"Are you going back to America soon?" the child asked when he'd disposed of the scone.

"I don't think so," Kate said, wondering if Gil was anxious for her to leave. She was probably disrupting some planned excursion with her unexpected visit.

"I hope you stay a long time," Gil responded. "You're not scared of Snidely and you don't go 'round saying he smells. I like that in a woman."

"It's certainly a trait I always look for," Sean agreed, deadpan.

Kate laughed and rumpled Gil's hair. "Well, I happen to like a discerning gentleman," she said.

"We'll try to dig one up for you," Sean replied.

Snidely was following his own tail in an endless circle. Outside, the winter rain drizzled against the windows, and the fire crackled on the hearth. Kate wanted to stay in that room with Gil and Sean forever.

As it happened, though, Sean rose out of his chair and said, "We'll leave you to yourself for a while. Dinner's in a couple of hours."

Kate wondered if she was supposed to dress up. It didn't seem likely that dinner would be formal when Mrs. Manchester was out of the house.

Feeling rumpled from her nap, she took a long, hot shower. Then, not knowing what was expected of her, she got into a striped dress in shades of pink and a pair of sandals. She wore her dark hair down and applied a small amount of makeup.

Sean's eyes lit up when she walked into the living room. He was wearing black pants and a beautiful cable-knit sweater, and his dark hair caught the light of the fire.

"Now I'm sorry we're having dinner at home," he teased, deliberately intensifying his accent. "I could make all me mates jealous if I showed you off."

Kate laughed, but his words pleased her. It had been a long time since she'd felt so attractive.

Sean offered white wine, and she nodded. When he brought her the glass, she asked, "Where's Gil?"

"He'll be along when he's done dressing. He had a bath—and Snidely got into the tub with him."

Kate laughed again at the picture that came to her mind, and then took a long sip of her wine because she felt so nervous inside. It was as though she'd regressed from thirty years of age to thirteen, and she couldn't for the life of her think of anything intelligent to say. She followed the sip with a gulp.

Sean was just about to say something when Gil bounded into the room, looking scrubbed and handsome in pants and a white shirt. "May I stay home tomorrow and look after Kate?" he asked with a hopeful lilt in his voice.

"Actually, no," Sean responded immediately.

Gil's disappointment was only momentary. After an instant, he was smiling broadly again. "Well," he said, "if you're going to be that way about it—"

"I am," Sean assured him.

Watching her nephew, Kate was thinking how much her parents would enjoy knowing him. She made a mental note to approach Sean, when the right moment arrived, about letting the boy visit.

The three had a simple dinner of meat pies and salad left behind by the very efficient Mrs. Manchester, and then Gil went off to do his homework. The next day was Monday, and school would be back in session.

"I'm sorry I haven't asked you before, Kate—how's your father?" Sean asked as they sat at a small table in a glass alcove, watching the rain fall.

"He's getting better every day," she answered. She studied Sean, wondering if she dared mention the possibility of a visit from Gil in the same sentence with her father. She decided against it. "I called home as soon as I arrived at the hotel, and Mother said he was almost ready to go back to Washington."

Sean turned his wineglass in one hand. "Have you let them know you're here?" he asked.

"I called the hotel and left word at the desk," she answered, yawning. "If any messages come in, they'll call me."

"You're still not over the jet lag," Sean remarked. "You'd better get some sleep."

"Will I see you tomorrow?"

Sean shook his head. "Not until late. I've got business meetings all day."

And Gil would be in school. A feeling of loneliness swept over Kate, and she lowered her eyes.

Unexpectedly Sean put his hand under her chin and raised her face. "Come away with me, Kate," he said hoarsely, getting to his feet and drawing her to him. "I'll show you the adventure of a lifetime."

Despite all her fine resolutions, Kate was powerless in his arms. Something melted deep inside her at the memory of that afternoon's erotic dream. "What kind of adventure?" she asked, her eyes wide as she looked up at him.

"I've got a little plane. I could show you some of the outback."

The idea intrigued Kate more than she would have dared to admit. "What about Gil?" she asked. "Would he go along, too?"

Sean shook his head. "He's got a school trip coming up. We could go then."

"When?" Kate wanted to know. She felt herself melting like a candle as Sean gently caressed her breasts.

"Day after tomorrow," he answered on a long, weary breath.

Kate closed her eyes. She wanted Sean to bare her as

he had that other time on her bed at home, but she knew he wouldn't. He was only torturing her, and himself. "Just the two of us," she mused aloud. "Interesting."

Sean bent his head and nibbled the covered peak of one breast. It went taut between his lips. "It'll be very interesting," he promised.

Kate was burning inside. The guilt she'd felt earlier was fading. Sean had a right to happiness, and so did she. No law, moral or civil, said the two of them had to stay apart for fear of defaming Abby's memory. "I think I should go back to my hotel," she said.

Sean lifted his head quickly, his green eyes full of questions. He voiced only one. "Why?"

"Because there I wouldn't feel as though Abby's watching me from beyond the veil," she answered.

"Gil won't understand," Sean reasoned.

Kate didn't want to do anything to hurt her nephew, especially when she was just getting to know him. "You're right," she conceded, deflated.

"There's another place we could go," Sean said thoughtfully. "Wait here."

Kate sat watching the fire and willing her agitated body to calm itself. Presently Sean returned, his hair sparkling with droplets of rainwater, accompanied by a teenage girl.

"This is Angie," he said to Kate. "She lives across the way, and she's Gil's favorite babysitter. Angie, this is my good friend, Kate Blake."

The pretty blond girl smiled at Kate. "That I am," she said. "Gil's favorite babysitter, I mean. Pleased to meet you, Miss Blake."

Kate nodded to the girl, but she was looking at Sean.

He beckoned to her with one hand, and against her better judgment, she stood and took his hand.

They were inside his car, a British sports model with a convertible top, and speeding down the driveway before Kate could catch her breath. She certainly hoped Sean didn't fly the way he drove.

"Where are we going?" she finally asked when it was clear that no explanation was forthcoming.

"You'll see," Sean answered.

A few minutes later they pulled into the parking garage of a towering building overlooking Sydney Harbour and the Opera House. Kate looked at Sean questioningly as he hauled her out of the car and strode off toward a bank of elevators, still gripping her hand.

"Sean!" she protested.

Inside, he pulled her close and kissed her so thoroughly that when he drew back, she was momentarily disoriented. He chuckled and kissed her again.

"Where are you taking me?" she demanded when she could gather the breath to speak.

The elevators whisked open on a small, beautifully decorated lobby. "This is the penthouse," Sean explained at last. "My company keeps it for visiting dignitaries."

Kate lifted an eyebrow as he unlocked the door. "Is that what I am?" she teased.

Sean winked. "Austra-Air wants to make sure your stay in Oz is memorable," he assured her. Then he opened the door, and Kate stepped into the penthouse, instantly bedazzled.

The outside walls were all glass, and Kate could see, through the rain, the lights of the bridge and the Opera House and the ferry boats crossing the water. All around them, in fact, lay the city like a kingdom made of colorful jewels.

"Oh, Sean, it's magnificent," Kate whispered.

He closed and locked the door. "So are you," he whispered, drawing her close again.

She reveled in the muscular hardness of his body as he bent and nibbled softly at her neck. When she was nearly too weak to stand, he led her into the darkened living room, where huge couches and chaise longues sat in the shadows. He removed her dress with a minimum of trouble, pleased to find she was wearing only panties beneath it.

Kate groaned as he laid her out on one of the large chaises, the city spread before her like a gift, and eased her panties down over her hips. Something nagged at her—the realization that she'd been so wrong about another man in what seemed to be another lifetime—but she couldn't break free of Sean's spell. It was entirely too powerful.

"Do you want me to love you, Kate?" he asked.

"Yes," Kate managed to whisper. "Oh, yes."

Gently he lifted her legs so that they rested over his shoulders. His hands caressed her inner thighs. "Prepare for some slight turbulence," he teased.

Chapter 5

After a few minutes of Sean's loving, Kate was frantic for fulfillment. A delirium of pleasure caused her to writhe and toss her head from side to side even as she pleaded, "Sean—I don't want to—not without you…"

Breathing very hard, he stripped off his sweater and tossed it away, then got to his feet. He lifted Kate into his arms and carried her into a nearby bedroom.

Her skin, covered with a fine film of perspiration from her exertions, felt deliciously cool. She watched her man as he removed the rest of his clothes and then came to her.

"Kate," he whispered hoarsely, just before his lips covered hers in a masterful kiss.

She responded with her whole being, her doubts falling away behind her like the tail of a comet. The throbbing heat in her body was building toward a crescendo again, and she began to twist and thrash beneath Sean. She was wildly impatient.

He buried his face in her neck, chuckling. "So it's like that, is it?" he teased in a husky rasp.

Kate arched her back, and in that moment, Sean's control snapped. He found and entered her in one fiery stroke.

For Kate, for that instant, all of creation froze like the slides in a broken kaleidoscope. In the next, the universe splintered into colorful pieces, for she had been too greatly aroused and too long denied. Her body bonded itself to Sean's, and with a primitive cry, she gave of herself, body and soul.

Her triumph excited Sean, and with a groan, he began increasing his pace. Kate urged him on with soft, breathless words and the motions of her hands. She met each thrust with a swift rise of her hips, taking him far inside her.

He muttered something that might have been either a prayer or a curse when the quest became urgent, and then, with a hoarse shout, he stiffened, gasping her name.

Her hands soothed the moist, muscle-corded expanse of his back. "I'm here," she whispered.

Sean trembled violently as he surrendered, then sank down beside Kate on the bed of shadows. "God," he muttered. "My God."

They lay still and silent for a long time, and then Kate started to rise from the bed. Sean immediately pressed her back down.

"I'm not through with you yet, love," he told her. "Not nearly."

Kate gave an involuntary groan as he found her breast in the darkness and weighed it in the palm of his hand. His thumb moved over the responsive nipple, shaping it. Preparing it.

She twisted onto her stomach, gasping, knowing she needed a few minutes to rest. But Sean was granting no quarter; he reached beneath her, and she flung back her head like a wild mare when he found what he sought.

"Stop," Kate murmured, even as she ground her hips in an involuntary response.

"Not until you're satisfied," Sean replied.

Kate could not turn onto her back again, for she was trapped by her own needs. "Oh, Sean—Sean—"

"Almost there," he told her, intensifying his efforts to drive her mad. "Almost there…"

Kate was damp with perspiration from her head to her feet. Her legs were stiff and wide apart, and her toes curled into the bedspread, seeking purchase. Her hands were pressed against the mattress, raising her upper body from the bed. "Oh," she cried, lifting her eyes to a ceiling she couldn't see. "Oh—*oh*…"

"It's going to be a long night, love," she heard Sean say gently from somewhere beyond the exploding lights and shooting flares of her climax. "A long, sweet night."

Kate awakened feeling as though she were lying in the light of a gentle sun, her sated body wrapped in the softest silk. Expertly Sean had put her through her paces, draining away all her tensions.

He bent and kissed her. "We'd better go, love. Mrs. Manchester will get the idea we're up to something."

Kate laughed and then stretched. "I don't think I can move from this bed," she said.

"That's fine, too," Sean answered. He was fully dressed again, but he pretended he was about to take off his sweater.

Kate bounded out of bed and hurried into the bathroom. One more session of Sean's singular brand of loving would turn her into a madwoman for sure.

She took a hasty shower and got back into her panties and dress, which Sean had thoughtfully brought from the living room. He was there when she came to him, looking out at the city lights and sipping from a crystal glass.

"What's that?" Kate asked.

"Vodka," he answered.

Kate wrinkled her nose. "Bad for you," she said.

"We're fresh out of carrot juice," Sean explained. "Let's go, love."

They took the elevator down to the parking garage and walked to Sean's car. When Kate was seated in the passenger seat, Sean walked around to the driver's side and got in. The engine roared to life and Kate felt sad to be leaving a place that had been hers and Sean's for a house that had been Abby's.

"I'll sell the house," Sean said, and Kate was convinced he'd been reading her mind. "It's that simple."

"It isn't, and you know it," Kate argued. "You have a child—my sister's child. I live in one hemisphere, and you live in another. There are just too many differences."

"What about tonight?" Sean argued. "Was that a difference?"

Kate swallowed. "A few more nights like tonight and I'll be a candidate for a nursing home. I must have had six…" Her cheeks went hot as she fell silent.

"Seven," Sean replied, "but who's counting?"

"That was only physical," she said. "You can't build a relationship on that." She prayed Sean would say he loved her, so she could tell him her real feelings for him.

"Come on, Kate. Men and women have been building 'relationships'—I hate that word—on *that* for a few million years." He shifted gears as they began moving uphill. "Beware of me, Katie-did—now I know how to bring you right into line."

Kate's face throbbed with renewed heat, and she was grateful for the darkness. "That was a chauvinistic thing to say!"

"Nevertheless," Sean replied with a shrug, "it's true."

And it was, although Kate would have died before admitting it. All Sean had to do was maneuver her into certain positions, touch her in certain ways, and she was lost.

"The way it is with us," he began after a long silence. "Was it like that with Brad?"

Kate knew he was really asking if what they had was new to her, so she didn't resent the question. "Brad and I never made love," she admitted, "so I wouldn't know."

Sean pulled the car over to the side of the street and

stopped so suddenly that Kate was stunned. "What?" he demanded.

"I said, Brad and I never made love—"

"How the hell did you manage that? You were engaged to the man!"

Kate's eyes were very wide. "You sound angry."

A closer look proved that he was more indignant than angry. "I feel so cheap," he said.

Kate couldn't help laughing. "I think that's supposed to be my line," she told him.

"You were saving yourself for marriage with him," Sean pointed out. "With me, it's a fast roll in the straw and 'thank you very much I've got a plane to catch'!"

Kate only shook her head, baffled.

Sean wrenched the car back into gear and pulled onto the road again, muttering a swear word.

Kate squinted at him in the darkness. "Did I miss something here? I haven't been to bed with anyone since college, and you're upset because you're the first?"

"Who was he?" Sean barked.

"Who?" Kate countered, getting angry herself now.

"The guy in college!"

Kate laughed again. "My God, I don't believe this!"

Sean's hands tightened on the steering wheel, then relaxed again. "Were you in love with him?"

Kate sighed, turning her eyes to the rain-misted view. Even in that weather, at that hour of the night, it was magnificent. "I thought so. His name was Ryan Fletcher, and we were going to be married."

"What stopped you?"

"Abby brought you home, and I realized what love really was."

Sean was quiet for a moment, then he said something that surprised Kate to the core of her being. "I married the wrong sister, I think."

Kate reached out and laid a hand on his thigh. She felt the muscles tighten to a granite hardness beneath her palm. "What went wrong between you and Abby?" she asked. "You were so happy once."

"Maybe I was. Abby changed her mind about life with me about five minutes after our plane took off from Seattle. She didn't like being married to a pilot, she didn't like sex, she didn't like Australia."

"Why didn't she leave you, then, and come home?"

Sean gave Kate a sidelong look. "This was home," he said flatly.

"Not to Abby," Kate pointed out.

"And not to you," Sean replied.

"We're not talking about me," Kate countered.

"I think we are," Sean argued. "You couldn't stay here with me and be happy any more than Abby could. You're a Yank, and you belong in the States."

Kate sighed. "I'll decide where I belong, thank you very much."

"You belong in my bed," Sean answered, "and if you think you can deny me, I'll have to prove my point."

Kate knew better. Sean could take her anytime, anyplace he wanted; her responses were evidence of that. All the same, her pride made her keep a defiant silence.

They had reached Sean's house, and the garage door

opened at a command from a button on the dashboard. The inside was only dimly lit.

Kate started to get out of the car, but Sean stopped her by gripping her wrist in his hand. He gave her a soft, savage kiss. When it was over, her knees were so weak that she could hardly walk inside the house on her own, but she wouldn't let Sean support her. He'd done quite enough.

In her room, Kate quickly undressed and put on a flannel nightshirt. She brushed her teeth and climbed into bed, determined to sleep.

She couldn't. For much of the night she relived the things she and Sean had done together, and by morning she needed him again.

With Sean in meetings and Gil in school, Kate had a day strictly to herself. The first thing she did was place a call to the United States, using her credit card.

Her mother answered on the second ring. "Hello?"

"Hi, Mother," Kate said, feeling shy with this woman, as though they were strangers with little common ground. In many ways, of course, they were exactly that.

"Kate," Irene confirmed, sounding a little annoyed. "Well, how is our world traveler?"

Kate suppressed a sigh. "I'm fine," she replied. "How are you and Daddy?"

"I'm very well, thank you, and your father is almost his old self again. We're off to the house in Washington tomorrow, as a matter of fact. Have you seen Gil?"

"I'm staying in the same house with him. He's a wonderful boy, Mother."

"Of course he is," Irene answered, sounding impatient. "He's Abby's child, isn't he?"

Kate could not have explained the emotions her mother's words aroused in her, and she was glad she didn't have to. She was also glad to be more than ten thousand miles away. "I think Sean had something to do with the project," she pointed out.

Irene sighed. "Which brings me to the most obvious question of all. What are you doing staying under that man's roof?" She made it sound as though Kate had taken a room in hell in order to have regular chess matches with the devil.

Kate thought of the sweet torments Sean had subjected her to the night before and wanted him more than ever. It was all she could do not to answer, *I'm here because I'm addicted to his lovemaking.* "It's a big house, Mother," she said instead. "They've got lots of room. Besides, this way I can be close to Gil."

"I'm not at all sure your father will approve. You haven't taken up with that man, have you?"

"*That man* has a name. It's Sean."

"Very well then, Katherine—are you involved with *Sean*?"

Kate wanted very much to answer yes, but she didn't quite dare to do it. "I'm his friend," she said, and her lips curved into a wry smile as she thought what an understatement that was.

"He's a monster—directly responsible for your sister's death."

Kate closed her eyes. "You know that isn't true, Mother. You remember what the coroner said. She'd been drinking and taking pills."

"Only because Sean Harris drove her to it. Australian men are chauvinists, Katherine. They use you up and throw you away when they're finished."

"I didn't call to argue about Australian men," Kate said firmly.

"Don't hang up!" Irene said quickly.

"We may not be the best of friends, Mother," Kate answered, "but we haven't reached that point."

"Your father will want to know whether or not you'll be bringing Gil back to the States and when."

Kate was developing a headache. "I haven't spoken to Sean about that yet. I need time."

"Just remember that your father isn't getting any younger, and he has a weak heart. It would mean the world to him to see his grandson."

Guilt swept over Kate like an ocean wave, but she stood strong against it. It wasn't her mission in life to effect a reunion between her parents and Gil. "I'll do my best," she said. "Goodbye, Mother."

"Goodbye, Katherine," her mother responded.

It would have been easy for Kate to lapse into a low-grade depression at that point, but she was determined not to let Irene get her down. She hung up and went to find Mrs. Manchester.

After conferring with the housekeeper about the best places to shop, Kate called a cab and ventured into downtown Sydney. Soon she was happily embroiled in purchasing the things she would need for her mysterious adventure with Sean. She bought several pairs of jeans, heavy flannel shirts, special underwear, socks and hiking boots. Then, lugging her bags, she found a model airplane for Gil, a fancy collar for Snidely, a book for Sean and a small box of imported chocolates for Mrs. Manchester.

It was midafternoon when she arrived back at Sean's house, where Gil and Snidely met her at the gate.

"I was afraid you'd gone back to America without saying goodbye," Gil told her.

Kate shifted all her packages so that she could ruffle his hair. "I'd never do that," she said gently. "Didn't Mrs. Manchester tell you I was out shopping?"

Gil shook his head. "All she said was to keep Snidely out of her clean house," he said. His brown eyes took in the bags she carried, one of which was clearly marked with the name of a local toy store. "What have you got there?"

"Help me get them inside and I'll show you," Kate answered, handing over half her burden to her nephew.

He accepted graciously, and the two of them went as far as the screened porch, Snidely at their heels. They dropped the bags and boxes on a wicker sofa, and Kate handed the model airplane to Gil.

His brown eyes widened. "Thank you, Aunt Kate," he said, accepting the gift.

"I believe the American word is 'wow,'" commented a quiet masculine voice from the inner doorway.

Kate looked up and saw Sean, and she went warm all over.

"Wow!" crowed Gil.

Kate felt almost shy, despite the fact that she'd thrashed beneath this man's hands and lips and body the night before. "I bought something for you, too," she said, handing him the book. It was an illustrated history of aviation.

"Thanks, Kate," he said. He accepted the book.

"And I didn't forget Snidely or Mrs. Manchester, either," Kate announced, perhaps too brightly. She felt awkward and inept all of a sudden.

Sean set aside the book to help a delighted Gil put the new collar on the dog. Moments later the boy rushed off to the kitchen to present Mrs. Manchester with her chocolates.

"What else did you buy?" Sean asked. The way his green eyes touched Kate made her feel a special intimacy with him, a deep need for more of what they had shared in the night.

Kate shrugged. "Jeans and shirts to wear when we go away," she said.

Sean was very close now. "Smart girl," he said. His hands rested on the sides of Kate's waist; his lips were a fraction of an inch from hers. "Did you buy a sexy nightgown?"

Kate eyes widened. "No," she admitted.

He gave her a light, nibbling kiss that set her senses afire. "Good, little sheila, because you aren't going to need one."

Kate trembled at the portent of his words. She was afraid and excited, wanting to run away and to stay, both at the same time. "Are you making an indecent proposal?"

Sean kissed her again, more thoroughly this time. "Absolutely," he answered, supporting Kate when her knees went limp beneath her.

She looked up at him, dazed. If he'd led her off to bed at that moment, she would have gone willingly, even eagerly, but he didn't. He gave her a swat on the bottom and nodded toward the bag of clothes she'd bought for their trip. "You'd better wash those before you wear them," he said.

Kate batted her eyelashes at him. "Thanks. I never would have thought of that on my own."

He gave her another swat and helped her gather up the bags. They were in the laundry room, cutting off tags and poking things into the washer, when Mrs. Manchester arrived, shooed them off and took over the project herself.

Sean took Kate's hand and led her into the living room. Since it was a bright, sunny day outside, there was no fire burning on the hearth, but Kate knew there would be later. Winter nights in New South Wales were cold.

"Where are we going on this adventure of ours?" Kate asked, perching on the arm of a comfortable sofa upholstered in practical navy blue fabric while Sean poured himself a drink.

"Queensland," he answered. "To a place out beyond Lightning Ridge."

"But it's winter," Kate reasoned.

Sean winked at her. "No worries, love. I'll keep you plenty warm of a night, and sometimes in the daytime, too."

Kate blushed and lowered her eyes. She could hardly wait to leave. "We'll go tomorrow?"

Sean nodded. "Can you wait that long, little sheila?"

Kate glared at him. Sometimes he carried his caveman routine just a little too far. "I can wait forever."

"Don't make me prove you a liar," Sean said, grinning. Then he set aside his drink and approached her.

Kate's breath caught in her throat when he placed gentle hands on both sides of her face and kissed her, his tongue claiming her almost as masterfully as his manhood had the night before.

"Maybe I'd better take you to bed," he said softly when the kiss was over and Kate was still trying to regain her balance.

Kate trembled. His delicious threat was empty, since Gil and Mrs. Manchester were home. Wasn't it?

Sean chuckled at her bemusement and gave her another soul-rendering kiss. When it was over, Kate had to sink down onto the couch, since she couldn't stand on her own any longer.

Gil came bounding in at that moment like a fresh breeze, carrying the box that contained his new model airplane beneath one arm. "Can we put this together tonight, Dad?" he asked eagerly, his brown eyes shining as he looked up at his father.

Kate felt such love for both Sean and Gil in that moment that she couldn't have spoken past the lump in her throat. Tears of emotion glistened in her eyes, but if Sean noticed, he pretended otherwise.

"We could get a start on it, I suppose," Sean agreed.

"Have you got all your things packed for the trip to Canberra?"

Gil nodded. "Mrs. Manchester took care of that," he said.

With a wink at Kate, Sean took the colorful box his son was holding out to him. "This looks like a three-man job to me," He said. "Want to help?"

Kate wanted to be near both of them. "Sure," she said with a sniffle.

Gil squinted at her. "Are you crying, Aunt Kate?" he asked.

Kate shook her head. "Yes," she said, contradicting her own gesture.

"Women," commented Gil.

Sean laughed, and even though he didn't touch Kate in any way, she felt as though she'd been held and comforted.

The three spent a happy evening putting the model airplane together, although Sean complained that it was a job Wilbur and Orville Wright wouldn't have wanted to tackle. By the time dinner was served, the plane was only half-finished.

"Looks like the rest of this will have to wait until you get back from your trip, mate," Sean told his son. "You've got lessons to do, haven't you?"

Gil nodded and went off to wash his hands before supper. When he joined Sean and Kate at the table, he was already yawning. "I'll bring you back a present from Canberra," he promised Kate. His eyes flickered to his father. "And you, too, Dad," he added.

"Thanks for remembering," Sean said with a grin.

Gil sighed contentedly. "This has been the best night since my birthday," he said.

Again Kate felt silly, sentimental tears stinging her eyes. She quickly lowered her gaze to the delectable seafood salad on her plate. In that moment she mourned all the birthdays and Christmases she'd missed with Gil, just as though he were her own son.

Sean's hand closed over hers, though only momentarily. "You're tired," he said.

Kate nodded. That was true enough. She'd never really recovered from jet lag, and then she'd spent most of the previous night in Sean's arms.

Sean's voice was almost unbearably gentle. "Maybe you'd like Mrs. Manchester to bring your dinner to your room? After all, it'll be an early morning tomorrow."

Kate wouldn't be pampered. She ate what she could of her dinner before excusing herself to hurry off to her room. After a brief shower, she collapsed into bed without even putting on a nightgown.

Chapter 6

That night was cold, but the next day dawned bright and warm. As Kate sipped the bracing tea Mrs. Manchester had brought to her, she looked ahead to the trip she and Sean planned to share and wondered what had possessed her to agree to it. She was not the daring type, as a general rule.

Abby had been the bold one. She'd been the one to skydive, get a pilot's license and go off to Australia to live with a new husband. Kate wondered what had changed her sister from a fearless woman to a little girl writing petulant emails home but refusing to do anything about her situation.

A knock on her bedroom door interrupted Kate's musings, and she uttered a distracted, "Come in."

It was Mrs. Manchester, back for the tea service. She

smiled at Kate and waited politely for an indication that she was through.

"You didn't work here when my sister was alive, did you?" Kate asked the older woman, frowning. "I'm sure I'd remember you."

Mrs. Manchester hesitated. Her warm eyes skirted Kate's. "I was here when she died, miss," she finally answered. "I'd just taken over from Mrs. Pennwyler."

"Is she still around anywhere, this Mrs. Pennwyler?" Kate asked. "I'd like to talk with her about Abby."

Mrs. Manchester shook her head. "Sorry, love. The old girl, bless her soul, has gone to live with her eldest son up in Darwin."

"What do you remember about Abby?"

"Mrs. Harris was very unhappy, miss."

Kate nodded. "I know. She emailed often. But I've never understood why she didn't divorce Sean—Mr. Harris—and catch a plane home."

"She had problems," the housekeeper said sadly.

Kate nodded, thinking of the coroner's report. A chill swept over her as she imagined what it must have been like for Abby hurtling off a high cliff that way, knowing she was going to die within seconds.

Mrs. Manchester was putting Kate's cup and saucer and the plate that had held a flaky croissant onto a tray. "Mustn't let the dead get in the way of the living," she said wisely. "Our time is limited enough as it is."

For the first time since she'd started thinking about Abby, Kate smiled. "You're right," she agreed. "Is Mr. Harris up yet?"

Mrs. Manchester laughed. "Up? He's been out and about for hours, miss—just got back a few minutes ago."

Kate looked down at her jeans, flannel shirt and hiking boots as Mrs. Manchester left the room. She hoped she was dressed for whatever Sean had planned.

As if summoned by the mere thought of his name, he appeared, looking around the door at Kate. There was an appreciative glint in his green eyes. "Everything's ready, love," he said.

A tremor of mingled delight and fear went through Kate as the man she loved stepped into the room. Like her, he was wearing jeans and a casual shirt. He carried a slouchy leather hat in one hand. "How do I look?" she asked.

"Good enough to eat," Sean responded hoarsely, and another shiver went through Kate even as her skin flushed hot.

She cleared her throat and averted her eyes for a moment, feeling shy again. "What about Gil? Did he leave on his field trip?"

"While you were still sleeping," Sean said. One moment he was in the doorway, the next he was standing so close to Kate that she could feel the heat of his body. He traced the outline of her mouth with a light touch of his index finger.

Kate trembled visibly, and her response embarrassed and angered her. "I could still back out, you know," she pointed out.

Boldly Sean cupped his hand over one of her breasts. The nipple hardened beneath the stroking of his thumb. "Could you?" he countered.

Kate groaned. "That isn't fair," she managed to say.

Sean was unbuttoning her shirt. Beneath it she wore a stretchy undershirt, rather than a bra, and her breasts and nipples were clearly visible through the thin fabric. Sean admired them for a long moment while Kate's cheeks flared pink. Although she was outraged, she was unable to stop him.

With one finger, he drew the neckline of the undershirt down until one breast was exposed, plump and vulnerable. "Just a little taste of what's going to happen when I get you alone," Sean said, and when he bent and touched Kate's nipple with the tip of his tongue, she tensed with sudden, violent pleasure. All thought of rebellion gone, she cupped her hands behind his head and pressed him to her.

But he was only playing. He abandoned the bare breast and turned to the one covered by the undershirt. Through the fabric, he nipped at it, grazing it lightly with his teeth, and Kate cried out softly, her head falling back.

Again she was disappointed. Sean caressed her naked breast once before covering it again, then he rebuttoned her shirt. She had never been more frustrated in her life.

"Sean, I need you," she managed to say.

He gave her a kiss as exciting as his dalliance with her breasts had been. "Later, little sheila."

Kate ached. "Now," she said.

Sean chuckled and gave her trim backside a swat. "Later," he repeated.

Kate was furious. Sean had aroused her on purpose

and now he was just going to leave her to suffer. "I want you now," she insisted.

"Tough," Sean replied. He grasped Kate by the hand, taking up her suitcase with the other. She allowed him to lead her through the house and out into the driveway where an open Jeep was parked.

"Damn you," she whispered angrily. "I want you to drop this Tarzan routine right now!"

Sean tossed her expensive suitcase into the back of the Jeep as though it were bargain-brand stuff. Then, grinning down at Kate, he lifted her by the waist and set her down inside the vehicle.

Although her pride dictated that she get out of the Jeep, storm into the house and call a taxi to take her back to the hotel, she buckled the seat belt instead.

Sean put the hat on and got behind the wheel. Looking over one shoulder, Kate noticed he'd brought a lot of other things besides her suitcase. She saw a tent, a single sleeping bag, fishing poles and a lot of packaged food, among other things.

"How come there's only one sleeping bag?" she demanded.

Sean grinned at her as he shifted into reverse. He was looking back at the road when he answered, "Spoiling for a fight, aren't you, sheila? Well, watch out, because you're about to get one."

Kate glowered at him and folded her arms across her chest. Her breasts still tingled from Sean's earlier attentions. He was a skunk, she decided, to get her excited and then leave her high and dry. "I wouldn't lower myself," she said.

"We'll see about that," Sean quipped, and then they were moving rapidly down the left hand side of the road.

Kate gasped, forgetting for a moment that all Australians drove that way. Sean put a hand on her thigh. Although Kate knew the gesture was meant to relax her, it only heightened her tensions.

"It'll be all right, Katie-did," he shouted over the noise of the wind.

Kate pushed his hand away and folded her arms again. That made Sean laugh.

They didn't attempt to speak after that. Instead, they raced through traffic rapidly, leaving the sprawling city behind. After an hour they reached a small airport.

Kate felt as though the breath had been buffeted from her. Her hair, so carefully plaited into a tidy French braid, was flying wildly about her face. Before looking at Sean, she grimaced into the side mirror to make sure there were no bugs in her teeth.

Sean caught her by surprise when he lifted her from the Jeep. Her body brushed the length of his as he lowered her to her feet, and the ache within her intensified until it was nearly unbearable.

"I ought to slap you," she said.

He kissed her until her knees were weak. "Patience, little one," he told her gruffly. "We're spending tonight on a friend of mine's station. You can do all your lovely little tricks for me when we're alone."

Kate decided then that she definitely *would* slap him. She raised her hand to do so, but Sean caught her by the wrist and pulled her close. She was breathless.

Sean kissed her forehead lightly. "Behave yourself,"

he ordered. Then he left Kate and started unloading the things in the back of the Jeep.

For lack of a better idea, Kate helped. He stowed the tent inside a small twin-engine airplane and went back for more baggage. Once they'd loaded the plane, he got inside and started the engines, then walked around the small craft, making a mysterious examination of everything.

Thinking she might lose her courage if she didn't take definite action, Kate climbed onto the wing, the way she'd seen Sean do, opened the passenger door and got into the seat.

Sean was wearing earphones now, and tuning in the radio. "Buckle up, love," he said to Kate.

She fastened her seat belt, trying not to think about how small and fragile that airplane seemed. As far as Kate was concerned, it was almost as flimsy as Gil's model. She bit down hard on her lower lip and clasped the edges of the seat in both hands.

Sean was talking with the control tower, but Kate didn't listen to his words. Her whole life was passing before her eyes.

Soon the plane was lumbering and jolting along the rough pavement toward the single runway. Kate closed her eyes tight and prayed silently for some last-minute reprieve, like a flat tire or an empty gas tank.

God was not listening to Kate's prayer. The airplane gained the runway and began taxiing along it at an ever-increasing speed.

"Open your eyes, Kate," Sean said reasonably, although he had to speak in a loud voice to be heard over the roar of the engines.

Kate obeyed him, not because of any desire to see, but because her first impulse was always to do just as Sean said. She was going to have to work on that, or she'd end up fetching his slippers and lighting his pipe. "Oh, God," she cried.

Sean laughed as the little craft hurtled into the sky. The ground fell away beneath them while they climbed toward the clouds.

Kate's knuckles were beginning to ache. She released her grasp on the seat and let out her breath. An exhilarating sensation of freedom and excitement had overtaken her horror, and her eyes went wide as she looked down upon farmhouses and fields.

"It's beautiful!"

"I know," Sean answered. They had gained enough altitude, it seemed, for he was leveling the plane off now. He muttered something into the speaker on his earphone and then grinned at Kate. "Control says they're glad you like it," he told her.

Kate made a mental note to watch what she said from then on. There were things she wanted to say to Sean that were none of Control's business. She rolled her eyes at him and gave him a shaky smile.

They'd been flying for over an hour when Sean switched the radio off and removed the earphones.

Kate was alarmed. "Don't you need to stay in contact with the tower?" she asked.

Sean smiled indulgently. "We're too far out for that, love," he said.

"Oh," Kate replied, and she was smiling, too. There were thoughts of revenge in her mind. "I suppose there's no reason I can't repay you for all the frustration you've caused me, then, is there?"

Sean looked a little worried. "I don't know what you're talking about," he said.

Kate unfastened her seat belt and turned sideways. "You will," she promised.

Sean stiffened and gave an involuntary groan as she ran her hand lightly up his thigh.

And that was only the beginning.

By the time the trees and craggy cliffs beneath them had given way to open grassland, Sean was as disconcerted and unsatisfied as Kate. He gave her a hard look as she settled back and refastened her seat belt.

She smiled at him. "How do you like the taste of your own medicine, Mr. Harris?" she asked.

"I'd step lightly if I were you, sheila," he told her. His jaw was clamped down tight, and he shifted uncomfortably in his seat. "As you Yanks like to say, you're on thin ice."

Kate tilted her head to one side. "Just what is it you're threatening to do to me?" she asked sweetly, batting her eyelashes and clasping her hands together beneath her chin. "Beat me? Strip me naked and leave me for the dingoes?"

Sean gave her a wry look. "Wrong. Except, of course, the part where I strip you naked. I like that one."

Kate laughed. "I think we're even," she said.

"Do you? Well, two can play at your game." With

that, he reached out and laid his hand on her upper thigh. She tensed as his fingers brushed her most sensitive and private place. Even knowing that he had no intention of satisfying her, any more than she'd satisfied him, she couldn't bring herself to push him away.

She felt a thin layer of perspiration cooling her heated skin. "Sean," she whispered as he tormented her with touches as light as the passing of a butterfly.

He chuckled. "The poet was right. Vengeance is sweet."

"I hate you," Kate gasped, even as her body jerked slightly in response to the whisper-light forays of his fingers.

"Absolutely," he replied.

"Oh," Kate moaned.

"Open your shirt, Kate," Sean said quietly. His tone was warm and inviting and terribly seductive. "I want to look at you."

"No," she murmured breathlessly, even as her fingers rose awkwardly to the buttons of her shirt and began working them.

When her shirt was open, Sean's fingers moved to her breasts. Their peaks strained against the fabric of her undershirt, longing to be free.

"You know what I want now, Kate," Sean said with a gentle kind of sternness that heated Kate's blood to a passionate simmer.

She did know, and it wasn't in her to refuse, even though she knew Sean was only dallying with her. He would leave her unsated until they were in bed that night, and that was hours away. With both hands, she raised the undershirt so that her breasts were bared for Sean's gratification.

He made an appreciative sound low in his throat and began to caress and shape her. With a groan, Kate sunk her teeth into her lower lip and turned her head, looking down at the distant ground, searching for anything that would distract her from Sean's delicious torment.

Half a dozen kangaroos hopped along the grassy ground, moving more rapidly than Kate had ever dreamed they could. She moaned as Sean continued to fondle her, arching her back even as she searched her mind for a way to rebel.

The plane began a gradual descent, and Kate scanned the horizon. There was no sign of a station anywhere in sight. She couldn't even see a single sheep.

"What are you doing?" she asked.

Sean withdrew his hand in order to concentrate fully on the controls. "You win, sheila," he answered cryptically. "I can't wait any longer."

"But this is the middle of nowhere!" Kate cried, coming swiftly to her senses. She pulled down her undershirt and then fastened her buttons.

"The perfect place," Sean answered.

Moments later the plane was bumping crazily along the ground. "What if we can't take off again?" she asked, wide-eyed.

"In a few minutes, love," he answered, "you're not going to need a plane to fly."

Kate's muscles went limp, then tensed again, going taut as piano wire. The plane came to a stop, and she closed her eyes in relief. Her heart was hammering, and she wasn't sure whether it was the unscheduled landing that had caused it, or the prospect of Sean's lovemaking.

He opened his door and climbed out onto the wing, then jumped nimbly to the ground. Kate was still trembling in her seat when he came around, got up onto the wing on her side and opened the door.

His eyes full of mischief and promise, he kept his gaze fixed to Kate's all the while he was unfastening her seat belt and turning her to face him. Her legs dangled outside the plane, on either side of his hips.

"Oh," Kate whimpered as he began unbuttoning her shirt.

He soon had that laid aside and her undershirt up beneath her armpits. Her breasts were warm and swollen under his gaze, their peaks pouting for his attention.

She cried out in mingled relief and despair when his mouth closed over one of her nipples. "A—aren't you even going to kiss me?" she asked.

He drew back long enough to answer, "I'm past that, thanks to your teasing. Now you'll have to pay the piper."

Sean took a long time at Kate's breasts, enjoying first one and then the other. When he finally pressed her back across her own seat and his, she was almost out of her mind with need. She felt the snap open on her jeans, trembled as they slid, her panties with them, down over her hips.

Ever so lightly, Sean kissed the tangled silk that sheltered Kate's femininity from all but him. She moaned and lifted her hips as an offering, but he only teased her with more kisses. At the same time, his hands were busy removing her boots, pulling her jeans and panties down and off.

When Kate was thrashing from side to side, frantic with need, he raised up. She felt all the familiar doubts and fears, all the old insecurities, but they weren't enough to stop her. She held her breath as he opened his zipper and freed himself. When he entered her, she became a wild thing, clutching at him with her hands and wrapping her legs around his hips.

Although she urged him to hurry, Sean's pace was slow and rhythmic. He meant to extract the last ounce of response from Kate before satisfying himself, and that knowledge only increased her frenzy.

When she was on the edge, he stopped to enjoy her breasts again at his leisure. Kate was woman at her most primitive; she pleaded, she threatened, she wheedled and bargained.

At last, with a low moan of his own, Sean gave in. He began to move more rapidly, and the friction made Kate cry out and stiffen as satisfaction overtook her. She was torn apart in those moments, and reassembled into a new, softer and gentler woman. She had been mastered, like a wild mare broken to ride, and the feeling was glorious.

Sean's release was a violent one. He lunged deep inside Kate and hurled his head back, his teeth bared over a string of savage endearments.

Kate cupped his taut buttocks in her hands as his powerful body bucked several more times, and then he fell to her breasts, gasping for air. Within moments, he was rolling a taut nipple between his lips and then suckling hungrily even as his torso heaved with the effort to breathe.

Kate plunged her fingers into his hair. She would have been content to hold him like that all day but, when he'd had a long turn at both her breasts, he raised his head and pulled her undershirt down. While he fetched Kate's panties and jeans from the wing, she hastily buttoned her shirt.

He bent and kissed both her knees before handing her the rest of her clothes. "You're a bad girl, sheila," he scolded. "Maybe that's why I like you so much."

Kate wished he would have said he loved her, but she'd long since learned that wishes were one thing and reality was very often another. "You're a scoundrel," she said, wrenching on her panties and jeans. "Where are my boots?"

Sean recovered them from the ground and handed them to her, rounding the plane as Kate shoved her feet into them.

He boarded the plane and reached across Kate to close her door, the back of his arm brushing her full breasts. "That'll keep you satisfied until tonight I hope," he said.

"Your arrogance is not to be believed!" Kate fussed.

Sean grinned broadly and quoted back some of the outrageous things she'd said to him during her climb to the heights.

"Bastard," Kate said.

The plane engines whirred and the propellers began to spin.

"Have you ever taken off from a place with no runway before?" she asked worriedly, now having something else to think about besides the obnoxious man beside her.

"Only about fifty thousand times," Sean answered, reaching for a pair of mirrored sunglasses on the instrument panel and putting them on with a flourish.

Kate was back to gripping the edges of the seat, although she was so relaxed that it was hard to hold on. She wanted nothing so much as to crawl into some warm, safe bed right there on the ground and sleep for twenty-four hours.

The plane jolted terribly as Sean increased its speed. Finally, with a rattling mechanical grunt, it flung itself into the air. Kate let go of her seat.

"I'm getting hungry," she said.

"I don't wonder," Sean answered, "considering the energy you've burned up in the past few minutes."

Kate hit him in the shoulder, but she was grinning. She felt too damn good to be angry.

After another hour in the air, an enormous flock of sheep came into view, shepherded by a man and three dogs. In the distance, Kate could make out a sizable house and a number of rustic outbuildings.

"Is that your friend?"

Sean rocked the plane from side to side, and the man below waved a hand. "Yes," he answered. "That's Blue. He's the best mate I ever had."

Kate continued to stare at the ground as Sean banked the plane into a wide sweep around the house and buildings and began a descent toward a dirt landing strip below. She could see another plane on the ground, as well as gasoline pumps and a pickup truck with rusty fenders.

"Does he live here all by himself?" Kate asked, thinking how lonely that would be. This part of Australia was so vast and empty, except for the occasional gum tree and the ever-present brown grass.

Sean shook his head as the plane nosed downward. "He's got a wife and kids."

"Kids?" Kate echoed. "Out here? Where do they go to school?"

Sean was busy landing the airplane, so he didn't look at Kate as they landed. "They don't. Ellen teaches them herself."

Any answer Kate might have made was prevented by the jostling impact of touching down. She breathed a silent prayer of gratitude for a safe landing and unfastened her seat belt.

Sean stopped Kate before she could open the door and jump out of the plane. "Don't be trying to put any fancy ideas in Ellen's head," he warned. "She likes her life the way it is."

While Kate was still thinking what an odd remark that was, Sean shut off the engines and got out himself. He came around to lift Kate to the ground as a slender blond woman came running from the direction of the house, her face alight.

"Sean!" she cried as she reached him and flung herself into his arms.

He gave her a hug and a sound kiss on the forehead and set her down. "Ellen," he said, "meet Kate."

Kate greeted the woman with a smile and an outstretched hand, even though she was wondering why Sean hadn't mentioned that she was Abby's sister. "Hi," she said.

Turquoise eyes sparkled in a suntanned complexion. "Hello, Kate," Ellen said, accepting Kate's hand with a strong grip. Momentarily she turned back to Sean. "Did you bring me books and chocolate bars?" she demanded.

Sean laughed and gestured toward the plane where the gear was stowed. "Enough to last you six months," he answered.

Kate heard dogs barking in the distance and the bleating of sheep. Soon, Sean's friend Blue would reach them.

She looked nervously at Sean. She wondered if Blue and Ellen had been Abby's friends, too.

Sean glanced at her, and once again she had the strange sensation that he could read her thoughts. He put one arm around her waist and pulled her close, his lips moving softly against her temple.

"Tonight," he whispered.

Chapter 7

When Sean had taken a large grocery box from the back of the airplane, he and Kate and Ellen started off toward the house.

It was a sturdy, practical-looking place, built mostly of natural stone. Smoke curled from two different chimneys, reminding Kate that the day was cool. She'd forgotten in the heat of Sean's lovemaking and its glowing aftermath that it was winter in Australia.

As they neared the house, three children, two girls and a boy, appeared at one end of a long, verandalike porch. "It *is* you!" one of the little girls cried, bounding down the steps to attach herself to Sean's right leg.

Sean laughed and shifted the box in his arms so that he could ruffle the child's flaxen hair. "Hello, Sarah," he said.

Now that Sarah had broken the ice, the other two children came running, too. They were introduced to Kate as John and Margaret.

"We were doing lessons," John confided. "I'm glad you're here, Uncle Sean, because it was a dead bore."

"John!" Ellen scolded, but there was a smile in her beautiful blue-green eyes.

The bleating of the sheep and barking of the dogs had grown much louder. Sean set the box down on the step and turned toward the mingled sounds, a broad grin stretching across his face. After a moment's pause, he strode off to meet his friend.

Kate started to follow and then stopped herself. Ellen was shooing the children back to their lessons.

"Come in," she said to Kate with a sunny smile. "Blue and Sean will be a while."

Kate returned the smile and went inside with Ellen, finding herself in a kitchen that ran the length of the house. Burnished copper pans and kettles hung on the walls on either side of an enormous brick fireplace. School books, pencils and papers were strewn over a long trestle table, and a rocking chair sat in a sunny alcove.

"Tea?" Ellen asked, going over to an old-fashioned electric stove and lifting a steaming kettle.

Kate was developing a taste for tea. "Yes, please," she said.

"You can sit here with us, Miss," little Sarah put in. She looked to be about ten years old.

Kate sat down at the end of one of the benches aligned with the trestle table. "Thank you," she said.

She tried to look at the work the children were doing without being too obvious.

Ellen had gone back outside to fetch the box Sean had brought while the tea brewed in a blue delft pot. When she returned, she set the box on the end of the table, opposite Kate, and pulled back the flaps.

Kate watched as she lifted out boxes of chocolate bars and stacks of books. "Bless that man," she said as John, Sarah and Margaret looked at the candy with round eyes.

"Just one between you," Ellen told the children, smiling as she handed them a chocolate bar. "Mind that you break it up evenly now."

While the kids were dividing the candy, Ellen turned her attention back to Kate. "Would you like one?" she asked.

Kate shook her head. "No, thank you," she answered. She was more interested in the books.

Ellen laughed as she handed one to Kate. It was a romance novel showing a sweet young thing being swept up into the arms of a dashing buccaneer. "They're better than candy," she said. "I can't get enough of one or the other."

Kate smiled as she looked through the other books. The covers were all quite similar, depicting almost every period in history as well as the present day. At the thought of Sean shopping for these books, her smile widened.

Ellen brought the teapot to the table, along with lovely china cups, too fragile for a station in the outback. "Do you think they're silly, those books?" she asked in a lilting voice, her expression worried.

"No," Kate said quickly. "As a matter of fact, this one with the sheikh on the cover looks pretty interesting to me."

Ellen's eyes sparkled. "Doesn't it, though?" she agreed, pouring the tea.

Before Kate could make further comment, a tall man with auburn hair and brown eyes entered the kitchen, followed closely by Sean.

"And who's this?" Blue demanded good-naturedly.

When Sean answered, there was a note in his voice that Kate had never heard before. "Katie-did, meet my best mate—Blue McAllister."

Kate nodded, feeling oddly moved. "Hello."

Blue hung up his hat and lightweight leather coat before progressing to the table. "Hello," he said, helping himself to one of Ellen's cherished chocolate bars. "I suppose you have a last name, as well?" he asked. "Or is it a well-guarded secret?"

"Blake," Sean said before Kate could answer, and this time he sounded angry.

Kate wondered why.

A look passed between Sean and Blue that wasn't entirely friendly. "You were related to Abby?" Blue asked in gentle tones.

Kate nodded. "She was my sister."

An uncomfortable silence descended, and Kate found herself wondering again why she'd given in to her passions when it was so clear that she and Sean could never have any kind of lasting relationship.

It was Ellen who smoothed things over. She laid a hand on Kate's shoulder and said, "Welcome. It isn't often I get a chance to talk with another woman. I'm glad you're here."

"Thank you," Kate answered, but her eyes had strayed to Sean's face, and she knew they mirrored all the questions she wanted to ask.

He turned away, ostensibly to gaze out the window. Blue suggested having a look at the starboard engine of his airplane, since it had been sputtering, and the two men left the house without a backward glance, John tagging after them when his mother nodded her permission to leave his schoolwork.

"Don't mind the men," Ellen said in her delightful accent after sending Margaret and Sarah off to play with their dolls. "I never met one yet that had half the tact he needed."

Kate wanted to cry, but she didn't. She couldn't quite manage a smile, however. "Were you and Abby friends?"

Ellen hesitated for a long moment. "Not really," she answered reluctantly. "The only time she ever came out here with Sean, she spent the whole of the weekend trying to convince me to leave Blue. Imagine it— me without Blue."

There *had* been a special spark between the McAllisters when Blue came into the kitchen, now that Kate thought of it. "Why on earth did Abby want you to leave your husband?"

Ellen sighed. "She said I was downtrodden, and that

I was going to seed out here with nobody to talk to but Blue and the kids."

The remark Sean had made when they landed came back to Kate in that moment. *Don't be trying to put any fancy ideas in Ellen's head. She likes her life the way it is.* "Abby could be pretty thoughtless sometimes," she said, taking a sip of her rapidly cooling tea.

Ellen smiled and shrugged. "She didn't know how it is with Blue and me," she said, and there was something in her tone and her manner that made Kate flash back to the explosive passion she'd felt in Sean's arms a short time before.

She nodded, a little shaken by the experience.

Ellen seemed to sense Kate's thoughts. She hid another smile behind the rim of her teacup. "You're in love with Sean?" she asked a moment later, keeping her face expressionless.

Kate swallowed. "I'm afraid so," she admitted miserably.

Ellen reached out for the pretty teapot and refilled Kate's cup and her own. "Troubles?"

Kate lowered her head for a moment. "You saw how he reacted when I told Blue Abby was my sister," she said.

Ellen looked genuinely puzzled. "Yes?"

"I'm a reminder of a very unhappy time in Sean's life," Kate told her new friend sadly.

Ellen's face brightened. "I think perhaps you're another kind of reminder altogether," she reasoned. "I can't remember when I've seen Sean look so relaxed."

Kate blushed. If Sean looked relaxed, it was no mystery to her.

Ellen chuckled. "I see I've blundered in where I don't belong," she said. Then she graciously changed the subject. "Earlier you said you'd planned to teach once. What did you take up instead?"

Kate gave Ellen McAllister a grateful look. "Political science," she said. "Daddy—my father thought it would be a better use of my time and his money. He wanted me to work on his staff."

Ellen broke off a square of chocolate from the bar she'd opened earlier and laid the morsel on her tongue. A look of ecstasy flickered briefly in her eyes, then she commented, "Do you like it—working for your father?"

Kate searched her heart. "Not really," she confessed.

"If you could do anything in the world," Ellen began, narrowing her eyes in speculation at all the possibilities, "what career would you choose?"

Kate didn't have to think. "I'd be like you, Ellen— making a home for the man I love. Raising his children."

Ellen put one hand to her mouth in feigned shock. "You mean, you'd actually like to be a—" she lowered her voice to a scandalized whisper "*housewife*?"

Kate laughed. "Yes," she answered.

Ellen squinted at her and took another square of chocolate. "I can't figure you as Abby's sister," she said.

Kate knew the remark was meant as a compliment, but she felt sorry that Abby had missed having Ellen for a friend. "According to Sean, she didn't like being a wife much."

Ellen glanced nervously toward the door, looking

for the men, then lowered her voice to a confidential tone. "She took a lover the first year they were married," she said.

Kate was stunned. She'd known that Abby had been unhappy from the first, but she'd never suspected such a thing. "Did Sean know?" she asked.

"Yes," interrupted a taut masculine voice from the doorway. "Sean knew."

Kate raised her eyes to his face. He looked grim and angry.

"I'm sorry," Ellen said quickly. She got up from the table and fled the kitchen in embarrassment.

"If you want to know anything about Abby and me," Sean said coldly, "ask me and not my friends."

Kate was quietly furious. "Now just a minute, Sean Harris. Don't you think you're being a little unreasonable here?"

He shoved a hand through his dark hair, and his broad shoulders slumped slightly. "Until about five seconds ago," he said hoarsely, "I thought Abby's affair was a secret."

Kate went to Sean and put her arms around him, her chin tilted back so she could look up into his face. "She was a fool," she said softly.

He kissed her forehead. "You're prejudiced, but thanks, anyway," he said.

Kate laid both hands on his chest, their torsos fitting together comfortably. "Go and talk to Ellen," she suggested. "She thinks you're mad at her."

Sean held her a little closer. "Couldn't that wait a

little while? I'd like to show you where we'll be sleeping tonight."

Kate thought of Sarah and John and Margaret. "We're not going to share a bed under this roof," she said firmly. "There are children here."

Sean moved her to arm's length, his hands gripping her shoulders. "What?"

"It wouldn't be right, Sean," Kate whispered. "We're not married."

"Then we'll get married."

"You're crazy. Where would we get a license? And a preacher?"

Sean sighed. Obviously those things would be impossible to find in the middle of nowhere. "Wouldn't being engaged make it right?" he asked.

"No," Kate said stubbornly.

Sean swore. "Then I'll just have to convince Blue that we should sleep in the barn," he replied.

Kate set the last bacon, tomato and lettuce sandwich on the platter with a flourish. Lunch was ready.

She started when she heard a sizzle behind her and turned to see Ellen cracking eggs into a frying pan. Kate could barely believe her eyes. "Eggs?" she asked.

Ellen smiled at her. "Blue and the kids really like them," she answered.

Kate cast a bewildered glance toward the pyramid of sandwiches she'd prepared, then looked at Ellen again.

"They'll just add them in," Ellen said.

"Oh," she finally answered, sounding a bit lame.

When they all sat down at the long trestle table a few

minutes later, it made for a merry group. The children were all talking at once, while Blue and Sean carried on a separate conversation.

She watched the men lift the tops off their sandwiches and add a fried egg, but she let the platter pass her by without taking one. She didn't usually eat this much for lunch but, keeping her eyes on her own plate, she ate what she could.

When the meal was over, Kate helped Ellen with the dishes. Blue and Sean and all the children had gone outside again.

"Are you feeling all right?" Ellen asked, looking genuinely concerned. "You didn't eat much."

Kate sighed. "I'm a little tired," she confessed. "I've never really gotten over my jet lag."

Ellen's lovely eyes were full of concern. "I'll show you where your room is, and you can lie down."

Kate shook her head. She didn't want to waste a minute of this experience on anything so ordinary as a nap. After all, she might never find herself on an Australian sheep station again. "I'd like to see more of the place," she said.

Ellen was obviously pleased. "Then you shall," she promised with a bright smile. They finished the dishes and walked outside.

"That's the shearing shed over there," Ellen said, pointing out a large building. "We have about two dozen lads come to help us when it's time to crop the sheep."

The bleating of the animals filled the air, and Kate could see them spread out all around the outbuildings like a sea of dusty clouds. "Do they make that sound all the time?" she asked.

Ellen smiled. "Mostly, yes. Of course, they're generally not this close to the house."

"Doesn't Blue have anyone to help him?" Kate asked, imagining what a task it must be to drive so many sheep from one pasture to another.

Ellen squared her slender shoulders and looked just a mite offended. "He has me," she answered.

"But you've got the children to take care of, and the house," Kate pointed out.

"I still have time to lend Blue a hand when he needs me." Ellen sounded proud and a little defensive.

Kate allowed herself to imagine living in such a place with Sean and she understood. When Ellen McAllister lay down beside her husband at night, she was probably bone weary, but she had the satisfaction of knowing that the work of her hands and heart and mind made a real difference.

Kate couldn't remember when writing speeches and booking hotel reservations for her father had ever given her such a feeling. "You're lucky," she said.

Ellen relaxed. "I know," she answered.

The two women walked for some time, while Ellen showed Kate the large patch of ground where she raised vegetables, the coops with the squawking hens that produced the McAllisters' eggs and provided the occasional chicken dinner, the building where the hired hands would stay when it came time to shear the sheep.

"Don't you ever get lonely, living way out here?" Kate ventured to ask as they entered the cool, spacious living room with sturdy, serviceable furniture and a fireplace that adjoined the one in the kitchen.

A large quilting frame was set up in the middle of the room, and a beautiful multicolored quilt was in progress. Ellen touched it with a fond hand as they passed. "I've got Blue and the kids and the people in those books Sean brings," she replied, starting up a set of wooden stairs. The banister was made of rough wood with bits of bark clinging to it in places. "Most of the time they're enough."

Kate sighed. "I guess nobody likes their life all the time," she said.

Ellen nodded as she looked back. They were on the upper floor when she asked, "What do you like best about your life, Kate?"

The question took Kate by surprise, and so did the realization that she hadn't really *had* much of a life before she came to Australia. "Sean," she answered, her eyes lowered, her cheeks warm.

"It's nothing to be ashamed of, loving a man," Ellen insisted. They had reached a doorway, and she led the way inside. "This is our room, Blue's and mine."

Kate saw a lovely hardwood bed covered with one of Ellen's colorful handmade quilts. There were several comfortable chairs, and two hooked rugs brightened the wooden floor. An old-fashioned folding screen stood in one corner of the room, and a wisp of a nightgown was draped over its top.

With a soft smile, Ellen pulled down the nightgown, folded it and tucked it into a drawer.

As much as Kate liked this woman, she was filled

with envy. It wasn't hard to imagine the happiness Blue and Ellen shared within the intimacy of these four walls; it was a charge in the air, like lightning diffused in all directions.

They went through each of the children's rooms, then Ellen opened a door at the end of the hall. It was a small room with a slanting roof, and contained an iron bedstead that was painted white. The spread was another of Ellen's elaborate quilts, this one in a floral design, and the curtains matched. A ceramic pitcher and bowl set was on top of an old wooden nightstand.

Kate drew in her breath. "It's charming," she said a moment later.

Ellen smiled. "I'm glad you think so, because you'll be sleeping here."

Kate was embarrassed again. "Sean...?"

Ellen's eyes sparkled with amusement and affection. "He can sleep downstairs in Blue's study. There's a chesterfield there that folds out into a bed."

Kate bit her lower lip and nodded.

Ellen laughed. "I dare say he'll have his due once you're away from here, though."

Kate had absolutely no doubt of that. She wouldn't be able to resist Sean when he set his mind on seducing her, so she didn't plan to waste her time trying. She looked toward the open window, where lace curtains danced on a rising wind.

"The sky looks angry," Ellen fretted, crossing the room to lower the window sash. "A storm's brewing, I think."

Kate felt an elemental yearning to be alone in this

room with Sean, to lie with him beneath the beautiful quilt and feel his arms tight and strong around her. "There must be things you need to do," she said to distract herself. "How can I help?"

Ellen remembered with a start that her wash was hanging outside on the line, and the two women ran to reach it before the rain did.

"What about the sheep?" Kate shouted over the increasing howl of the wind as she and Ellen swiftly wrenched sheets and shirts and dish towels from the clothesline.

"They don't mind a little rain," Ellen called back.

Enormous drops began pummeling the ground, the roof and the windows only moments after Kate and Ellen were inside. They stood near the sputtering fire to fold the fresh-smelling laundry. The kids were back at the trestle table, working at their lessons.

About half an hour had gone by when Blue and Sean came in from looking after the sheep. They were both soaking wet, and Ellen rushed to peel away Blue's jacket and hat. As she was leading him toward the fire, Kate's eyes met Sean's.

She longed to fuss over him in the same way, but she wasn't certain she had the right. After all, this wasn't her house and Sean wasn't her husband.

Both mischief and appeal flickered in his eyes as he gazed back at Kate. Then, rather dramatically, he sneezed.

Kate went to him. "You're wet," she said helplessly.

"And cold," he answered.

Kate shivered, although she was dry and warm. After

a moment's hesitation she took his hand and led him toward the hearth. There was something sweetly primitive in making a fuss over Sean while a storm raged at the windows, and she wished they were alone.

Sean smiled and kissed her forehead, then began stripping off his shirt. Drops of water shimmered in his hair, catching the firelight like diamonds. His chest glistened with moisture.

Using all the determination she possessed, Kate turned away. "I'll get you some tea—"

"They'll be needing more than tea," Ellen said wisely. She took a bottle of brandy down from a cupboard, along with a jar of instant coffee.

Kate stood by and watched, since there was nothing else to do, while Ellen brewed two mugs of coffee and added healthy doses of sugar, milk and brandy. Kate's hands trembled a little as she carried the nutritional disaster to Sean and held it out.

He accepted the offering with a little ceremony. His eyes, linked with Kate's, seemed to strip away her dry clothes, until she felt naked in front of him. She'd lost all awareness of the others.

Sean lifted the brew to his lips and drank, and when he swallowed, Kate felt the brandy coursing through her own system, warming her, melting her muscles and bones.

"You need to lie down," she heard Sean say. The words didn't seem to go with the movements of his lips.

A moment later he set the mug aside and lifted Kate into his arms. She could feel the wetness of his skin seep through her lightweight flannel shirt.

He carried her to the room Ellen had showed her earlier and laid her gently on the bed.

"The children," she whispered in sleepy despair.

Sean grinned as he unlaced her hiking boots and pulled them off. "It's all right, Katie-did. I'm only putting you to bed."

"I wish we could—make love," Kate said with a long yawn.

Sean chuckled. "Believe me, sheila, so do I. But you're right—we can't with the nippers about."

It felt so good to have her shoes off that Kate stretched and gave a little groan, curling her toes as she did so. Sean unsnapped her jeans and slid them down over her hips, thighs and legs. It was so different from the last time he'd removed them.

He stripped her to her undershirt and panties, then tucked her underneath the quilt and bent to kiss her forehead. "Sleep, love," he said softly.

Kate snuggled down between the crisp, chilly covers, giving a little sigh. "It's so—nice here..."

Sean kissed her again, this time on the lips. "All the comforts of home," he agreed. "Except for one, of course."

Kate opened her eyes, but they fell closed again. She hadn't realized she was so tired. "I'm afraid of thunder," she confessed after the sky was rent by a deafening roar.

Sean drew up a chair and sat down beside the bed, holding her hand in his. "I'll never let anything hurt you," he promised.

Kate couldn't remember a time when she'd felt so safe and wanted. Her mouth seemed to be moving without permission from her brain. "I wish we lived in a place like this," she said, punctuating her words with a yawn. "Just you and me and Gil and our babies..."

Sean's chuckle was a rich, sweet sound. "Oh, love, you are making it hard for me to keep my hands to myself. Go to sleep, before I disgrace us both."

Kate stretched and burrowed deeper into her pillow. Soon the rain and the wind and even Sean receded into nothingness, and she was dreaming dreams.

When she awakened hours later, the room was dark and cold and she was alone. For a reason she could never have explained, she turned onto her stomach, buried her head in her arms and wept with grief.

Chapter 8

At dinner Kate was puffy-eyed and quiet, wishing she'd never come to Australia. Maybe she wouldn't be so deeply, hopelessly in love with Sean Harris if she'd stayed where she belonged.

Later, when the dishes were washed and dried and put away, Ellen sat down at her quilting frame and showed Kate how to work a simple stitch. While they sewed, Sean and Blue played a cutthroat game of chess. The children were sitting in front of a television set, watching a picture that intermittently faded and jiggled on the screen.

"Is that good for their eyes?" Kate asked, worried.

"They'll soon tire of it," Ellen answered with a contented sigh, and she was right. Minutes later, the TV was silent and the kids were getting out various books and toys.

Because they got up early and worked hard, the McAllisters liked to be in bed by eight. Kate, having had a long nap, was wide awake, but she didn't want to disrupt the household, so she helped herself to one of Ellen's romance novels, gave Sean an innocuous good-night kiss and went off to her room.

About a hundred pages into the book Kate realized she'd selected the wrong reading material for keeping her mind off Sean and all the sweet delights she'd known in his arms. She closed the paperback and turned out the light to stare up at the ceiling with unblinking eyes.

She tried counting sheep next, and was certain she got through the McAllisters' entire flock without missing so much as a lamb. She was still sleepless, and her body was still wanting Sean.

She turned the light back on and started to read again. This time she didn't stop until the happily-ever-after ending, and a glance at her watch told her that it was nearly dawn. Kate got out of bed and quietly got dressed.

Sean was in the kitchen, drinking instant coffee by the hearth, when she arrived there. He'd already built the fire to a crackling blaze.

"Where do they get wood?" Kate asked. She hadn't stopped to wonder before, but the land was barren for miles around.

Sean set aside his coffee and drew her into the circle of his arms as though she'd asked some romantic question. "There's an occasional stand of gum trees about," he answered, his lips a fraction of an inch from Kate's. "And they have some of it shipped in by rail, from a town about ninety-five kilometers south of here."

Kate's breasts were pressed into the hard wall of Sean's chest. "Oh," she said weakly. She was still holding the romance novel she'd read during the night in one hand, and it dropped to the floor.

Sean released her to retrieve it, and his eyes danced in the dim light of the fire as he looked at the cover and then at Kate. "Katie-did," he teased, "I'm surprised at you."

Kate was quietly defiant. "I liked it," she said, sticking out her chin. "In fact, I can't wait to buy a supply for myself."

Sean tossed the book onto the table with a chuckle and then pulled her close again, his hand grasping the waistband of her jeans. His fingers were warm against the bare skin of her abdomen, and he seemed in no hurry to withdraw.

Kate gave a trembling sigh. She was helpless where this man was concerned. "A-are we leaving today?"

Sean nodded, bending his head to nibble at her lips. "Yes, sheila. Provided the runway isn't knee-deep in mud, we're taking off after breakfast." He turned his hand to caress the nest of silk at the junction of Kate's thighs. "If we stay," he continued, answering the question Kate hadn't the breath to voice, "I'll have to take you somewhere private and have my way with you."

At the sound of footsteps on the stairs, Sean stepped back, ending the intimate embrace. Kate swayed on her feet, and he gripped her shoulders, pressing her onto one of the benches beside the table. She was trying to catch her breath when Blue came into the kitchen, whistling softly.

"Good morning," he said, his grin taking in both his guests in a single sweep. "Off to the blue sky, are you?"

"If the runway's clear," Sean answered, and he sounded as distracted as Kate felt.

Blue took the kettle from the stove and poured steaming water into a mug, adding instant coffee and sugar to that. He stooped slightly to look out the window and assess the sky. "Should be all right," he said. "Then again, you could be here for weeks."

"Now there was a conclusive statement," Sean remarked.

Blue's eyes were twinkling in the dim, cozy light of the warm kitchen. "Anxious to see the last of us, are you?" he teased. "I don't mind telling you, I'm insulted."

Sean laughed. "Who's insulted?" he returned. "You and Ellen haven't been to Sydney in six years."

While the men went on arguing good-naturedly, Kate went to the cupboard for a cup, then to the stove for hot water and coffee crystals. She stood at a far window, looking out at the sky. As she watched, streaks of gray shot through the black velvet expanse, following by tinges of crimson and apricot. The spectacle was stunning.

Sean appeared beside her. "What do you see out there, sheila?" he asked softly.

"Magic," Kate replied, glad to be next to him.

Soon the sky had performed all its tricks and the

kitchen was full of noise and laughter. Kate set the table for breakfast, while Ellen prepared oatmeal, toasted bread, sausage and eggs.

When the meal was over, Blue put on his coat and hat. Ellen and the children gathered around him in a happy ritual of hugging and kissing. Kate's throat felt thick as she watched.

After Blue had said a morning farewell to his wife and children, he shifted his eyes to Kate. "It was good to meet you, Kate Blake. Come back and see us again soon."

Kate nodded and muttered her thanks as Sean put on his own hat and coat to follow his friend outside.

Ellen was busy clearing the table, her motions too swift and intense for the simple job. It was plain to see that she already missed her husband, even though he would be back in time for supper.

"Daddy forgot his tucker!" Sarah cried suddenly, running to fetch the canvas bag that contained a hearty homemade lunch and dashing for the door.

John and Margaret ran out behind her.

Kate felt a pang at the prospect of leaving this family. She'd never seen one quite like it before, and she hadn't dreamed such simple, unadorned happiness really existed.

When Sean came back inside minutes later, he announced that the runway was dry enough for a take-off. Kate went to gather her things, bringing her small leather suitcase downstairs with her.

The time with Ellen and Blue and their children had

been precious to Kate. She hugged her new friend and said a soft goodbye.

There were bright tears in Ellen's eyes. "Don't be a stranger," she said, before turning to embrace Sean.

Kate didn't let her tears fall until she and Sean were inside the airplane and racing along the runway to meet the blue sky.

"What's wrong?" Sean asked with genuine concern in his voice as the small craft shot into the air. The landing gear made a *ker-thump* sound as it moved back into the belly of the plane.

Kate sniffled and dried her cheeks with the back of one hand. "They're so happy," she said.

"And that's something to cry about?" Sean persisted, frowning in puzzlement.

"It is if you realize you've never even *seen* that kind of happiness before, let alone had it for yourself."

Sean was quiet for a long time. When he finally spoke, they were flying at a level altitude. Far below, a small stream looked like a long mud puddle in the brown grass, and kangaroos paused to drink. "Abby thought Ellen ought to leave Blue and get herself a career in the city," he said, and his voice was flat, emotionless.

Kate supposed it was hard for him, even now, to speak of Abby. "Ellen told me," she answered. "Did Abby want a career?"

Sean made a raw sound in his throat that was probably meant to pass as a chuckle. "Definitely not. She made a life's work out of telling other people what to do."

Kate regretted bringing Abby's name up in conversation, but she knew that she and Sean had to talk about her sister. If they didn't, she would always hover over them like a ghost. "You sound as though you hated her," she said.

"Toward the end," Sean answered, "I did."

The subject was too painful; Kate had to back away. "Where did you meet Blue McAllister?"

There was relief in Sean's voice when he answered, "Flight school. He and I went to work for Austra-Air at the same time."

"And Ellen?"

"She was a buyer for a chain of department stores. They met on one of Blue's flights."

Kate was surprised. She'd pictured Blue and Ellen growing up close to the land. "How on earth did they end up way out here on a sheep station?"

"The station was Blue's dream. Ellen loved him enough to share it."

Kate was quiet for a long time. She looked out at the raw panorama spread out below, trying to remember how it had felt to live and work in Seattle, to be mainly concerned with the course of her father's career. The whole scenario had about as much reality for her as a rerun of a TV movie.

"What's your dream, Sean?" she finally dared to ask.

Sean had one hand on his knee, the other on the control lever. "I want to keep on flying," he answered in a noncommittal tone without looking at Kate.

"There has to be more than that," Kate ventured.

Sean sighed, and she knew by the angle of his head

that his eyes, hidden behind a pair of mirrored sunglasses, were fixed on the horizon. "All right," he said, "I'll tell you. I'd like to have a wife who looked at me the way Ellen looks at Blue."

Kate smiled. "That shouldn't be hard to manage. I would imagine you have women falling at your feet, Captain Harris."

At last Sean spared her a glance. "Most of them are only looking for a good time," he said. "I want a woman who can say her wedding vows and mean them."

Back to Abby again. Kate let out her breath. "How about you? Did you keep your vows, Sean?"

His jawline hardened visibly. "I've never gone back on my word in my life," he replied, and Kate knew he was telling the truth. He had been faithful to Abby, even when he was desperately unhappy.

Kate reached out and rested a gentle hand on Sean's leg. "We need to talk about my sister," she said.

"Personally," Sean responded, "I'd like to forget she ever existed."

Kate was annoyed, sensing the depths of Sean's stubbornness. "What about Gil? He's a part of Abby. Do you want to forget about him, too?"

"Of course not," Sean snapped. "If it hadn't been for him, that part of my life would have been a total waste."

Kate drew a deep breath and let it out slowly. "Was it really that bad?"

He turned his head in Kate's direction, but she couldn't see his eyes because of the sunglasses he wore. "It was that bad," he answered.

"Then why didn't you divorce her?" Kate asked, exasperated.

Sean's answer stunned her. "I did," he said. "Two days after I moved out of the house, she drove her car off a cliff."

Several long moments passed before Kate could speak. Even now she was afraid to ask the question that had plagued her ever since Abby's death, but she made herself do it. "Did you take Gil away from her? Is that why she did it?"

Sean shoved splayed fingers through his dark hair. "She didn't want him," he said in a voice so low that Kate could barely hear it. "She brought him to my office that afternoon and left him with my assistant—along with a note saying she was going to meet her lover in Brisbane. They were planning to be married once the divorce went through, according to her."

Kate closed her eyes. As painful as any reminder of Abby was to her, it was a tremendous relief to know that her sister hadn't died on purpose. "Why didn't you tell us that before? My parents and I have always thought she killed herself."

"No one seemed very interested in anything I had to say at the time," Sean answered.

It was true. Everyone had been so caught up in their own feelings and conclusions about Abby's death that very few questions were asked. "I'm sorry, Sean," Kate said softly.

Sean had evidently spotted their destination. He began guiding the small plane downward, and the conversation was clearly over.

* * *

The campsite was in the shelter of a grassy canyon, where a small, spring-fed lake was hidden away. Since they had landed a mile off, by Kate's calculations, she and Sean had to carry their supplies a considerable distance.

When several trips had been made, and Sean was satisfied that they had everything they needed, he set about putting up the tent. Kate, exhausted by the treks back and forth between the plane and camp, collapsed onto the ground.

"I wouldn't do that again if I were you," Sean commented without looking up from his task. "We get the occasional milk snake 'round here."

Kate shot back to her feet and looked frantically around. When there was no sign of a snake, she sat down again. "Next you're going to tell me there are crocodiles in the water," she said, gesturing toward the lake.

Sean's white teeth showed in a grin. "Just don't expect me to wrestle one for you, love."

Kate sniffed. "You mean, you wouldn't even try to save me?" she asked, insulted.

"I'd say it would be the croc who needed saving," he replied, going on with his work. He tossed his head, as if to shake away some dreadful image. "Poor devil," he added.

"What kind of Australian are you?" Kate grinned, folding her arms across her chest.

"The kind who can manage the likes of you," Sean responded, finishing with the tent and dusting his hands together at a job well done. "Come on," he said, taking up a tackle box and two fishing poles. "Let's go catch our supper."

"Supper?" Kate echoed. "We haven't even had lunch."

Sean dropped the fishing poles and the tackle box and came toward her, grinning. "Lunch, is it?" he teased. "Now there's an idea I can warm up to. Come here, Katie-did, and give me lunch."

Kate's cheeks were hot, and she retreated a step, unconsciously holding the buttoned front of her shirt together with one hand. She wanted Sean as much as he wanted her—but she wanted him *later*, in the privacy of the tent. "I think we should go fishing after all," she said formally.

Sean was still advancing. Then, suddenly, he stopped in his tracks. A look of absolute horror contorted his features, and he yelled, "Look out!"

Kate sprang into his arms, her heart hammering against her breastbone, only to find that he was laughing. A wild turn of her head showed her that there was nothing behind her. "Bastard," she said, doubling up her fists and slamming them against Sean's chest.

He caught her by the waistband of her jeans, opening the snap with a motion of his thumb. A slight pull made the zipper come undone. "You were awake all night, wanting me," he said in a low, hoarse voice.

It was true, and Kate couldn't deny it, much as she wanted to. "How do you know?" she threw out lamely.

Sean's hand slid up under her shirt, over her rib cage to the rounded underside of her breast. "It was a wild guess," he replied, and a grin spread across his tanned face as Kate flinched at the passing of a fingertip over her nipple.

"S-someone might see us," Kate managed. As much as she longed for and needed this man, something deep inside her always wanted to erect a barrier. She needed a place to hide.

"Only the 'roos and the snakes," Sean answered with an easy shrug. He was unbuttoning Kate's shirt now, and there was nothing she could do to stop him. Her hands hung uselessly at her sides.

"We c-could go inside the tent," she suggested.

Sean shook his head. "I want to have you in the bright light of day, Katie-did," he answered.

A tremor went through Kate as he slid her flannel shirt off over her shoulders and arms and tossed it onto the grass. Her full breasts swelled against the scanty cloth of her undershirt, straining to be free.

He squatted to untie and remove her boots, then peeled away her stockings. The feel of his hands on her bare feet was so unexpectedly erotic that she shivered. He claimed her jeans and panties next, leaving the undershirt for last. After he'd pulled it ever so slowly over her head, Kate stood naked before him.

She felt no more shame than Eve had before the fall from grace.

"My God, you're beautiful," Sean whispered, his hands resting lightly, almost reverently, on the curves of Kate's hips.

Kate reached back to undo her French braid, delighted by the catch in Sean's breathing as her bare breasts rose. Then she shook her head until her hair lay about her shoulders. In those moments it was easy to believe that she was the only woman on earth, and Sean the only man.

He took off his hat first, tossing it into the grass. Then he removed his shirt. Goose bumps appeared on his skin as the cool breeze touched him, but Kate doubted that he felt the cold any more than she did.

She stepped forward to unfasten his belt and open his jeans. Sean groaned and let his head fall back when she clasped him boldly in one hand, taking his measure with long, gliding strokes of her palm.

He dug his fingers into her bare shoulders as he dragged her close and propelled her into a hard, elemental kiss. When it was over, Kate ached to possess and be possessed. Her body had long since made itself ready for Sean.

"I need you so much," she whispered. "Please don't make me wait this time."

Sean uttered a hoarse chuckle. "I don't think I could manage that," he admitted. Then, in a motion that dated back to Adam, he clasped Kate by the waist and lifted her to the top of his shaft.

She drew in her breath as she felt him nudging the portal of her womanhood, and it came out as a ragged rendering of his name.

He lowered her slowly, begrudging every fraction of an inch she gained, making her pay for it with pleas and promises. By the time she'd taken all of him, she was delirious with need.

Kate shivered as he unsheathed himself rapidly, then

began the sweet process of entering her again. "Oh, Sean," she whispered, "please."

But he stopped and tilted her back, only partly joined with him, so that he could take one of her nipples into his mouth. A jolt of pleasure went through Kate at this new contact, and she thrust herself down upon him in response, taking matters into her own hands.

Sean groaned and lifted her again, slowly, slowly, all the while feeding greedily at her breast.

She wrapped one arm around his neck and entangled her free hand in his hair, whispering his name over and over again as a litany and a plea.

Finally Sean reached the limits of his control. He dropped to his knees in the grass without ever breaking contact with Kate, and allowed her her freedom. She began to rise and fall and writhe upon him, her body taking over her entire being while her mind spun in another universe.

When Kate cried out in unbearable pleasure, Sean thrust her bountiful breasts together with his hands and ran his tongue back and forth across the nipples. Kate gave cry after primitive cry while her body bucked spasmodically in release.

She was still in a daze when Sean's moment came. He stiffened violently beneath her and then thrust his hips upward, spilling himself into her.

She prayed silently that he had given her a child, so that she would have something left of him when the inevitable happened and they parted. All her dreams and fears entangled with one another and Kate dropped her head to Sean's bare shoulder and sobbed.

He was still breathing too hard to speak, but his hands roved soothingly over the naked skin of her back and buttocks, and his lips moved against her temple. "What is it, sheila?" he asked softly when he could speak. His hand was under Kate's chin then, and he was looking deep into her eyes.

Kate couldn't speak of parting, not when she and Sean were still joined together. She simply couldn't. She shook her head wildly and pressed her wet cheek against his shoulder. The ghosts of people she'd trusted—Abby, Brad, her father—were all around, taunting her. "Hold me," she said.

He reached out and found his shirt, which he draped gently over Kate's trembling shoulders, and then he put his arms around her. "I love you," he told her.

For a moment Kate couldn't believe she'd heard the words. "What?" she sniffed.

He chuckled, holding her even more tightly. "I said I love you," he answered.

Kate drew back far enough to search his face and the depths of his green, green eyes. "You do?" she marveled.

Sean sighed in a put-upon way. "That isn't the customary response to such a declaration, Katie-did," he pointed out. "Do you love me or not?"

Kate pretended to consider the question. "I love you," she professed in the tone of one making a sudden decision. Then she couldn't tease any longer. "I always have," she added softly.

He kissed her, deeply and thoroughly, and she could feel him stirring inside her. He slipped his hands beneath the shirt and around her rib cage, rising unerringly to her breasts. "Marry me," he said when the kiss ended.

Kate was dizzy, and she could barely see for the stars in her eyes. "Anytime," she answered.

Sean opened the shirt and lifted her breasts in both his hands. "I'll be a demanding husband," he warned, chafing sensitive nipples with the pads of his thumbs. He was getting harder inside her.

"I'll be a demanding wife," Kate answered, giving a small sigh as she began to move upon Sean.

He stopped her movements to prolong the delicious friction. Nibbling at her ear, he said, "I'll want you often."

"Good," Kate breathed, writhing slightly.

Sean groaned at the sensation this produced, then pressed Kate backward into the grass. The fabric of his shirt protected her from the chill of the ground as he withdrew and then drove into her, and she bent her knees in order to receive him.

Satisfaction came to Kate first, so she had the special pleasure of guiding Sean through his. She ran her hands up and down the smooth flesh of his back and whispered soft, soothing words as he fought against the inevitable and then succumbed.

He fell to Kate when it was over, gasping and exhausted, and still she held him. Presently he rolled onto his side, drawing Kate close as he moved. He kissed the top of her head and squeezed her tightly.

"I hope I'm pregnant," she said dreamily.

Sean sat bolt upright and stared down at her. "What?" he rasped.

"I said—"

"I know what you said, damn it!" Sean growled. Then he swore roundly, got to his feet and fastened his jeans.

Kate stared up at him, startled and scared. "Sean—"

"I thought you were protected," he said.

It was like being slapped. "You thought…" She snatched up her clothes and began scrambling back into them. "Damn you, Sean Harris!" she screamed.

He turned away, shoving one hand through his hair. "I won't be able to bear it if you leave carrying a child," he said in a voice so low that Kate barely heard him.

Her eyes were hot with tears—tears of relief and confusion and love. She went around to face him, snapping her jeans as she moved, then pulling her undershirt into place. "Sean, I don't have any plans to leave."

He looked at her with mingled hope and contempt. "You will, love," he said. "As soon as your beloved daddy crooks his finger, you'll be on a plane home."

Kate had to vent her frustration somehow, so she stomped one foot. "I'll give you a *finger*, you officious creep!" she yelled, holding up the pertinent digit.

Sean laughed in spite of himself. "God, but you do need taming, sheila," he said.

Kate kicked dirt at him with her bare foot. "You go to hell!" she shouted, still furious over his remark about her allegiance to her father. Deep down inside, she was terribly afraid he might be right.

"Come here," Sean ordered quietly.

"Drop dead," Kate answered, storming off in the direction of the plane. In that moment she would have given her soul for a pilot's license.

Not to mention her boots.

Chapter 9

Midway between the campsite and Sean's plane, Kate stepped on a thistle and began hopping about awkwardly on one foot in a ceremony of pain.

Sean made an affectionately contemptuous sound as he lifted her into his arms to carry her back to the camp. "You're lucky I don't believe in spanking," he said with a philosophical air about him. "If I did, I'd turn you over my knee right now and blister your delectable little rear end."

Kate glared at him. "Put me down," she said.

"It'll hurt if I do," Sean warned.

The thistle in Kate's foot was already stinging. "Then don't," she conceded grudgingly.

Sean chuckled and set her carefully on a large stone near the tent. Then, squatting down in front of her, he lifted her wounded foot and examined it with a frown. "Nasty bit of business, that," he commented. "Next time you stomp off in a rage, sheila, wear your boots."

"Don't patronize me," Kate hissed, squeezing her eyes shut when she saw that Sean was about to remove the thistle. There was a biting sting and then relief.

Sean set her wounded foot on her knee. "There's still the iodine," he said, rummaging around in one of the packs they'd brought.

Kate figured the medicine would hurt worse than the injury, and she was right. Tears burned in her eyes when Sean applied the iodine, and her teeth sank into her lower lip.

Gripping her foot in a gentle grasp, Sean put a Band-Aid over the wound and followed that with a light kiss.

Kate braced herself. "Would it really be so terrible if I had your baby?" she asked.

Sean handed Kate her stockings, then her hiking boots. "It would if you got on a plane and went back to the States," he answered, looking not at her but at the sparkling waters of the hidden lake. "I won't have my children living on different continents."

"You asked me to marry you a little while ago," Kate reminded him. "Did you mean it?"

Sean got to his feet. The winter sun was at his back, casting a golden aura all around him. "I meant it," he said. "But there won't be any babies until we're sure it's going to work out."

"That's the stupidest thing I've ever heard," Kate argued, lacing up one of her boots. "If you don't think we can make it, why the hell did you bother to propose?"

Sean cupped his hand under her chin and made her look up at his face. "Because I love you, and I need you," he said forthrightly.

"Well, then," Kate pressed, standing.

"I felt the same way about Abby," he answered tightly. Then he took up the fishing poles and the tackle box again, and he walked away.

Kate still didn't know whether he'd really meant his marriage proposal. It had seemed so, but then he'd made that ominous remark about Abby. She followed him down to the rocky bank of the lake and took one of the fishing poles when he set them down. "I guess you don't trust me much," she observed.

Sean took a jar of fish eggs from the tackle box, opened it and baited his hook. "I think we should live together for a while," he announced.

"No way," said Kate, thinking of Gil as well as herself and Sean. "If you don't have enough confidence in what we have together to marry me, then we're better off to stay on separate continents."

Sean handed Kate the pole with the baited hook. "What do we have, Katie-did? Besides the sexual thing, I mean?"

Kate cast her hook into the water and reeled in the slack in her line. "I don't know. But if it's what I saw back there at the McAllisters', I want a shot at it."

Sean looked at her and grinned. "Me, too," he answered.

They fished in silence for a while, neither getting so much as a bite, and then Sean said, "I've got a flight to Hong Kong day after tomorrow. Come with me."

Kate hesitated. "I don't think so."

"Why not?"

"Because I want to spend some time with Gil, for one thing. And I need to think about what's happening between you and me. In case you haven't noticed, Sean Harris, it's hard for me to put one sensible thought in front of another when you're around."

He grinned. "I have the same problem."

Kate drew a deep breath. Since they were talking calmly, now seemed as good a time as any to broach the subject of taking Gil back to America for a visit with his maternal grandparents. "Mother and Daddy would love to see Gil," she ventured.

Sean stiffened slightly. "Fine. Let them fly down here."

Kate sighed. "Sean, my father is getting older, and he's not in the best of health. I think the trip might be too much for him."

Sean was quiet for a long time. Out of the corner of her eye, Kate could see that his jawline was as hard as the volcanic rock embedded in the walls of the canyon rising around the lake. "I don't trust him," he said finally.

Kate gave her line a few tugs, hoping to interest a fish. "Okay," she answered, "but it's only fair to tell you that if we get married, I plan to make regular trips back to the States. And if we have a child, I'm taking him or her with me."

Sean's resentment was almost tangible. "Fine," he said. "Let's just forget about having babies and getting married. That will make everything simple."

"Damn," Kate muttered through her teeth. "What did my father do to make you hate him so much?"

"He tried to steal my son."

Kate's pole trembled in her hands. "I know you think Daddy was behind that, Sean, but you're wrong. He would never do a thing like that."

"A month ago you would have told me that what's-his-name wouldn't sell cocaine," Sean pointed out, reeling in his line with a furious motion of his hand and then casting it again.

The reminder of Brad shook Kate's confidence in her own instincts. She *had* trusted her fiancé with her whole heart, and she'd been so terribly wrong. She bit into her lower lip and said nothing, and her pole and the lake blurred into each other.

Sean finally put his hand on hers. "Kate, I'm sorry," he said. "I shouldn't have thrown that in your face."

Kate couldn't look at him. "No. You were right—I trusted Brad. I would have married him."

"Kate."

"What's your secret, Sean?" she asked miserably, still avoiding his eyes. "What terrible thing am I going to find out about you now that I'm so much in love with you that there's no going back?"

He took her pole and set it aside with his own. "I've never lied to you about anything, Kate, and I don't plan to start." He spread his hands. "I'm just what I represent myself to be—a man who loves you."

Kate went into his arms and held on tight to his waist. "If this falls through," she whispered, "I won't be able to stand it."

Sean entangled his fingers gently in her hair and drew her head back to make her look at him. "I'm not going to betray you, Kate," he promised hoarsely.

She gazed into his eyes, letting all her fears and insecurities show. There was no hiding from this man who could turn her mind and body inside out at will. "I'll marry you, if you still want me," she said softly. "As soon as you get back from Hong Kong, we'll arrange for the license."

Sean nodded. "It's a deal, Yank," he said with a grin.

Kate put her arms around his neck and kissed him. "There's one other thing, Sean," she said after a long time. "I can't live in Abby's house."

"Fair enough," he answered. "We'll shop for one of our own after the honeymoon."

Kate was silent a moment, gathering courage for what she wanted to suggest. "We could take Gil with us," she said cautiously.

"On our honeymoon? Not likely, sheila."

Kate forged bravely ahead as though he hadn't spoken. "It's summer in the States," she said. "Gil would love Seattle, and on our way home, we could take him to Disneyland."

Sean's face hardened. "Is that what this is all about? You want to get married so your parents can get a look at Gil?"

"Of course not!" Kate protested, insulted.

He smiled, but the expression wasn't pleasant. "Maybe they'd like to come down for the wedding," he suggested. "I'm sure they'll be pleased to learn that

The Fiend has started in on their second daughter after using up their first."

"That's a terrible thing to say!" Kate cried.

"The truth is the truth, Kate," Sean said stubbornly. "When your parents find out I'm back in the family, all hell's going to break loose. You might just have to choose between them and me."

The thought was appalling—and all too possible. "Is that what you wanted Abby to do? Choose between you and them?"

Sean threw down his fishing pole without even bothering to reel in the line. "No!" he shouted. "Damn it all to hell, no!"

Kate put her pole down carefully, just to show him that some people in this world were civilized and could control their temper. With her chin high and her shoulders back, she turned and walked toward the camp.

Sean strode after her, grabbing her by the shoulders and wrenching her around. "I never asked anything of Abby but love and loyalty," he rasped. "She repaid me by getting rid of our baby and taking a lover. *Don't you ever* accuse me of trying to hurt her in any way, because I gave her everything I had!"

With that, Sean abruptly released Kate and walked away, leaving her to stand alone by the lake, staring after him. He disappeared around the canyon wall without once looking back.

Kate's emotions were in such a dither that she couldn't stand still. Her mind rang with words she wanted to forget—*She repaid me by getting rid of our baby and taking a lover.*

The solution, she knew, was to get so caught up in some task that she didn't have time to think. She busied herself gathering rocks to make a circle around the place where the bonfire would be, as she'd seen people do in the movies. After that, she gathered what stray pieces of brush she could find and piled them inside the ring of stone.

An hour passed and there was still no sign of Sean.

Kate dragged a box of canned goods over near the nonexistent fire and sat down to wait, her chin in one hand. Sean would be back, she told herself. He couldn't stay away forever.

She began to tap one foot against the ground. One thing was clear—marrying Sean Harris in the near future was out of the question. He wasn't emotionally ready for such a commitment, and neither was she.

An overwhelming sadness overtook Kate, and she sighed beneath the weight of it. When they got back to Sydney, she would pack her things and return to the hotel. Once she'd had a few days to get to know Gil, she would get on a plane, go home and try to pick up the scattered pieces of her life.

The trouble was, none of them fit anymore. She was no longer Brad's fiancé or her father's press secretary, and that left her with nothing to be. She was shamed anew by the realization that, for all her efforts, she'd never built a life for herself.

Kate was chewing listlessly on a cold piece of Mrs. Manchester's meat pie when Sean finally returned to camp. He looked at Kate's attempt at a fire and grinned.

"What's so funny?" Kate demanded. She was through putting up with his patronizing manner.

Sean dumped an armload of dry, broken branches beside the carefully arranged rocks. He ignored Kate's question and squatted down to go through the supplies for a meat pie of his own.

"Don't you have anything to say?" she asked when the silence stretched to interminable lengths.

Sean looked up at her, chewing. "Yes," he answered. "Can you cook?"

Kate gave a strangled cry of fury and kicked dirt at him. "No, and I don't intend to learn," she said, "so you can just forget any ideas you might have of getting me to fetch and carry for you!"

"Fine," Sean told her calmly.

"Furthermore, I have no intention of marrying anybody with a temper like yours."

"Good," Sean replied, serenely consuming the rest of his meat pie.

Kate sank to her knees beside him and shoved one hand through her hair. "Aren't you going to ask me to forgive you for deserting me like that?" she asked.

"No," Sean answered. "I'm not."

"You're not sorry?"

Sean shook his head. "It was leave or wring your neck, sheila. I'm still not sure I made the right choice."

Regally Kate got to her feet, marched over to the tent and crawled inside. Then she summarily zipped the zipper.

A marriage to Sean would never work out anyway, she assured herself. And then she lay down on the sleeping bag she was going to have to share with him that night and cried until her nose was red.

Some time later the zipper on the tent made a rasping sound as Sean opened it. He crawled in to lie beside Kate, gathering her into his arms. "Don't cry, sheila," he whispered, holding her close.

Kate slipped her arms around his neck; she couldn't help it. "We're hopeless," she said.

He chuckled. "No. Where there's this much love, there's always hope. But you were right before." He paused and sighed. "We need time to think this through, both of us."

For all the reassurance in his words, there was a note of resignation, too, and Kate was anything but comforted. She couldn't pretend that nothing was wrong, either, because something was. "What did you mean when you said Abby got rid of your baby?" she asked, her voice barely more than a whisper.

Sean didn't put her away from him, but his arms didn't hold her quite so tightly. "Exactly what you think I meant," he answered after a long time.

Kate closed her eyes. "I'm sorry, Sean."

"So am I, but it's over and done. It's a mistake for us to talk about Abby. We're both scared, and we keep dragging her memory out and throwing it between us."

Kate knew he was right, but she wasn't sure they'd ever be able to make a relationship work. Sure, they had passion, but Sean and Abby had probably had that in the beginning, too. Would their lovers' quarrels become vicious battles at some point in the future?

Kate couldn't bear the thought. "Make love to me,

Sean," she whispered, desperate for some distraction from her confusion.

He laughed, but the sound had elements of a hoarse sob. "There's a request I'll never refuse, Katie-did," he said. But instead of kissing her, or opening her shirt or jeans, he caught her by one hand and hauled her out of the tent.

"I think you may be an exhibitionist at heart," she commented, disgruntled, and Sean laughed again.

He kept right on walking toward the lake, though, pulling Kate after him.

When he finally let go of her hand, he immediately tossed aside his hat, then kicked off his boots. His socks, jeans and shirt soon followed.

Kate looked at the water with concern. "Are there snakes or crocodiles in there?" she asked.

"Probably not," Sean answered, wading into the water.

He was as magnificent naked as he was dressed, and Kate couldn't help staring at him. "Come back here," she said lamely.

Sean grinned. "Come and get me," he challenged.

"Damn it, it's winter," Kate pointed out, hugging herself.

"Chicken," he replied.

His insolence made Kate get out of her boots and her clothes and stomp furiously into the water that could be infested with creatures she wouldn't even recognize. When she stood face-to-face with Sean, he chuckled at her angry expression and began to bathe her.

The water was cold, but Kate was transfixed by the

gentle splashing motions of Sean's hands. He washed her face, her shoulders, her back and breasts and beneath her arms, and it was a strangely sensual experience.

When he proceeded to the lower part of her body, her breath caught in her lungs and the already taut tips of her breasts grew tighter still. She ran her tongue over her lips as he parted her, cried out when he claimed her with a sudden thrust of his fingers.

"Easy," he said, as the water began to churn around them from the frantic motions of Kate's hips. "Take it slow and easy, sheila."

"I—oh, God—I can't!" Kate cried. His thumb was moving around and around on her, making her slippery even though she was waist-deep in water. "Oh, Sean…"

He bent to take one of her nipples into his mouth, and Kate clutched at him, driven by a need she hadn't been prepared for. Her nails left pink curves in the flesh of his shoulders, but she didn't care. She moved wildly in the water, seeking him.

"Take me," she pleaded.

"Later," he replied. "Right now I want to see your pleasure, Kate. I want to watch you respond to me."

"Oh," she whispered, *"oh…"*

Sean intensified his efforts, greedy at her breasts, a merciless conqueror. When she stiffened violently and cried out in relief, she knew he was watching her every reaction, and that made her gratification even keener.

When the water was still at last, he kissed her and maneuvered her gently onto his shaft. Soon the lake was wild again, and the cries that filled the air were Sean's.

They didn't dress immediately, but dried each other and crept into the tent to lie entwined in sweet silence and sleep. When Kate awakened, Sean was outside, whistling, and she could hear the cheery crackle of a campfire.

Hastily Kate found the clothes Sean had left for her and put them on. When she crawled out of the tent, he was squatting beside the fire, stirring something in a frying pan, and dusk was deepening the shadows that sprawled across the lake.

"What's that?" Kate asked, sniffing.

Sean grinned at her. "No worries, love. It's nothing on the endangered species list."

"Don't tease me," Kate fussed, going to sit near him on the ground. "I just woke up."

He treated her to a brief, smacking kiss but said nothing.

Looking at him, she wondered how she was going to live without him—for a few days or for a lifetime. "Do you absolutely have to go to Hong Kong?" she asked.

"Yes," he answered. "You can still come with me, you know."

She shook her head. "There will be other trips," she said, hoping against hope that what she was saying was true. "Right now I need some time and space, and so do you."

Sean only shrugged and went back to his cooking. It looked to Kate like some kind of chops, and it smelled wonderful. Her stomach grumbled.

Sean chuckled. "Hungry, sheila?"

Kate nodded, licking her lips.

"Strange thing about love," Sean philosophized. "It either takes your appetite away completely or makes you eat like a crazed shark." He reached out to give the contents of another kettle a knowledgeable shake. "I probably shouldn't give you any dinner, since you refuse to do your share of the cooking."

Kate found metal plates and utensils for them both. "Does setting the table count?" she asked.

"That depends," Sean said, pausing to look at Kate's chest. Her buttons were open, and she was straining against the undershirt.

"On what?" she breathed.

Sean reached over and lowered the undershirt, revealing both her breasts. He bent and kissed each nipple lightly. "On whether or not you're willing to provide dessert," he replied.

Kate held a breast for him with one hand and entangled the other in his hair. "Does this answer your question?" she asked, her voice husky with pleasure.

He suckled for a few moments, then withdrew and righted her undershirt. "Absolutely," he answered belatedly.

The mosquitoes were thick that night, so they retired to the tent after their meal. Kate couldn't see a thing in the darkness, but she could hear Sean undressing as she took off her outer clothes. She was kneeling, clad only in her panties and undershirt, when he reached out for her.

"What do you want, Kate?" she heard him ask in a low, raspy voice. He was close; his hands were resting on her bare thighs and she could catch the clean scent of him.

Kate drew her undershirt off over her head and then took his hands in hers. For an answer, she laid his palms against her swollen breasts. Her nipples hardened.

Sean caressed her for a while, then gently turned her so that her back was to him. He moved one of his hands between one breast and then the other, fondling them in turn, while he moved his other lightly over her belly.

Kate's breathing was quick and shallow, and despite the chill of the night, she was so warm that she was perspiring lightly. She squirmed backward until she found what she wanted and needed, and she took it.

Sean had not expected to be taken prisoner, and he gave a sharp gasp of pleasure.

Bracing herself against the tent floor with her hands, Kate allowed her instincts free rein and became the conqueror. Sean groaned helplessly as she had her relentless way with him, now teasing, now tempting, now taking him in earnest.

He gave up what Kate took from him with a defiant, adoring shout, then turned her and pressed her to the sleeping bag. She still could not see him, but she could feel the caresses of his hands and the touch of his lips, and that was enough.

"You'll have to give an accounting for that, sheila," he promised between deep, ragged breaths. He found her with his strong fingers and began a rhythmic, circular massage that soon had Kate writhing, her hands stretched above her head.

Sean found them and imprisoned them in his fist,

holding them where they were. Kate's back arched, and a whimper escaped her as he continued to soothe and torment her at once.

"I love you," she managed as he worked her skillfully toward frenzy. "Oh, God, I love you so much."

"Then stay with me," he answered, showing her no more mercy than she had shown him. "You belong with me, Kate—in my house and my bed."

She moaned.

He took her to the east and west and north and south of heaven itself before allowing her a slow descent to earth.

In the morning they rose early to fish. It was their last day alone together, and that gave everything they did a note of sad festivity.

After lunching on their catch, they took down the tent, packed up their gear and hauled the lot of it to the airplane, where Sean stowed it neatly away. Looking back, Kate could see only a ring of stones surrounding a dead fire to mark their passing. Except for that, the ancient land was undisturbed; they might never have been there, loving and living, laughing and crying, shouting and whispering.

"We'll be back someday," Sean assured her, lifting her chin and planting a soft kiss on her mouth.

Kate nodded and turned her face toward the future, half excited and half afraid.

The small plane left the land with a roar that scattered birds and sent kangaroos hopping wildly toward the horizon. A magical time in Kate's life was ending, and she knew it, and she wanted to cling to it with both hands.

Of course, there was no way to do that.

They landed once, around noon, at an isolated place that sold hamburgers and gasoline to truckers and pilots, and took off again immediately.

"I didn't bring you out here to make you sad, Kate," Sean remarked, having caught the forlorn expression on her face.

She nodded, her hands clenched together in her lap. "I know," she said. How could she explain the feeling of loss she had, and the sense that it would be permanent?

They landed at the small airport outside of Sydney a few hours later, and neither of them spoke as they carried their gear from the plane to the waiting Jeep. Sean had a word with a mechanic, and then they were off.

"I'm moving back to the hotel," Kate said, uttering her first sentence in over an hour.

"Tonight?" Sean asked. There was no challenge or recrimination in his voice.

"Yes."

"Why?"

"Because of Gil. Because of Abby," Kate whispered. "Because we can't be in the same house together without ending up in each other's arms."

Sean shrugged and took Kate to the hotel where she'd stayed her first night in Sydney. He waited until she'd booked a room, then kissed her lightly on the cheek and left.

An hour later her suitcases arrived by cab. She was on the telephone when the bellhop brought them up, but she managed to tip him and wave her thanks without interrupting the call.

"So," she said when the door had closed behind the young man. "What would you and Daddy think if I married Sean Harris?"

Her mother's stunned silence was answer enough.

Chapter 10

"How long will you be in Hong Kong?" Kate asked, holding the telephone receiver to her ear with one hand and towel-drying her freshly shampooed hair with the other.

"Three or four days," Sean answered. He sounded as glum as Kate felt. "You might as well come here and stay, since I'll be gone."

She smiled. "That was a very transparent attempt to get me to feel sorry for you," she said.

He chuckled ruefully. "Did it work?"

"Yes," Kate answered, "but I'm still staying here."

"Have it your way, sheila."

Kate drew a deep, weary breath. "I would like to spend some time with Gil, if that's all right with you."

"It's fine. Listen, love, I'm not very good at small talk. Will you have dinner with me tonight?"

"No," Kate answered, remembering the chops he'd cooked by the campfire. "I had dinner with you last night. I'll see you when you get back from Hong Kong."

Sean sighed. "Good night, Kate."

"Good night," she responded gently before hanging up.

The evening news was flickering on the television screen, so Kate went over and turned up the sound. As events happening overseas were recapped by a brisk Australian voice, a picture of her father's face filled the screen. He was standing behind the president's desk, witnessing the signing of an important bill he'd been trying to push through the Senate for months, and he looked justifiably proud of his accomplishment.

Kate felt a certain homesickness, then cinched the belt of her heavy terry cloth robe a little tighter and sat down on the edge of her bed to eat a supper brought to her by room service. As much as she loved Sean and Gil, it was going to be difficult to live so far from friends and family.

When a silly game show came on, she got up to turn off the TV. She thought of Abby, and wondered how many of her sister's problems could have been solved by an extended visit home.

In a moment, Kate's sister and mother were both inside her head, yammering that it would be a mistake to marry Sean. She shut them up by turning the game show back on.

Kate slept in the next morning, then spent a few leisurely hours shopping. She and Sean weren't planning a formal wedding, but she wanted a special dress just the same.

It was midafternoon when she arrived at Sean's house to see Gil. He and his dog, Snidely, were playing with a Frisbee on the front walk, and his eyes lit up when he saw Kate.

"Is it true?" he demanded, racing toward her but stopping just short of a hug.

"Is what true?" Kate laughed, resisting an urge to ruffle his hair. She knew that some children resented gestures like that, and she wanted very much for Gil to like her.

"Dad said you and he have been talking about getting married," Gil told her, and he looked genuinely pleased by the prospect. "Are you going to be my mom?"

So Sean had said they'd *talked* about getting married, not that they definitely would. Kate put an arm around Gil's shoulders, and they proceeded up the walk. The driver of the taxi she had arrived in honked his horn as he drove away, but she barely heard the sound. She was too busy searching her mind for the proper answer to Gil's question. "I'd be your stepmother," she said at last. "And your aunt. But my sister was your mom, and nothing is ever going to change that."

Worried brown eyes scanned her face. "You wouldn't make me give Snidely away, would you?"

"Of course not," Kate answered quickly. They had reached the steps of the porch, and they sat down side by side at the top. "I think Snidely is a nice dog."

Gil was happy again. "Thanks," he said.

Kate wanted to kiss his forehead or his cheek, but checked herself. He'd probably hate that, think it was corny. "Say, handsome," she said as though struck by sudden inspiration, "how about having dinner with me tonight, since your dad's away? We'll go wherever you like."

The child nodded eagerly. "McDonald's!"

Kate laughed and slapped her hands against her blue-jeaned thighs. "McDonald's it is, then, but we'd better tell Mrs. Manchester before she goes to any trouble making you dinner."

The two went inside and found the older woman in the kitchen, rolling out dough.

"Aunt Kate's taking me to McDonald's," Gil announced importantly, "so you don't have to cook."

Mrs. Manchester smiled. "Well, that's good news," she said with enthusiasm to match Gil's. "I'll just watch the telly, then, and have something simple for supper."

"We could bring you a hamburger," Gil volunteered.

Mrs. Manchester glanced at Kate, her eyes twinkling. "I don't think that will be necessary," she said. "You just go and have a good time, young man, and don't worry about me."

Kate told the housekeeper when she would bring the boy back and called another taxi while Gil dashed upstairs to change his clothes.

"I wish you'd come back and live at our house," Gil told her when they were riding toward the nearest McDonald's in the backseat of a cab.

Kate thought of the plans she and Sean had made to buy another house, one where Abby's memory wouldn't haunt them at every turn. "I think we might end up living together at some point," she said cautiously. "Maybe you wouldn't like it, having another person around when you're used to just your dad and Mrs. Manchester."

Shyly Gil moved a little closer to Kate on the seat. "I'd like it," he assured her in a quiet voice.

Kate was so moved that her throat thickened and, for a minute, she didn't dare look at her nephew for fear of bursting into sentimental tears. "Have you ever thought about visiting America?" she asked when she'd recovered herself.

Gil considered for a long time. "Dad says the place is overrated," he told her finally. "But I'd like to see it for myself—especially Disneyland."

Kate smiled at that. "Disneyland is one place that's everything it's cracked up to be," she told Gil.

He looked concerned. "Disneyland is cracked up? What happened to it?"

Kate laughed. "We seem to have a language barrier here. When an American says something is everything it's cracked up to be, that means it's all that you'd expect of it and more. Disneyland is wonderful."

"Oh," Gil replied, and his expression betrayed both puzzlement and relief. "That's good."

Once they'd reached McDonald's and were happily consuming their hamburgers, french fries and milk shakes, they exchanged idioms and tried to guess at their meanings. This made them both laugh so hard that people turned to look at them.

Kate would have liked to spend more time with Gil, but it was getting late and he had school in the morning. The day after that, however, would be Saturday, and Sean wasn't returning until Sunday.

"Do you have plans for this weekend?" she asked.

Gil's eyes were bright with anticipation as he shook his head.

"Then how about going to the Taronga Zoo with me? It's been a while since I've seen a platypus or a wombat or even a koala."

Gil liked the idea immediately, and he recounted the school field trip he'd just been on all the way home in the cab. Kate had the driver wait while she saw her nephew safely inside the house and said good-night.

When she got back to her hotel room, a bouquet of twelve yellow roses was waiting on her nightstand. The card read simply, "Now and always. Love Sean."

Kate bent to sniff the luscious scent of the flowers, feeling optimistic about all the problems and differences she and Sean would have to work out in order to make a life together. Didn't all couples have to do that?

She took a long, hot bath, read a third of the thick romance novel she'd bought that afternoon while shopping for her dress and fell into a sound sleep.

Since she hadn't found a dress she liked the day before, she went out shopping again after breakfast. At a pricey little boutique tucked away between a pawnshop and a bookstore, she found a lovely ivory silk gown with a trimming of narrow lace around the hemline and along the V-shaped bodice. It was perfect.

After paying for the dress, Kate took it back to her hotel room and hung it carefully in the closet. She was just turning away from doing that when the telephone rang.

She answered with a questioning, "Hello?"

Sean's voice came over the wire as clear as if he were in the next room instead of on another continent. "Hello, sheila," he said. "Did you get the flowers?"

"Yes," she answered, smiling. "They're beautiful—thank you."

"I'll have to exact a certain price for them, of course," Sean teased.

Kate felt warm all over, and she wished he could be right there in that room with her. "Of course," she retorted in a low, sultry voice.

"How's Gil?" was his next question.

"He's just fine. We went to McDonald's for supper last night, and we're off to the zoo tomorrow."

"Sounds like he's pretty comfortable with you."

Kate smiled. "He asked me if I was going to be his mom."

The warmth seemed to fade from Sean's voice, at least for the moment. "What did you tell him?"

Kate sat down, feeling deflated. "I said I'd be his stepmother, *if* you and I were to get married."

"I see." Sean still sounded uncomfortable, but that awful chill was gone from his voice.

Kate was never sure where her next question came from, because she hadn't given it a moment's thought beforehand. "I don't suppose you'd let me adopt him?"

There was a long silence.

"Sean?"

"That would give you the same legal rights that Abby had," Sean reflected.

"I know," Kate answered. She knew she was walking on thin ice emotionally, and she was practically holding her breath.

"We'll talk about it when I get back," Sean said abruptly. Kate wished she could look into his eyes, for then she'd be able to read his thoughts.

"Which will be Sunday?" Kate asked brightly, anxious to soothe him.

"Probably," Sean replied. "I love you, Kate."

"And I love you."

A few moments later they hung up.

The telephone immediately jangled again, and when Kate answered, she was surprised and a little alarmed to hear the operator say, "You have another overseas call, Ms. Blake. This one is from the States."

"Thank you," Kate said, and bit down on her lip as she waited. She felt inexplicably nervous.

"Your mother tells me you're thinking of marrying that Australian," Senator Blake boomed, without so much as saying hello to his daughter first. "Don't you think that's a little idiotic, given what he did to your sister?"

Kate braced herself. "He didn't do anything to Abby. She manufactured her own set of problems, just like the rest of us."

"He'd like to have you believe that. Katherine, I want you to get on the next plane and come home. I need you here in Washington, anyway."

"I'm not going anywhere," Kate answered flatly.

She could feel the storm brewing in and around her father. "Katherine," he said in an ominously quiet voice, "I expect to see you in this office within seventy-two hours. Is that clear?"

She sighed. "I'm sorry, Daddy. I'm staying here, and I'm marrying Sean."

"If you do, by God, I'll disinherit you. You'll be left with nothing but your grandmother's trust fund!"

Kate didn't care about the money she wouldn't inherit, and her trust fund was quite adequate for her needs. But she did care about losing the senator's love and approval. "Do whatever you have to do. I've made my decision, Daddy."

At that, the senator hung up on his daughter with a resounding crash.

Kate was still upset the next morning when she set out to pick up Gil at Sean's house. Her father had no right to behave like such a tyrant, and she was going to tell him so the next time she saw him.

Gil greeted her at the front door, dressed for a day at the zoo. His smile seemed as wide as the distance between Kate and the senator. Once she was inside, the little boy gave her a shy hug. "I've been thinking about going to the States," he told her. "I think I should, since I'm half-Yankee."

Kate grinned. "I think you should, too, but your dad might have a different opinion."

"I could go if he changed his mind, though," Gil told her enthusiastically. He brought a passport from the pocket of his jacket. "See?"

Kate nodded. "You'd better put that away before you lose it or something," she said.

She was distracted from Gil by Snidely's unmistakable bark. "You get out of my kitchen, you great hulking beast!" Mrs. Manchester cried, affronted.

"I think maybe you should go and tie up your dog," Kate told her nephew.

He nodded his agreement and disappeared.

When the boy returned, he and Kate went outside and got into another taxi. They rode to Circular Quay, which was down near the Sydney Opera House, and boarded a ferry that took them across the harbor to the world-famous zoo.

They spent a happy morning examining one creature after another. Some were indigenous to Australia, while others might have been seen in any zoo.

Kate took a picture of Gil holding a baby koala. The little animal crunched nonchalantly on eucalyptus leaves all the while, willing to tolerate the idiosyncrasies of human beings.

When midday came, Kate and Gil had hot dogs and sodas for lunch. Kate reflected that her diet was going to hell on greased tracks; she'd have to get herself back on healthy food soon.

By early afternoon Gil was getting tired, so they took the ferry back to Sydney proper, found a movie house and bought tickets. Kate was glad to sit down, and she didn't really care what the show might be.

It was an action-adventure story, as it turned out, and both Gil and Kate were soon drawn into the plot, as much a part of things as the main character. When they came out two hours later, they were blinking in an effort to focus their eyes.

A quick check of her pocketbook showed that Kate was nearly out of money. "Let's go back to the hotel for a few minutes," she said to her nephew. "Then we'll have supper somewhere."

"Great," Gil agreed. It was an expression he'd heard in the movie, and he seemed pleased with himself for picking it up.

The hotel was several blocks away, but it felt good to walk after sitting for a couple of hours, and Kate and Gil played their game of exchanging idioms again as they went.

When they reached Kate's room, she opened one suitcase, and then another, and then another, searching for her Australian money. She finally found some in her overnight case, which was sitting in the bathroom on the counter.

A knock at the door brought her out, smiling and curious, her wallet in one hand. The room looked as though it had been ransacked, she thought, as she passed by the trail of open suitcases she'd left behind her.

Sean was standing in the hallway when she opened the door, and she was so surprised that she just stood there for a moment, staring at him.

"When I go to America," Gil was saying cheerfully in the background, "I'm going to spend a whole month at Disneyland."

There was a slight change in Sean's expression, but his words sounded normal enough. "Aren't you going to kiss me, sheila?"

Kate realized that he was really there, and not a product of her overworked imagination, and she hurled her arms around his neck. "You're back early."

He removed her arms gently. "Surprised?" he asked, backing her into the room.

"Dad!" Gil shouted, hurling himself at his father. "We went to the zoo and saw a movie and once we had supper at McDonald's!"

"Good," Sean said quietly, ruffling Gil's hair with one hand. He was smiling, but there was something odd in his face as he looked around the room at Kate's suitcases.

Kate felt uneasy without knowing why. "Lucky we came back to get some money," she said to Sean. "If we hadn't, we would have missed you."

Sean was still looking at the suitcases, and it seemed to Kate that he was a little pale beneath his suntan. "Is that so?" he asked.

Kate wanted to shake him. "What's wrong?" she asked, keeping her voice as even as she could.

Sean wouldn't look at her. Instead, he turned his gaze toward Gil, who still stood at his side, looking up. "So, you're planning a trip to America, are you?" he asked.

Dread went through Kate like a cold wind when she realized the conclusion Sean was drawing from the rifled suitcases and his son's comment about Disneyland. "You don't understand," she said lamely.

"I think I do," Sean said, and his voice was like dry ice.

Gil chose that moment to whip his passport out of

his jacket pocket and present it. "I could go anytime I wanted," he said proudly.

"I want you to wait for me by the elevators," Sean told his son, speaking in a voice that was all the more ominous for its quiet, measured tones.

Disappointment flashed in Gil's upturned face. "But we were going to have supper—"

"Go," Sean said flatly.

After casting one baffled, injured look in Kate's direction, Gil obediently walked out of the room and down the hallway. Kate would have gone after him, but Sean closed the door and barred her way.

"Pretty damned clever," he said.

Kate let out a furious sigh. "I wasn't planning to take your son away," she told him, shoving one hand through her hair.

Sean looked at her with contempt, but behind that she saw the pain of betrayal. "I was a fool to trust you. All of it—the talk, the lovemaking—you did it all to get into my good graces, so I'd leave you alone with Gil!"

"That's not true!" Kate cried. "You're deliberately misunderstanding the situation. Gil and I went to the zoo and then to the movies, and I was out of money, so I came back here to get some—that's why the suitcases look the way they do."

Sean didn't seem to hear her. He was like a geyser about to spew dangerous steam, and Kate had a terrible feeling that nothing she could say or do would move him. "Why did he have his passport, then?" he hissed, moving to grab Kate and then stopping himself at the last second. "Why was he talking about going to Disneyland?"

"I don't know why he brought his passport," Kate answered. "He got it out earlier to show it to me, and he probably just stuck it in his pocket."

"Why were you interested?" Sean demanded.

It was no use, and Kate knew it. "We did talk about going to America," she confessed. "But it was a someday kind of thing—not something immediate."

"You're just like your father," Sean accused. "You'll do anything, step on anybody, to get what you want!"

"No," Kate argued, her eyes filling with tears as she shook her head.

She might not have spoken at all for all Sean seemed to care. "You're like her, too—why didn't I see that you're no better than she was?"

Kate couldn't bear any more. She grabbed Sean by the lapels of his windbreaker and shouted, "Listen to me, damn you. I'm not my father, and I'm not Abby— I'm just Kate! And I'd die before I'd betray you, Sean Harris, because I love you more than I've ever loved anything or anybody!"

With a gentle kind of cruelty, Sean brushed Kate's hands away, turned on his heel and walked out, leaving the door open behind him.

Kate stepped into the hallway, her face wet with tears. "Sean, please…" she called after him, desperate.

"Goodbye," he said coldly without even turning around to look at her.

Kate sagged against the doorframe, closing her eyes as she heard the sound of an elevator bell. When it chimed again moments later, she knew Sean and Gil were gone.

She went back into her room, like something wounded, and, after closing and locking the door, she sprawled across the bed, too sickened to think or move. It was a long time before she gathered the strength to call the airport.

There was a flight leaving for Los Angeles in two hours. Numb from the core of her soul out, Kate booked a reservation on that flight, refolded everything in her suitcases and called the desk for a bellhop. While she was waiting, she dialed Sean's number.

Fortunately Mrs. Manchester was the one to answer.

"This is Kate," the caller said brokenly. "May I please speak to Gil?"

The housekeeper sounded bewildered and kindly. "He's right here, Miss Blake," she said.

Gil came on the line a moment later. "Are you going, Aunt Kate?" he asked.

New tears welled in Kate's eyes. "I have to, sweetheart," she said. "You understand, don't you?"

Gil was silent for a long time, then he answered, "I guess I won't get to see Disneyland."

Kate dried her cheeks with the back of one hand. "Maybe another time," she said with forced cheerfulness. "I want you to promise to email me, Gil, and tell me all about school and sports and Snidely. Okay?"

"Okay," he replied.

"I love you, darling."

"And I love you, Aunt Kate," the little boy responded bravely.

Kate swallowed. "G-goodbye, Gil."

"Goodbye," came the forlorn reply.

Just as Kate was hanging up the telephone, a knock sounded at the door. The bellhop entered at her hoarse call of, "Come in!"

The young man loaded Kate's bags onto a luggage cart and started off toward the elevator. After a few moments spent struggling for composure, she followed.

All the way down to the desk and all the way to the airport, Kate kept hoping that Sean would show up. She had the scenario all worked out in her mind. He would say he was sorry, that he knew she would never do anything to hurt or betray him, and then they'd kiss and everything would be all right again.

Only it didn't happen that way.

There was no sign of Sean at the airport.

Kate had her passport checked and boarded the plane. Her last fantasy died when the doors of the craft were slammed shut. Sean wasn't going to come down the aisle and collect her and take her home.

She didn't have a home anymore.

Kate curled up in her seat, a bundle of despair and confusion, and stared out the window, watching the city of Sydney recede. She was really leaving—the dream was over.

After a while Kate slept. It was a fitful rest, and she awakened with a violent start when she felt someone's hand on her shoulder. Sean. Somehow, someway, he'd come for her. Maybe he'd been in the cockpit of the airplane all the time....

But it was only a blond flight attendant, smiling apologetically down at Kate. "I'm sorry, miss," she said, "but we're about to land in Auckland. You'll have to fasten your seat belt."

Kate sat up grumpily and fixed the belt. Maybe she'd get off in New Zealand, take a couple of days to compose herself and then go back and talk to Sean again. By now he had to be sorry for what he'd thrown away so thoughtlessly.

But even before the plane touched down, Kate had decided to go on to the States.

She'd done enough compromising. If Sean Harris wanted to talk to her, he was going to have to make the next move.

Chapter 11

The child flung himself at Sean in a rage of pain and disbelief. "I hate you, I hate you!" he screamed, hammering at his father's chest with knotted fists. "You made her go away!"

Mrs. Manchester, who had inadvertently witnessed the scene, hurried off to another part of the house—but not before giving Sean a look that said her thoughts on the matter were similar to Gil's.

Feeling as though he were being torn in two, Sean grasped his son by the wrists to stop the attack. Then he knelt down on the floor of the entryway to look into his son's eyes. "Listen to me," he said hoarsely. "Please."

Gil still looked miserable, but he gave up the struggle. "Kate wasn't going to take me away," he insisted. "We were just going to have supper at a restaurant."

Sean gave a heavy sigh. "I know that now," he confessed. "And I'm sorry."

Gil's lower lip trembled and tears glistened in his eyes. "What good does being sorry do?" he challenged. "Aunt Kate's gone, and she'll probably never come back."

Kate was gone all right. While Sean had been agonizing over the fact that he'd been a fool not to trust her after all she'd been to him, she'd checked out of her hotel room, taken a cab to the airport and gotten on board a plane. By now she was probably halfway to New Zealand.

Sean rose to his feet. He was hurt and he was remorseful, but he wasn't really surprised. Kate had only done what he'd expected her to do all along—she had run back to Daddy when the first misunderstanding arose. Sean sighed, ruffled his son's hair and walked away.

"You could go and get her," Gil called after him in hopeful despair. "You could tell her you're sorry and bring her back."

Sean closed his eyes against his son's pain and his own. In time the hollows and canyons Kate's passing had left in their lives would fill in. All they needed was time.

"It's better this way," he answered, and kept walking.

The first thing Kate did when she reached home was take a long, hot shower. When that was done, she slept for thirty-six hours.

She opened her eyes to a world without Sean and Gil,

and cried all the while she bathed and dressed and set out for the supermarket to buy food. She had no appetite at all, but her refrigerator was empty, and she knew she would eventually have to eat.

She encountered Brad in the yuppie section, where the miniature corn cobs and pickled crab apples were sold. He smiled and introduced the woman beside him.

"Allison, meet Kate Blake. Kate, my wife, Allison." He said "my wife" with a spiteful little twist, as though he expected Kate to fling herself down at his feet in despair.

"Allison," Kate acknowledged, properly shaking the hand of Brad's new bride. She was obviously a career woman—she wore a classic suit and there was a briefcase in the shopping cart, with the initials ABW engraved on the brass trim.

The brown-eyed, attractive blonde nodded, reserve evident in every supple line of her body. "Kate," she confirmed.

Kate excused herself and went wheeling off toward the produce section, hoping Brad had given up the life of crime once and for all, for his own sake as well as Allison's.

When Kate arrived home, loaded down with shopping bags, the doorman helped her carry them into her apartment. She was just handing him a tip when the telephone rang.

Until that morning Kate had kept it unplugged, and she wished now that she'd left it that way. She wasn't ready for a round with the senator or her mother.

The caller was Irene Blake. "Welcome back, darling."

Kate sighed. "Hello, Mother."

The doorman waved and slipped out, closing the door behind him.

"I can't tell you how glad your father and I are that you've finally come to your senses. I'm certainly disappointed, though, that you didn't bring Gil back with you."

"Hold on a moment, please," Kate said politely. Then she laid down the receiver, walked into the kitchen and took two aspirin from the bottle she kept in the cabinet by the stove. After washing them down with water, she went back to the telephone.

"I guess I'm not surprised that Sean wouldn't give an inch where the boy is concerned," Irene went on, and Kate wondered if her mother had been talking the whole time she was in the kitchen. "Australian men are notoriously stubborn, you know."

"And American men aren't?" Kate retorted, singularly annoyed.

"Your father is going to be stunned when he learns you didn't bring Gil home with you," Irene continued. "It's little enough to ask, I should think—"

"Mother," Kate interrupted with terse politeness. "I couldn't just grab the child and carry him off. That would be a crime."

"I'll tell you what is criminal, Katherine Blake—"

"Please don't," Kate broke in.

Irene took a sharp breath. "What's happened to you?" she demanded. "You're different."

"I'm older and wiser," Kate replied with a sigh.

"When are you joining your father in Washington?" Her mother pressed on.

"I'm not. He disinherited me, remember?"

"The senator didn't mean a thing by that, and you know it."

"He could have fooled me," Kate said.

"You're deliberately being difficult!"

Kate bit her lower lip. "I don't mean to be, Mother." She let out her breath in a rush. "Maybe we should talk later. We don't seem to be getting anywhere."

"All right," Irene agreed stiffly, "but I wish you were the kind of daughter we could depend on."

And I wish you were the kind of mother I could call "Mom," Kate thought. *I wish I could cry on your shoulder and tell you how much I'm hurting right now.* "Goodbye, Mother," she said.

The following Monday morning Kate returned to college. Although she had a degree, she wanted to teach in elementary school, and that required a few credits she didn't have.

Soon, her life became a lonely round of going to class, studying, sleeping and eating. When she was at home, she invariably wore her bathrobe.

"You know," her friend Maddie Phillips remarked one night as she sat filing her nails and watching Kate watch a rerun, "you're going to seed. Look at you— you've got all the personality of a doorstop."

Kate gave the glamorous redhead a look meant to be quelling. "Gee, thanks, Maddie. I admire you, too."

Maddie shook her nail file at Kate. She owned a

small travel agency and lived one floor down in a two-bedroom with a terrace. *"And,"* she rushed on, as though her friend hadn't spoken, "you're getting fat in the bargain."

Kate picked up the remote control for the TV set and pushed the volume button until Maddie's voice was drowned out completely. Never one to be ignored, Maddie scrambled out of her chair and plopped down beside Kate on the couch. She wrenched the control from her hands and turned off the TV.

"The trouble with you, Kate Blake, is that you're in denial."

Kate glared at her. "You've been reading too much pop psychology," she said. "I'm not denying anything."

"Oh, no? I'll bet you've put on ten pounds in the past month—true?"

Kate sighed. "True," she admitted.

"And you're not sleeping very well, either," Maddie went on.

There were shadows under Kate's eyes, and she knew it. "Can't deny that," she said.

Impulsively, for Maddie was nothing if not impulsive, she took Kate's hand in hers. "What happened down there in Australia?" she asked. "It's time you told somebody."

Kate felt tears pressing behind her eyes. She'd been back for six weeks, and there hadn't been a word from Sean—not a letter or a telephone call. Apparently he still believed Kate had planned to kidnap his son.

"I fell in love," she said, and then the whole story

spilled out of her. She told Maddie everything, except for the intimate details.

"That's so romantic," Maddie murmured when the tale ended.

"Romantic? I love that man and he hates me, Maddie. What's romantic about that?"

Maddie ignored the question. "You've got to go back there. Or contact him."

Kate folded her arms. "Not on your life," she said stubbornly. "Sean's the one who's in the wrong, not me."

"Hell of a comfort that will be when the baby comes," Maddie said shrewdly.

Kate's gaze shot to her friend's face. She hadn't consciously considered the possibility that she might be pregnant, but now she was forced to. And she knew all the signs were there; she'd just been ignoring them.

Maddie folded her arms and nodded sagely. "Denial," she said.

"Oh, God," Kate replied, and she began to cry.

Maddie slipped an arm around Kate's shoulders. "Sean has a right to know," she said softly.

Kate shook her head. If Sean knew about the baby, there would be all sorts of problems. Hadn't he said he wouldn't have his children living on separate continents? No, it was better if he never learned he'd fathered another child.

"You're not being fair," Maddie insisted.

"Was it fair of Sean to accuse me of trying to steal his son?" Kate paused to sniffle. "He claimed to love me, Maddie, and yet he wouldn't even let me explain."

"There must have been a reason."

Kate sighed, remembering the kidnapping attempt against Gil, the one Sean had blamed on the senator. She had to admit, to herself at least, that he had more cause to worry than the average parent. "Maybe," she said grudgingly.

Maddie gathered up her purse and handed the TV control back to Kate. "Here. Watch reruns till your eyes cross," she told her friend. "See if I care."

Kate looked up at Maddie. "You do care," she said. "Thank you for that."

Maddie smiled sadly, touched Kate's shoulder, then left. Kate switched off the TV, crawled into bed and cried.

The next morning, a Saturday, her father returned from Washington and summoned her to his study in the fancy house on the hill. Because she had no classes that day, Kate put on her roomiest pair of jeans and a loose T-shirt and drove up there.

Her mother met her at the front door, elbowing aside a uniformed maid to do so. "Look at you," she said, running her eyes over Kate with an expression of horror. "You're a wreck!"

"You don't know the half of it, Mother," Kate replied, stepping past Irene to enter the house. "What does Daddy want?"

Irene made a face as she closed the door. "You needn't sound so cynical, Katherine. Your father is merely trying to bridge the gap between you, and it's more of an effort than *you've* made, I dare say."

Kate followed her mother down the hallway and into the familiar study.

"I want you to go back to Australia and fetch my grandson," the senator said, the moment he and his daughter were alone in that room full of books and expensive leather furniture.

Kate bit her lower lip, then answered, "I can't do that."

"Nonsense," John Blake retorted. "You simply pick the boy up when his father's not home, then the two of you get on a plane and come home."

Kate groped for a chair and fell into it. She felt dizzy and just a bit sick to her stomach. "You're serious, aren't you?" she whispered, her eyes round.

"Of course I'm serious," the senator replied.

"Why do you want Gil so badly?"

"He's my flesh and blood, that's why. He's all I have left of my firstborn child."

Kate closed her eyes for a moment. The room seemed to be spinning around her. "It's really true," she marveled. "You *were* behind the kidnapping attempt."

"Harris forced me into that by denying me my grandchild..." the senator began.

Kate held up one hand in a plea for silence and eased herself out of her chair. "Please," she whispered. "I don't want to hear any more."

"Katherine!"

Kate stumbled out of the room, closed the door and leaned against it, as though to hold back something ugly.

After leaving her parents' house, she drove straight to the cemetery where Abby was buried, parked her car and made her way awkwardly over the slippery green grass to the family plot.

Abby's headstone was a giant angel, with a trumpet pressed to its lips. *Fitting,* Kate thought, kneeling nearby. "I thought you were so wonderful," she said sadly. "Know what, Abby? It hurts to find out you were only human."

A light breeze blew through the sunny graveyard, ruffling Kate's hair. She ran her hand gently over the place where her only sister lay. "I'm going to have Sean's baby," she went on. "I don't expect you or anyone else in the family to understand, but I had to tell someone."

Kate paused, looking up at the blue, blue sky with its lacy white clouds. "I'll never understand why you didn't want Sean, Abby. He's so wonderful—"

It seemed that Abby challenged her then, although Kate knew the exchange was happening only inside her own head. *If he's so wonderful, why did you leave him?*

Kate bit down on her lower lip, her eyes on the ground. "I know now that I shouldn't have," she answered softly. "It was all a misunderstanding—we could have talked it out."

Give it up. You're Daddy's little girl and you always were. You wouldn't have been happy anywhere but right here in Seattle.

"That's not true," Kate argued. "I was happy in Australia. Happier than I've ever been."

Then go back. You have my blessing.

Kate shook her head. "I haven't the courage," she said.

Why not?

"I've been so wrong about everybody in my life—

you, Brad, Daddy. The one time when I was right, I
didn't stay and fight—I ran away like a coward. I'm
afraid of doing that again."

After a long time, she rose, touched the face of the
trumpeting angel and whispered, "Goodbye, Abby."

Sean nodded and left the cockpit. The passengers
were still trailing out, and he had to struggle to keep
himself from hurrying them along.

At last he was able to escape. His suitcase in one
hand, Sean strode along the walkway and left the ter-
minal. It was a chilly September day—down under it
would be spring. Here it was the fall of the year, and
the leaves were beginning to turn.

Sean shook his head. This part of the world was a
strange place, whether the Yanks liked to admit it or not.

He got a cab right away, but he had to repeat the address twice before the driver understood. Sean grinned
to himself. Everybody here had an accent—it was no
wonder they didn't comprehend plain English.

Kate's glasses were riding on the tip of her nose as
she read from her algebra textbook and got her prenatal
vitamins down from the shelf at the same time. Without looking away from the book, she dumped a capsule
onto the counter, lifted it to her mouth and swallowed it.
She nearly choked and was gulping down water when
the doorbell rang.

Muttering, she meandered into the living room. It
was probably the Henderson kids selling candy or cal-

endars so some team they were on could buy new uniforms.

When she opened the door, however, Sean was standing there, looking like an ad for flight school in his spiffy blue uniform. He took off his hat in a shy gesture and said, "Hello, Kate."

Kate's throat constricted around the prenatal vitamin capsule. "Hello," she managed, taking off her glasses.

Sean grinned slightly, bringing on a poignant pain in the region of Kate's heart. "May I come in?"

She stepped back, her glasses in one hand and her algebra book in the other. "Sure," she said, long after the fact.

Sean set his hat on a table. He had a bag, too, and he put that on the floor at his feet. "I was wrong," he said, just like that.

Kate stared at him. Even if she could have spoken, she wouldn't have known what to say.

He looked at Kate for a moment with his heart in his eyes, and then he went to the windows and stood with his back to her, gazing out at the city. "I'm living in San Francisco now," he told her.

At last Kate found her voice. "You're still with Austra-Air?"

Without turning around, Sean nodded. "Yes. So Gil and I are giving the States a chance to win us over."

Kate's heart was beating faster than it had since she'd returned from Australia. "Take him to Disneyland," she suggested softly. "That'll cinch it for you."

Now Sean turned. "I'm sorry, Kate," he said, meeting her eyes. "I should have trusted you."

"You're right," Kate said. "You should have."

"Will you give me a second chance?"

Kate had prayed to hear those words, but she hadn't really expected an answer. For that reason, she hadn't rehearsed a reply, and she just stood there, stricken.

Sean came closer, laying his hands gently on her shoulders. "Kate?" His voice was low and hoarse. "I'm ready to make some compromises, to prove I love you enough to make this thing work."

Kate swallowed. "Like what?" she managed.

"Like living in San Francisco. Like letting you adopt Gil if you want."

Kate was so moved that her voice came out sounding strangled and squeaky. "You'd do that? You'd make him legally my child?"

Sean nodded. "I would," he affirmed.

Tears welled in Kate's eyes—happy tears. Her arms went automatically around his neck. "What's my part of this bargain?" she asked with a half smile.

He chuckled. "Ah, sheila, I'm glad you asked that," he answered, slipping his arms around her thickening waist. "Come closer and I'll show you."

"I want a proposal first," Kate protested primly.

Sean laughed. "All right, then," he agreed. "Will you marry me, Kate Blake? Will you share my life and my bed? Will you be a mother to my son?"

"I will," Kate vowed, raising one hand to prove the oath.

That was when Sean kissed her. At first it was a gentle, tentative kiss, but then she felt his body harden into a familiar readiness. His tongue plundered the depths of her mouth, and Kate's knees turned to mashed potatoes.

When he lifted her into his arms without breaking the kiss, she didn't demur. She wanted whatever he had to give her.

"There is one little thing I should mention," she said breathlessly when they reached the bedroom and Sean was lifting her sweatshirt off over her head.

He bent and kissed the rounded tops of each of her breasts. "What?" he asked.

Kate drew in a sharp breath as he unfastened her bra and quickly tossed it aside. "You're probably going to be mad," she warned.

Sean lifted her, so that she was forced to wrap her legs around his waist. That put her breasts at mouth level, and he took immediate advantage of the situation. "I'll get over it fast," he assured her between suckles.

Kate was moaning. "Maybe I should—oh, God— wait."

Sean turned to her other breast. "Tell me," he said.

"I'm pregnant," Kate blurted out.

He eased her slowly, gently to the bed, bending over her. "Damnedest thing," he murmured, shaking his head. "I could have sworn you just said you were pregnant."

"I did, and I am. That is, *we* did and I am."

Sean laughed, and the tears glistening in his eyes were a touching contrast. "My God, sheila—that's won-derful."

Kate drew him down toward her lips and her body. Both were his to claim. "I'm very glad you think so,

Captain Harris," she said, and then she kissed him, unbuttoning his shirt at the same time.

The warm, hairy hardness of his chest felt good under her palms. She squirmed as he unfastened and unzipped her jeans.

"I thought you had changed," he remarked when the kiss had ended. His lips were against her bare belly then, and Kate was trembling in anticipation.

"Thanks a lot," she muttered.

He laughed again. "As soon as you've gotten over having this one," he said, moving lower. "We'll start another."

Kate was already writhing slightly, for he was very near his destination. She felt the downy curtain part and she moaned. After that, all her words were incoherent.

Once the first shattering pinnacle had been reached, Kate lay gasping on the bed, watching Sean as he removed the rest of his clothes. When he was naked, he stretched out over her on the bed.

"I thought I'd die for missing you," he said hoarsely, and his eyes glinted in the half-darkness of the bedroom.

Kate ran her hands along his magnificent back. She didn't speak, for her body told him everything.

With a groan, Sean entered her, murmuring words of love and need as he completed that first long, delicious stroke.

Kate welcomed him, thrusting her hips upward to draw him into her very depths.

"You'll make a madman of me yet," he moaned, withdrawing slowly and then gliding into her again.

Fire had been ignited inside Kate, and the flames were rising higher and higher. She whimpered as her temperature climbed, and hurled herself at Sean in a wanton search for what only he could give her.

"That's it," he whispered, tucking his hands under her bottom to urge her on. "That's it, Katie-did—I want everything."

She was soaring toward a molten sky, borne high on tongues of fire. "Sean—Sean—"

He buried his face in her neck even as he buried his manhood in her depths. His strokes were the fierce lunges of a conqueror, and Kate's surrender was complete.

With a cry of jubilation, she exploded like a nova, and Sean was only moments behind her.

When it was over, they lay still. For Kate, Sean's rapid heartbeat and ragged breathing were music. She'd thought she'd never hold him like this again, never feel the unique planes and hollows of his body fitted to hers.

"The least you can do," she said when she was capable, "is buy me dinner."

Sean gave her a playful swat. "Buy you dinner, is it? I ought to turn you over my knee for not telling me about the baby sooner."

"I've only known about it for a few weeks myself," Kate defended. "Shall we send out for Chinese or walk down to the corner for fish and chips?"

"I'm not walking anywhere," Sean said. He'd slid down to her breast and was rolling his tongue around her nipple. "Besides, chow mein isn't what I'm hungry for."

Kate shifted slightly to give him better access. "We deliver," she said.

Later, when the loving was over, she told him about her estrangement with her father and her decision to become an elementary school teacher.

Sean thought teaching was a grand idea, since Kate liked kids so much, but he surprised her where the rift with her father was concerned. He said she should try to make things right, or she might come to regret it someday.

Chapter 12

The senator stepped uneasily through the front door of the gracious home overlooking San Francisco Bay. He held his hat in one hand and clutched the front of his overcoat closed as though he expected someone to snatch it away. Beside him, Irene slipped out of her snow-dusted mink coat and gave Kate a cautious kiss on the cheek.

"You look wonderful, darling," she said.

"Are you my grandparents?" Gil asked forthrightly.

Irene was crying, and the senator looked at the little boy with a helpless expression Kate had never seen on his face before.

"Yes," Sean said quietly when no one spoke. "These are your grandparents." He stood behind Gil, one hand resting on the boy's shoulder.

The senator's weary blue eyes moved from Kate's face to Sean's. "I apologize for everything," he said.

Sean nodded without speaking, took Kate's hand and led her out of the room.

"I wish I didn't have to leave for Honolulu tonight," he said, drawing her as close as he could, given her bulging stomach.

She laughed and laid both her hands on his cheeks. "Oh, you poor man," she teased.

Sean's hand rested on the rounded sides of Kate's stomach. "You'll take very good care of my daughter, won't you?"

"The best," Kate assured him.

He kissed her, and Kate was sorry he was going away. If they'd been alone, she might have taken him by the hand and led him up the stairs to their spacious bedroom.

"Keep that up and I'll have my way with you right here, Captain Harris," she said in a conversely prim voice.

He laughed and squeezed her bottom. "I'm shocked, Mrs. Harris," he scolded. "What would the PTA think if they heard their vice president carrying on like this?"

Kate shrugged. "Kiss me again," she said.

Sean obliged graciously.

When he'd left for the airport, Kate went back to the living room. Her mother was sitting in a chair next to the fireplace, watching fondly as Gil and the senator plundered the brightly wrapped gifts under the Christmas tree.

"No fair shaking," Kate protested.

The old man and the boy looked at her with similar smiles.

"Can I give Grandpa his present now, Mom?" Gil asked.

"No," Kate answered, settling into her favorite chair and spreading the colorful afghan she was knitting over her knees. "Christmas is still three days away."

"Scrooge," complained the senator.

"Please?" Gil wheedled.

Kate caved in. After all, it was Christmas and she was no disciplinarian, anyway. "All right, but just one," she conceded.

"Our gifts are arriving later," the senator confided to his daughter as Gil ran up the stairs to fetch the special set of Australian stamps he'd set aside for his grandfather.

"By boxcar," confirmed Irene.

Kate chuckled and tended to her knitting.

The snow had stopped in the early morning, two days later, when Sean crawled into bed beside her and drew her into his arms.

"Hello, Mrs. Harris," he said, his lips moving against her temple.

"Exactly who are you?" Kate retorted, yawning. But she snuggled closer.

He placed a warm hand on her stomach. "Very funny," he said. "Did you lay down the law to the senator, by the way?"

"Uh-huh," Kate said. "He won't be bothering me about coming back to work for him after this. I told him that being vice president of the PTA at Gil's school is the closest I'm ever going to get to politics."

"How did he react?" Sean asked, stretching and making himself comfortable beside Kate.

She giggled at the picture that came to her mind. "He blustered, but I wasn't intimidated. After all, he was wearing Gil's Mickey Mouse ears at the time."

Sean laughed and stretched again. "I'm going to sleep," he announced.

"No, you're not," Kate replied.

* * * * *

Dear Reader,

I was first inspired to write *His Only Wife* several years ago while staying at my weekend home in Young, Arizona. The town was hosting the Payson Hotshots, feeding them and giving them a place to sleep, while they battled a nearby wilderness fire—a fire I could see from the front porch of my house.

As I watched, I wondered about the amazing individuals who chose to work in such a dangerous profession. I also wondered about the people who loved them and made up their families. Soon after, the idea for *His Only Wife* was born, a book that, I'm thrilled to say, went on to become my first Harlequin American and the start of a seven year and still going strong career!

My newest series, Sweetheart, Nevada, due out the summer of 2013, was also inspired by wilderness firefighters, and the incredible impact one fire can have on the lives of hundreds of people as they struggle to survive in the wake of a horrific disaster. And because the books are from Harlequin, you can bet the characters will somehow manage to find satisfying love along the way.

I do hope you enjoy *His Only Wife* and my forthcoming Sweetheart, Nevada series. As always, I love hearing from readers. Visit my website at www.cathymcdavid.com to drop me a line.

Warmest wishes,

Cathy McDavid

HIS ONLY WIFE

Cathy McDavid

This book is dedicated to the courageous men and women who serve as wilderness firefighters in the western United States and all over the world. It has been a joy writing about you and an honor to make your acquaintance.

Chapter 1

Tourists in motor homes, cowboys in pickup trucks, and teenagers in hot rods with the radios blasting.

Not much had changed about the Pineville service station over the last decade from what Aubrey Stuart could see, except maybe the price of gas.

And her.

She guided her mini SUV toward the far island and parked beside a pump. Pushing the door open with one hand, she grabbed her tiny purse off the front passenger seat and stepped outside. In the blink of an eye, she exchanged air-conditioned comfort for the heat of Arizona high country in late June.

While waiting for her credit card purchase to be authorized, she removed the cap from her gas tank and eyed the constant stream of vehicles coming and going.

Everything about this place was familiar to Aubrey. During the four-hour drive from Tucson, she'd steeled herself against the pain that the sight of Pineville always brought on during those few short visits she'd made through the years. But to her vast relief, there wasn't any. Only a twinge of melancholy.

Could it be she was really and truly over Gage Raintree?

A high-pitched electronic beep drew her attention to the gas pump and the message scrolling across the panel in vivid green letters.

"Cash only, see clerk inside," Aubrey read out loud and sighed. With another hour's drive still ahead of her, she had wanted this to be a quick in-and-out stop.

Better to be safe than sorry, she decided. Thirty-foot drop-offs in some places made the winding dirt road to her grandmother's home in Blue Ridge treacherous. Running out of gas halfway there would be at best an inconvenience, at worse a disaster.

Slamming the door of her SUV shut, she headed toward the minimart, extracting a twenty-dollar bill from her purse as she went. Ten years earlier, on the day she left Blue Ridge, she'd walked through this same door. In some ways, it felt like a lifetime ago. In other ways, only yesterday.

Back then, she'd been all innocence, painfully shy, and skinny as a broomstick. The brainy older daughter of renowned heart surgeon Alexander Stuart. Her younger sister, Annie, used to call her a nerd, and rightfully so. Aubrey hadn't just fit the description, she'd defined it. With the exception of Gage Raintree, the male population at large hardly noticed she existed.

"Enough already," she grumbled, snapping out of her reverie. An hour away from Blue Ridge and already she had a bad case of Gage Raintree on the brain. What would it be like when she arrived at her grandmother's?

Her movements purposeful, Aubrey strode into the minimart and went straight to stand in line behind several other people. The store was packed, taxing the sole clerk's limited abilities. She felt sorry for the poor kid when the man ahead of her vehemently complained about the inconvenience.

Her turn finally came. "Twenty dollars on pump three." She smiled pleasantly, handing the clerk her money. "And I need a receipt, please."

He appeared grateful that she wasn't going to bite his head off like everyone else. "Anything else, ma'am?"

"No, thank you." She took the receipt and started toward the door. At the sound of a familiar voice, her knees locked.

"Aubrey?"

She stood immobile and willed her gaze not to fly around the store.

"Aubrey, is that you?"

What were the odds of him being here? In this convenience store, at the exact same moment as her? Well, this was the last gas station on the road out of town.

"Aubrey Stuart?" the voice called again.

She had to look. There was simply no avoiding it. And, well, he didn't sound mad. That was a good sign, right? Mustering her courage, she turned slowly around and came face-to-face with her ex-husband.

"I thought you weren't arriving until tomorrow," he said.

"Hello, Gage." Her voice quivered. It had a tendency to do that when she was nervous or uncomfortable or, like now, both. "How are you?"

"Good. How 'bout yourself?" He moved ahead in line, closing the distance between them. "You look great."

His lingering appraisal of her appearance caused Aubrey's cheeks to heat. Never was she more aware of the fact that her younger, stick-figure self had filled out in all the right places.

"So do you," she blurted. "Look great, that is."

Of all things to gush forth from between her lips. Complete mental dysfunction was her only excuse. Gage did that to her. He always had.

But, sweet heaven, he did look great.

Tall to start with, he'd outgrown his once lanky form. There was no shortage of muscles bunching beneath his T-shirt. He wore his nearly black hair shorter than before. The wavy ends poked out from beneath his weathered cowboy hat to curl attractively at the base of his neck. His boots were scruffy, as always, and he needed a shave. Not that the dark stubble shadowing his jaw detracted from his good looks. Quite the contrary.

Rather than risk another embarrassing blunder, she forced her stiff legs to take a step toward the double glass doors at the front of the store. She'd known seeing him again would be a bit awkward, but she hadn't expected it to be so…disconcerting. "Guess I'll see you around."

"Hold up." He retrieved his change and plastic sack containing his purchases. "I'll walk you to your car."

"No!" At his bemused expression, she checked herself. "That's not necessary. You're obviously in a hurry."

"Actually, I'm not."

The sexy half smile he turned on her was potent as ever. Hoping to minimize its effects, she grabbed for the door handle nearest her and yanked, almost tearing her hand off in the process. The door rattled, but didn't open. Too late, she realized she'd pulled instead of pushed. Gage came up behind her, reached around and braced his hand on the glass panel near her head.

"Here. Let me get that for you." The door swung open, and a hot breeze struck Aubrey in the face.

She glanced over her shoulder. *Big* mistake.

His face hovered a few inches above hers. If she shifted slightly, she could find herself nestled in the crook of his arm. It was a place she'd been often enough as a teenager and remembered well.

A warning bell the size of Liberty herself rang inside Aubrey's head.

"Thanks." She shoved through the door and flashed him a smile she hoped radiated confidence. "See you around."

He followed, his long strides easily keeping pace with her. "Is this yours?" he asked when they reached her SUV.

"Mine and the bank's," she answered. Not wanting Gage to sense her discomfort, she made an effort to relax.

"Four-wheel drive. That'll come in handy around here." He gave the car the standard once-over typical of men, then hitched his chin at the neighboring island of gas pumps. "I'm still driving a pickup."

The long-bed crew cab he indicated was considerably newer and nicer than the one he'd driven in high school. And from what she could see, loaded to the hilt with lumber and various other building materials. He must have come into Pineville to purchase supplies for his family's cattle ranch. There was some sort of emblem on the driver-side door that she couldn't make out from this distance.

"It's big," she said and returned to filling her SUV with gas.

"I heard you were staying with your grandmother for a while. That's nice of you. A broken hip is no picnic, and I'm sure she appreciates your help."

"Yes." Small-town gossip, thought Aubrey. Nothing stayed secret for long. Everybody from the local sheriff to the clerk at the feed store had probably been informed of her arrival.

"Look, Aubrey," Gage said. "I know you probably feel a little…weird after what happened. Is there any chance we can get together and talk?"

"I'm not sure that's a good idea." She squeezed the gas nozzle until her fingers turned white. "I mean, what's to talk about? It was ages ago, and we've both moved on."

"But I don't want you feeling like you have to run for cover every time you see my pickup truck coming down the road. Blue Ridge is a small town. You can't walk across your front lawn without having to stop and chat with at least three people."

"I'm not going to run for cover every time I see you," she scoffed.

He gave her a skeptical look.

"Really." She hated that he knew her so well. But then, how could he not? They'd spent fifteen straight summers together, the last one as Mr. and Mrs. Raintree.

A loud click sounded, signaling her gas tank was full. Grateful for small favors, Aubrey jammed the nozzle back into the side of the pump. "I have to go. Grandma's expecting me." She slid in behind the wheel.

"Drive carefully. There's a lot of loose gravel on the roads." He shut her door for her.

Aubrey wiggled her fingers in farewell, then started the SUV. Without meaning to, she sped out of the parking lot, succumbing to the urge to put as much distance between herself and Gage as possible.

Two miles outside of Pineville her heart rate finally dropped to double digits, and her breathing slowed. The worst was over, she told herself. She ran into Gage and had lived to tell about it. Next time wouldn't be so hard. Right?

Aubrey fervently hoped so. If not, this could be the longest six weeks of her life.

* * *

Something must have happened. An accident maybe? Aubrey hit the brakes and came to a stop behind a Hummer hauling a trailer loaded with ATVs. She flipped up the sun visor and, squinting, stared out the windshield. For as far up the highway as she could see, traffic was at a standstill. It was then she realized there were no cars coming from the opposite direction.

After several minutes, people started getting out of their vehicles and milling around. Resigned to wait, Aubrey lowered her window and shut off her engine.

She didn't relish being stuck in a traffic jam, but at least she was safely away from Gage. Closing her eyes, she leaned back against the headrest and allowed the memories to come. Pain and hurt accompanied the steady stream of images filling her mind, convincing Aubrey that, despite her earlier conviction, she was anything but over Gage.

He'd been her first for many things. Her first kiss. Her first real date. Her first love. Her first—and only—husband. Without warning, her eyes began to tear.

"You okay?"

Aubrey sat bolt upright at the intrusion. A middle-aged man stood next to her open window.

"Ah…yeah," she mumbled, embarrassed at being caught on the verge of crying. "Just tired."

"I'm going down the line, passing the word. There's a wreck a mile or two up the road."

"Is it serious?"

"A semi and four cars, they're saying. Road's completely blocked in both directions."

The distant wail of a siren grew louder. As the ambulance passed, adrenaline flooded Aubrey's system, one of the many side effects of working in a hospital E.R., she supposed. Though, for her, it had recently become worse.

"Hope you brought a good book to read." The middle-aged man rapped her door and gave her a toothy smile before moving on. "We're gonna be here a while."

"Thanks," she called after him, her breathing, thankfully, slowing.

No book, but she had brought along some medical periodicals on health care for the aged and how to live independently after a hip fracture. She took one from the seat beside her and thumbed through it. Hopefully, she'd find something beneficial to her grandmother and compelling enough to keep her mind off the traffic jam. And Gage.

"Aubrey." He stood at her window.

Her hands involuntarily jerked, and the newsletter dropped onto her lap. "What are you doing here?"

"I'm about a dozen cars behind you. I walked up to check on you."

A dozen cars? He must have pulled out of the gas station right behind her.

"I'm fine." She collected the scattered newsletter pages.

"So we're back to that?"

"What?"

He leaned down and rested his forearms on her open window. "One-or two-word sentences."

Damn. He did know her well. "I guess."

His arms were tanned, the dusting of soft brown hair on them denser than she remembered. She shouldn't stare, but it was easier looking at his arms than his face.

"Is talking with me that tough?" he asked, readjusting his cowboy hat. "I remember when we'd stay up half the night talking. After we got married, we'd stay up half the night making l—"

"Details aren't necessary. I remember."

As did Gage, if his wide grin was any indication.

What was with him, anyway? They'd seen each other occasionally through the years, most recently at her grandfather's funeral. Those encounters had always been on the tense side and notably brief. Had enough time finally gone by that they could relax in each other's company and be themselves? It appeared so for Gage.

"Two whole sentences. That's a start." He chuckled and strode away.

But not to his truck. Instead, he cut behind her SUV and came up the passenger side. Before she could protest, he'd settled in beside her. Her glower had no dimming affects on the twinkle lighting his dark brown eyes.

"I don't remember inviting you in."

In response, he removed his cowboy hat and set it on the dash.

"Forget making yourself comfortable, you won't be staying long."

"Another thirty minutes, I'd say. The sheriff's office called in a special tow truck for the semi, and it hasn't arrived yet."

Siren wailing, the ambulance passed them going in the opposite direction toward Pineville. Momentarily distracted, Aubrey looked out her window. "I hope no one's injured."

"Two. Seriously, but not critically."

"How do you know all this?" She shot him a quizzical glance.

"I made a call on my cell phone. I have a friend who works in the newsroom at the radio station in Pineville."

"A friend?"

He turned toward her. "A *good* friend." His expression hinted at more.

"I'm happy for you." She crossed her arms over her middle and told herself it was indigestion and not jealousy gnawing at her stomach. For all she cared, he could have a thousand good friends.

"He and I went to fire academy together."

Aubrey groaned inwardly. Shame on her for walking right into his trap.

She remembered a very brief conversation they'd had at her grandfather's funeral when Gage mentioned joining the Blue Ridge Volunteer Fire Department. It was on the tip of her tongue to ask if he'd stuck with it, but she refrained, not certain she wanted to learn everything about him yet.

"You still a nurse in the emergency room at Tucson

General?" He moved his seat back to accommodate his six-foot-plus frame.

Aubrey rolled her eyes and shook her head. The man had a lot of nerve. "Not at the moment."

"You quit your job?"

"I took a leave of absence."

"Wow." He stopped fiddling with the seat position and faced her. "I thought you loved nursing."

"I do." Aubrey heard her voice crack and swallowed before continuing. "Just not the E.R. lately."

She thought of Jesse and Maureen—saw them as she had at their thirtieth wedding anniversary, a hundred family members and friends in attendance to join them in celebrating. Dear friends of the Stuarts, Aubrey had known "Uncle" Jesse and "Aunt" Maureen practically her entire life. She remembered being deeply touched at the way they gazed sweetly into each other's faces. How wonderful it must be, she'd thought, to still be in love after so many years.

But then another, different image of Jesse's and Maureen's faces came to her. Broken and battered and covered in blood. Less than a week after the anniversary celebration, the couple had been brought into the E.R. while Aubrey was on duty, victims of an automobile accident. Upon glimpsing them, Aubrey had froze.

All of the E.R.'s staff vast skill and expertise proved inadequate. They couldn't save her parents' friends. Within the hour, Uncle Jesse and Aunt Maureen were both dead.

Aubrey lost more than two patients and more than

two family friends that sad and terrible day. She lost a part of herself. And though she wouldn't admit it to anyone, she was terribly afraid she might never find it again.

"Hey, you okay?" Gage reached over and tucked a stray lock of hair behind her ear, a gesture so familiar, Aubrey's heart ached. He let his fingers linger. "You seemed lost for a second there."

He couldn't be any closer to the truth.

Something stirred inside her at the intimate contact, and it wasn't revulsion. Her eyes involuntarily sought his. Emotions, some old, some new, filled her. Without intending to, she let out a soft, "Oh."

A horn beeped, then another. The moment, or whatever it was, abruptly ended.

Gage grabbed his hat off the dash and swung around. "Traffic's moving. I'd better get back to my truck."

"I think that's a wise idea." Aubrey started the SUV with shaky fingers. She was never so glad to be surrounded by rude and impatient drivers.

"How about you and me pick this up later where we left off?" Without waiting for her answer, he stepped outside.

Another chorus of horns blared. Aubrey began to inch ahead, forcing Gage to slam the door shut. "How about we not?" she muttered under her breath.

In the next instant, he was on the run, his arm raised high in a parting wave.

Aubrey let out a frustrated grumble. Five minutes alone with him and look what happened. She let him touch her and stare at her…and…comfort her. Did she not possess so much as a smidgen of self-control?

Gage picked up his cell phone and punched in his friend's number.

"KSLN newsroom."

"Marty, it's me."

"Hey, buddy. What have you got?"

"Traffic's moving," Gage said. "Slow, but steady. I'll let you know more when I reach the accident scene."

"The tow truck just hit town. Should be in your vicinity within the next few minutes. My guess is only the northbound lane's open."

"Nothing coming at me, so I'd say you're right."

Gage kept Aubrey's silver SUV in sight. He planned on tailing her the entire way to Blue Ridge. The road was notoriously rough in places and in her present distracted state of mind, she might not be paying close attention.

"Did you hear the latest on the Denver fire?" Marty asked.

"Got the call a half hour ago. Thirty-five percent contained as of this afternoon. Assuming the weather holds, it'll be fifty percent by the morning."

"Kelli's already unpacked my bags. She was furious I might miss our six-month anniversary."

"Newlyweds. Every month is a reason to celebrate."

"That's fine with me." Marty chuckled. "Kelli really knows how to celebrate, if you catch my drift."

Gage did. All too vividly, in light of his recent encounter with Aubrey.

"You disappointed about the fire?" Marty asked.

"Not at all."

"Huh! I figured you'd be raring to go. It's been almost two weeks since the last one."

"Aubrey arrived today."

"Ah. That's right. The ex-wife is back in town. How'd it go?"

"Good and bad." Gage gunned the accelerator and passed a van. Only three vehicles now separated him and Aubrey's SUV. "Good because she let me get within ten feet of her without clamming up. Not that she talked a mile a minute."

"And bad because…?"

"She looks great." *And feels great, too.* Gage's fingers still tingled from when he'd brushed her hair back from her face.

"Gage," Marty said, his tone patient. "Need I remind you the lady ran out on you without so much as a 'see ya around, it's been swell'?"

"She didn't run out on me. The divorce was a mutual decision."

"Thanks to her father's interference."

"Can't blame him for everything. If she'd really wanted to stay married to me, she wouldn't have left." *Or, I could have gone with her,* thought Gage. "But I see your point."

"You were a walking train wreck afterward. Are you sure you want to put yourself out there again?"

"No. But you should have seen her."

Gage recalled Aubrey hurrying across the gas station parking lot. Short denim skirt. Short little top. Short red hair. The only thing long about her had been her legs. He'd never seen so much of their tanned length exposed in public. The Aubrey he remembered lacked the confidence to show off her body. Gage had to admit he liked the change in her.

In fact, everything about her was different, including her green eyes. They were the same color, but their former vividness had been replaced by wariness and a sadness he didn't think had anything to do with him or their breakup.

He often wondered what might have become of them if her father hadn't shown up that night, waving a carrot in front of Aubrey's face. Her decision to return to college hurt Gage, but the passing years had given him an adult perspective he lacked at twenty. He understood, at least in part, some of her reasons and didn't disagree with them.

Blue Ridge offered little opportunity for anyone with an ambition outside of ranching. He of all people knew that. Aubrey dreamt of following in her father's footsteps her whole life. Bombing her first year at college took a little of the wind from her sails, but it hadn't thrown her off course.

No, Gage did that when he proposed marriage.

Marty made a disgruntled sound into the phone, distracting Gage.

"Be careful, buddy. A hot ex-wife back in town is no reason to go all stupid."

"Quit your worrying," Gage answered, returning his focus to Aubrey's SUV. "I'm not planning anything."

But he was. He'd seen the spark igniting in Aubrey's eyes when he'd touched her. And while he wasn't ready to go "all stupid" as Marty put it, he did want to explore possible options. Risky, yes, but the plain truth was, he'd never cared for a woman the way he had Aubrey. One look at her again and he wasn't sure he ever would.

The only way to discover for sure if Aubrey reciprocated any of his feelings was for him was to see her again.

Already his mind was formulating a plan. One that would ensure he and Aubrey crossed paths frequently during her stay in Blue Ridge.

Chapter 2

Aubrey flopped over onto her side, pulled the bedsheet up around her neck and cracked open one eye. A field of tiny pink tulips filled her vision, more faded than they'd been the last time she slept in this room, but still the same.

She and her sister chose the wallpaper, back when she was four and Annie three. It was the first summer they'd stayed in Blue Ridge. Grandma Rose had wanted the girls to feel at home, so she and Grandpa Glen drove them into Pineville for the day and let them pick out paint, wallpaper, bedspreads, matching sheets and a lamp at the home decorating store. Being little girls, they went with a pink color scheme.

Grandma Rose never changed a thing. Every summer for the next fourteen years, Aubrey and Annie spent their nights in twin beds, slumbering amongst pink tulips. Until the summer ten years ago when, fresh from a quickie Las Vegas wedding, Aubrey had moved out of her grandparents' house and into an old motor home parked behind the barn on the Raintree ranch.

Thinking of Gage reminded her of the two of them in her SUV yesterday. One little touch of his fingertips, one brush of her hair, and she'd gone soft and gooey inside. Old habits were definitely hard to break. Groaning, Aubrey drew the bedsheet over her head and buried her face in her pillow.

"Aubrey," her grandmother hollered from her bedroom across the hall.

"Coming!" Aubrey sprang out of bed, glancing at the alarm clock as she did. The red numerals glowed 8:16 a.m. *Yikes!* No wonder her grandmother was hollering. Throwing a robe on over her pajamas, she hurried through the door.

"Were you still sleeping?" Grandma Rose asked when Aubrey entered her room.

"I could have sworn I set the alarm before I went to bed."

"It's all right. You needed your sleep. I could tell when you arrived yesterday that you were tired from the drive."

More frazzled than tired, thought Aubrey. She'd seen Gage tailing her the entire way from Pineville to Blue Ridge and couldn't shake the feeling he was going to prove as difficult to outrun during her stay here as he was on the road yesterday afternoon.

"That's no reason for me oversleeping." Aubrey positioned the wheelchair by the side of the bed, then helped her grandmother to a sitting position. "Do you need to use the bathroom?"

"If you don't mind."

"That's why I'm here."

Over the next thirty minutes Aubrey saw to her grandmother's needs, getting her bathed and dressed and otherwise ready to face the day. When they were done, she wheeled her grandmother to the kitchen and got her situated comfortably at the table. It still shocked Aubrey to see how small and frail her grandmother had become. When she'd arrived yesterday and glimpsed the older woman napping in a recliner, only the presence of Mrs. Payne, the neighbor, had kept Aubrey from crying out in alarm.

"What do you feel like eating this morning?" Aubrey asked as she made a pot of coffee.

Like the bedroom she and her sister had shared, there were no significant changes in the kitchen's decor, either. Coffee was stored in the second largest of four ceramic windmill canisters on the counter. The others held flour, tea bags and sugar, in that order.

"Just toast. And maybe some of that calcium-enriched orange juice," her grandmother answered.

"Is that all?"

"I haven't recovered my appetite since the accident."

No wonder her grandmother had lost so much weight. Aubrey remembered the breakfasts served in this kitchen as being hearty enough to satisfy a crew of lumberjacks.

"Well, maybe we can fix that while I'm here." She placed two steaming mugs of coffee on the table, then opened a cupboard where she knew she'd find a loaf of bread.

"I'm so glad you came, dear." There was genuine pleasure in her grandmother's voice, along with a hint of sorrow. "I'll try not to be a burden."

Aubrey went over to her grandmother and placed an arm around her shoulders. "Don't talk like that. You're no burden whatsoever."

"I suspect your father didn't want you coming here. As far as sons-in-law go, he's everything a mother could ask for. But he can be a little dictating at times."

"A *little?*" Aubrey laughed and took the chair beside her grandmother.

Dictating did indeed describe Alexander Stuart. He was a man used to wielding authority. And though he meant well and loved his family dearly, he sometimes treated his wife and daughters like rookie interns who needed to be browbeaten into shape.

The first time Aubrey openly defied him had been the end of her freshman year at college. Unable to cope with the pressures and high expectations put on her, she'd escaped to Blue Ridge and married Gage.

It wasn't the last time she defied him, either. And while her father had backed off over the years, he still attempted to sway her when he felt she was making a wrong decision.

Like now.

Alexander Stuart had preferred to hire a caregiver for his mother-in-law so that Aubrey could remain in Tucson and face her career crisis head-on. He disapproved of her "running off and hiding in Blue Ridge again" as he'd called it. But Aubrey didn't tell her grandmother that.

"I'm so glad you're here." The older woman smiled warmly. "I've missed you."

Aubrey covered her grandmother's hand. "I've missed you, too."

Sitting there in the homey kitchen she remembered so well, Aubrey was glad she'd returned to Blue Ridge. She wanted nothing to tarnish or otherwise ruin her stay. So, for her grandmother's health and well-being and her own peace of mind, she'd learn to live—temporarily—in the same town with Gage.

She rose from the table, brimming with determination. "How about some eggs with that toast, Grandma?"

"Maybe one. Fried." The smile tugging at her grandmother's lips was conspiratorial. "I'm supposed to be watching my cholesterol."

"One fried egg coming up. And we won't tell your doctor I corrupted you." Aubrey fixed an egg for herself, as well.

The two of them enjoyed a leisurely meal that started with a discussion of Grandma Rose's care and diet and ended with an unexpected barrage of banging noises emanating from the front porch.

Aubrey put down her coffee mug and automatically stood. "What is that?"

"I have no idea." Grandma Rose peered through the doorway leading into the living room.

At the sound of the front door opening, Aubrey hastily retied her knee-length robe, which suddenly felt tissue-paper-thin, then plucked her tousled hair. "Somebody's here." She'd forgotten what it was like living in a small town. Friends and neighbors frequently stopped by without phoning first and doorbells were for strangers.

"Morning," Gage called from the living room. "Anybody home?"

Aubrey dropped back into her chair.

"We're in the kitchen," Grandma Rose called back, obviously delighted at the prospect of a visitor. "Have you had breakfast yet?"

Gage stopped in the doorway, smiling broadly. Rather than his cowboy hat, he wore a baseball cap, which he removed as he entered the room and bent down between the two women to plant a kiss on Grandma Rose's cheek. "Mom already fed me. But I'll take a cup of coffee if there's extra."

Grandma Rose tittered like a schoolgirl. "Why, of course there's extra."

He leaned toward Aubrey. She shied, momentarily alarmed he intended to kiss her cheek, too. But he just winked.

"Stay put," he said. "I'll get my own."

Aubrey had every intention of staying put. Silly, she supposed. Gage had seen her wearing far less than pajamas and a thin robe during their marriage. Heck, the outfit she wore yesterday exposed more bare skin than this one. Her fingers gravitated toward the hem of the robe. The movement must have caught his eye, for he looked down, and his smile widened.

Damn him.

Her first instinct was to lower her head. She resisted and met his gaze head-on.

Like the previous day, heat crept up her neck, all the way to the tips of her ears. Still she stared. "Clean mugs are in the cupboard to the right of the sink," she said.

"What brings you by this morning?" Grandma Rose asked. "And don't tell me it's the smell of brewing coffee."

She appeared oblivious to Aubrey's discomfort. The Raintrees had always been friendly with her grandparents. Fortunately, Aubrey's and Gage's impulsive and short-lived marriage hadn't affected that friendship. Given the two families' long-standing history together, Gage was probably a frequent visitor to her grandmother's house.

"I'm here to start work on the handicap renovations."

"What?" Aubrey and her grandmother said in unison.

"You did advertise for a handyman?" Gage peered at them from over the brim of his mug, then took a sip of coffee. "I saw the notice posted on the bulletin board outside of Cutter's."

There were two markets, if one could call them markets, in Blue Ridge. Cutter's was the larger of the two, not much more than a convenience store with a modest produce bin, while the town's one and only gas pump could be found at the Stop and Go.

"I did," Grandma Rose exclaimed. "But surely you can't be answering the ad. When in the world would you have time, what with working at the ranch and all?"

Gage propped a hip on the edge of the counter in a casual stance that somehow managed to be sexy, too.

"Well, it's not just me. We're splitting the job between all of us in the volunteer fire department. I'm building the wheelchair ramp for the front porch. Gus will change out your round doorknobs for lever ones, and Mike's installing a grab bar in your bathtub. Anything else you need, Kenny Junior will handle."

"Gage is the captain." Grandma Rose beamed. "He was promoted after Bob Stintson and his wife moved to Show Low."

"Really?" So, Aubrey thought, he had stuck with firefighting. No surprise. Gage always had a sense of adventure. He was the one who suggested they elope, after all.

"You know we're raising money for some new equipment." Gage directed his statement at Grandma Rose. "We figured this would be a good chance to build the fund and help out a loyal contributor at the same time."

"Why, I'm…." She placed a hand at her throat. "I'm just thrilled. Thank you, Gage. Thank all the boys for me. Now you swear this won't be an inconvenience? I heard from Martha Payne yesterday your father has suffered another gout attack."

"He's not so bad. I think he'll be up and around in a couple of days. Hannah can handle things for one morning," Gage said, referring to his younger sister.

Aubrey thought she noticed a bit of tension in the

lines around Gage's mouth. She remembered Mr. Raintree as being a somewhat hard and inflexible man, on par with her own father. She and Gage always shared that commonality. If Mr. Raintree was laid up, he probably depended on Gage and Hannah to run the ranch. The work was constant and difficult, she knew firsthand from her brief residence there.

"Are you sure?" her grandmother asked. "I don't want to be the cause of any…discord."

"Forget it." He dismissed her worries with a casual shrug. "I'd be here helping even if you hadn't advertised for a handyman."

Aubrey believed him. Gage adored her grandmother, and she him. But, as Aubrey watched their exchange, she couldn't help feeling something was amiss in the Raintree family.

"Dad's just being his usual grumpy self," Gage went on.

Her grandmother nodded in understanding. "Gout is no picnic."

"Probably less painful than a broken hip." He shifted his weight to his other foot, looking quite at home and in no hurry to start the renovations.

"It's been tough going so far," Grandma Rose said, smiling, "but I expect to improve rapidly now that my granddaughter is here. I couldn't ask for a better nurse."

Gage toasted Aubrey with his coffee. "Here's to granddaughters."

Bringing her mug to her lips, she drained the last bit of coffee. "Grandma, we should probably get a move on."

Her grandmother's appointment wasn't until early afternoon, but Aubrey wanted Gage out of the house. The three of them sitting around the kitchen having a friendly chat reminded her too much of days gone by.

"Where you headed?" he asked, not taking the hint and not moving an inch.

"Physical therapy," Grandma Rose told him.

"Sounds like fun."

"It's hard work," Aubrey corrected him.

"I don't doubt it." Unfazed by her brusque tone, Gage polished off his coffee, rinsed out his mug and placed it in the dishwasher. "And speaking of hard work, I should get cracking."

Aubrey blew out a huge sigh when she heard the front door shut behind him. How long, she wondered, would it take to build the wheelchair ramp? More importantly, how long until she could comfortably share the same air space with him?

Getting Grandma Rose ready for their trip to Pineville didn't take long. She obviously wished to be self-sufficient eventually and would do whatever was required of her to achieve that status. Because morale played an important part in the recovery of someone in her grandmother's condition, Aubrey encouraged her.

Afterward, she helped her grandmother into the recliner so that she could watch her favorite soap opera. During the show, Aubrey showered and dressed. When she finished, they still had a good half hour to kill before they had to leave for the rehabilitation center in Pineville.

"Wheel me out onto the porch, dear," Grandma Rose said, using the remote to shut off the TV, "so I can see how Gage is doing with the ramp."

Aubrey tried to come up with a valid argument. "Are you sure? You have a big afternoon ahead of you and don't want to overdo it."

"I'd like to know how I can overdo it by just sitting."

"It's warm out there."

"Nonsense." Grandma Rose leaned forward and braced her hands on the armrests. "I can tolerate a little heat."

Aubrey reluctantly complied with the request, the wheelchair bumping as it rolled over the threshold and onto the porch. She thought about asking Gage if he could replace the threshold with a flatter one, then caught herself. Asking one of the other guys might be a better approach.

The first sight to greet her as she stepped outside was Gage's pickup truck parked in the driveway. The emblem on the door, she now noted, was some kind of flame with initials in the center. He'd lowered the tailgate and was using it as a makeshift workbench. The second sight to greet her was Gage. He stood with his back to them, bent over a circular saw and cutting wooden planks. She tried not to notice him, but her eyes kept darting across the yard to where he worked.

His shoulders were broader than she remembered, the muscles more defined and prominent. He might have grown another inch or two. Then again, maybe he just stood straighter and taller. Either way, maturity agreed with him. Were he another man, Aubrey might find the changes appealing.

When the plank Gage was cutting split neatly into two pieces, he shut off the saw and looked up. "Hey, there." Removing his ball cap, he ran fingers through sweat-dampened hair, then flung it onto the tailgate as he came toward them. "Need a hand?"

"No, I—"

"Good heavens, Gage," Grandma Rose interrupted. "You must be dying of thirst. Get him a glass of lemonade, will you, Aubrey?"

Setting the brake on the wheelchair, she gratefully retreated into the house. Maybe by the time she came back with his lemonade, he'd be working again.

No such luck.

He was sitting in the chair closest to Grandma Rose when Aubrey stepped outside.

"Thanks," he said, as he shot to his feet and reached for the plastic tumbler she carried.

She gave it to him and when he'd sat back down, she inched toward the door. "I have a few things to do around the house before we leave for Pineville."

"There's nothing that can't wait until later," Grandma Rose said, motioning with her hand. "Sit down and visit for a while."

Gage grabbed one of the other chairs and dragged it over next to his. Flashing his trademark sexy grin, he patted the seat. "You heard your grandmother. Sit and visit for a while."

To a casual observer, the invitation appeared innocuous enough. Aubrey knew better.

He drank half the lemonade in one long swallow. "Whew! That hit the spot." He then lifted the plastic tumbler to his forehead and rested it there. "Awfully hot for June."

"Do you remember the day you and Gage first met?" Grandma Rose didn't wait for a response and just prattled on. "It was at Sunday school. You were about four and Gage must have been, oh, five or six. You had on that pretty pink dress I liked with the big white sash. We had such a time with your hair, trying to make it look nice." She made a tsking noise. "A few weeks before arriving here, you and your sister decided to play beauty parlor. Annie, the little dickens, cut a huge chunk of hair out of the left side of your head. Your poor mother cried for days."

Aubrey had no desire whatsoever to walk down memory lane. Gage clearly didn't share her sentiment and enthusiastically participated in the discussion, bringing up one youthful indiscretion after the other.

Crossing and uncrossing her legs, Aubrey endured the small talk. Because of Gage, she'd lived exclusively for the summer when she and Annie would stay in Blue Ridge. For nine straight weeks, their parents visited various hospitals across the country where their father would demonstrate the latest medical advance he'd made in the field of cardiovascular surgery.

Their mother, Carol May Stuart, had been raised in Blue Ridge, having met their father at college. They both liked the idea of their daughters being exposed to the same grassroots upbringing she experienced. The girls loved Blue Ridge; their grandparents loved having them stay. It had been a perfect arrangement. Until the summer after Aubrey's freshman year at the University of Arizona when everything went to hell in a handbasket.

"Do you remember the day you came home and announced you'd eloped?" Grandma Rose's smile turned sentimental. "I was so happy for you both."

If Gage was ill at ease with her grandmother's reminiscences, he didn't show it. His attention didn't waver from Aubrey once while the older woman recounted the incident. Not that Aubrey had made eye contact with him. But she could feel his stare just as surely as if he'd reached over and laid a hand on her.

"I remember everything," he said in a husky voice.

She remembered everything, too. And despite the scalding temperatures, a shiver ran through her.

Perhaps sensing Aubrey's discomfort, Grandma Rose slapped the arms of the wheelchair. "Would you look at the time." No one had so much as glanced at their watch. "We'd best be on the road, hadn't we, Aubrey?"

"Yes," she mumbled and gratefully rose.

Gage also stood and grabbed the back of her chair, pulling it out. She couldn't help herself and looked at him. Given the sexually charged atmosphere in the SUV yesterday, she fully expected desire or longing to be reflected in his features. What she saw there caught her off guard and affected her far greater.

Sadness and, unless she was mistaken, regret. For

their marriage, she wondered, or that it ended? She couldn't tell, and maybe that was for the best.

"And I need to get back to work. That ramp won't build itself." Gage's smile vanquished all trace of negative emotion from his face. "Can I help you into the car, Rose?"

"Yes, thank you. That would be nice. Aubrey, fetch my purse for me, will you? It's on the kitchen counter."

"Sure, Grandma."

They were leaving at last. Retrieving her grandmother's purse first and then hers, Aubrey headed back outside just as Gage was assisting Grandma Rose into the SUV. The scene was tender enough to give Aubrey pause.

He had no sooner buckled her grandmother's seat belt when a series of loud beeps cut the air. Stepping away from the SUV, he reached for the radio hooked to his belt. Aubrey remembered seeing similar communication devices being used by the local ranchers. After listening to a garbled voice, Gage depressed a button and returned the radio to his belt, a frown creasing his brow. "I have to leave."

"Problems at home?" Aubrey asked.

"No."

Without so much as a wave goodbye, he abandoned Grandma Rose and hopped into his truck. Throwing it into Reverse, he tore out the driveway, the tires spewing a shower of gravel and dirt. He hadn't even bothered to put the tailgate back up. His ball cap sailed out and landed at the end of the driveway.

"What the heck was that all about?" Aubrey asked after retrieving the cap and loading the wheelchair into the back of her SUV. It annoyed her that Gage would take off and leave the ramp half-done, not to mention a mess in the front yard.

"I suppose he got called to a fire," Grandma Rose answered.

"What fire?" She scanned the nearby rooftops. No telltale plume of gray-black smoke billowed skyward.

"In the mountains somewhere, I suppose." She peered out the window. "Or anywhere in the state. Once they went to California and twice to Colorado."

Aubrey jammed the key in the ignition, inexplicably irritated. "The volunteer fire department doesn't travel outside Blue Ridge."

"No. But the Blue Ridge Hotshots do. Gage is also a wilderness firefighter."

Aubrey's mind grappled with the unexpected information. "Since when?"

"For a while now. During the summers, mostly. He does something else with them the rest of the year, too, but I don't know what. Part-time, of course. He still works the ranch with the family."

"You're kidding."

"He didn't tell you?" Grandma Rose looked surprised.

Aubrey shook her head. "No one did."

Her family seldom talked about the Raintrees after the divorce. Aubrey's father resented Gage and flew off the handle every time his former son-in-law's name was mentioned. Because his outbursts had accounted for any number of unpleasant family gatherings, Aubrey opted to keep the peace and stopped asking about Gage. News occasionally made it her way via her grandmother, but not with any regularity.

She had yet to start the SUV, and the vehicle's interior temperature quickly escalated. Turning on the engine, she set the air-conditioning on maximum before pulling out of the driveway.

The drive to Pineville took about an hour, not all of which was filled with conversation. During the frequent lulls, Aubrey's mind drifted to Gage. Besides being captain of the Blue Ridge Volunteer Fire Department, he was also a wilderness firefighter. Amazing.

Mountain fires had been in the news too often during the last few years for her not to know what a Hotshot was and how important they were to the safety and preservation of Arizona's endangered high country.

She'd always assumed—along with most people in Blue Ridge—that Gage would follow in his father's footsteps and take over management of the Raintree Ranch. To discover he'd chosen a different profession, one as dangerous and challenging as a wilderness firefighter, intrigued her.

And being intrigued by Gage was a complication she neither wanted nor needed in her life right now.

Chapter 3

The smell of chicken enchiladas, homemade pizza and hot apple pie commingled, filling Aubrey's SUV as she drove the main road through town the following morning. From their resting place on the floor in front of the passenger seat, the foil-wrapped food dishes rattled and shook in protest with every bump, pothole and sharp turn.

Buildings and landmarks marked Aubrey's short trip, most familiar, a few new. The feed store, the one-room public library and Mountain View Realty's log cabin-style office building were the same as she remembered. A life-size wooden statue of a bear now stood in front of the Blue Ridge Inn, its big paw raised in greeting.

How, Aubrey asked herself, had she let her grandmother coerce her into running this errand? Some of the Hotshot crews, as reported by her grandmother's neighbor, Mrs. Payne, had taken over the Blue Ridge community center. "A satellite fire camp of sorts," she'd said, and explained a little about how the twenty-member crews rotated shifts. In a show of support, many of the townsfolk prepared food for the wilderness firefighters, who used the community center to eat, sleep and otherwise relax before returning to action.

According to recent reports, the blaze had been raging in the mountains twenty-five miles east of Blue Ridge since yesterday, apparently started from the smoldering remains of an illegal campfire left by recreationists. It didn't take much to ignite a fire during the hot, dry Arizona summers.

Originally, Mrs. Payne had planned on delivering the food items. But the two older women got to chitchatting and decided Aubrey should do it. That way, they could work on a baby quilt for Mrs. Payne's newest grandchild. Aubrey agreed, only because she didn't have the heart to deny her grandmother the opportunity to spend an enjoyable hour with a friend. And it was for a good cause.

Besides, what were the chances of Aubrey running into Gage anyway?

That's what you said at the gas station, a small voice inside her teased.

"Shut up," she told the voice as she pulled into the community center parking lot.

Aubrey had spent every spare minute not dedicated to her grandmother's care thinking about Gage and his second job. She remained glued to the radio and TV news for updates on the fire. She'd even gone so far as to research Hotshots on the internet, using the laptop computer she'd brought with her.

Holding the box of food dishes to her chest, she used her shoulder to push open the heavy door leading into the community center. From the number of vehicles in the parking lot, she expected quite a few people to be inside. The actual count was considerably more.

A dozen or so cots took up one corner of the huge, airy room, many of them occupied. Metal chairs surrounded a TV, which sat on the small, homemade stage. Several stations had been created by arranging long tables into Us or Ts, their various purposes indicated by a cardboard sign taped to a corner.

"Hi, there. You bring a food donation?" The woman greeting Aubrey was about her age and looked vaguely familiar. Before she could place the face, the woman said, "You're Aubrey Stuart, aren't you? I heard you were back in town."

"That's me," Aubrey said, wishing she could remember the woman.

"You don't recognize me, do you?"

She smiled apologetically and shook her head.

"It's been a long time." The woman returned her smile. "I was Eleanor Carpenter. I'm Eleanor Meeks now. I used to live about a half mile up the road from your grandparents. You played sometimes with my younger sister, Beth. When you weren't playing with Gage, that is." Eleanor's eyes remained warm and friendly, but her smile turned impish.

"Of course." Aubrey was surprised by the delight she felt at running into a former acquaintance. "Nice to see you again." She shifted the box of food to her hip. "Are you volunteering here?"

"Yep. When I can arrange for someone to watch the kids, that is." She took Aubrey by the elbow and led her toward the kitchen located in the rear of the huge room. "Let's find a place for this food and then we can talk."

"Is your husband a Hotshot?" Aubrey asked.

"Was." Eleanor's smile faded. "He was killed two years ago in a burnover incident when the wind suddenly changed direction."

"Oh, my gosh! I'm so sorry." Aubrey instantly flashed on her parents' late friends, Jesse and Maureen. "I didn't—"

"It's all right." Eleanor reached into the cardboard box and removed one of the covered dishes. She placed it in an empty spot on the counter. "I won't lie and say things are always easy. But me and the kids, we're doing okay. Volunteering with the Hotshots helps." A shadow of grief crossed her face. It lasted only a moment and then she was smiling again.

Aubrey couldn't help thinking of Gage. Was he all right? Was he in danger? How long until he returned?

Some of the internet websites she'd visited the previous night portrayed wilderness firefighting as a glamorous and exciting profession, the men and women as heroes. They were, but as an E.R. nurse, Aubrey knew better than most the not so glamorous and exciting side of firefighting.

"Hey, Eleanor," someone called. "Can you give us a hand? This idiot fax machine won't print."

"I'm the local Jane-of-all-trades." Eleanor sighed wearily, though she acted more pleased than put out. "Hang around, why don't you? If you're not in a hurry." She started off, then stopped and turned. "It's good to see you again, Aubrey. Welcome home."

Welcome home.

The phrase echoed in Aubrey's head. Though she had lived most of her life in Tucson, Blue Ridge had been home to her, too. Certainly the home of her heart.

"Thanks," she told Eleanor. "I think I will hang around."

Whatever malfunction had struck the fax machine, it perplexed not only Eleanor, but several others. While the group of workers stood over the machine—reminding Aubrey of surgeons and nurses in an operating room—she finished unloading the food dishes and went wandering the community center.

As she neared the front door, it flew open. A large group of Hotshots entered, dressed in dark brown pants, black T-shirts and heavy work boots with thick rubber soles. They were covered in grime, and the smell of smoke clung to them, nearly overpowering Aubrey.

She couldn't avoid hearing their conversation as they passed.

"I'm going to grab a quick bite to eat," said one of the tallest of the group. "What about the rest of you?"

Most concurred.

"I'm gonna hit the sack for a while." The speaker yawned noisily. "I haven't slept in two days."

The taller man slapped his buddy companionably on the back. "Take care of that arm first."

"This?" He held out the affected limb, and Aubrey noticed an ugly gash running the length of his forearm. "It's just a scratch."

"I don't care if it's a pinprick," the taller man said. "Take care of it."

"Yes, sir." The injured man veered away from the others and went behind a U-shaped station, where he dropped down into a metal chair and rolled up his sleeve. The cardboard sign taped to the table read First Aid.

Without stopping to think, Aubrey went over to him. "Can I help you with that? I'm a nurse."

He peered up at her, and his face brightened. "Sure."

She came around the tables and conducted a quick inventory of the available medical supplies. Then she took the man's arm and examined the cut. It was long and inflamed, but not deep.

"How did this happen?"

"A tree branch attacked me." His smile widened and took on a new appearance—that of a man interested in a woman. "You got to watch out for those fellows. They're sneaky. Catch you when you're not looking."

She released his arm, giving him the kind and helpful smile she reserved for patients. "I'm going to the kitchen for some water to wash this. I'll be right back."

"And I'll be right here."

In the kitchen, she found a small basin that she promptly filled with warm water from the faucet. She also found a stash of industrial paper towels and grabbed a handful. Not the best for cleansing wounds, but they'd do in a pinch.

True to his word, the man was waiting for her when she returned.

"You're back." He didn't mask his delight at seeing her.

Aubrey set the basin and paper towels down on the table near him and donned a pair of latex gloves. While she treated his wound, he engaged her in lively conversation. He was a good-looking man, despite the dirt and grime. And he didn't come on so strong that he offended her with his mild flirting. Another woman would probably flirt right back. But not her.

Aubrey met, and subsequently dated, any number of available, attractive men. With every one, she waited for that telltale flutter of awareness in her middle. It rarely came, and the relationships tended to fizzle out, some sooner than others. Yet one glimpse of Gage bent over a circular saw cutting planks and she'd had enough flutters to lift her three feet off the ground.

"Are you a volunteer medic?" The injured man's question jarred Aubrey from her musings.

"No. I really just came by today to drop off some food donations." Aubrey had finished cleansing the wound and was applying an antibiotic ointment to the affected area.

"You live here?"

"Uh…yes and no." She opted for the condensed version, not wanting to go into her life story. "I'm staying with my grandmother for an extended visit. She's recovering from a broken hip. How about you?"

He shook his head. "Sacramento. Born and raised."

"And you belong to the Blue Ridge Hotshots?"

"No way," he scoffed and pointed with his free hand to the emblem on his T-shirt. It bore a resemblance to the one on Gage's truck. "I'm with the Sierra Nevada Hotshots."

"Really? I didn't know there were other firefighters here."

"There are four crews working the fire right now. Us, Blue Ridge, Albuquerque and the Tucson Hot Shots. More are scheduled to arrive tonight if the fire continues to spread."

"I just learned yesterday that Hotshots traveled to different states."

"We go wherever we're needed. Kind of like the marines." A dimple appeared in his cheek when he gave her a crooked grin. "So, are you free for dinner when this fire's done making the morning headlines, or do you have a boyfriend?"

"I…ah…." Why was she even hesitating? She absolutely did not have a boyfriend, and this seemingly nice, definitely handsome man had just asked her out. She tried to make her lips form the word no. "N-not really."

"Uh, oh. Too slow." The man—whose name Aubrey didn't even know—chuckled good-naturedly. "And the eyes were a dead giveaway, too. Is he with the Blue Ridge Hotshots?"

"I don't have a boyfriend," she said, strong and firm with no hesitation this time.

"A wannabe boyfriend? Are you one of those Hotshot groupies?"

"Absolutely not!" She huffed indignantly. "May I remind you I'm holding your injured arm in my hands, and I'm not above inflicting pain."

His chuckle developed into a full-blown belly laugh. "As much as I'd be tempted to in this case, I don't steal another man's girl. But if you ever get tired of him, or he doesn't treat you right, give me a call. Sacramento's not so far away I can't find my way back here."

"Honestly, there's no one—"

"MacPherson! You're not giving this young lady a hard time, are you?" The taller man from earlier appeared, his jaw set in a no-nonsense frown.

"Who, me?" MacPherson pretended to be insulted.

"You'll have to excuse him, ma'am. He has a tendency to run off at the mouth. You have my permission to boot him where it counts if necessary."

"It's all right," Aubrey answered.

"Hey, Captain." MacPherson held up the arm that Aubrey had finished dressing. "She's a nurse."

"Are you?" the captain asked.

"Yes, I am."

"Are you a volunteer here?"

"Her boyfriend's one of the local crew," MacPherson interjected before Aubrey could answer.

"He's not my boyfriend," she protested, but no one paid her any heed.

The captain had made an attempt to wash up. His face and hands were scrubbed clean, if not the rest of him. "Have you ever considered volunteering? I'd be happy to introduce you to Marty Paxton, the Blue Ridge commander."

"Thanks, but no."

"Wilderness firefighting teams can always use skilled medical personnel."

Aubrey glanced around the community center, seeking a diversion. Where had Eleanor gone off to? "I can't. I'm the sole caregiver for my invalid grandmother." That sounded better than the truth.

Jesse and Maureen's deaths had done a real number on Aubrey, shaking her confidence to the core. No matter how hard she tried not to, she saw their faces in every trauma patient she treated. Aubrey believed she owed her patients the best possible care. How could she explain to the captain that she feared she might freeze the first time a seriously injured firefighter was brought in?

Thankfully, he took no for an answer. "Well, if you ever change your mind, I'm sure there'll be an opening for you."

"And you could always come to Sacramento if you get tired of this place." MacPherson bounced to his feet and shot her a look loaded with innuendo. "Thanks for the bandage job. See ya around, I hope."

"Nice meeting you, ma'am." The captain nodded curtly. "Let's go, MacPherson. We got a call while you were under the knife. Playtime is over."

"But we just got here."

The rest of MacPherson's complaint went unheard as the two men were joined by the remaining members of their crew. Moving as one, they rushed out the door. If they'd been riding horses, Aubrey would have expected to see a cloud of dust billowing behind them.

"You done?"

She turned at the voice and, seeing Eleanor, smiled. "There you are. I missed you earlier."

"Sorry about that. I got suckered into making a bunch of copies at the real estate office next door where I work. The owner is good about letting the Hotshots use his equipment."

"That's nice." It seemed to Aubrey the locals were more than willing to assist the firefighters however they could. She'd forgotten how much she liked the we're-in-this-together attitude prevalent in small towns.

"Someone just brewed a fresh pot of coffee. Can I interest you in a cup?" Eleanor asked. "Or an iced tea? I'm scheduled for my break. We could catch up on old times."

If the promise of a caffeine pick-me-up wasn't enough, the hope shining in Eleanor's face would have persuaded Aubrey. "Sounds great." She reached into her jeans pocket for her cell phone. "Let me check in at home quick. Make sure everything's okay with my grandmother."

Home. There was that word again. She should probably be careful how she used it before someone—herself included—got the wrong impression. Look at the conclusion MacPherson had drawn thanks to one little slip of the tongue.

Why would anyone think she had a boyfriend?

"Have you seen Gage yet?" Eleanor asked after she and Aubrey found a quiet spot in which to curl up with their iced teas.

"Yesterday," Aubrey answered with forced nonchalance. "He and the other volunteer firefighters are doing the handicap renovations on my grandmother's house."

"Mmm. I think I heard that. Funny how neither one of you ever remarried."

Aubrey didn't rise to the bait Eleanor dangled. "Not really. I've been focused on my career for the past several years. Serious relationships have been low on my list of priorities." Not exactly the truth, but not a lie, either.

"I can certainly understand."

"What about your sister, Beth? Has she gotten married?"

Aubrey's attempt to change the subject backfired.

"Last spring. To an insurance salesman in Show Low. You know, after you and Gage…after you left town, she made quite a play for him. He turned her down flat, which she took pretty hard. Of course, we all told her she was wasting her time. He was never interested in anyone but you. Oh, he's dated some. I mean, no man is made of stone. There was one gal in Pineville he hooked up with for a while. A technician for the phone company, I think." Eleanor smiled coyly. "But like you, serious relationships have been low on his list of priorities."

As it had yesterday on the porch with Gage and her grandmother, reminiscing made Aubrey fidgety. "Tell me about your children," she said. "Do you have any pictures?"

Trust a mother's pride in her offspring. To Aubrey's vast relief, Eleanor immediately switched gears and for the next several minutes they enjoyed an amiable conversation. One that didn't twist Aubrey's stomach into knots.

"I've really enjoyed visiting, but I need to get back to work," Eleanor said with reluctance. "I'm on duty until seven."

"It's been great. I hope we can do it again while I'm here."

"Oh." Eleanor's eyebrows lifted. "You aren't staying for good?"

"No. Only until my grandmother recovers."

If she did recover. The chances of an elderly person leading a fully independent life after breaking a hip weren't good. But Aubrey refused to dwell on statistics. Rather, she and her grandmother would take it one step at a time.

After a goodbye hug, Aubrey and Eleanor parted company. The TV blared in the background as Aubrey headed down the center of the large room. Men still slept in the cots, some of them snoring soundly.

She was about ten feet from the front door when it swung open and another group of Hotshots entered. These firefighters were wearing navy blue T-shirts, as opposed to black, she noted, and included a woman

among their ranks. Knowing they must be tired and
hungry, Aubrey stepped aside to let them pass, smiling at their nods and hellos, until the last man stepped
through the door.

Upon seeing him, her smile froze.

Like the other Hotshots, he was dirty and grimy and
smelled of smoke. Black smears covered his face and
arms. Sweat plastered his short black hair to his head.
A combination of sun, heat and wind had turned his
tanned complexion dark and ruddy. Bits of debris clung
to his clothing, and there was a jagged tear in the knee
of his pants.

He looked tough and rugged and strong enough to
hammer nails with his bare knuckles. He also looked
sexy as hell.

The fluttering thing started again in Aubrey's middle. Only today it resembled propellers on a twin-engine
plane rather than butterfly wings.

"Aubrey! What are you doing here?"

"Hi. I…uh…brought some food."

As a boy, he'd been cute. As a teenager, handsome.
But Gage Raintree as a man fully grown was utterly
breathtaking.

"Are you leaving already?" he asked.

"Actually, I've been here a while. And yes, I am leaving."

The other Hotshots had moved on ahead, leaving the
two of them as alone as they could be in a large room
full of people.

Gage took a step back and pushed open the door with

one hand, the corded muscles of his arm standing out. "Here. I'll walk you to your car."

Oh, no, thought Aubrey. What now? Nowhere to run, nowhere to hide. The problem was, after getting one look at him, she really didn't want to do either of those things.

Gage entertained no doubts he would somehow get Aubrey alone and harbored no qualms about doing whatever was necessary to accomplish that end. He didn't blame her for her obvious reluctance; they had a lot of unresolved stuff still hanging over their heads. And just because he was ready and willing to tackle some of that unresolved stuff didn't mean she felt the same.

A sense of satisfaction filled him when she finally relented and agreed to let him accompany her outside. As a result, he now had the enjoyment of following her to her SUV. And it was definitely enjoyable.

She wore jeans today. Low-riders. And a snug little blouse that revealed a modest band of creamy flesh. When she moved just right, he could see her belly button. A definite plus. Her short, bouncy hair had been pulled off her face with a headband, but several tendrils escaped, falling into her eyes.

Eyes that watched his every move.

Since running into Aubrey, Gage had dwelled on little else except her. Even the fire had taken a mental backseat, which was unusual for him. He tended to throw himself into firefighting to the exclusion of everything else, which caused a significant number of rifts with his family. To say his father disapproved of Gage being a firefighter was the understatement of the century.

When he and Aubrey reached her SUV, she reached for the driver-side door handle. Anticipating just such a move, he blocked her with his body.

"Sorry about leaving everything a mess yesterday," he said, leaning against the door. "When I get called, I have to report immediately."

"It's no problem." She dug impatiently through her purse for her car keys. "I moved what I could into the garage, if that's all right."

"I'll call Hannah. Have her stop by and pick it up."

"Don't bother. It's not hurting anything."

"Thanks. That'll save me making a second trip between the ranch and the house."

"How's the fire? I saw on the news it's only five percent contained."

A question. Good. Maybe she wasn't as skittish as she appeared. "We had a lucky break today with the weather, which is encouraging. But you can never predict for sure when it comes to fires, so I'm not packing my gear just yet."

"I admit I was a little surprised to learn you're a wilderness firefighter. When did that happen?"

"About four years ago. My friend Marty recruited me. I told you about him. He's with the Pineville radio station. We met when the old Hunt Museum and General Store burned down, and he came out to do a live broadcast."

"I took it for granted you ran the ranch with your dad." She gave a little shrug. "Since that was, well, that was always…"

"My plan. Yeah, well, it's still my dad's plan."

"He doesn't like you being a firefighter?" Her eyebrows knitted, then lifted. "I'd think he'd be proud."

Gage expelled a long breath. "It's not that he doesn't like me being a firefighter, just not now. Between his gout attacks and Hannah commuting back and forth during the week to the agricultural college in Pineville, running the ranch falls mostly to me."

"And firefighting has a tendency to cut into your chores."

"In a big way. It's a forty-hour-a-week job during the season. Double that when we're at a fire."

"What do you do when you're not fighting fire?"

"Clear roads of hazards, burn control fires, training. It's never-ending."

"You've taken on quite a load," she observed.

"More so now that we're participating in the drought study."

"Drought study?"

"For the federal government. All the ranches in the area have lost a lot of grazing land because of the drought. We didn't think we were going to make it for a while, and wouldn't have without the extra income from the study." He didn't tell Aubrey how very close the Raintrees had come to losing the ranch that had been in their family for five generations.

"I thought you liked ranching."

"I do." He caught her gaze and held it. "But I love firefighting, and I'm going to keep doing it despite my dad's objections."

"Good for you, Gage."

"Do me a favor, will you? The next time my dad and I have an argument, repeat those same words to me."

He grinned, attempting to lighten the mood and fend off the resentment perpetually gnawing at him. His father bent over backward to support his younger sister's ambitions, which were in keeping with the Raintree tradition of cattle ranching, but not his son's.

She smiled back. "Is he really that tough on you?"

"Tougher."

"What about hiring help?"

"We can't afford it."

"I hope you can find a compromise. Firefighting is special. Not that ranching isn't," she quickly amended. "But you make a real difference in the world." Genuine admiration tinged her voice, and his chest swelled.

"Like being a nurse?"

"Firefighting is nothing like being a nurse. You put your life on the line for others. That takes courage and daring."

"It's just a job."

"It's not just a job." She tilted her head and stared him square in the face. "I have to say, Gage, you really impress me. Not that I wasn't—"

She didn't have a chance to finish because he hauled her into his arms, lifted her onto her toes and brought her mouth to within a tiny fraction of his.

Her green eyes went wide. "If you're thinking of kissing me, think again."

"Oh, I'm going to kiss you, all right."

Deciding this was exactly the opportunity he'd unconsciously been hoping for, he swung her around and pinned her against the SUV door. She didn't run screaming, which was all the encouragement he needed. He then made good on his threat and kissed her soundly.

For the second time that day, he felt the searing sting of flames licking his body. Only these flames were the product of his own desire.

She didn't respond initially, and he could sense her struggle to remain unaffected. Gage would have none of it. He didn't merely seek entrance into her mouth with his tongue, he demanded it. And once inside, he made it his personal mission to affect Aubrey as much as possible. She held out for another few seconds, then conceded with a soft moan.

Mindless of the warm summer sun beating down on them and the occasional passing car or pedestrian, he kissed her over and over. Venturing from her mouth, he tasted a delicate earlobe and the sweet curve of her neck where it joined her shoulder. She shuddered and sighed, and he took her mouth again.

"Enough," she gasped when he finally allowed her to catch her breath.

Because he was fast approaching the point of no return, he eased back a step.

Aubrey pressed her palms to her flushed cheeks. "We can't do this. It's crazy."

"I want to see you. I think it's pretty obvious there's still a lot of attraction on both sides."

She worried her bottom lip and shook her head. "Not a good idea."

"I disagree." Gage's heart rate had finally slowed to something his overcharged system could tolerate. "Have dinner with me later this week. We'll talk."

Her dubious expression spoke volumes. "You're right about one thing. There is still a lot of attraction on both sides. But I've only been back in town a few days, and it's not like we've remained close through the years."

"Okay, w—"

She cut him off with a raised hand. "I'm not ready… not going to start dating you again. It would be a mistake. For a lot of reasons."

"Aubrey…"

"I'm out of here in six weeks when my leave of absence is over. And I don't think either of us wants another miserable parting. One was more than enough."

Gage was struck by the sudden pain clouding Aubrey's eyes. Pain because she'd hurt him and regretted it? Or had he hurt her? Truthfully, he'd never stopped to consider the possibility that his refusal to accompany her to Tucson might have been viewed by Aubrey as a form of rejection. Well, maybe he should consider it and consider it hard.

"I really have to go."

"Aubrey—"

She grabbed the door handle of her SUV and got in. This time, he didn't stop her.

"Goodbye, Gage. And good luck with the fire." She shut the door.

He stayed, watching her pull out of the parking lot and replaying the last five minutes in his head. Kissing her had been great. Unbelievable. He didn't regret it for one second. But it was clear he'd pressured Aubrey for more than she was prepared to give. And if he didn't want to scare her off, he'd have to take a less headstrong approach.

Fortunately, Gage counted patience as one of his strong suits, along with perseverance.

If he'd learned anything as a Hotshot, it was when to fight and when to back off.

And that backing off didn't signify quitting.

Chapter 4

Gage was dirty, hungry and more tired than he could remember being in a long time. He wanted a hot shower, food—any food would do—and fourteen hours of uninterrupted sleep. In that order.

Standing at the back door of the ranch house, he indulged himself in a good, long stretch. When he finished, he treated the family dog, Biscuit, to an ear-scratching and head-patting combo. The fire hadn't been the worst one Gage had fought by any means, but there had been a few hairy moments, thanks to Mother Nature and her unpredictable whims. In addition, they were shorthanded, forcing all the Hotshots to work double shifts. The one time he'd visited the community center and saw Aubrey was his only break in three full days. But what a break it had been.

Since then, he'd repeatedly relived those minutes they kissed, lingering in particular on the taste of her warm and giving mouth. Not to mention the exact moment she melted against him, abandoning all efforts to resist. He thought less about her sudden turnaround. It surprised him how she'd gone from searing hot one minute to icy cold the next, and he intended to focus the sum total of his mental energies on resolving whatever prompted it.

Tomorrow, when he actually had some mental energy in supply.

He guessed it to be somewhere between ten and ten-thirty in the morning, if his blurry vision could be trusted. Good. His father and sister would be out somewhere working the ranch and not in the house. He'd persuade his mother to fix him breakfast while he showered, assuming she was home and not at work, then sleep until supper. She'd cover for him, and he could avoid a confrontation with his father until he'd had a chance to refuel and reenergize.

Luck, unfortunately, wasn't on Gage's side.

He stepped into the bright, sunny kitchen of the Raintree home and nearly collided with his father, who had apparently been on his way out the door.

"Morning, Dad." Gage quickly recovered and blustered through a friendly greeting. "How's the ankle?" He sidestepped the older man, making straight for the refrigerator.

Having raised two children, one headstrong and the other a handful, Joseph Raintree long ago perfected a stare worthy of freezing a guilty twelve-year-old in his tracks. Gage wasn't a kid anymore, but the stare still had the ability to immobilize him. He came to a grinding halt.

"You've been gone since Tuesday," Joseph said in a low voice. His lips hardly moved, yet each word struck Gage like a tiny bullet.

There wasn't more than a half-inch difference in their heights or the widths of their shoulders. And before the gout had gotten so bad, his father regularly gave Gage a run for his money in arm-wrestling matches. Steel-gray hair and a pronounced limp were the only visible signs Joseph had aged in the last twenty years. Inside the man, Gage knew, was a different story. Chronic pain had taken a toll on his father, in more ways than one.

"No message. No phone call. Your poor mother was worried sick."

"Wait just a minute." Gage exhaled and steadied himself. "I called home the minute I hung up from dispatch and talked to Hannah."

"Who didn't tell us until that evening where you were."

And this was somehow Gage's fault? "Her lack of communication skills isn't my problem."

"You're part of this family, which makes it your problem."

"Dad, even if she never said a word, you knew where I was." Gage bent over the sink, ran the cold water and splashed a handful on his face. "All you had to do was listen to the local news or pick up the phone and talk to a neighbor," he said after toweling dry. "Maybe leave this damn ranch once in a while and go into town."

"You will not take that tone with me."

"Dad—"

"What you *will* do is get dressed and finish the chores that need doing around here. Between you being gone and my gout, we're behind. The herd hasn't been moved to the south range yet, and we're almost a week late in filing the latest grazing study report."

"Didn't Hannah do anything while I was gone?" Anger and resentment built inside Gage, fed in large part by his utter exhaustion. His younger sister, it seemed to him, got away with as little work as possible. He didn't understand it, given her intention of taking over management of the ranch one day from their father. "I'm not the only one in this family capable of filling out forms." He looked past his father into the family room. "Where is Hannah, anyway?"

"Registering for summer school."

Gage slumped against the refrigerator and scrubbed his bristled jaw. "Summer school. How could I forget?"

How could he?

Hannah majored in agricultural management at Pineville College. She made the two-hour round-trip drive three days a week, arriving home too late to get much work done on the ranch. If not for a scholarship, she wouldn't be attending college at all.

Gage didn't begrudge his sister an education. Since he had no plans to follow in their father's footsteps, he was all for Hannah doing it. And he himself had attended firefighting academy. But he did begrudge her their father's blatant favoritism. Hannah was separated from Gage by eight years and three miscarriages. As the long-awaited and much-wanted second child, she could do no wrong in the eyes of her doting parents.

"I thought we agreed Hannah was going to stay home this summer." Convinced his argument fell on deaf ears, Gage nonetheless persisted. "You know June and July are the busiest months of year for me."

"Can't be helped. She needs some class for next semester."

Gage pushed off the refrigerator. One class might be doable, if they all worked together.

"You'll have to pick up the slack," Joseph continued. "No more taking off for hours or days on end whenever the mood strikes you."

"I'm a Hotshot, Dad. Our job is to fight fires and save the very land your cattle graze on. What's left of it after four years of drought." A part of Gage's brain recognized the futility of his words, but the other part wouldn't shut up. "I also head the Blue Ridge Volunteer Fire Department. If this house were to go up in flames, I'd be the one driving the engine here. But I suppose even then you'd accuse me of taking off when the mood struck."

"You're twisting the situation around to suit your own purposes!"

"If I am twisting the situation around, I'm not the only one," Gage replied.

He broke eye contact first, ending their staring match,

and tugged his filthy T-shirt free from the waistband of his pants. "I'm tired, Dad. I've had at most ten hours sleep in the past three days. Let me shower and take a nap. I'll fill out the reports and fax them in before supper. If sending them in sooner is that critical, Hannah can do it when she gets back."

Gage was well aware his sharp tone made him sound more like a frustrated teenager than an adult, but he was too tired to care. Both men turned when the back door flew open, and Hannah burst into the kitchen, her long black hair caught up in a bouncy ponytail.

"Hey, big brother." The smile she showered on Gage lit up the room. If she ever put that smile to serious use, half the male population of Pineville College would be throwing themselves at her feet. "The prodigal son returns." Her glance traveled from Gage to their father, causing her smile to droop slightly. "Did I walk in on the middle of something? Oh, I get it," she said when no one answered. "None of my business."

"Actually, it is—"

Joseph didn't let Gage finish. He limped over to Hannah and bent down so she could plant a kiss on his cheek. "Did you get registered for your class?"

A stab of resentment penetrated Gage's empty and growling stomach.

"Two classes." Hannah extracted a paper from the back pocket of her jeans and waved it. "Remember?"

"Two?" Gage said, "I thought you were taking only one class."

"Agricultural accounting and animal industry 101.

I start next week, Monday through Thursday. Sorry, Gage." The dark eyes she turned on him were the mirror image of his own in shape, size and color. Hers, however, were dancing and not the least bit apologetic despite her words. "These are accelerated classes, three hours each. I won't be home until afternoon. Hope that's not too much of a problem. Dad said you wouldn't mind covering for me."

"Funny, he didn't tell me that."

Joseph Raintree countered Gage's sarcasm with some of his own. "You weren't here to tell."

Gage made an abrupt dive for the door. He felt like if he stayed in the house a minute longer, he'd suffocate. "I'll do my best, but no promises. If I get called to a fire, I'm out of here. And speaking of getting out of here…"

"Where to you think you're going?" Joseph called after him.

"Somewhere quieter."

Gage no sooner shut the back door than it flew open and Hannah appeared.

"Wait. A letter came for you yesterday from the Forest Service. You might want it."

Gage took the letter from her outstretched hand and glanced at the return address. Could it be? So many weeks had passed, he'd long since lost hope. Tearing open the envelope, he prepared himself for bad news.

His luck, however, had taken a turn for the better.

Pleasure spread through him as he read the first paragraph. "I made it." The lowness of his voice took him aback, considering he wanted to shout his good news.

"Made what?"

Hannah stood at his elbow, trying none too discreetly to read the letter over his shoulder. Biscuit also stood nearby, tongue lolling and tail wagging, though his interest clearly lay in another petting.

"The list of candidates being considered for promotion. To crew leader." Gage surrendered to the grin tugging at his mouth. "I report Monday morning for my initial interview."

"Congratulations, big brother! That's awesome." She grabbed his arm and gave it an enthusiastic shake. "You so deserve this promotion."

"It'll mean more hours for me if I get it."

Hannah's expression said she couldn't believe he was worried about such an insignificant thing. "We'll manage."

"Thanks." Without thinking, he reached up and yanked affectionately on her ponytail.

Suddenly, his hand went still. How often had he done this exact thing in the years they were growing up? Too many times to count.

His resentment for his younger sister instantly faded.

"The monthly grazing reports are late. Think you can fax them out this afternoon, Hannah?"

"No problem."

"Call me on my cell phone if you have any trouble with them." He replaced the letter in the envelope and stuffed it in the front pocket of his T-shirt.

"I can handle the reports."

Gage nodded. "You've got what it takes to run this

place, you know." And she did, if she ever quit fooling around and really applied herself.

His compliment brought a smile to her face. Gage was again struck by her prettiness.

"You sure you won't stay?" she asked. "Dad'll cool off in a couple of hours. He just likes to, you know, parade his authority."

"Parade his authority? That's a pretty big mouthful for an agricultural major."

"You'd be surprised at all the stuff I've learned in animal psych class that applies to people."

Gage chuckled. "See ya later, squirt. Tell Mom I'm sorry I missed her."

Ten minutes later he reached the end of the dirt road leading from the Raintree ranch to town. The pickup truck bumped as the tires hit pavement, tossing the various loose items that littered the front seat into the air. Gage headed east. He'd known his destination all along. It was the same place he always went to whenever he craved solitude.

Next to the community center sat a small block building that housed the volunteer fire department's sole engine. It wasn't the ragtag couch in the back room that drew Gage, but rather the small, run-down motor home parked behind the station.

The same motor home he and Aubrey had occupied during their brief marriage—only then it had been parked on the Raintree ranch.

Gage had continued to live in the motor home for several months after she left, foolishly hoping she might one day return. Even after he moved back into the ranch house and his old bedroom, he occasionally escaped to the motor home for some peace and quiet. A couple years ago, Joseph Raintree decided to dispose of the eyesore. Gage hooked the motor home to his pickup truck and hauled it to the fire station rather than the landfill, claiming it was for the guys to use.

So far, he was the only guy to use it.

The mattress in the motor home's sole bunk was lumpy and sagging, a condition fresh sheets and new pillows didn't improve. At the moment, however, it appealed to Gage more than the finest quality feather bed. And yet, when the driveway leading to the fire station appeared, he drove right past it and instead took the turnoff farther up the road, the one leading to Aubrey's grandmother's house.

He told himself he was just checking on the handicap renovations—to see what progress the others had made, if any, during his three-day absence.

It was a bald-faced lie, of course, and he darn well knew it.

At the sound of a vehicle door slamming, Aubrey placed the can of tuna fish she'd just opened on the kitchen counter and went into the living room. One of the volunteer firefighters must have stopped by to make another repair. Probably Kenny Junior. When he left the previous day, he promised to return and replace the front door threshold with a lower one.

His timing was actually good. Aubrey and her grandmother had recently finished a strenuous, yet productive, round of physical therapy. Bound and determined to walk on her own again, Grandma Rose had pushed herself hard. But rather than take a quick nap before lunch, as was her habit, she'd asked Aubrey to wheel her next door to Mrs. Payne's. The two friends were engaged in a heated race to finish the baby quilt before Mrs. Payne's grandchild made his grand entrance into the world.

Aubrey flung open the front door, ready to greet Kenny Junior, only it wasn't him. A different volunteer firefighter climbed the porch steps. This one younger, taller and…filthy from head to toe.

"Gage! What are you do—" She pushed open the screen door and stepped out. Her hand stopped just short of taking his arm. "Jeez, are you all right? You look awful."

"Thanks." He moved as if each step resulted in excruciating pain.

"What happened? Were you injured?"

"Only a little." The crooked smile he aimed her way lacked its usual luster. "And not in the line of duty."

"Is that a joke?" By way of invitation, she opened the screen door and he followed her inside.

"Yes, it is. And evidently a bad one. You can blame my warped sense of humor on my dad. He didn't exactly give me a hero's welcome when I got home this morning."

"Oh, Gage." Because he obviously wanted to make light of an upsetting situation, Aubrey changed the subject. "I heard on the news this morning the fire is nearly contained."

"Pretty much done, except for the cleanup."

Once they were in the kitchen, Gage half sat, half tumbled into the nearest chair. He did look awful. She started to tell him he should be home in bed, then caught herself. Home, apparently, wasn't an option.

But that didn't explain why he was here, in her grandmother's kitchen.

"You hungry?" she asked instead of one of the dozen questions running through her head.

"I'd eat if you're offering."

"I am. And how about a shower?"

In response, a spark flickered in his tired eyes.

Her comment hadn't been the least suggestive, yet he'd taken it that way. Or was it she who'd subconsciously implied something suggestive?

"You can shower in the hall bathroom while I fix lunch," she added, just in case he'd misunderstood her. "I think there's still some of Grandpa's old clothes around here. They won't fit well, but they're clean."

He nodded, his smile tired, but grateful.

Some minutes later, she returned from rummaging through an assortment of cardboard boxes stacked in the corner of the basement. The faded T-shirt would be too big around the waist and the men's cotton pajama bottoms too short in the leg for Gage, but it couldn't be helped.

She set the folded clothes on the floor outside the bathroom door. Her hand poised to knock, she instead waited, breathing slowly and listening to the sound of the running shower. Her heart beat a fraction faster. Gage stood on the other side of the door—stark naked and with hot water streaming down every inch of his body.

They'd showered together frequently during their marriage, the two of them squeezing into the motor home's tiny bathroom. She didn't recall lack of elbow room as being a problem. In fact, finding creative ways to utilize the cramped space had proven a thoroughly enjoyable experience.

Aubrey's vivid imagination went far afield before she roused herself and stifled it. Gage naked and showering wasn't something she needed to be thinking of, particularly after her little speech the other day about not being ready to date him again.

Besides, she doubted they could still fit in that tiny shower. She'd been skinnier then and so had Gage.

It might be interesting to try, the pesky voice inside her teased.

Yeah, interesting. And stupid.

Her leave of absence was up in five weeks, and she'd be returning to her job in Tucson, free, God willing, of whatever unreasonable fear had gotten a hold on her since Jesse and Maureen's deaths.

You hear me? she told the voice. *Stupid.*

The voice didn't answer.

Firming her resolve, Aubrey knocked briskly on the bathroom door and hollered, "The clothes are on the floor outside the door."

"Thanks," came a muffled reply, and then the water shut off.

Oh…my.

Since continuing to stand there would only invite images of Gage drying himself, or drying her, Aubrey retreated to the kitchen, stopping first at the pantry for another can of tuna fish.

She made two sandwiches, slicing them diagonally before arranging them on a plate. Guessing Gage's appetite hadn't decreased in the intervening years since they'd dined together, she spooned out a bowl of cottage cheese and topped it with some of Mrs. Payne's home-canned peaches. Aubrey was just pouring a glass of milk when Gage came into the kitchen and promptly fell on the meal.

Conversation came to a complete standstill as he consumed the food with the speed and voracity of a grizzly bear newly awakened from a winter-long hibernation.

"Slow down," she warned, sitting in the chair beside him. "You'll choke if you're not careful."

He mumbled something that might have been, "Good," or "More." She wasn't sure which.

"Would you like another sandwich?"

Mouth crammed with peaches, Gage tilted his head from side to side.

"A half a sandwich?"

He nodded vigorously.

She took the liberty of pouring him a second glass of milk before rising and then took her sweet time fixing the half sandwich, all the while studying him discreetly from the corner of her eye.

Her late grandfather's clothes were indeed a poor fit, yet Gage managed to look sexy as hell in them. It might have been his still-damp, uncombed hair falling forward over his brow, or the bare feet and impressively muscular length of calf extending out from beneath the hems of the too-short pajama legs.

Yes, maturity definitely agreed with Gage Raintree. As did firefighting. No small miracle some woman hadn't snapped him up. In a town the size of Blue Ridge, he was surely one of the most eligible bachelors, if not *the* most eligible.

Having at last satisfied the need to gorge himself, he slowed his rate of eating to something resembling that of a human being.

"Thanks. That hit the spot." He used the napkin she'd set out to wipe his mouth.

"When was the last time you ate?"

"Yesterday. Breakfast. Not counting the PowerBar I had for dinner last night."

"And before that?"

He arched one eyebrow. "Lunch the previous day. At the community center."

Ah. Where they'd kissed. Like Aubrey needed reminding.

Gage pushed his plate away, and she reached for his dirty dishes, thankful for the distraction.

"Leave them," he ordered in a low voice and placed his hand over hers.

"But—"

"The dishes can wait. Talk to me for a few minutes."

Aubrey watched, spellbound, as he folded her smaller hand into his larger one. "A-a-about what?"

His thumb traced small circles on the sensitive skin behind her knuckles and though she knew it was wrong as wrong could be, she let him continue.

"Why did you leave me?"

She tried to jerk her hand away, but he refused to relinquish it.

"Tell me," he said, holding her gaze as firmly as he held her hand.

Aubrey went still. "You know why. To return to school."

"Is that the only reason?"

"We were just kids, not ready for marriage. We couldn't even support ourselves without your parents' help."

"A lot of couples start out on a shoestring. They manage."

"Yes, if they're committed to each other they do."

"And you weren't committed to me?"

She chewed her bottom lip, debating on how to simplify a complicated answer. "High school was always easy for me. I aced every class, sometimes without cracking a book. But college was a whole different story. You know that. I finished the second semester of my freshman year two-tenths of a grade point away from being expelled. My father didn't understand and came uncorked. I headed to Blue Ridge the day after school let out. To escape, though I told myself I was just taking a break. And then, there was you."

"Just like every summer," Gage said, his expression hard to read.

"No, you're wrong." She swallowed before continuing. Twice. "That summer we made love for the first time, and you proposed."

"You didn't have to accept my proposal if you really wanted to go back to school."

Aubrey stared out the kitchen window, seeing not her grandmother's yard but a view of the Raintree ranch from the motor home's back door.

"I didn't think I wanted to go back. I was in love in you." And she had been, body and soul. Probably from the first day they'd met in Sunday school.

"I'm glad to hear you say that."

She turned to look at him. "Tell me your proposal wasn't spontaneous and that you thought everything through before making it."

"It was spontaneous," he admitted. "But I don't regret it."

"Neither do I."

"We had six great weeks of marriage."

"One great week of marriage and five weeks of fighting," she corrected him.

He grinned. "That's not they way I remember it."

"Are you kidding?" She shot him a disbelieving look. "We fought more in those five weeks than most couples do in five years."

"We also made love more than most couples."

Yeah. At least ten of those times in a shower the size of coat closet.

"A great sex life isn't enough to base a marriage on."

He chuckled. "At least you admit the sex was great."

She smiled along with him as resisting was an exercise in futility. "That wasn't all we did right. We had a lot of fun, too, when we weren't at each other's throats."

"Not enough for you to stay married to me." His remark sobered them both. "Did you call your father and tell him to come get you?" His fingers tightened on hers.

"God, no! Is that what you thought?"

"It crossed my mind."

"I swear, Gage. His visit was entirely unexpected."

"So you hadn't planned on switching your major to nursing and not tell me?"

"That was strictly my father's idea." She sat up straight and squared her shoulders, steeling herself for the hard part. "But it was good one, and I'm grateful to him for having it. If I hadn't returned to Tucson and college, I might never have become a nurse."

Aubrey's father had appeared one night out of the blue, midway through the summer. He'd banged on their motor home door, insisting he speak with her. Once inside, he'd presented her with a proposition that included her changing her major from premed to nursing—a still difficult study course but with less pressure and less competition. He'd pulled some strings at the university and gotten her admitted into the nursing program. The catch was she had to return the third week of August in time for the fall semester.

Gage's grip on Aubrey's fingers relaxed. "I never wanted to hold you back. That wasn't the reason I proposed."

"You could have come with me to Tucson."

"And lived off your parents' charity? I don't think so," he scoffed.

Alexander Stuart had generously offered to supplement the newlyweds' income, enabling them to live in an apartment off campus while Aubrey attended school full-time. Gage's pride hadn't allowed him to accept the offer. She understood now what she hadn't then. It was important to Gage he be able to support himself and his wife without assistance. Not an easy task for a twenty-year-old with no college and no job skills besides ranching.

"We basically lived off *your* parents when you think about it," she ventured.

His eyebrows drew together. "That wasn't the same. We both worked on the ranch and earned our keep."

"You're right," Aubrey relented. She saw no reason to rehash a ten-year-old argument.

She didn't think her father had intended to break up her and Gage's marriage, not consciously anyway, but his attempt to facilitate her return to school had done exactly that by driving a wedge between her and Gage that grew wider with each day. Had they been older and more experienced, they might have found a solution. As it was, tensions mounted in the days following her father's visit, escalating in a final blowout that ended with Aubrey packing her bags.

"I couldn't win for losing," Gage said, letting go of her hand. "Not after your dad dropped his bomb."

"How so?" Her fingers felt oddly vulnerable without his wrapped around them.

"What choice did we have but to divorce? If I insisted you stay in Blue Ridge, you would have come to resent me for forcing you to give up your dream of working in medicine. Don't tell me you wouldn't have," he interrupted when she started to speak. "And if I went with you to Tucson and let your father support us, I'd have lost my self-respect and been miserable. Probably made both our lives miserable. The only other choice was a three-year separation, and I don't think our marriage could have survived while you finished college." He blew out a breath. "Whichever way I turned, I was screwed."

"Oh, Gage, I'm sorry." She hadn't realized until now how cornered and helpless he must have felt, and it saddened her.

He shrugged. "So, I admitted I was wrong. Then came the divorce."

"I wish I'd known that at the time."

"Would it have made a difference?"

"To be honest, I'm not sure. Maybe we were doomed from the beginning."

"Have you ever wondered what would've happened to us if we stuck it out?" he asked.

She considered lying. There was still a considerable attraction between them and she'd be courting trouble by giving him false hope. In the end, she opted for the truth. She owed him that much.

"Sometimes, sure. More so in the beginning."

Closing his eyes, he ran a hand through his nearly dry hair and down the back of his head. He looked so tired.

"You're ready to keel over," she said. "What say we call it a day, and you get some sleep?" Speaking for herself, Aubrey could use a break from all the emotional unloading.

"All right."

"Nap on the couch if you like. Grandma's next door at Mrs. Payne's. I'll take lunch over to them and stay awhile, leave you alone to get some rest."

"Nah." He stood, bracing one hand on the table and using the other to hold the sagging waistband of the pajama bottoms. "Think I'll head over to the volunteer fire station."

"You can't possibly work in your condition," she insisted in her best bossy nurse voice.

"Believe me, I'm going to sleep," he said with a laugh. "The old mot—" He stopped laughing and closed his mouth before continuing. "There's a bunk at the station where I can crash."

"Okay. In that case, you're free to go."

"Yes, ma'am."

He gave her a mock salute, and Aubrey shoved him through the kitchen door, laughing at the sight he made in her grandfather's pajama bottoms.

On the front porch, she waved goodbye as he backed

his pickup out the driveway, her emotions bouncing from one end of the spectrum to the other.

She was glad they'd talked and cleared the air of a few lingering issues. But by doing so, she opened herself to him, and the walls between them, walls she'd erected for both her own and his protection, had begun to crumble. If he kept holding her hand, kept staring into her eyes like he did, those walls might topple down completely.

Then where would she be? And more importantly, what would she do about it?

Chapter 5

Aubrey lightly pressed the back of her hand to her grandmother's forehead. The older woman lay in bed, her papery cheeks flushed a deep shade of pink and her eyes unusually bright.

"You mean to tell me, with all those years of training and all that fancy equipment, you still take someone's temperature by touch?"

"Why mess with success?" Aubrey didn't require a digital ear thermometer to tell her Grandma Rose's temperature was well over a hundred degrees and climbing.

"I'm fine. A bit of allergies is all." She pushed aside the sheet covering her as if to rise. "Happens every summer."

Aubrey snatched the edge of sheet and deftly replaced it. "Stay put."

"Like I have a choice," Grandma Rose groused. She'd made excellent progress during the past week with her physical therapy, graduating to short bouts around the house with a walker. But she was still a far cry from getting out of bed or a chair unassisted.

The past week had also been noteworthy for another reason. Aubrey hadn't seen or heard from Gage once since the day she'd made him lunch. Not that she had any reason to see or hear from him, she reminded herself firmly, nor did she necessarily *want* to. She would, however, like to know if everything was all right with him at home and if he'd resolved his differences with his father—strictly from the standpoint of a concerned friend, of course.

As promised, Kenny Junior had shown up to replace the threshold and Gus to change the round doorknobs to lever ones. She'd casually queried them both about Gage, but they hadn't seen or heard from him, either.

"How sore is your throat?" she asked her grandmother, banning thoughts of Gage to the back of her mind where they rightfully belonged.

"What makes you think I have a sore throat?"

Aubrey sighed. "You haven't touched the breakfast I brought you and made a terrible face when I forced you to take a few sips of apple juice."

"Are you always so mean to your patients?"

"Only when they try to pull the wool over my eyes. Now, how sore is your throat? Scratchy or agonizing?" She gently prodded her grandmother's neck beneath her jaw.

"Leaning more toward the scratchy side." Her grandmother winced and jerked away.

"Uh-huh."

"You don't believe me?"

"I believe you," Aubrey lied. She cradled her grandmother's face in her hands and turned her head toward the window.

"What are you doing?"

"Open your mouth."

Her grandmother obliged, but made it clear she didn't like Aubrey peering down her red and swollen throat.

Aubrey went into the small bathroom and returned a minute later brandishing a bottle of extra-strength acetaminophen. She leaned down and kissed her grandmother's burning forehead.

"I'll be right back. I'm going to the kitchen to break these up into smaller pieces for you."

There was no doubt in her mind Grandma Rose needed to see a physician. When she obediently popped the tablet pieces in her mouth and accepted the glass of water, Aubrey realized her grandmother was sicker than she let on.

"I'm taking you into Pineville, Grandma."

"What for?"

"To see your doctor. If he's not available, we'll go the hospital emergency room."

"Nonsense."

Aubrey went to her grandmother's closet and slid open the door. "Would you like to change first or go in your nightgown?"

"All this fuss over a little fever."

"You have a *high* fever."

"How would you know? You never even took my temperature."

Aubrey rolled her eyes and returned to the bed with a floral dressing gown she'd found hanging on a peg just inside the door.

"In addition to a fever, your glands are swollen, and your throat looks like it's on fire. You're sick." She located her grandmother's slippers beneath the bed and pulled them out. "When people get sick, they visit the doctor."

"I hate going to the doctor." Grandma Rose stared into space, her chin set at a stubborn angle. "Ever since the accident, all I ever do is go to the doctor. I'm tired of it."

"I understand." Aubrey sat on the edge of the bed and took her grandmother's weathered hand in hers. "Getting old stinks. But it beats the hell out of the alternative." The blunt observation delivered with such candidness earned her a slight lowering of the chin from her difficult patient. "I love you, Grandma. And I don't want anything to happen to you. Certainly not anything I can prevent with a simple doctor visit."

The chin came down another inch.

"Now, quit being such a grump and let's get you dressed."

"All right," her grandmother said. "I'll go. But not to Pineville. Today's Thursday and the clinic is open."

"The clinic? I don't know…"

Blue Ridge lacked sufficient population to support a full-time physician and state-of-the-art medical facility. What the town did have was a two-to-three-day-a-week doctor and a one-room clinic built beside a ramshackle thrift store. The proceeds from the volunteer-staffed thrift store went to fund the clinic and the connecting helipad. In instances of serious illness or injury and when time was of the essence, patients were airlifted by helicopter to the hospital in Pineville.

Though she was well aware it had saved numerous lives, Aubrey didn't like thinking about the helicopter. Her grandfather had been airlifted out of Blue Ridge twice. And while reason told Aubrey neither the helicopter nor the clinic had anything whatsoever to do with her grandfather's death, she's still felt better taking her grandmother into Pineville.

"That Dr. Ferguson is a nice enough young man, I suppose. You haven't met him, he came here some years back after old Dr. Hunt retired," Grandma Rose babbled. "You remember Dr. Hunt, of course. He's the one who removed the fishhook from your scalp."

"How could I forget?" Aubrey slipped the dressing gown over her grandmother's head. "I still have the scar."

She'd been twelve and Gage thirteen. They'd hiked the two miles to Neglian Creek crossing alone, promising to return with enough trout for dinner. Gage took her hand in his the moment they'd left the main road and never let go. Midway through the afternoon, a misaimed cast on Aubrey's part resulted in disaster, made worse by their botched attempts to remove the hook. Gage, poor kid, had gone pale and shaky at the first drop of blood.

Aubrey had sympathized, given him a quick peck on the cheek and told him she'd be fine. He'd surprised them both when he took her by the shoulders and pressed his lips to hers. It had been their fist kiss. More followed each summer thereafter, increasing in frequency and intensity.

They'd discovered their secret spot earlier that same day. Tucked into the steep bank on one side of the creek and completely sheltered by the overhanging branches of a willow tree, it provided the perfect hideaway. For years afterward, they'd escaped there whenever opportunity presented itself.

It was the place they'd made love for the first time and, minutes later, where Gage had proposed.

"Dr. Ferguson is competent, mind you." Grandma Rose appeared oblivious to Aubrey's mental meanderings into the past. "But he's no Dr. Hunt. Still, I'd rather visit him than go all the way into Pineville."

Seeing as her grandmother's health was what mattered the most and not which doctor she visited, Aubrey relented with a weary, "Okay."

Perhaps the sorely outdated and grossly underequipped clinic had improved during the last decade. One could only hope.

Dr. Ferguson turned out to be staring fifty square in the face. But, Aubrey supposed, from her grandmother's considerably older vantage point, fifty made him a young man. And, as reported, he was competent, if a bit brusque. Aubrey could see why her grandmother didn't like him as well as his predecessor.

"You think she has strep throat?" Aubrey asked when he'd completed his exam and taken a throat culture.

"I think it's likely, given her symptoms and the fact I've treated three cases in town since last week. Here's enough penicillin to last ten days." He handed Aubrey a box containing the capsules. "Bring her back to see me next Tuesday when I return for a follow-up."

Aubrey didn't need to read a book on body language to know when she was being dismissed. "Is there any chance you can come back tomorrow? Just in case she gets worse."

"I'll be fine, Aubrey," Grandma Rose assured her.

"Aren't you a nurse?" Dr. Ferguson asked. "I thought I remember your grandmother telling me you were."

"Yes, but—"

"She couldn't have a more competent caregiver than you."

Her grandmother pulled at her arm. "Aubrey, honey, can we go home? I'm tired."

"Of course." She did look bedraggled. It was thoughtless of Aubrey to prolong the visit. "We appreciate your help, Dr. Ferguson."

"How long are you staying in Blue Ridge?"

"Another four weeks or so."

"I'm glad to finally meet you. No offense, but I hope this is the last time." He took firm hold of Grandma Rose's left arm and helped her stand. "We want your grandmother to make a speedy and full recovery without any complications."

"Thank you, Doctor," Grandma Rose said feebly, latching on to Aubrey's elbow.

The three of them shuffled outside to Aubrey's SUV. Being hoisted into the passenger seat robbed Grandma Rose of the last of her strength, and she dozed during the five-minute drive home. They arrived to find Gage's pickup truck parked in the side driveway. Like before, a circular saw had been set up on the lowered tailgate and building material was strewn across the lawn.

Aubrey attributed the flash of joy filling her to relief at having someone to help her with her grandmother and not that the someone was Gage. The argument might have held water if her heart didn't execute a full somersault at the sight of him emerging from the garage. He'd grabbed the hem of his T-shirt and was using it to wipe his face, exposing a wide expanse of flat, muscular stomach.

Spying them, he dropped his shirt and broke into a brisk walk, meeting Aubrey just as she stepped out of the SUV. "Need a hand?" he asked.

"Thank you!" Okay, some of the joy Aubrey felt really *was* relief. The trip to the clinic had exhausted her, too. "If you could help me get Grandma out of the car and stay with her while I bring the wheelchair, that'd be great."

"I have a better idea." Without waiting for her reply, Gage strode to the passenger side and opened the door. "How about it, Rose? You ready?"

"For what?" she asked, blinking as she came more fully awake.

"A ride."

Gage slipped one arm under her knees and the other behind her back. He lifted her out of the car and carried her up the front porch steps as if she were a small child.

"I can walk, young man," she said, but her protest lacked conviction.

Aubrey dashed ahead of them and opened the door.

"Where to?" Gage asked.

"Her bedroom, please. Down the hall, last door on the right." Aubrey followed behind and watched Gage gently set her grandmother down on the bed, touched at the pains he took not to cause the older woman any discomfort.

Aubrey came up beside him. "I don't know how I would have managed without you."

"No problem."

"How about some lunch in return for the favor?"

"I've eaten, thanks. But I'll take another glass of that lemonade, if you have any."

The drawl and the grin were a potent combination, and hard to resist.

"Coming right up. Just give me a few minutes to give Grandma her medicine and settle her in bed."

It took more than a few minutes to accomplish everything and longer still to leave a message with her grandmother's regular doctor and make a pitcher of fresh-squeezed lemonade. By the time Aubrey brought Gage a tall, icy glass, a good hour had passed.

"Is your grandma doing better?" he asked, taking the glass from her.

"She's resting, finally."

"Good." He'd made impressive headway with the ramp.

"Wow! I can't believe you did all this in an hour."

He raised the glass of lemonade to his lips and guzzled almost the entire contents in one swallow. What was it with him? Did the man not know how to eat or drink like a normal person?

"I didn't do it all in an hour." He stopped to wipe his damp forehead with the back of his arm, the gesture pure Gage and cover-model sexy. "I built the ramp at home in two large pieces. Figured it would be easier and faster constructing it that way."

She smiled at his ingenuity. "It looks good."

"Care to take it for a test-drive?"

Would she ever become immune to that grin of his? "Very funny."

"I'm serious. I need to test the ramp before I bolt the pieces together. Go get your grandmother's wheelchair and ride it down."

"She pretty much uses a walker now."

"The wheelchair will be a better test."

And there would be days her grandmother might still use the wheelchair. Like today, when she was sick.

"Okay. I'll be right back." She returned shortly, pushing the wheelchair ahead of her. "Are you sure you wouldn't rather be the first one to try the ramp?" she asked Gage. "You built it, after all."

"Nah. I have less experience with wheelchairs than you do. I might crash." He stood at the bottom of the ramp. "I'll be your spotter."

Aubrey hesitated only briefly, then sat in the wheelchair and rolled it to the edge of the porch.

"Watch that a wheel doesn't go over the side," he warned. "I haven't nailed on the guards or put up the handrails yet."

The first part of the descent went without a hitch, but maneuvering the L-turn required some skill. Aubrey would have to be sure and practice with her grandmother before she left for Tucson. Her level of concentration was so intense, she didn't realize she was at the bottom of the ramp until Gage's jean-clad legs came into view.

"Hey, I did it!" She laughed. "The ramp works."

The toe of his raised work boot made contact with the wheelchair's footrest, and she came to a sudden stop. Her laugh stuck in her throat when his hands came down on the armrests, trapping her where she sat. Instantly, her Gage-meter kicked on, and she didn't have to see him to know his face hovered two tiny inches above hers.

"Look at me, Aubrey."

His low voice somehow managed to awaken every nerve ending in her body and start them tingling. Luckily, the emergency fail-safe in her brain went on red alert.

"Maybe I should go inside and ch—"

"Look at me."

Talk about manufacturing trouble where none existed. If she looked up, he'd kiss her. She knew it sure as she knew migrating birds flew south for the winter. And kissing Gage would be foolish and stupid and… and…unbelievably fantastic if their last kiss was any indication.

"I can't," she whispered, maintaining her reason, but only by a slim margin.

"Yes, you can."

She kept her eyes glued to his work boot. *Don't do it. Don't look at him.*

But then she did, and reason went the way of migrating birds.

Chapter 6

Aubrey looked up at Gage, and just like that, the control he'd fought so hard to maintain snapped. Desire crashed through him with the delicacy of a piano being dropped from a third-story window. He sucked in a breath of much needed air hoping to counter the effects. It didn't work. Nothing would work if he continued staring at her.

She had the most expressive green eyes he'd ever seen. He swore he could read her mind just by observing their subtle changes in color. Back when the two of them were married, her eyes would darken from emerald to almost hazel as he moved over her naked body, then grow darker still when he entered her. It had been—and judging by his body's reaction, still was—the most incredible turn-on.

Today, hesitation and a hint of suspicion clouded the vivid depths of those irises. She wanted him, but she was as yet unwilling to surrender to that want. Maybe she never would.

He wished he weren't so adept at this mind-reading stuff. Given the opportunity, he'd have rather gone with his first instinct and kissed her socks off. Playing it cool didn't come naturally to Gage, but he'd made up his mind she'd be the one to make the next move. Given the way he felt at the moment, he might live to regret his decision.

"You forgot to apply the brake."

"I did?"

She angled her head in question or, dare he hope, invitation. The roaring in his ears and the pounding inside his chest made it impossible for Gage to decide which.

"Uh-huh. You should apply it when you reach the bottom of the ramp." He stared at her mouth and let his eyes linger there. "You don't want to lose control and have a runaway."

"Are we talking about the wheelchair, or…" She hesitated, parted her lips, "Something else?"

She had a great mouth, too. Soft, sweet and, when she was so inclined, wonderfully wicked. He remembered the sensation of her lips trailing down his neck, his stomach, his…

Whoa, buddy, he cautioned himself. *Better not go there.* If he weren't careful, the neighbors would have one humdinger of a free show.

The threat of public shame had little effect on his

raging hormones. "I was talking about the wheelchair. Did you have something else in mind?" He sure as hell did, and it involved her mouth, a place with considerably more privacy, and some *serious* loss of control.

"No." She didn't quite crack a smile but almost. Encouraged, Gage lowered his head. Seconds ticked by, then a full minute. Just when he was about to break his promise to himself and make the first move, she turned and put her lips to his ear. "Aren't you going to..."

Kiss you, his mind eagerly supplied the rest of her sentence while his muscles tensed in readiness.

"Get back to work?" Her low, throaty laugh filled his ear.

It wasn't the reaction he'd been counting on. "Yeah, right. Work."

Give credit where credit was due. The lady was good. She'd rejected him, but lessened the blow by giving him back some of the same teasing he'd given her. Gage stood and retreated a step, accepting defeat and freeing her from the confines of his arms.

"How's your family? Is your dad's gout still bothering him?" She set the brake and rose from the wheelchair, smoothly shifting the conversation from pillow talk to small talk, much to Gage's disappointment.

"Better these past couple weeks." He strolled over to his truck, which was parked a few feet away. Picking up the glass of lemonade he'd put down earlier, he swallowed the bits of melting ice cubes, then located a tape measure from the open toolbox.

"I have an article on gout and diet in the house, if

you think your father'd be interested." Aubrey had followed him to the truck. "It discusses how eating the right foods can reduce the frequency and severity of attacks. I'm sure your father's doctor has already counseled him about diet, but the article details an innovative approach."

"Mom might be interested. I think she'd try anything just about now. Dad hasn't exactly been a barrel of laughs since the attacks started." Gage measured off one of the ramp guards.

"Gout is very painful."

"On everybody." He was well aware he'd let some of his resentment toward his father creep into his voice. Forcing his mouth into the shape of a smile, he said, "I'll take the article for Mom, if you don't mind. I can drop if off on my way home. She's working today."

"Your mother has a job?" Aubrey hoisted herself onto the tailgate next to the toolbox. Kicking off her sandals, she let them drop to the ground.

"Part-time. At Mountain View Realty." Gage pushed a button on the tape measure. As the mechanism sucked up the tape with a noisy whirr, he studied Aubrey. She'd sat in that exact same spot, watching him work, chatting about nothing in particular, and passing him the occasional tool more often than he could count. Old habits, he told himself. No big deal.

Yet, it felt like a big deal. She could have, *should* have, gone inside, particularly since she was determined to keep matters on a strictly casual basis between them. But she hadn't. Instead, she'd hopped onto the tailgate

of his truck and dangled those gorgeous legs in front
of him.

He searched in vain for the level he'd been using earlier, his mind unable to focus on much else besides…
bare skin. Lots of it.

"What does she do?" Aubrey asked.

"Who?"

"Your mom. Did she get her real estate license?"

Right. They were talking about his mom's job. *Focus,*
he told himself.

"No, more like secretarial stuff. Answers the phones,
does the filing, runs errands. She works with Eleanor,
your old friend Beth's sister."

Aubrey nodded. "Does she like it?"

"She likes it a lot, and I think it's been good for her
to get away from the ranch."

Very good.

Gage saw the dulling effects decades of hard physical labor had on his mother's once cheerful personality.
Working outside the home restored a small measure of it.

"And your dad? He's okay with your mom working?
If I remember, he was sort of…old-fashioned."

"No." A derisive chuckle escaped before Gage could
stop it. "He hates it."

But he sure didn't hate the extra income, thought
Gage. There had been a few weeks during the worst of
the drought season when Susan Raintree's paycheck had
been the only thing putting food on the table.

"After our ranch was chosen to participate in the
grazing study, Dad tried his best to get Mom to quit."

This time, Gage's chuckle rumbled with genuine mirth. "She refused."

"You and your dad getting along better?" Aubrey dug around in the toolbox beside her and came up with the level, which she passed to Gage.

How had she known what he was looking for? Old habits, again, no other explanation for it.

"We're not fighting. As long as I don't get called to a fire, we manage to stand each other's company."

They didn't talk for several minutes while Gage went over to the ramp and measured for the handrails. Pulling a carpenter's pencil from his back pocket, he jotted the different lengths he'd need on a scrap piece of wood.

"What's Hannah up to these days?" Aubrey asked when he returned.

"Taking summer classes at Pineville College. She's getting her degree in agricultural management."

"Good for her! She's always loved ranching."

"Yep. And she'll be able to use that degree when she takes over for the old man."

"Hannah's going to manage the ranch?"

"So she says."

Aubrey broke into a sunny smile. "And with her taking over, that leaves you free to be a firefighter."

"*Will* leave me free. She has another year and a half to go before she graduates, possibly longer." Depending in part on the family's finances, Gage added silently. He picked through the stack of two-by-twos on the ground beside the truck.

"The Raintrees are actually going against tradition."

Aubrey shook her head in disbelief. "Who'd have believed it?"

"Well, not all traditions. Dad still has trouble with Mom working."

"But not your sister?"

"Apparently, a woman taking over the family business is okay, but holding a job outside the ranch is not okay. Yeah," he continued before she could comment, "the rest of us have a little trouble with the distinction, too." He laid the two-by-twos on the ground, one next to the other, sorted by size.

"When do you sleep?" Aubrey's green eyes narrowed on him, more thoughtful than critical

"At night, usually. Like most people."

"Seriously, Gage. The ranch doesn't run itself. Someone has to cover for your mom working part-time, your sister going to college and when your dad has a gout attack. Process of elimination leaves you."

"It's not as bad as you think."

"What about your firefighting?"

"What about my firefighting?" Her line of questioning reminded him too much of the arguments he had with his father. On the plus side, it took his mind off her legs.

"Does anyone do the chores while you're gone or do they accumulate?"

"The chores get done, sooner or later." Some days, a lot later.

If they had an extra couple hundred dollars to spare, he'd hire Kenny Junior for a week. But there never seemed to be an extra ten dollars lying around, much less two hundred. Hannah's summer school costs had depleted the family expense fund. Gage's hazard pay was being used to build it back up in preparation of the fall roundup when they'd have no choice but to hire help.

"You forget," Aubrey said. "I lived on your ranch for six weeks, I know the work is never ending. No one person can do it all in without sacrificing something. I figure it's sleep. Tell me I'm wrong."

"I get enough sleep." And he did, if one considered four to six hours a night enough sleep. Maybe he should risk his father's wrath and push Hannah to help more. She didn't offer unless asked, using school as an excuse to avoid pitching in.

"If you don't take care of yourself, you'll wind up sick, or dead from exhaustion."

"Okay, Nurse Stuart. I promise to get more sleep if it'll make you happy."

"Joke if you want," Aubrey snapped.

He heaved a long sigh.

"I'm sorry." She was immediately contrite. "It's not my place to tell you what to do."

"Forget it. I'm used to bossy women. I was married to one once."

She picked up a screw and threw it at him.

"Hey!" He ducked, and the screw glanced off his shoulder.

"I admit I'm bossy. But only because I care about you."

He was tempted to ask how much she cared, but held his tongue. "Thank you."

"Which reminds me." She planted her fists on her hips in a classic pose. "What the heck are you doing here anyway?"

"Building a handicap ramp?"

She scowled at him. "You're busy. Can't one of the other volunteer firefighters build it?"

"I want to help your grandmother. You're not the only one in town who cares about her."

"I know, but—"

"Dad's having a good day. He's handling the chores while I'm away. And if you quit your nagging, I'll be finished in another hour. Then I can go home and get some of that sleep you insist on."

He reached out and cupped her chin in his palm, his fingers stroking her cheek. The gesture was automatic, something he'd done often when they were younger to shut Aubrey up and not hurt her feelings.

Old habits again, and apparently impossible to break.

Their gazes connected, and something akin to the sweet rush of emotion that once lit up their lives passed between them.

The moment lasted only until the phone rang from inside the house.

"That's probably Grandma's doctor. I called him earlier." Aubrey hopped off the tailgate and slipped on her sandals. "I'll be right back." She dashed toward the house.

"I'll be waiting."

Gage watched her until the screen door slammed shut behind her before returning to work, already missing her company and counting the minutes until she returned.

She didn't, however, come right back. An hour dragged by, during which Gage did all he could on the ramp and then some. Eventually, he ran out of excuses to stay. From the periodic snatches of muted conversation drifting through the screen door, he knew she was still on the phone.

Who could she be talking to for so damn long? Not her grandmother's doctor, that was for sure.

A boyfriend maybe? Gage's gut turned to stone. He'd assumed because she hadn't remarried, she was unattached. But what if her reluctance to get involved with him again was because she had some bozo in Tucson on the string?

Venting his frustration on his tools, Gage chucked them into the back of his truck, missing the toolbox more times than not. The debris followed the way of the tools. Within a few minutes, his truck bed resembled a war zone. The ruckus had the neighbor, Mrs. Payne, popping out onto her porch for a look-see, but not Aubrey. She stayed inside.

He was just climbing into the truck when he decided to say goodbye before leaving. Opening the screen door, he hollered, "Hey, in there, I'm leaving. See you later."

Aubrey materialized in the doorway leading to the kitchen, a portable phone stuck to her ear and a grim expression on her face. "Oh, okay. See ya later. And thanks."

Gage tromped back to his truck, his mood decidedly sour. He took some pleasure in the knowledge that if Aubrey were indeed talking to a boyfriend, the conversation wasn't going well.

Aubrey closed the medicine cabinet in her grandmother's bathroom, shut off the light and padded through the bedroom toward the door.

"Good night, dear." Her grandmother's tired voice traveled to Aubrey from across the darkened room.

She paused, a hand resting on the doorjamb. "I thought you'd be asleep already."

"Not quite."

Her grandmother had rallied after her long afternoon nap, and the two of them ate a light dinner together in front of the TV. Neither were hungry, her grandmother because of her strep throat and Aubrey because of her terse phone conversation with her father.

Shortly after dinner and not long into *Wheel of Fortune,* a flushed and feverish Grandma Rose retired to bed. Aubrey hoped the antibiotics would kick in soon.

"I assume the call with your father didn't go so great." The bedsheets rustled as Grandma Rose changed positions.

"How'd you guess?"

"I woke up a couple times and heard bits and pieces of your conversation."

"Was I loud?" Aubrey retraced her steps back into the room.

"No, dear. You weren't loud." Grandma Rose patted the edge of the mattress, and Aubrey obediently sat down. "But you looked a little downtrodden during dinner. Care to tell me what's wrong?"

"Nothing's wrong." Nothing *new,* at least. Not keen on discussing her father, Aubrey attempted to divert the conversation. "Annie was there, visiting the folks. She and some friends just got back from a trip to L.A. Guess they tried out for some reality television show."

During the fifteen minutes she'd spoken with her younger sister, Aubrey learned more than she cared to about the audition process. In many ways, she envied Annie and her free-spirited, take-life-as-it-comes attitude. Being the serious, overachieving firstborn had its drawbacks.

"Sounds just like Annie," Grandma Rose said with amusement. "Did she and her friends make it onto the show?"

"They won't find out for a few weeks. Mom sends her love and says to drink lots of fluids." After Annie, Aubrey had talked with her mother. "She was upset to hear you have strep throat, but glad to know you're making such excellent progress with your physical therapy. I promised I'd call her tomorrow with an update on how you're doing. I would have brought you the portable phone if I'd known you were awake."

"That's all right. I'll talk to her tomorrow. How's your father doing?"

Grandma Rose might have been physically weak, but she was mentally sharp as a tack. There was no way Aubrey was going to get out of talking about her father.

Everyone said she and him were too much alike. They frequently knocked heads, although even in the midst of their most heated confrontations, Aubrey understood her father loved her and only wanted what was best for her.

"He's fine and concerned about your recovery."

"He didn't want you to come here. He wanted you to stay in Tucson."

"No, Grandma," Aubrey instantly protested. "That's not true."

"Yes, it is. I haven't been his mother-in-law all these years for nothing. I can read him almost as well as your mother. Where you and your sister are concerned, anyway."

Aubrey expelled a long sigh. She would have rather lied but found it impossible. "You're right. He did want me to stay in Tucson. Not for the reasons you think," she hurriedly added. "He loves you and would have hired the best possible nursing care for you."

"You're the best possible nursing care I could ever want or need." Grandma Rose linked fingers with Aubrey, much like she had when Aubrey was little. "So, tell me, why didn't he want you to come?"

"It has to do with Uncle Jesse and Aunt Maureen's deaths."

She sensed more than saw her grandmother's sorrowful expression.

"They were such lovely people. Good friends of your parents."

"You know I was on duty the night of the accident when they were brought in?"

"Your mother told me. She said you took it pretty hard."

"Yeah, I did. Mom and Dad were in Chicago at a seminar. I hated giving them the news on the phone, but I didn't want them hearing it from a stranger."

It felt good to finally talk with someone about that night. As an E.R. nurse, Aubrey had become accustomed to setting her emotions aside. It was, she'd found, the only way to survive a job where heartache and tragedy were a daily occurrence.

"I was shocked when I recognized Jesse and Maureen beneath all the blood, and, well, I panicked briefly." In truth, she fell into a stupor. "It took me a couple seconds to compose myself." She'd stood like a stone statue until another nurse grabbed her by the arm and shook her.

"It's amazing you were able to function at all. That speaks very highly of your skill and dedication."

"Maybe."

"How can you think otherwise?"

"Because since that night, I've suffered three more… moments of indecisiveness." Aubrey looked down at her lap.

"Oh, you poor thing."

"Grandma, I'm afraid." Tears pricked Aubrey's eyes. "If I can't overcome this problem, I might have to quit the E.R. and change my specialty to something where I'm not required to treat accident victims."

A very long, very silent pause followed. Aubrey's laugh verged on desperate.

"Say something, will you?"

"What does your mother think of your situation?"

"I haven't told her."

"Can I ask why?"

"Dad feels the fewer people who know, the better."
It had occurred to Aubrey her father might be ashamed
of what he perceived as a failure.

"Well, he may be right," Grandma Rose said reas-
suringly.

"He wanted me to stay in Tucson. Face my problem
head-on." Not run away like she had in college. "And I
can see where he's coming from, even if I don't agree."

"I have no doubt after a short break from the E.R.,
you'll return to work and this difficulty you're having
will become a thing of the past."

"And if not?"

"You go into another specialty," Grandma Rose said
simply.

But it wasn't so simple for Aubrey. "I don't want to
go into another specialty."

She could cite any number of reasons: the training
she'd had, the certifications she'd earned. The plain
truth was she thrived on the fast-paced environment of
the E.R. Her aspirations were to one day manage the
emergency department of a large metropolitan hospital. Oh, sure, she could find a modicum of enjoyment
in other fields of nursing, but would she find the same
satisfaction?

The desolation filling Aubrey abated, and some of the
determination her grandmother had been talking about
rushed in to take its place. "Maybe Dad was right and

coming here was a mistake. I should be at work. Not hiding out in Blue Ridge."

"You're going back to Tucson?"

Aubrey heard her grandmother's panic and quickly reassured her. "I promised you I'd stay for six weeks. But afterward, yes. I have to go back. You understand, don't you?"

"I do." Grandma Rose lowered herself onto her pillow. "Will Gage?"

The question, from out of left field, gave Aubrey a start. "I'm sure he will."

"And if he doesn't?"

"It really makes no difference."

"He's still in love with you, Aubrey."

Okay. She hadn't seen that coming, either. "We're friends is all." Did friends usually flirt and kiss?

"And *you're* still in love with him."

"I am not!"

"Hmmm," was Grandma Rose's only comment.

Aubrey collected her thoughts and tried to put them in a semblance of order. "We were married once and, yes, in love for a long time before that. There are bound to be lingering feelings."

A lot of lingering feelings. If her grandmother, a sick, elderly woman, had noticed, it was worse than Aubrey realized. She really had to keep Gage at a distance, not encourage him as she'd done today.

"After you, work is my number-one priority," Aubrey said with conviction. "Whatever it takes, I'm going to overcome this freezing problem."

"You will. What you went through, seeing someone you love die in front of your eyes…" Grandma Rose's voice thinned and trailed off. "Takes a body a while to get over it."

Her grandmother would know, having been at her grandfather's side when he'd passed away in the hospital.

She found and squeezed Aubrey's hand again. "I'm so proud of you, sweetheart. Always have been. You'll survive this ordeal and be a better nurse for it in the long run."

Tears pricked Aubrey's eyes anew; tears of sentimentality rather than sadness. She was glad she'd come to Blue Ridge, especially glad she'd had this talk with her grandmother. It made all the recent disagreements with her father fade into nothingness.

"You're tired." She stood and rearranged the mussed bedsheets. "It was wrong of me to keep you up."

"I'm glad you did."

"So am I." Aubrey kissed her grandmother's cheek. "But you need your rest. It's the only way you'll get better."

"Good night, sweetheart. See you in the morning."

Aubrey closed the door on her way out and shuffled across the hall to her room. It had been a trying day from beginning to end, her emotions all over the place. Tomorrow, when her mind was clear and her body refreshed, she'd address the problem with Gage. If she didn't take immediate steps to tone down their highly charged attraction, her leaving in another four weeks would wind up a carbon copy of the last time, complete with hurt and anger.

Unfortunately, thoughts of Gage refused to be put off until tomorrow. After tossing and turning for a good half hour and mashing her pillow into an unidentifiable lump, Aubrey got up and prowled the quiet house, stopping first to peek in on her grandmother.

The hall clock told her it was past ten. A cool breeze wafting in through the screen door convinced her a breath of fresh air might be just the ticket to calm her jangled nerves. Aubrey switched on the porch light. Outside, the breeze followed through with every tantalizing promise it had made, sifting through her hair and caressing the parts of her not covered by the gym shorts and tank top she'd worn to bed.

She went to the far end of the porch and leaned against the column. Eventually, she relaxed, lulled by chirping crickets and a pair of hooting owls. Both nature's symphony and her respite came to an abrupt halt when a pair of headlights swung into her grandmother's driveway, accompanied by the sound of spitting gravel.

"Who in the world…"

Pushing off the column, she walked tentatively toward the porch steps. She wasn't worried. Being Blue Ridge and not Tucson, her late night visitor was, in all likelihood, no stranger.

The vehicle, a large, looming shadow in the moonless night, came to a stop behind Aubrey's SUV. The headlights flicked off and the driver's side door opened.

A lone figure emerged—tall, broad-shouldered and undeniably male.

Aubrey's heart recognized Gage long before her brain did and beat wildly in anticipation.

So much for toning down their highly charged attraction.

Chapter 7

Gage stared his fill. He wasn't the kind of person to hurry a good thing, and Aubrey in shorts and a tank top was one incredibly good thing.

"I lost my cell phone earlier," he stammered. "I think it might have fallen off my belt while I was working."

He stood at the bottom of the porch steps, Aubrey at the top. Their positions put him on direct eye level with her breasts. With her back to the light, he couldn't see much. Imagination and memory filled in the blanks.

"Oh." She hugged her waist. "I can't help you much, I haven't been outside until just now."

"Do you mind if I have a look around?" Given the fact he hadn't been able to tear his gaze away from her, his remark could have been construed differently.

"Go right ahead. Do you need a flashlight?"

"I brought one." He produced a miniflashlight from the back pocket of his jeans.

Neither of them moved. "Gage," she began, then faltered. Lifting her arm, she brushed back the hair from her face. One breast raised and strained against the fabric of her pajama top.

"Uh-huh?" His attention remained fixed on her. She was more sexy, more beautiful in that moment than he ever remembered.

"About today..." She rubbed the back of her neck.

Gage watched, his mouth dry as an old bone baking in the hot sun. She let her arm fall, and he narrowly avoided groaning with frustration.

"I'm leaving in another four weeks and returning to Tucson."

"Okay." He knew that and wasn't sure he liked it.

"It's uh..." She shifted her weight to her other foot and blew out a breath. "It's probably a good idea for us to keep a little distance between us. Just to avoid any problems when the time comes for me to leave."

Gage moved forward until he was toe to toe with the bottom porch step. "You think we'll have problems when you leave?"

"Possibly... Yes," she said with more confidence.

He returned the flashlight to his jeans pocket and climbed the bottom step. His new position put him on eye level with her mouth. Not a bad place to be, either. "Why?"

"Because..." She swallowed nervously, her strength

apparently deserting her. "We have a lot of history to-gether and shared memories."

Gage sensed a brush-off coming and refused to go down without a fight. "A lot of *intimate* history."

"Well, yes."

From his raised vantage point, he had a great view of her cleavage. "And you don't want to start anything we can't finish, right?"

"Exactly."

"No."

"What?"

"I said no." He leaned closer, inhaled the freshly showered scent of her. "I, for one, want to start some-thing with you, and I'm pretty sure you want to start something with me, too. But you're scared and under-standably so."

"You're wrong." Her protest sounded weak, thank God.

"About you wanting to start something, too, or you being scared?"

"Gage, please."

"Tell me something, Aubrey. When I had you trapped in the wheelchair this afternoon, did you want to kiss me? Not *would* have, but *want* to?"

"I…uh."

Gage eased forward and angled his head upward as if to meet her lips. He stopped a few inches short. "Yes?"

If he turned his head marginally to the left, his mouth would graze the underside of her jaw. He resisted. For their relationship to develop into something more, Aubrey had to stop being a participant and start being the initiator.

"The truth, Aubrey. No more games." He closed the distance between their mouths by several more millimeters. "Do you want to kiss me?"

Her breath hitched. "You don't fight fair."

"Not where you're concerned."

"Fine," she said with what sounded like forced resignation. "I want to kiss you. Will you leave now that I've confessed?"

"No way."

"How come?" Her brow furrowed in surprise and then indignation. "Because I won't kiss you?"

"Because I haven't found my phone." He chuckled and moved closer still. "And because you haven't kissed me."

"If that's what it takes to get you to leave..." She dipped her head, bypassed his mouth and brushed his cheek with her lips.

Gage went completely motionless, waiting.

She didn't pull away. Good, but not enough. Difficult as it was, he kept his arms locked at his side, silently pleading for her to end his torture, either by going inside or giving them what they both wanted. Seconds stretched into an eternity.

At last, she cradled his cheeks in her hands. "Happy?" she crooned and pressed her mouth to his smile.

"Ecstatic." His tongue traced the outline of her bottom lip as his arms circled her waist.

"This changes nothing. We're not getting involved."

She tilted her head back as he tasted the silky column of her neck and the hollows above her collarbones.

"Quit your jabbering and give me a real kiss."

She obliged him by fully fusing her mouth with his.

Since she'd technically instigated the kiss, he let her control it. He had no complaints about the arrangement and, evidently, neither did she. They started out slow, familiarizing themselves with each other through tender and tentative explorations—something they'd missed out on during their frantic kiss at the community center.

Their leisurely pace didn't last, however. Aubrey slid her hands from his face to his shoulders, pulling him to her. Gage took her invitation a step further. Without separating their mouths, he lifted her off her feet, walked up the remaining two porch steps and stumbled blindly in the general direction of the lawn chairs.

They almost made it.

A shrill chirping sounded from a distance. "Dammit," he grumbled and set Aubrey down, though he didn't release her.

"What's that?" she asked dazedly.

"My cell phone."

"Your cell phone?"

"I told Hannah to call the number in thirty minutes. I figured I could follow the ringing to the phone."

Aubrey disengaged herself from his arms and straightened her pajamas. "You'd better go find it while it's still ringing."

"Yeah." He could see the change coming over her. Already, she regretted kissing him, possibly questioned

her momentary loss of sanity. The chances of them picking up where they left off once he found his phone were
slim to none. "I'll be right back," he said and beat a path
to the front yard.

Flashlight in hand, he followed the sound of the
chirping, which quit as he was closing it on it. Gage
was considering asking Aubrey to go inside and call
the number for him when he found the phone near the
ramp. He picked it up and hooked it to his belt. Only
then did he look for Aubrey.

She stood near the screen door, one hand on the knob.
He walked to the porch, ready to put up a fight. She
wasn't going inside without first talking to him. At the
top step, he paused.

"Aubrey—"

She silenced him with a raised hand. The other one
clutched the doorknob like a lifeline.

"I'm not ready for this, Gage. As tempted as I am to
be with you, I can't. I'm leaving soon, and it wouldn't
be fair to either of us."

At least she admitted to being tempted.

"You could always stay."

She shook her head. "I have my job to consider."

He understood. In a town the size of Blue Ridge,
employment opportunities on a whole were limited and
virtually nonexistent for nurses. He could hardly ask her
to give up her career for him. Not when he resented his
father for making just such a demand. And even if Aubrey were willing, she'd come to resent him, too.

"More importantly," she said, "there's a...situation I've been ignoring that needs resolving."

He had no right to ask, but nonetheless, did. "A boyfriend situation?"

"No." She shook her head, her green eyes a little lost. "Work and family."

"I'm sorry." Gage's apology was sincere. He well knew the obstacles of balancing work and family. "Anything I can help with?"

"This is something I have to deal with on my own."

"Sounds serious."

"It is." Eyes closed, she massaged her forehead. "I'm having a bit of a career crisis, I guess you could say. And my dad and I don't exactly agree on how I should handle it."

Gage knew Alexander Stuart regularly attempted to impose his will on his daughters, Aubrey in particular. Funny, where their parents were concerned, she and Gage really were very much alike.

"If you ever want to talk, I'm a good listener."

"Thanks. Maybe another time. It's getting late and I have an early morning." Opening the door, Aubrey stepped inside. "Good night, Gage." Her face was a dark shadow behind the screen. "Thanks for building the ramp. You're a good friend of the family."

He started to say he could be a whole lot more than a good friend if she'd let him but kept his mouth shut. Pressuring her for more before she was ready would only reverse the tentative inroads he'd made. And besides, he was coming away with considerably more than just his cell phone.

At least he now understood a little better what was bothering Aubrey and how it was contributing to her case of cold feet where their relationship was concerned. He just didn't know what to do about it.

Yet.

"See ya later."

Gage bounded down the porch steps, digging his keys from his pocket when he hit bottom.

No doubt about it, Aubrey still cared for him. If she didn't, the thought of getting involved wouldn't scare her like it did. And most importantly, she didn't have a boyfriend. At least one who mattered.

For the first time since her return, Gage felt like he had a fighting chance with Aubrey.

"More mashed potatoes, honey?"

"Thanks, Mom." Gage accepted the serving bowl from his mother's outstretched hands and ladled a second helping onto his dinner plate.

He wasn't particularly hungry but didn't want to hurt his mother's feelings. She'd spent half the afternoon in the kitchen laboring over their meal. Neither was he particularly talkative. None of the Raintrees were, which was a little unusual. Then again, they were all pretty tired.

Hannah, a notorious chatterbox, had stayed up late the previous night doing homework then gotten up at the crack of dawn to leave for class. For his part, Gage had ridden out bright and early to check the water level of the stock tanks and round up any strays. His father, enjoying a second straight week free from gout, had come along. Too proud to admit he'd overextended himself, he was paying the price in the form of sore muscles and aching joints. Gage's mother, evidently weary of trying to jump-start family mealtime conversation, settled for seeing that everyone got enough to eat.

Gage's excuse wasn't as much fatigue as his inability to keep Aubrey and the searing kiss they'd shared last night off his mind. He still didn't know if he should be mad at his sister for interrupting them, or thank her for doing so. Chances were good if she hadn't called his cell phone when she did, Gage and Aubrey would have yielded to their impulses and given new meaning to the word *reacquaint*.

He need only close his eyes to recall the feel of her as she came into his arms, warm and lush and, for a few heart-jarring moments, willing. If Gage didn't know better, he'd think he was seventeen all over again.

"Peach pie anyone?" his mom asked, getting up from her chair and reaching for her husband's empty plate. "It's homemade."

"You sit, Mom," Hannah said. "Gage and I will get the dishes and serve dessert. Won't we, big brother?"

"Absolutely." Anything to stop thinking of Aubrey. Gage snatched the platter of leftover roasted chicken from the center of the table.

Outside, Biscuit barked, announcing the arrival of a vehicle in the Raintree driveway.

"Who could that be?" his dad demanded and hobbled toward the door.

"Bring some extra pie," his mom called to Hannah in the kitchen. "We have company."

Gage's cousin, Chase, entered the great room behind Joseph, cradling his seven-year-old daughter, Mandy, in his arms. One of her feet was bare, and she was whimpering.

"Sorry to barge in on your dinner," Chase said, visibly distressed. He turned in a half circle as if he didn't know quite what to do with his daughter.

"What's wrong?" Gage asked and went toward them.

Chase wasn't one to fluster easily, or hadn't been until he'd become a single dad six months earlier when his wife—make that his ex-wife—walked out. The change in family structure had turned him into a chronic worrier where Mandy was concerned.

"She was playing out behind the shop and cut her foot on a piece of sharp metal. It's deep, but I don't think she needs stitches. I was hoping you could have a look and give me your opinion."

"Sure." Gage led the way to the kitchen.

"She's had such a rough go of it lately," Chase said as they walked, "I hate to put her through any unnecessary trauma."

In the kitchen, Gage patted the end of a long counter inlaid with colorful ceramic tile. "Sit her down here why don't you."

"Hi, Mandy, honey." Hannah, who was serving up the last of the pie, greeted them. "What happened?"

The little girl clutched a tattered stuffed toy to her side and sniffled. "I hurt my foot."

"Aw, that's too bad. Well, Uncle Gage will fix you right up."

"I don't want no stitches."

"Who does?" Hannah licked a dribble of pie filling from her finger.

Gage pulled a chair from the breakfast set over to the counter and sat down in front of Mandy. He tickled the back of her ankle and when she automatically lifted her leg, he deftly captured her foot in his hand.

Mandy giggled. "Quit it, Uncle Gage."

"What have we here?" He removed the bandage Chase had put on the cut and tsk'd as if her injury was something awful to behold. "I say surgery's in order. What about you, Dad?" He looked to Chase for confirmation.

She squealed and tried to jerk her foot away. "No!"

"I'm kidding, pumpkin." He tickled her ankle again, glad to see she wasn't in a lot of pain. "It's not so bad. I'm sure a butterfly bandage will be enough."

"You don't by chance have any?" Chase asked. "I'm out."

"Not here. Maybe at the station. We could ride over and dig through the first-aid supplies." Gage reexamined Mandy's cut. "Has she had a tetanus shot recently?"

"When she started kindergarten. I called SherryAnne before we left the house." Chase's flat answer discouraged any further questions about his ex-wife. "What about antibiotics? Do you have any of those at the station?"

"Just topical." Gage reapplied the bandage. "But I agree she should have some. Lacerations on the foot are prone to infection."

"I don't want a shot." Mandy's bottom lip protruded in a pronounced pout, and her eyes brimmed with tears.

"No shot," Gage said. "Just some bad-tasting medicine."

Mandy scrunched up her face but didn't object.

"Doc Ferguson won't be back in town until Tuesday." Chase gathered his daughter in his arms. "Maybe I should take her to the E.R. in Pineville after all. I'll call you tomorrow and let you know how it went."

"You won't get home until ten or later," Hannah said. "Stay and have some pie with us. You can leave in the morning."

"I have appointments all day." Chase was a veterinarian, the only one for thirty-five miles in any direction.

"Maybe Mom can take Mandy," Hannah suggested.

"She's working tomorrow." Gage stood and returned the chair to the table.

"Thanks anyway." Chase headed out of the kitchen with Mandy in his arms. "But it's probably better for everyone if we just go tonight."

"Wait." Gage reached for his cell phone. "I have an idea." He hit a speed dial number on the key pad and waited while the call went through.

"Hello."

A small jolt of anticipation went through him at the

sound of Aubrey's voice. "Hi, it's Gage. Are you busy at the moment?" He winked at Mandy. "I have a patient who requires the services of a good nurse."

Aubrey leaned her back on the front door of the clinic and shielded her eyes against the setting sun. In the distance, Gage's pickup truck rumbled down the road, headed straight for her. Grandma Rose had insisted she'd be fine alone for a short while, leaving Aubrey with no legit excuse to refuse Gage's request.

Not that she would have refused to help Chase and his daughter.

She'd met Mandy only once, at her grandfather's funeral. Mandy had been a toddler then, Chase and SherryAnne happily married. Aubrey liked Gage's older cousin, though she hadn't known him well and Sherry-Anne hardly at all. During her summers in Blue Ridge, Aubrey's attention had been fixed exclusively on Gage.

The truck swung into the drive and parked beside her SUV. Both doors opened and Gage emerged from the driver's side. He paused, his bare arm resting on top of the open door.

His searching gaze landed on Aubrey where it remained. She could feel the effects of his intimate scrutiny clear to her toes. A very small, very wistful sound escaped her lips, and for one fleeting moment, she considered disregarding every one of her resolutions about Gage.

"Thanks for agreeing to see us."

Chase appeared by Aubrey's side, intruding upon

her and Gage's interlude—for which she was grateful. Something went haywire with her reasoning every time she found herself near Gage. It was a distraction she didn't need, especially while working.

"Hi, Mandy." Aubrey smiled at the little girl in her father's arms, clinging to both him and a velveteen pony for dear life. In a cheery voice, she said, "I bet you don't remember me. You couldn't have been more than two when we met."

Mandy answered by burrowing her face in her father's shirt.

"Don't be shy," Aubrey cooed and moved closer.

"I hate shots," came a muffled reply.

"Want to hear a secret?" Aubrey uttered the last part in a conspiratorial whisper. "So do I."

One eye peeked out and peered at Aubrey. "But you're a nurse."

Aubrey shrugged. "Doesn't mean I like shots."

The eye went back into hiding.

"You know what?" Aubrey was acutely aware of Gage as he passed by. She tried her best to hide the current of sensation winding through her. "Because I don't like shots, I'm real gentle when I give them. The patients at the hospital took a vote, and they said of all the nurses, my shots hurt the least."

The eye reappeared. "Is that really true or are you just making it up?"

"Well…" Aubrey scrunched her mouth to one side and squinted. "A little of both, maybe."

The eye crinkled, and Aubrey suspected Mandy

might be enjoying the teasing. She pivoted to face Gage, who was unlocking the clinic door.

"You have a key to this place?"

The dead bolt gave, and he pushed open the door. "Yeah, the volunteer fire department works closely with the clinic."

Aubrey supposed that made sense. Just like she supposed Gage had received some EMT training.

"You understand I can't dispense antibiotics to Mandy without Dr. Ferguson's consent?"

"Give me just a minute." Gage walked into the clinic and went straight to the phone sitting on a scarred metal desk that was more junk than antique. He referred to a list of phone numbers taped to the desktop and dialed.

Aubrey stowed her purse on the counter. "Let's see about that foot." She gestured toward the narrow examination table.

The little girl was loathe to leave the sanctuary of her father's arms. He finally got her to sit on the table but not without a fuss.

Aubrey bent down to inspect Mandy's foot. "I promise I won't touch you, sweetie, unless you tell me it's okay. Agreed?"

Mandy nodded, her mouth compressed into a tight bud.

"All right, hold your foot up so I can see it."

She complied and, after more coaxing, allowed Aubrey to remove the bandage.

Halfway through her examination, Gage got Dr. Ferguson on the line. "He'll talk to you."

Aubrey went over to Gage and took the phone from him. His fingers lingered on hers far longer than necessary.

"H-h-hello, Dr. F-Ferguson." She gripped the phone tight to counteract the sizzling effects of Gage's touch.

"Hello, Aubrey. I wasn't expecting to speak to you again so soon. How's your grandmother doing?"

"She's better." A brief update on Grandma Rose gave Aubrey a chance to compose herself. Afterward, she filled in the doctor in Mandy.

"Give her some cephalexin." He told Aubrey where the prescription medicines were stored. "Would you mind writing up a short report for me before you leave and putting it on the desk?"

"Not at all. Thank you, Doctor."

"Thank you. This has been a great help to me." For once his voice was warm. Almost friendly. "I've no right to ask but would you perhaps consider volunteering at the clinic one or two afternoons a week? I could really use someone with your skills."

"I..." Aubrey's refusal stuck in her throat.

In all honesty, she missed practicing nursing. Treating minor injuries and checking sore throats might not compare to the fast-paced environment of Tucson General's E.R. and the addictive rush of adrenaline, but she'd no doubt enjoy herself. And heaven only knew the shabby little clinic could use a strong administrative hand.

From the corner of her eye she watched Gage talking to Chase. Could she handle something else that would put her in close contact with Gage? Doubtful. Nor did she need more ties to Blue Ridge—ties that would be hard to cut when the time came to leave.

"Aubrey?" asked Doctor Ferguson.

"I'm sorry. I got sidetracked." *And how.* She swallowed before speaking. "As much as I'd like to volunteer, I'm afraid I can't. I'm leaving the end of the month and would hate making a commitment only to break it." She noticed Gage watching her and averted her head. Hadn't she done as much to him when they were young—made a commitment and then broke it?

"I understand." Doctor Ferguson's voice was once again clipped. "If you change your mind, give me a ring."

"I will."

Aubrey disconnected after saying goodbye. Expelling a long sigh, she spun around—and found herself nose-to-chest with Gage. When had he moved? Bracing a hand on the edge of the desk saved her from losing her balance and falling straight into him.

"Is everything okay?" he asked, giving her not one spare inch of space in which to maneuver.

"Fine."

"You sure?"

It was obvious he wanted to ask her about her conversation with Doctor Ferguson, and he might have if not for Mandy.

"Am I gonna get a shot?" Huge, worry-filled eyes pleaded with Aubrey.

"No, sweetie. I promise." Aubrey reassured her with

a big smile. "And no stitches, either. But I'm going to have to wash your foot real good and put some medicine on it that might sting a little."

The little girl hugged her stuffed pony to her like a shield.

Aubrey sympathized, wishing she, too, had a shield to protect herself from the man standing in front of her.

Chapter 8

Gage flung the spark-plug wrench he'd been using into the toolbox at his feet, swore in frustration and contemplated what kind of trade-in value he could get on the old tractor. Forty-five backbreaking minutes in the sweltering sun and he still hadn't figured out why the worthless piece of junk kept stalling out.

Yeah, right. Who was he kidding? The Raintrees could barely afford a new wheelbarrow much less a new tractor.

Climbing onto the front wheel, he leaned down and poked around the engine for the umpteenth time, hoping to identify the problem before his knees and his patience gave out.

He had his right arm buried up to his shoulder in the bowels of the engine when his cell phone rang.

"Great," he growled, straining to reach a loose wire that hopped about with a life of its own. "Who could that be?"

As he reached around with his left hand to unclip his phone from his belt, it suddenly hit him how much he sounded like his father.

The thought took him aback. Way, way aback.

Before he could answer his phone, the radio on his belt emitted a series of tones. Instantly, Gage's heart rate accelerated to Mach speed. He hopped off the tractor wheel and, listening to the radio, sprinted to the house.

By the time he reached the back porch, his phone had stopped ringing. Ignoring the number on the caller ID, he called dispatch.

"We have a fire," the voice said upon answering his call. "Seventeen miles northwest of Saddle Horn Butte."

"Where do I report?"

He was given the various details of the fire and the meeting location for his crew. Not bothering to stop for a pencil and paper, Gage committed the information to memory as he tore through the kitchen, gathering his keys and wallet. Anything else he needed was stored in a metal container in the bed of his truck. Within minutes, he was behind the wheel.

He didn't make it to the end of the driveway.

His father hobbled toward him from the side yard, hollering and waving his arms. "Where are you going?"

Gage slammed to a stop and rolled down the window. "There's a fire," he called out. "I just got the call."

"What about the tractor?"

"I'll finish repairing it when I get back."

"And when exactly will that be?"

"I don't know."

"You can't just leave." Joseph reached the side of the truck. He was panting slightly. "We need the tractor to move those boulders blocking the lower access road."

"The access road's been blocked for months. Another few days won't make a difference."

"Kenny Junior's coming tomorrow to help dig post holes for the new fence. He can't get his truck past those boulders."

"Not now, Dad." Gage started to roll up the window.

"Hold it right there, young man." Joseph jabbed the air with his index finger. "Your first duty is to this family. Fighting fires is something you can do in your spare time."

"And when do I ever have any spare time around here?"

Countless trees and brush were being destroyed while Gage and his father argued. Possibly summer homes and recreation sites. Ranches and grazing land by the acre. Gage couldn't wait any longer. He let up on the brake, and the truck rolled forward.

"I'll call when I have a minute."

"You leave now, you might as well not come back." Joseph's scowling expression could have been carved from stone.

"Is that an ultimatum?"

"Yes."

"Whatever." Gage was in no mood for idle threats.

"I mean it this time, son."

Did he? Gage didn't think his father was any more serious than the last two times he'd issued similar warnings.

But Gage was—serious as a heart attack. He wasn't just a firefighter these days, he was up for promotion to crew leader and not about to ignore his increased responsibilities.

"Be careful about giving ultimatums, Dad. You might not like the answer you get."

Joseph's jaw went slack, then clenched.

Gage peeled out of the driveway and barreled down the road. More than one rabbit and lizard saw him coming and executed a mad dash for safety.

At the main gate leading into the Raintree Ranch he met up with Hannah who was returning from the college. He debated stopping to chat with her and decided he had thirty seconds, and thirty seconds only, to spare.

She shoved open the gate, the rusty mechanism objecting with a high-pitched squeal. "You were going fast enough." She walked over to lean on Gage's open window. "Where's the fire?"

"Northwest of Saddle Horn Butte."

"Oh, wow!" Her face registered shock. "I was just kidding."

"I don't know how long I'll be gone. Sorry to dump everything on you."

"Don't sweat it."

"Dad's in a bitch of a mood."

"What else is new?"

"He's mad because the tractor's still not working."

"I'll get Kenny Junior to look at it when he comes out tomorrow."

He had no doubt Kenny Junior would move a mountain for her if she so much as batted an eyelash at him.

She rapped the side of his truck. "You get a move on. We'll be fine."

"Thanks, sis." Some of the weight on his shoulders lifted. "I appreciate you taking care of things while I'm gone."

"Hey, it's cool. That's what family's for." She waved him off. "You be careful, you hear?"

Gage hit the gas. A glance in his rearview mirror told him Hannah was already in her car and on her way home. Good. If anyone could cajole their dad out of his bad mood, it would be her.

He didn't realize until he reached the highway that Hannah had never before offered to handle things for him while he was at a fire. She was usually too caught up in her own little world to think beyond personal wants and wishes.

Maybe his younger sister was finally growing up.

And if that were the case, his life might have just become a tiny bit easier.

"You should really have that looked at by a doctor." Aubrey laid an ice pack on the Hotshot's knee. The joint was swollen to half again its normal size. She'd had to cut a hole in his pants to get at it. "You probably tore a ligament."

He lifted the ice pack and inspected the soft bulge where his kneecap should be. "I'll be fine."

Aubrey had insisted he elevate the injured leg and used one of the metal folding chairs in the community center as a prop. She handed him two ibuprofen and a bottle of water.

"Take these."

"You have anything stronger?"

He *was* in pain, she thought, and not nearly as tough as he tried to appear. "Not here and not without a doctor's orders."

"It's okay." He downed the tablets. "I want to be clearheaded if they call us for another shift."

She gave him a wet washcloth, and he used it to clean his face and hands. The rest of him would have to wait. With one bathroom and twenty Hotshots wanting to shower, he had a good two hours to kill before his turn came.

"You're not thinking of going back to the fire?" Aubrey asked, not quite believing her ears.

He lifted one shoulder in an indifferent shrug.

"Put too much pressure on that knee and you could cause permanent damage to the ligament."

"It's just a sprain." He dismissed her concern in favor of a plate of spaghetti, courtesy of another volunteer.

Aubrey shook her head in dismay.

She'd treated a dozen Hotshots for minor to moderately serious injuries in the last two days and not one of them even remotely considered calling it quits. They were either raving lunatics or the bravest individuals she'd ever met.

"Hey, Aubrey," her friend Eleanor called. "Can you run next door to the Wash-o-matic and pick up that last load of laundry?"

"Sure." It would be her fourth trip of the day. Aubrey would hate to count the number of bath towels, dishtowels, bedsheets, rags, tablecloths and assorted clothing she'd washed and folded.

As she crossed the large room to the main door, her gaze gravitated toward the TV, where a reporter was broadcasting live a few miles from the fire. Smoke filled the sky behind her, a swirling, billowing mixture of white and gray. The news, however, was encouraging. At last report, the fire was sixty-five percent contained. Experts predicted it would be ninety-five percent contained by morning.

So, why hasn't anyone heard from Gage?

When Aubrey showed up at the community center the day before with a food donation, she told herself it was the neighborly thing to do. It was the same excuse she used when she returned that morning and then stayed all day. In truth, she'd been hoping for information on Gage, who'd been gone three days without a single word.

She tried not to concern herself. After all, Gage was an experienced firefighter, and they'd been receiving regular updates on his crew via radio transmission. At least, that's what Kenny Junior told Aubrey earlier when he dropped off some planks to finish the handicap ramp.

And it wasn't like she and Gage had a relationship

or anything. They were friends. Period. Friends and former spouses.

So, did former spouses go around kissing each other like they were crazy in lust?

No point denying it. She *had* kissed him, *wanted* to and *did* it. Gage might have egged her on, but he hadn't coerced her. Not by a long shot. What must he be thinking? One minute she'd told him they needed distance in order to avoid problems when she left town. The next minute she was kissing him like she couldn't wait to jump naked into bed with him.

Aubrey grabbed the empty laundry basket and trudged out the door into the deepening light of early evening. The Wash-o-matic was a short hop, skip and jump from the community center. Just far enough to work up a sweat.

While dumping clean laundry from the dryer into the basket, she asked herself, not for the first time, why she'd returned to the community center, not once but twice, and why she was doing exactly what she'd told the Sierra Nevada captain she wouldn't—namely, help out.

The answer, she knew, had as much to do with being useful as it did with finding information on Gage. Aubrey missed her job, plain and simple. Though an entirely different environment, there were similarities between a busy E.R. and the community center.

Both hummed with excitement and energy, not to mention that they both existed in a state of constant tension. The highly trained and dedicated staff members were united in a common purpose: bringing comfort and relief to the people who walked through the door. Aubrey may have been a stranger to most people in the room, but she felt right at home, and they sensed that about her.

Was that the reason Gage and the other Hotshots fought fires? Did they have the same desire—no, compulsion—to help those in need as Aubrey and her co-workers?

Maybe she'd been wrong. Maybe she did understand what motivated Gage. But nursing didn't usually require one to risk their life on a regular basis as firefighting did.

She stood, slamming the dryer door shut. Where was Gage? Why didn't he call? Balancing the basket of clean laundry on her hip, she made her way back to the community center.

In her absence, a mud-splattered minibus had parked near the front entrance of the community center. The last of its occupants, a man wearing brown pants and a navy blue T-shirt, slipped through the door. Aubrey's step faltered. Those were the colors of the Blue Ridge Hotshots. Had Gage's crew finally returned?

Running while carrying a full laundry basket proved cumbersome, but Aubrey didn't drop so much as a sock. Not that she would have stopped to pick it up.

Inside the community center, she quickly scanned the new arrivals, searching for Gage. Her chest heaved, and her temples pounded. From the back and side, all the Hotshots looked alike; their damp hair mussed, their clothes rumpled and every inch of them streaked with grime and soot.

Aubrey wove her way through the large room, her eyes going from one to the other. Smiles greeted her. Not one, however, belonged to a familiar face. Damn! Where was Gage? The emblems on the navy blue T-shirts identified the firefighters as Blue Ridge Hotshots. His crew. He had to be with them, didn't he?

She went up to the nearest one, moving the laundry basket to her other hip. "Excuse me. Did Gage Raintree come back with you?"

He gave her a curious and then appreciative once-over. "Are you Aubrey Stuart?"

"Yes." How did he know her name?

A smile lit his sun-burned and wind-reddened face. "Nice to meet you. I'm Marty Paxton, Gage's captain. I've heard a lot about you."

"Nice to meet you, too." She shook the hand he offered, more interested in news of Gage than social pleasantries. "Can you tell me where Gage is?"

"I can do better than that." His smile grew. "I can show you."

Relief swept through Aubrey, followed by anticipation. The one-two punch left her wobbly in the knees. "Okay."

Marty raised an arm and pointed at the open doorway leading to the kitchen. "In there."

The laundry basket hit the floor with a thud. Deep laughter followed Aubrey as she darted through the maze of folding tables and chairs blocking her route to the kitchen. She assumed the laughter was Marty's. The hell with him. He could think what he wanted, she didn't care. So long as she confirmed with her own eyes that Gage was safe and in one piece.

He was standing at the sink, his right hand under the faucet, water running full blast. Eleanor stood beside him and stared at his hand, her lips thinned in concentration.

They both glanced up as she skittered to a stop. Gage's expression conveyed surprise. Eleanor's didn't. In fact, her eyes twinkled with an I-thought-so mirth.

Aubrey dismissed her as she had Marty. What did they know anyway?

"Hey."

"Hey."

Eleanor reached around Gage and shut off the water. "Titillating as this conversation is, I'm afraid I simply must tear myself away."

"Huh?" Gage turned to look at her. "Sure. Thanks, Eleanor."

"You're welcome." She smirked at Aubrey on her way out. "To both of you."

Aubrey didn't remember deciding to throw herself at Gage the second Eleanor left the kitchen, yet somehow she wound up in his arms.

"Thank God you're all right." Her voice hitched with emotion. "I got worried when no one heard from you."

Gage could have gloated, she supposed. He could have told her he knew all along she was lying and still had feelings for him no matter what she said, but he didn't. Instead, he squeezed her tight as if he couldn't bear to be parted from her ever again. Aubrey's heart sang.

"I was worried about you, too," he murmured into her hair.

Though she would have gladly let him, he didn't attempt to kiss her.

"Why didn't you call?" she demanded when they finally broke apart.

"Sorry. I would have if I'd known you wanted to hear from me. Did you want to hear from me, Aubrey?"

"Yes." The admission came out softer than she intended.

"Seems to me you made it pretty clear the other night at your grandmother's house you wanted to put some distance between us."

How could she explain her reasons to him when she didn't understand them herself?

"I talked with your mother this morning at the real estate office," she said, avoiding his question. "You haven't checked in with your family, either."

"They know where I am."

"But they don't know you're safe."

"I'll call later."

She'd obviously struck a sore spot with him and let the subject drop. "How's the fire? I heard earlier it was sixty-five percent contained."

"It's closer to eighty now."

"Wow. That's great news. When do you report back?"

"We may not have to. We're supposed to stick around

here for the next few hours just in case." He cradled his left hand inside his right one.

Aubrey's nurse's eyes zeroed right in. "What happened to your hand?"

"Just a small burn."

"Let me see."

He obediently placed his hand in hers, and she gently uncurled his fingers. His palm was bright red. Blisters the size of dimes covered the pads of each finger, including his thumb. A single large blister an inch long cut across the center of his palm. Charred particles were imbedded in the skin alongside the blisters. It had probably looked worse before he washed it.

Aubrey took a second to compose herself. "How did this happen?"

"I got a sticker or some damn thing inside my glove. It hurt like a son of a bitch. I took the glove off for just a second to get whatever it was out. Right about the same time this burning log decided to roll down the hill at us."

"And you had to stop it," she said, turning the cold water back on and sticking his hand under the flow. She didn't release his wrist.

"Actually, Ernesto stopped the log. Not intentionally. He tried to jump clear of it but tripped and was knocked flat on his butt. The log rolled onto his legs."

"Oh, my God, Gage."

"I didn't think and just reached down to shove it off him."

"Is he all right?"

"Yeah. They took him to Pineville hospital. He may

need plastic surgery." Gage indicated his injured hand with a nod. "This is a scratch compared to him."

"This is hardly a scratch. You have second-degree burns."

Aubrey pictured a burning log rolling down a hill toward Gage and went ice cold, inside and out. She had to fight the debilitating numbness threatening to turn her limbs into deadweights and reminded herself she wasn't in Tucson General's E.R. No one's life hung by a thread, depending on her quick responses to save them.

She clenched her jaw and tried to concentrate on the present. Enough was enough, she chided herself. This ridiculous nonsense had to end, and soon. She was a nurse. A professional. Someone who—

"Aubrey? What's wrong?"

"Nothing."

"You don't look very good."

"I'm fine," she said, drawing deep, even breaths. The infusion of extra oxygen helped warm her frigid blood. "Just tired."

"Me, too."

"I bet you are." Feeling a little better, Aubrey shut off the water and wrapped Gage's hand in a clean towel. "Let's dress this for you."

She led him out of the kitchen and toward the folding table that served as the first-aid station.

"Why are you here?" he asked as they walked.

"I'm volunteering."

"Since when? I thought you didn't want to make any commitments only to break them."

"It's just for today." And yesterday. She didn't inform him that one of the main reasons she'd returned to the community center was to learn if he was safe. "Have a seat." She motioned to an empty chair.

"I have a better idea." A mischievous grin deepened the lines of fatigue bracketing his mouth.

"What?" Aubrey sensed a wild scheme about to be hatched.

"Grab what you need, and let's ditch this place."

"To go where?"

"I'll show you."

She shook her head. "You need to rest."

"That's exactly what I have in mind." The gleam in his eyes far from instilled her with confidence.

"Let me take you home," she insisted.

"I'm not going home. Not yet." The finality of his statement left no room for argument.

Aubrey again pondered what had happened between Gage and his family, but curbed her curiosity for the moment.

"Please." He flashed her the same woeful expression that had broken her resolve so often when they were younger. "It's not far. I promise."

"Okay." She gathered up the medical supplies she'd need, ignoring the warning bell clanging inside her head. "On one condition."

"Name it."

"You agree to see Doctor Ferguson first thing in the morning and have him check out your hand."

"I'm fine. It's no big deal. I've had rope burns worse than this."

"Gage."

"All right. If I'm not called back to the fire."

"You can't go back with your hand like th—"

He cupped her cheek in his palm, effectively silencing her—something he'd also done often when they were younger. "Quit being a nurse for one hour, okay?"

"Okay." She didn't correct him. Her concern for his well-being had little to do with her profession and a lot to do with her much-denied-but-there-nonetheless feelings for him. "What about food? Are you hungry?"

"Starving."

"There's some leftover pizza in the fridge. I'll get us a couple slices. And something to drink."

This time, Gage took the lead. As promised, they didn't go far. Just next door, to the volunteer fire department station. Only they didn't enter the station as Aubrey anticipated. He took her out back, and the sight that met her caused her to screech to a grinding halt.

Parked in the shade of the building stood a motor home. The same one they'd resided in during their short marriage. Memories inundated Aubrey, one after the other, in rapid-fire succession. Some were heartwrenching and agonizing, others tender and sweet and incredibly wonderful.

She gulped, unable to move.

"Come on," Gage urged, taking her elbow with his good hand.

Did he have any idea what he was asking of her?

"Give me a second." She seriously considered making a beeline straight back to the community center as fast as her legs could carry her.

Going inside the motor home with Gage wouldn't be wise. She'd be inviting trouble on the grandest of scales. When it came to Gage, she was far safer surrounding herself with as many people as possible. Something always seemed to happen—something that involved mouths and bodies coming together like high-powered magnets—every time they were alone.

But he was hurt, she reminded herself. And in pain. Tired, hungry, battered and bruised. He probably had nothing more dangerous in mind than a nice long nap. Right?

Her feet remained glued to the ground.

"I figured we could talk in private while you bandaged my hand."

Talk in private?

She wasn't reassured. Talking with Gage inevitably left her feeling like an emotional dishrag.

Her gaze traveled between the motor home and Gage and back to the motor home. Aubrey had a vivid recollection of Susan Raintree helping her sew curtains for the many little windows. Were the curtains still hanging? The exterior had taken a serious beating from the elements. If the inside in any way resembled the outside, the motor home should have been condemned years ago.

"Come on," Gage urged again. Quietly. Beseechingly. Seductively.

She let his voice slide over her, and the small shiver

that coursed through her as a result wasn't unpleasant. If anything, it was tantalizing.

A momentary flash of insight penetrated Aubrey's fog-filled brain. She was, she realized, at some sort of turning point in her relationship with Gage. She either went back to the community center and the situation remained status quo: a constant state of sexual tension flowing between them that would continue until the day she left Blue Ridge. Or, she accompanied him into the motor home, a course of action that pretty much launched them on a path from which there was no turning back.

Did she want to be with Gage badly enough to risk an agonizing separation when she returned to Tucson? And what about him? Could he handle a repeat of what happened ten years ago?

"I'm leaving at the end of the month," she said in a choked whisper.

"So you've told me."

"Nothing that happens today or any day between now and then will change my plans."

"I know."

"Do you?"

"Yes."

She studied his face for several long seconds and saw that what he said was true. He was indeed resigned to her eventual leaving.

"All right." Aubrey squared her shoulders and took a tentative step forward. "We can talk."

Climbing the steps of the motor home was like walking through a time portal. She placed her hand on the doorknob and pushed. In an instant, the last decade faded away. Her skin prickled, her toes curled and her pulse drummed. Gage coming up behind her worsened her strange symptoms. Entering the small and achingly familiar domain, she had the distinct impression talking wasn't all they'd do, especially when she glimpsed the faded curtains hanging from crooked rods.

Chapter 9

Gage strained not to move as Aubrey treated his injured hand. Every touch of her fingers, every brush of her arm, elevated his sense of awareness to a higher level. He hadn't brought her to the motor home in an effort to seduce her, but seducing her was pretty much all he could think of at the moment.

"Gage?"

"Sorry. Did you say something?" He tried to recall her question, but his brain function had been reduced to zilch.

She sighed and delicately probed a blister. "I said, you really should be taking antibiotics. Dr. Ferguson can prescribe one for you when you see him tomorrow."

Gage tensed, though not from pain, and reminded himself to breathe regularly. She definitely wasn't lying to Mandy when she told the little girl the patients at Tucson General voted her the gentlest nurse. Aubrey's careful ministrations, combined with her proximity, pushed him to the very limits of his tenuously held control.

He sat at the compact dining table, the sole available seating in the motor home. Only one of his long legs fit in the cramped space beneath the table. The other one stretched across the narrow walkway, the toe of his boot butting the front panel of a lower storage cabinet. Aubrey barely had room to maneuver, which accounted for their constant—and he assumed unintentional—physical contact, along with his fast-growing state of arousal.

Gage wriggled in the seat and tugged on a pant leg.

"Does that hurt?" Her worried glance flitted to his face and then back to his hand.

"Not at all. I'm just a little stiff."

"I bet you are."

She had no idea.

"Is your shoulder bothering you? I noticed you rubbing it earlier."

"A bit."

"I brought some liniment." She inclined her head at the assortment of medical paraphernalia lying on the table.

A pain-relieving cream probably wasn't going to help Gage with what ailed him. If anything, Aubrey massaging liniment into his sore muscles would only increase his discomfort. Nonetheless, he picked up the tube with his left hand and attempted to unscrew the cap—*at-*

tempted being an apt description. Gage was anything but ambidextrous.

"Here. Let me." Aubrey relieved him of the tube. "Take off your shirt."

Gage rose, inadvertently crowding Aubrey.

She lowered her gaze, watching him unbuckle his belt. He watched her watching him, and deliberately slowed his movements, hoping for a reaction.

"Do you need help?" she asked.

He figured he could succeed one-handed, but where was the fun in that? "Sure, thanks."

He raised his arms over his head, and Aubrey whisked off his shirt. Unfortunately, she did it like a nurse undressing her patient and not like a woman stripping her lover.

So much for wild, crazy fantasies coming true.

What, Gage wondered, did she think about the two of them being there together? Did she want him as much as he wanted her?

"Sit," she ordered.

He plopped back down in the seat. Aubrey came to stand in front of him, squeezing a dollop of liniment into the center of her palm. The outside of her thigh pressed lightly against the inside of his. Her movement appeared innocent, much as Gage wished she had an ulterior motive. One sign, one teeny tiny sign from her and...what? Throw her on the floor and take her right there?

She soothed the liniment into his shoulder using strokes that were strong, competent and incredibly gentle. Gage closed his eyes, hovering midway between heaven and hell. He silently pleaded for her to stop while simultaneously hoping she'd go on touching him until dawn tomorrow.

He got his first wish.

"Is the water connected?" She turned and moved to the sink.

"Last I checked." Gage had run a garden hose and extension cord from the station so that the motor home would have, if not all the comforts, at least the minimum necessities of home.

She flipped on the faucet. Water sputtered and spit before flowing in a steady, albeit thin, stream. After washing and drying her hands, Aubrey picked up a box of sterilized gauze pads.

"I'm not sure the best way to bandage your hand." She narrowed her eyes contemplatively. "You don't by chance have an old glove hanging around we could use?"

"I'd like to shower first. Get out of these filthy clothes."

"Oh." She caught his stare and something flickered in her eyes, giving his innocent comment an entirely different meaning.

Gage responded with a rush of heat that made the fire he'd been fighting the past three days seem like a marshmallow roast.

They'd showered together often in this motor home. He recalled in minute detail the sight of her bare skin glistening beneath the spray of hot water and the enjoyment they'd both derived from him toweling every inch of her dry. Seeing her cheeks flush, he thought he might have finally broken through the barrier of her professional demeanor.

"I should go," she said in a controlled voice. "Give you some privacy."

Before she could execute the backward step she obviously wanted to take, Gage reached out with his good hand and grabbed hers. "Stay."

"I can't. I…shouldn't."

His thumb toyed with the band of her wristwatch, burrowing under it and worrying the sensitive spot on the inside of her wrist. She was leaving soon, very soon, returning to the career she loved and the life she'd made for herself in Tucson. He had no business whatsoever starting something with her, especially when he had nothing better to offer. Yet he couldn't bring himself to let her walk out of the motor home.

"I won't pressure you into anything you don't want or aren't ready for, Aubrey. I swear."

"I know. And that's just it." She squeezed her eyes shut and gave a small, nervous laugh. "You wouldn't have to pressure me."

There was no thinking involved. No moment of indecision. Gage came out of his seat like a rocket. In the next second, he had Aubrey pinned against the counter.

Green eyes met his, an array of emotions flaring in their smoky depths. Surprise. Curiosity. Arousal. Nothing to indicate displeasure or unwillingness. It was all the invitation he needed.

"I'm filthy." He bent to nuzzle her cheek and ear. "And I stink."

"So I noticed." Sighing, she linked her arms around his neck. Her breasts fit snugly against his chest, and Gage could discern her taut nipples through the fabric of her shirt. He longed to tease them with the tips of his fingers or, better yet, the tip of his tongue.

"Take a shower with me."

She wrapped an ankle around his calf and adjusted her hips to align with his.

"Will we still fit?"

"Hell, yes." He'd find a way or die trying.

Mouths meshed and tongues tangled in an explosive, heat-generating kiss that left them both shaking and short of breath. He fumbled with the top button of her shirt, desperate to be skin to skin with her. Body to body. Soul to soul.

With a smile both coy and shy, Aubrey brushed his hand aside and unfastened the buttons herself. She didn't stop there.

Giving her room to maneuver, Gage eased backward until his behind hit the table. He would have liked to participate in her undressing, but his injured hand pretty much prevented that. No matter. Standing idly by and watching Aubrey shuck out of her clothes wasn't exactly torture.

Then again, maybe it was.

She paused, one finger hooked beneath the strap of her skimpy pink bra. A rumble of desperation emanated from his chest. Had she changed her mind? He hoped not. Almost as much as he hoped his radio wouldn't go off for at least an hour or so.

"Do you have any protection?" she asked.

She hadn't changed her mind. *Thank you, God.*

"Uh, yeah. I think so." He dove through the door to the bathroom and snapped on the dim overhead light.

An unopened box of condoms sat on the medicine cabinet shelf, and he could have cried with joy. His foot caught on the doorjamb in his haste to exit.

"Sorry." He offered a half smile in way of apology for his clumsiness.

Her eyebrows lifted. Not so the corners of her mouth. "You keep condoms in the medicine cabinet?"

Gage realized how sleazy he must look to her. "These are Kenny Junior's," he hurriedly explained. "They've been here for I don't know how long. When I first moved the motor home to the station, he planned to use it for a bachelor pad."

"Kenny Junior?" Aubrey cracked a smile, and they both burst out laughing. The volunteer firefighter had the heart of a teddy bear and a physique to match. She eyed the box of condoms speculatively when their laughter finally died. "Are they still good?"

Gage held the box in a death grip and read the label. His sharp burst of laughter bordered on giddy. "They don't expire for another six months."

Aubrey tipped her head to one side. "Okay."

"Really?" The single word hardly summed up everything he was thinking and feeling, but coherent sentences were beyond his present capabilities.

"Yes, really."

Her smile was warm and genuine and filled Gage

with an elation he hadn't felt in years. Ten years to be exact. She sauntered toward him, picking up where she left off and easing the straps of her bra down her shoulders. He dropped the box of condoms on the table and opened his arms.

Like the teenagers they'd once been, they tumbled into the bathroom. The remainder of their clothes landed in a heap on the floor. Gage cursed his inept hand more than once.

"Take it easy." Aubrey reached inside the shower and adjusted the spigot. The ancient plumbing squeaked and gurgled before releasing a sputtering spray. "You'll hurt yourself."

In that moment, a thousand needles could have pierced Gage's flesh and he wouldn't have noticed. Aubrey was exquisite. All feminine curves and angles in exactly the right proportions.

She spun around, and her wide eyes followed a path from his face, down his chest, and then lower. There, it lingered. Gage couldn't hide his very obvious desire for her, nor did he try.

"Water's taking a sec to heat up," she said in a thready voice.

"We can wait." He made the offer strictly for Aubrey's sake. A dip in the Arctic Ocean wouldn't diminish his ardor, much less a little cold water.

"I'd rather not." Her eyes met his again and she moistened her lips.

The dozen or so inches separating them instantly diminished to one. Pushing the plastic curtain aside, he scooped her up in his arms and deposited her in the shower. Water pelted her, collecting in rivulets and streaming down the length of her body to pool at her feet. He stared, mesmerized. She was so incredibly beautiful.

"Aren't you going to join me?"

"In a minute."

"Gage." She laughed self-consciously and reached for the plastic curtain.

"No way." He stopped her before she pulled it closed and climbed into the shower with her.

There was enough room for the two of them if they stood plastered against each other, an arrangement that suited Gage just fine. He wrapped his arms around Aubrey's waist, liking the feel of her slick, wet skin sliding along his. He'd missed this, missed her, more than he let himself admit.

Before he could kiss her, she picked up a sliver of pink soap from the recessed dish and rubbed it in her palms until a frothy lather dribbled between her fingers. She spread the lather over his shoulders and chest and across the flat plane of his stomach. Repeating the process, she washed his hips and thighs. Gage didn't dare move, anticipating her next move.

To his surprise and pleasure, she cradled his cheeks in her hands and washed his face and neck. The sweet, tender treatment of his sunburned skin affected him far more greatly than any bold strokes in more intimate places might have.

"My turn," he said after rinsing his face beneath

the spray and then snatched the soap from her slippery fingers.

Rotating her around so that they stood with her back to his front, he rubbed the soap back and forth over her breasts until they were covered with suds. He paid special attention to the plump undersides before focusing exclusively on her nipples.

"You don't have to." She sighed contentedly as he continued soaping her with his uninjured hand.

"Try and stop me." He had plans, and they included giving better than he got.

He traveled down her belly, making large, sweeping circles with the soap, and eventually ended at the junction of her legs. She parted her thighs and let her head loll back into the crook of his neck.

"Do you want me to touch you?" he asked, nibbling the side of her neck and fitting his erection into the cleft of her buttocks.

In answer, she moved her hips.

"Say it," he urged.

"Touch me. Please, Gage. I'm going crazy."

She wasn't the only one.

He dropped the soap, reached between her legs and began exploring. His left hand didn't possess the dexterity of his right one, and he cursed it. Showing no hesitation whatsoever, she covered his hand with hers and gently guided him. Her lack of inhibition was such a turn-on, he very nearly lost it then and there.

Aubrey hadn't climaxed their first several attempts at lovemaking. They were both too young and inexperienced. Fortunately, sex improved as the weeks passed. Gage was an apt student, paying careful attention to what she liked. He put his learning to good use now, adding the patience he'd acquired as a grown man. The results were incredible.

"Like that?" he croaked when she arched her back and moaned seductively.

"Just like that."

When the first tremor took her, he wrapped his right arm around her middle and held on for the ride. He didn't loosen his grip until she fell limp against him.

"Let's get out of here," he suggested.

Without waiting for her answer, he turned off the spigot, ripped open the shower curtain and grabbed a towel. Laying it across her shoulders, he stepped out of the shower, then helped her do the same. Gage then had the enjoyment of toweling Aubrey dry. It was as much fun as he remembered.

She giggled when he knelt and picked up her foot to dry her toes. "What about you? Is there another towel in here?"

"I don't need one."

Most of the water on his skin had already evaporated due to extreme temperature—*his* internal temperature, not that of the motor home. Sensing her watching him, he glanced up.

"That was nice," she said in a throaty whisper.

Not sure whether she was referring to the shower, the toweling off or her climax, he said, "I enjoyed it, too."

"Hurry." Aubrey spun sideways and dashed out the door.

Gage chased after her, grabbing the box of condoms as he flew by the table. She got only as far as the overhead bunk before he caught her. Considering her impish grin, that may have been her plan all along. He boosted her into the bunk before crawling up after her. Laughing, they fell onto the sagging foam mattress.

"Just like old times." She toyed with a lock of his damp hair, twirling it between her fingers.

"Better." He kissed and nibbled her lips. Lightly. Playfully.

Their mood turned serious when Gage rolled Aubrey onto her back and positioned himself over her. He removed a condom from the box before tossing it in a corner. Extracting the condom from the foil package with his left hand defeated his abilities.

"I'll do it."

Aubrey not only opened the package, she placed the condom over his erection. She didn't hurry, testing the very limits of his willpower. When she at last finished, he settled himself between her legs, looked into her eyes, and watched them darken from emerald to hazel. It was like coming home after a too long absence.

"Make love to me, Gage." She elevated her hips in an urgent plea.

"Aubrey. Oh, God."

She *did* want him. Every bit as much as he wanted her, and Gage was able to put their uncertain—if not impossible—future from his mind. For the moment, at least. Today, she was his. He'd worry about the consequences tomorrow.

* * *

Aubrey took a small bite of food and grimaced. She wasn't a fan of cold pizza, but eating gave her something to do while Gage inhaled his meal. She washed the cheese-and-pepperoni combo down with a swallow of soda, wondering how to start a conversation and when. They really needed to talk, which was the reason they'd come to the motor home in the first place. More so now that they'd made love. But Gage also needed to eat and sleep.

Maybe she should wait for another day.

"You okay?" He caressed the back of her hand, a tentative smile on his face. "You seem a little preoccupied."

The rumpled, just-flopped-out-of-bed look gave him a sexy edge that would be difficult for any woman to resist, especially one who'd finally accepted she was starting to fall for him all over again.

"I'm fine." She smiled back, also tentatively.

They sat across from each other at the small dining table, knees knocking and feet scuffling. While Aubrey had dressed in the bathroom, Gage scrounged up an old pair of jeans from the bottom of the closet. No sooner were they dressed than an awkward tension descended upon them. It had yet to ease. Talking, Aubrey mused, might only increase the tension.

And not talking is going to relieve it?

The metallic crunch of an aluminum can being compressed jarred her from her reverie. Gage leaned over, opened the cabinet under the sink and deposited his trash in the plastic container stored there.

"You done?" He reached for her soda.

"Not yet. Thanks."

Aubrey still had half her pizza slice left and most of her drink, which she was reluctant to give up. Picking at the remains of her food would give her something to do while they talked—that was if they ever got around to talking.

Damn. She really needed to say something. Gage might have...expectations...given the manner in which they'd spent the last hour. Unrealistic expectations.

Screwing up her courage, she blurted, "This changes nothing. No matter what happens, I'm—"

A shrill chirping cut her off. Gage's cell phone. He lunged for the bathroom where he'd left his dirty pants on the floor. Aubrey wasn't so much frustrated at the interruption as she was worried that Gage might be called back to the fire. She'd yet to bandage his injured hand.

"Raintree here," he said from the bathroom, slightly out of breath. "Yeah, Marty." A pause. "No, I didn't leave. I'm in the motor home." Another, longer pause. "All right. I'll stick around for a while just in case." He emerged from the bathroom, the phone wedged between his shoulder and ear. "No problem. Thanks for calling." Disconnecting, he dropped the phone on the dining table. "Looks like we've been relieved of duty."

"That's good news." And it was. For Gage, for the thousands of wilderness acres spared and for the people living near Saddle Horn Butte. Aubrey pushed away the remains of her meal. "Let's finish bandaging your hand."

Doing something routine might put them—put her—at ease enough so they could converse comfortably.

She operated by rote, applying an antibiotic ointment and bandaging the tip of each finger. A break in the conversation didn't come, mostly because there was no conversation.

Now or never, she told herself and opened her mouth to speak.

Gage beat her to it. "Do you remember our secret spot?"

"Sure I do."

He grinned. "And the day we found it?"

"How could I forget?" She fitted a gauze pad over the blister on his palm and taped the dressing in place. "I still have a scar from your fishhook."

"That was the first time I kissed you."

"I seem to remember it was me who initiated the kissing. You were all freaked out over a little blood."

"I wasn't freaked out." His grin went from amused to sly. "It was an act to trick you into kissing me."

"You're terrible." She shot him an appalled look, entirely feigned.

"That was also the place where we first made love." His voice dropped in volume. "Then decided to elope right afterward."

Her hands stilled, as did her breathing and, she was relatively certain, her pulse.

"Gage…"

"Don't you freak now. I'm not going to suggest we elope again."

"Good." The single word came out on a rush of relief.

"But I do have feelings for you." His tone was reassuring and reasonable, two things she didn't feel at the moment. "And I think you have feelings for me, too. I know you, Aubrey. You wouldn't have made love with me if you didn't."

He was right, of course.

"What do you want from me?" she asked. More importantly, what was she willing to give?

He cupped her chin in his bandaged hand. "I'd like for us to try and make a go of things for the remainder of your stay in Blue Ridge."

"A go of things?" she asked hesitantly. "As in boyfriend and girlfriend?"

"Yeah. Pretty much."

Aubrey mulled this over with amazing calm, considering her chaotic frame of mind. She supposed she could blame their sleeping together today on raging hormones trapped in close, familiar quarters. Or nostalgia, even. But dating Gage? Dinner at her house Friday night and a movie in Pineville Saturday afternoon? That would involve a conscious decision, one she might eventually regret.

"What if we do make a go of things? What happens when it's time for me to leave?"

"We'll figure something out. Find a way to be together."

"Oh, Gage." He could be so sweet. So optimistic. The complete opposite of Aubrey, who tended to anticipate trouble around every corner. "It's not that simple."

"You have a job, I know."

"Not just a job, a career. One I've worked hard for. As have you."

"Okay." He nodded jerkily. "So we compromise. Tucson isn't the only place with a hospital. Pineville has one. Granted, it's not as large."

Aubrey rubbed her temple, though it was her chest that really hurt. "If it were merely a matter of me finding another nursing job, I'd say yes. But there are other factors to consider. What about your obligation to your family's ranch?"

"Hannah's taking over in another year and a half. Two at the most."

"Which means you can't move to Pineville until she's graduated college."

Tightly thinned lips were his only concession to her point.

"There's another reason I need to go back to Tucson General. One I haven't mentioned."

He waited for her to enlighten him, one eyebrow quirked.

Aubrey hesitated, worried he might view her as incompetent once she revealed her problem. She took pride in her skills and abilities, and her periodic freeze-ups had carved a huge hole in her confidence.

"You remember our family friends, Jesse and Maureen Donaldson?" she started out slowly. "They died a few months ago in an automobile accident."

"Your grandmother told me. I never met them, but you talked about them a lot and I know you were close."

"I was on duty the night they were brought into the E.R." She paused, waiting for the lump in her throat to shrink enough for her to continue.

"Oh, jeez. I'm sorry, sweetheart. That must have been awful for you."

"When I recognized them, I froze. It was like my brain stopped communicating with the rest of me. While they lay there, dying, I did nothing."

"You were in shock."

The prickle of impatience she felt was directed at herself, not Gage, but it was him she snapped at. "An E.R. nurse can't afford to be in shock."

"Okay."

"Sorry." She was instantly contrite. "This is hardly your fault."

He accepted her apology with a shrug. "So you're human like the rest of us."

She shook her head. "When you work in a large metropolitan E.R., someone you know and care about is bound to be brought in eventually. You have to be able to detach yourself from any personal involvement until the crisis has passed. I didn't detach myself," she finished on a miserable note.

"There's not a firefighter I know who hasn't had a moment of indecision, including myself."

"A moment of indecision isn't the same thing as a complete inability to respond." She lifted his injured hand and turned it over, palm up. "When that burning log rolled onto your friend's leg, did you hesitate? No.

You acted on instinct and did what was necessary to save him without regard to your personal safety."

"Ernesto's life wasn't hanging by a thread, either."

"Would you have reacted differently if it had been?"

"I hope to hell not."

"I only wish I could say the same thing and with as much conviction." Unshed tears stung her eyes. Staring out the small window over the sink didn't dispel them. Neither did Gage's compassionate tone.

"I remember feeling like I was walking underwater," she continued. "Everything was blurry and wavy. Sounds ran together. That's never happened to me before, and I've seen some truly terrible things."

She stopped for a ragged breath. "Neither Uncle Jesse nor Aunt Maureen regained consciousness, which I suppose was a blessing. Aunt Maureen died first. Her neck broken."

"That's awful."

"What if it's my fault Uncle Jesse and Aunt Maureen died?" She choked, trying to regain her composure. "How many moments were lost while I just stood there, doing nothing? Moments that could have been utilized to save their lives."

"Their deaths weren't your fault," Gage said adamantly. "They were beyond saving. I know it sounds cruel, but a few minutes, a few hours, wouldn't have made a difference."

"But what about the next time I freeze up?" The ball of misery inside Aubrey's chest expanded until it pressed against her lungs, cutting off her air supply. "And the next?"

"How often has it happened?"

"Often enough."

"When was the last time?"

"Oh…" She glanced at her watch. "About seven o'clock. In the kitchen when I saw your hand."

"You didn't freeze up."

"No. But I had a serious panic attack."

"Which you obviously conquered."

"Covered, not conquered." She turned toward him, fear welling inside her. "I'm scared, Gage. Scared I won't be able to practice emergency nursing ever again."

"Would that be so bad?"

"How would you feel about having to give up fire-fighting because you couldn't handle the pressure?"

"I'd hate it and be angry with myself for being such a wimp."

"Exactly." Gage had hit the nail squarely on the head. She *was* angry with herself. Flat-out furious. "I have to go back to Tucson when my leave of absence is up and face this problem. If I don't, I might lose my nerve altogether. Dad thinks I shouldn't have left in the first place."

"He's not always right."

"True." Had Aubrey not been so well acquainted with Gage, she wouldn't have detected the trace of bitterness in his voice. "But in this instance, he may be." His hand still lay near her arm, and she clasped it gently. "I'm going back, Gage. I have to. Please understand."

"I do. I care about you, remember? And I'm behind you 100 percent." He brought her fingers to his mouth and kissed the knuckles. "But I still want to see you while you're here."

"I couldn't take a repeat of the last time I left. My heart isn't up to the stress, not after the beating it's had the last couple of months."

"No strings. I promise."

"You're not exactly a no-strings kind of guy."

"I won't make a stink when you leave."

She believed him, or maybe she just chose to because she, too, wanted to see him again.

"Come on." She stood, pulling him out of his seat. "Finish getting dressed. Then I'll drive you home."

"And tomorrow?" Gage drew her into his arms.

"You call me, and I invite you over for dinner."

"Count on it."

His kiss was demanding and possessive, verging on wild. Had Aubrey been wearing socks, they would have disappeared in a wisp of smoke. The spellbinding effects lasted only until they left the motor home.

As they walked hand in hand to the community center, Aubrey's tendency to expect trouble kicked in. She began to question her reasons for sleeping with Gage and inviting him over the following night—not because their farewell would be difficult and sad when she left, but after nearly three weeks of being with him on a steady basis, she might not want to leave Blue Ridge.

What, then, would become of the nursing career she loved?

Chapter 10

Gage jerked back as a flame unexpectedly leapt up in front of his face, the heat from it stinging his skin.

"Hey, buddy," Marty said from beside him. "Watch it. You almost lost an eyebrow."

"You think I'd know better." Gage adjusted the controls on the front of their gas barbecue grill. The blue flame flickered once then promptly extinguished with a soft puff. Gage cursed under his breath. "The automatic ignition on this thing has never worked right."

"You guys ready for these?" Kelli came across the lawn toward them carrying a large platter heaped with hamburger patties.

"Not yet." Marty leaned over and gave his wife a peck on the check. "Gage can't get the grill lit."

"Firefighters." Kelli rolled her eyes and handed her husband the platter. "Here, let a layperson have at it."

Turning the knob ever so slowly, she depressed the ignition button twice in rapid succession. A small flame appeared, caught, then spread evenly beneath the artificial coals.

"Okay." Kelli straightened and swiped her hands together. "Give that a few minutes to warm up, and we're ready to rock and roll."

Gage looked first at her, then Marty. "Did she just whip my butt?"

"Hard," Marty said and broke into laughter.

"How'd you do that?" Gage asked. The temperamental grill had been giving the Raintree family grief for years.

Kelli waved her hand in the air. "Magic fingers, my friend."

Gage took out a scrubber and began to clean the grill. "Maybe after we eat you can show me your magic fingers again."

Marty put a possessive arm around Kelli's waist. "You got your own girl. Go play magic fingers with her and leave mine alone."

Yeah, thought Gage, he did have his own girl. At least for another two weeks.

"And speaking of girls…" Kelli sidled closer to Gage, who'd finished cleaning the grill and was now coating it with a nonstick spray. "I like Aubrey. A lot. I can't believe you two ever divorced."

"Kelli," Marty warned.

"I'm sorry." She gave an apologetic smile. "But you two are just so cute together."

"It's all right," Gage said, setting the can of spray down and picking up the hamburger patties. "I'm glad you like her."

When faced with the prospect of a rare Sunday afternoon off work, Gage had invited Marty and Kelli out to the ranch for a cookout. Now that he and Aubrey were officially dating, he wanted her to get to know his friends and for them to know her.

His mother, delighted with the prospect of entertaining Gage's captain, had outdone herself, whipping up her special recipe potato salad, pineapple coleslaw and corn on the cob to go with the hamburgers. Aubrey had brought two kinds of dessert. She and her grandmother were in the house helping his mother, along with Hannah. Gage's father, also in the mood to relax for once, was watching a ball game on TV.

"You going to ask her to stay in Blue Ridge with you?" Kelli smiled expectantly.

This time her husband's warning was accompanied by a stern scowl. "None of your business, sweetheart."

"I'm fond of Gage, I like seeing him happy. Aubrey makes him happy."

Gage couldn't agree more. Aubrey did indeed make him very happy.

The burgers sizzled as he set them on the grill. Kelli observed him with an eagle eye and when he was finished, went behind him with the spatula and rearranged all the hamburgers.

"I didn't know burgers cooked better in straight rows."

"That way the heat is more evenly distributed." She sighed impatiently. "Clearly you two only know how to put fires out, not cook with them."

"Is she this obsessive-compulsive at home?" Gage asked.

"Worse." Marty knocked back a swig of iced tea.

Both he and Gage would have preferred a cold beer but they made it a practice to avoid alcohol during fire season.

"Well, just so you know," Gage said, stepping aside so Kelli could more closely supervise the cooking hamburgers, "I'm not asking Aubrey to stay."

"Why?"

"Because she has her job to return to, for one." The conversation he and Aubrey had in the motor home last week came back to Gage in bits and pieces. "It's not fair of me to ask her to give it up." He didn't mention her freezing problem.

"I suppose you could commute and have a long-distance relationship." Kelli sprinkled seasoning on the hamburgers. "Vacations, holidays, three-day weekends."

Marty murmured, "Give it a rest," under his breath but she ignored him.

Gage tried to remember the last three-day weekend he'd had off and couldn't. Hell, he hadn't had a Sunday afternoon off in two months.

"I'm sure we'll work something out," he said with far more assurance than he felt.

Because of his promise not to pressure Aubrey, he hadn't brought up the subject of life after Blue Ridge with her. Lately, however, as the days flew by, he'd begun to question his ability to hold out.

The back door opened, distracting Gage. Aubrey emerged with Hannah in tow, the two of them carrying plates and bowls and chatting a mile a minute. They headed for the table and chairs they'd set up earlier under the branches of a sprawling cottonwood tree.

She smiled at him from across the distance, and Gage felt a strong emotion tug at his heart. He wasn't just going to miss Aubrey when she left, he was going to be lost without her.

Again.

From inside the house, the phone rang. Gage could hear a distant echo of it coming from the barn. He told himself to relax. A ringing phone didn't automatically mean a fire. After all, his radio hadn't gone off and his cell phone remained silent.

But when his mother rushed through the back door, concern written all over her face, Gage knew this phone call wasn't social.

"Christine Peterson's on the line. Their haystack is on fire."

"Get a hold of the guys," Gage hollered to his mother. "Tell them I'll meet them at the station. And tell Mike to ready the engine."

In a small town the size of Blue Ridge, there was no dispatcher. Calls for the volunteer fire department came by telephone.

Before Gage could turn all the way around, Kelli took the spatula from his hands.

"Go," she said without preamble.

"I'll come with you." Marty jogged alongside Gage.

"You don't have to."

"This is a volunteer fire department, right? I'm volunteering."

Gage didn't refuse. They could always use the help. Hay fires could smoulder for days or turn nasty and burst into flames.

He spotted Aubrey on their race to his truck. "Come with us," he shouted. "In case there are any injuries."

She paused, uncertainty shadowing her features. It lasted only a second, long enough for Gage to wonder if he'd asked too much of her. In the next second she passed her stack of paper plates to Hannah and ran to join Gage and Marty at the truck.

The three of them piled into the cab and, without another word, tore out of the yard.

They could see the plume of white smoke for several miles before they arrived at the Petersons' place. Aubrey sat in the backseat of the engine, squished between Marty and Kenny Junior. Gage was up front with Mike, who drove, and Gus rode on the top. Aubrey hoped to God everything would be okay.

It had been over twenty minutes since the call had come in at the Raintree ranch. Fire could cause an amazing amount of damage in that time. And while it seemed to take forever, the Blue Ridge Volunteer Fire Department was the closest help. The *only* help. A house would burn to the ground long before an emergency vehicle from Pineville arrived.

Their wailing siren had drawn numerous onlookers. Adults spilled from their houses to watch the engine pass, and children waved at them from front yards. Two cars followed closely behind, to help, Aubrey hoped, not hinder.

The Petersons' place was in the middle of town on six acres. The possibility of the hay fire spreading to neighboring houses was slim, but the proximity of the Petersons' house and barn presented a danger. Burning embers carried on the breeze could easily ignite a roof, tree or woodpile.

As the engine screamed toward the driveway, someone Aubrey didn't recognize pushed open a rolling gate. A half-dozen horses, evidently freed from their stalls in the barn, trotted around the front yard, bucking and kicking, and whinnying at all the commotion.

Mike drove the engine across the finely manicured lawn and past the small herd of horses to the barn in back of the house.

"Holy crap," Marty said when they got near the barn, his fingers poised on the door handle.

The reason for his expletive became quickly clear. The shade covering the haystack was in flames, the wooden posts and trusses holding the tin roof ablaze. Smoke poured from the haystack in a huge funnel, going up at least thirty feet before veering off at an angle.

John Peterson stood between the burning haystack

and the barn, spraying water on the fire with a garden hose. He could have been spitting on it for all the good he did. A single garden hose was no match for this inferno.

Before the engine came to a complete stop, the guys were already piling out and donning the rest of their gear. Within the next minute, they had the hose unrolled and hooked up to the water tank on the engine. Kenny Junior turned a valve, and a blast of water a hundred times the size of the garden hose exploded from the nozzle.

"What can I do to help?" Aubrey asked. Since none of the Petersons appeared injured, her nursing skills weren't in demand.

"Unload the other hose from the back of the engine and unroll it," Gus told her. "We may need to pump water from the Millers' stock pond across the street if the tank runs dry."

"Okay." Aubrey glanced over her shoulder as she headed to the back of the engine. Gage held the nozzle, his feet planted solidly in place, and aimed it at the fire. Kenny Junior backed him up. The rest of the guys cleared the area around the fire, dragging, pushing, or driving anything and everything away.

"Jeremy, come back," Mrs. Peterson cried. She ran after a young boy—Aubrey assumed he was her grandson—who'd escaped the confines of the house.

The boy, no more than three, must have had aspirations to be a firefighter when he grew up. He refused to listen and kept running up the hill leading to the barn until he was alarmingly close to the fire.

"Get the hell out of here," his grandfather yelled. He'd gone over to the barn wall closest to the fire and was wetting it down with the hose.

Jeremy stopped in his tracks, evidently startled by his grandfather's brusque outburst, and began to cry.

"Come back," his grandmother called, huffing and puffing. She'd lost speed halfway up the hill, unable to catch her agile grandson.

Aubrey dropped the hose and bolted. She reached Jeremy and swooped him up in her arms.

"I've got you, sweetie pie."

Jeremy didn't want to be rescued. He wiggled and squirmed and hollered, "Snowflake," over and over in Aubrey's ear.

She was more than a little glad to present him safe and sound to his grandmother.

"Jeremy, honey, I told you to stay in the house. It's not safe out here."

Aubrey glanced back up the hill to the fire. The flames still raged despite being saturated with water. The four wooden posts holding the shade covering blazed like giant matchsticks.

Other than on TV, she'd never witnessed firefighters in action. A burning haystack might not compare to a city skyscraper in terms of danger, property damage and potential loss of life. But it was nonetheless terrifying, especially when Gage and his crew ventured close to the flames.

Beside Aubrey, Mrs. Peterson struggled to hold on to her rambunctious grandson. "He wants to find Snowflake."

"Is that one of the horses?"

"Heavens, no," Mrs. Peterson exclaimed. "She's our barn cat. A stray we recently took in. And wouldn't you know it, she produced a litter of kittens three weeks ago. In the haystack of all places."

Aubrey had been watching Gage fight the fire, only half listening to Mrs. Peterson. The older woman's last remark, however, had Aubrey paying rapt attention.

"The cat and kittens were in the haystack?" she gasped in horror, unable to consider the dire consequences.

"They got out. At least, we *think* they did. John saw Snowflake carrying one of the kittens into the barn right when we first noticed the smoke."

"One?" Aubrey asked. "How many did she have?"

"Four," Jeremy answered. He'd quit wiggling quite so much and hung on his grandmother's arm, attempting to move her. She stood steady as an iron post.

"He's been enthralled with the kittens," she explained. "Playing with them all week."

"Cats are very resourceful," Aubrey said. "And resilient. I'm sure Snowflake's fine." And at least *one* of her babies.

"Can't we go look for her, Grandma? Please?" Jeremy's whining intensified.

"No."

"But the kittens…"

Her voice softened. "We'll look for Snowflake the minute the fire's out. I promise."

"It is out." Though not fully extinguished, the firefighters' efforts had started to pay off. Already, the fire looked smaller in size and considerably less threatening.

"What do you think?" Mrs. Peterson asked Aubrey. "Is it safe to go into the barn?"

"The fire hasn't spread, and I don't think it will at this point."

Mrs. Peterson's glance alternated between her grandson and the barn. "I'll just take a quick walk through and see if I can spot Snowflake."

"Can I go with you?" Jeremy chirped.

"Absolutely not!" Aubrey and Mrs. Peterson said in unison.

Jeremy frowned. "Not fair."

Aubrey reached out and rumpled his hair. "Maybe next time, kiddo, when you're a little older."

After returning Jeremy to the house, Mrs. Peterson went to the barn. Aubrey started up the hill, watching the firefighters. Gage and his crew had done their job. Smoke continued to pour from the blackened remains of the haystack but the fire was pretty much done for. The shade covering the haystack stood at an odd angle, the wooden columns now nothing but charred twigs.

If only there was something more she could do to help. Aubrey wasn't used to standing around in an emergency situation. Her adrenaline rush, which had kicked in back at the ranch when Gage asked her to accompany him and Marty, had yet to abate.

She was halfway to the engine when she heard a loud crash. She looked over and gave an involuntary shriek. One of the burnt columns had collapsed, and a piece of the tin roof the size of a door had fallen and hit the ground with a horrendous clatter just inches from where Gage stood.

He jumped back. So did Kenny Junior. They momentarily lost control of the hose.

Aubrey stared, transfixed, her heart lodged in her throat, her stomach twisted in knots. Had the piece of roof hit Gage, he would have been seriously injured. Possibly disfigured. Killed if it had landed on his head.

"We're all right," Gage hollered when Marty, Gus and Mike came running. He regained control of the hose, stepped back several feet and continued dousing the smouldering haystack.

And still Aubrey didn't move. She wanted to cry but no tears would come. It had happened again. In a moment of crisis, she'd frozen.

For how long she stared at Gage she didn't know. Seconds. Minutes.

"Man down!" Gus yelled.

Aubrey turned her head, though her feet remained anchored in place. Mr. Peterson sat on the ground, evidently dazed, his arms hanging loosely at his sides. Gus, who was working only a few feet away, reached Mr. Peterson first, then Mike. The two of them knelt down to talk to the older man.

Aubrey's legs at last responded, and she hurried to join them. "What's wrong?"

"Not sure yet," Gus responded.

"Mr. Peterson?" She also knelt, noting his pasty pallor and rapid breathing. She automatically reached for his wrist and took his pulse. It was uneven and accelerated.

"I'm okay. Just need to rest a minute." Sweat dotted his forehead.

He could be having a reaction to the roof collapsing or a touch of smoke inhalation but Aubrey suspected something more.

"Are you currently on any medications?"

"Yes."

"What kind?"

He listed his prescriptions. Aubrey recognized the names as those taken for a heart condition.

"You may have overdone it a bit." She eyed the fire. Gage still had the situation under control. They were safe where they were, for the moment anyway. "I want you to rest while I get something from the engine." She patted his arm. "I'll be right back."

Earlier, on the drive over, Aubrey had automatically taken a mental inventory of the available medical supplies and equipment and remembered seeing a portable oxygen tank.

She walked to the engine on shaky legs. Marty was there, unloading some shovels. At her request, he carried the oxygen tank to Mr. Peterson and helped her set it up. Mrs. Peterson arrived just as Aubrey was adjusting the valve.

"What happened?" she asked, her expression one of alarm.

Aubrey filled her in on the details.

"John! How many times have I told you to take it easy?"

"I'm all right," he grumbled.

"He probably is," Aubrey confirmed, "but I encourage you to call his doctor."

Mrs. Peterson fussed over her husband for several minutes. Aubrey was relieved to see him grow stronger with each passing minute. They'd be able to move him into the house soon.

"Any sign of Snowflake?" she asked.

"Yes, thank goodness," Mrs. Peterson replied. "I found her and all four kittens in a bucket under the workbench."

"Jeremy will be glad to hear it."

Aubrey had been crouched beside Mr. Peterson and shifted so she could see the fire. Mike had taken over the hose with Marty backing him up. For all intents and purposes, the fire was out, though it continued to smoulder and hiss.

Gage came toward them, rolling his shoulders to relieve tension, a tired smile on his face.

"How's our patient doing?"

Aubrey couldn't help thinking if the piece of tin roof had fallen just a few inches more to the right, Gage might be the patient in her care along with Mr. Peterson.

"Better," she said, fighting to keep her voice steady.

"You really should consider becoming a volunteer

medic for the Hotshots." Gage gazed down at her, his eyes filled with affection and admiration. "You're a natural at this."

But Aubrey didn't feel like a natural. Far, far from it.

Chapter 11

Gage clipped his radio to his belt and walked into the kitchen. His mother stood at the counter, wrapping four large chocolate chip cookies in plastic. She dropped them in the ice chest he'd left on the counter.

"Hey." He came up behind her and gave her an affectionate squeeze. "That's my job."

"I baked these this afternoon. Thought you might like them for your picnic."

"Thanks, Mom."

Gage had invited Aubrey on an evening picnic and told her he'd bring the food. Not much of a cook, he'd made arrangements with Harold Sage, the owner of Sage's Bar and Grill. Some of the stuff Harold fixed seemed a bit strange, but he promised Gage that Aubrey would be delighted at the gourmet fare.

"I can't believe she's leaving next Friday," his mom said. "It seems like she just arrived."

Removing a bottle of chilled wine from the refrigerator, Gage placed it in the cooler, the perpetual lead weight in his stomach growing heavier. He hadn't been able to stop thinking of Aubrey's imminent departure for days now.

They'd spent every free minute together since that day in the motor home two and a half weeks ago—which, because of their hectic schedules, wasn't nearly enough. Gage had been gone for four of those days working a fire in Utah. Because his departure coincided with semester break at summer school, his sister was able to pick up most of the slack at the ranch.

Right after the fire at the Petersons', she gave in to Dr. Ferguson's persistent needling and agreed to volunteer at the clinic every other afternoon. News spread fast and before long, she had more patients than she could handle.

He hadn't yet been able to convince her to volunteer with the Hotshots. Her personal demons continued to haunt her and Gage wished there was more he could do for her than lend the occasional ear.

For his part, he sailed along on a tide of contentment. He and Aubrey took long walks, went horseback riding, had dinner and then went dancing at a honky-tonk in Pineville, and generally hung out together.

They'd also had sex. Lots of it, frequenting the motor home whenever possible. One night, they tossed a sleeping bag and pillows in the bed of his truck and went on a drive to Signal Point. Gage would always remember the sight of Aubrey, naked and sitting astride him, moonlight glinting off her auburn hair as she bent down to kiss him.

He'd be lying if he said he didn't want their picnic tonight to end much the same.

"Look, honey." His mom took a sip of her iced tea as if to fortify herself. "It's none of my business, but I'm asking anyway. What's going to happen with you and Aubrey when she leaves? Have you two discussed it?"

"We have. Though not recently." Difficult as it was for him, he'd kept his word and not pressured Aubrey into any kind of commitment. "She's leaving, and I'm staying. For now," he added on impulse and then wondered why he did.

"Does that mean she's coming back in the near future? Or are you moving to Tucson?"

"How would you feel if I did?"

His considered before answering, rubbing the condensation forming on the outside of her glass with her thumb.

"Ranching's a funny thing. It's either in your blood or not. You might look like your father, but you take after me in a lot of respects. I married into the lifestyle and accepted it because I love your father. I refuse to impose that same lifestyle on my children if it's not what they truly and honestly want. Hannah does, I think. You, on the other hand, have fought to get away from ranching since you were a kid."

"For all the good it's done me."

"You're an adult now. No one can stop you from leaving, including your father." Susan smiled ruefully. "Though he probably thinks he can."

Gage shut the lid on the ice chest. "I can't leave the ranch. Not while Hannah's in college."

"Granted, you being gone would make things harder, but not impossible."

"We wouldn't be having this conversation if Dad weren't ashamed to ask people for help. That's the real reason he wants me to stay. All that talk about family responsibility and obligation is just so he can save face."

"Don't be so hard on him, sweetheart. Growing older is rough, more so on some of us than others."

"It doesn't have to be. We live in a town where nine-tenths of the population would bend over backward to help a friend and neighbor. Insisting I stay is selfish and unfair."

"He has his pride," Susan said, her tone sharp.

Gage realized he'd gone too far and made an effort to control his temper. "No one would think less of him if he asked for an occasional hand."

"Of course they wouldn't. But he doesn't see it that way. His gout has done as much emotional damage as physical."

What would it be like to live with reoccurring and debilitating pain? Gage tried to imagine. Like his father, he'd probably resent having to slow down and rely on others. But he doubted he'd force his family to give up their goals and ambitions in order to compensate for his loss of abilities.

Susan went back to rinsing dishes and stacking them in the dishwasher. "If you want to leave with Aubrey next week, do it. We'll manage one way or another."

"How?"

It was probably just as well Gage's dad had ridden over to the Double S Ranch on the other side of Neglian Creek and wasn't home to hear their conversation.

"I'll quit my job," Susan answered.

"You love working at the real estate office."

"I can always go back to work when Hannah graduates college."

"Forget it."

His mom was attempting to compromise, and while he appreciated the effort, he'd have none of it. She'd already made enough sacrifices for the sake of their family. Gage wouldn't be the reason behind another one. Nor would he put his family in worse financial straits. They needed his mom's income.

"What about Kenny Junior?" she asked. "He might be willing to work part-time in exchange for room and board."

Gage's mental wheels began to spin. "Maybe."

"We could fix up the old bunkhouse," Susan went on to say. "All it really needs is a good cleaning, a fresh coat of paint and a couple minor repairs. Kenny Junior's not fussy."

"I'll talk to him," Gage said, liking the arrangement more and more by the second.

"And I'll talk to your dad. But I need to approach him just right." Susan folded the dish towel she'd been using, hung it over the oven handle to dry and faced Gage. "Put it to him like we're doing Kenny Junior a favor and not the other way around."

The lead weight in Gage's stomach felt suddenly lighter. Was it possible? Could he leave with Aubrey next week and move with her to Tucson? Excitement grabbed hold of him as his mind soared in a dozen different directions.

He'd have to put in his notice with the Blue Ridge Hotshots. Hopefully they'd give him a good recommendation, as Gage had no intentions of quitting firefighting anytime soon. The Tucson Hotshots were a top-notch outfit and if they weren't hiring, he'd look elsewhere. With a little grooming, Kenny Junior could take over as head of the Blue Ridge Volunteer Fire Department.

All at once his mind ground to a screeching halt.

What about Aubrey?

Gage realized he'd been making one very large assumption. His and Aubrey's agreement to date was only for the duration of her stay in Blue Ridge. She might not welcome him tagging along with her to Tucson, moving into her apartment with her. Just because the last couple of weeks had been unbelievably great for him didn't mean they were great for her, too.

But, oh, they *had* been great weeks. Better than their marriage. Gage and Aubrey hadn't argued once. Come to think of it, they'd never argued before they were married, either. Did their problems start only when they were cohabitating?

He'd talk with Aubrey tonight, he decided. Try and

get an inkling of how she felt about him—*them*—before springing any plans on her.

"Your dad will dig in his heels at the beginning," Susan continued. "He won't like it that you're leaving."

"Dig in his heels?" Gage had to laugh. "He'll blow his stack. And make everyone's life miserable."

"Only because he'll miss you." His mom went to Gage and gave him a hug. "And so will I. Terribly."

"I'll miss you, too."

"Tucson isn't so far. You can come up for a visit every few months." She stepped back, and her eyes glistened with tears. "I've always loved Aubrey. She's a very special person. Nothing would make me happier than to see you two married again."

"Wait just a second." Gage put out a hand. "Who said anything about marriage?"

"Well, I…"

"Let's take this one step at a time. I have to talk to Aubrey first."

Not that Gage wasn't in favor of walking down the aisle with Aubrey again. He just didn't want to rush things. Too much too soon was what had landed them in trouble the first time.

"She loves you. It's obvious."

Did she?

Susan's smile spoke volumes. "And I think the feeling's mutual."

Was it?

He lifted the ice chest off the counter. "I'd better load

up the truck and head out of here. I told Aubrey I'd pick her up at six-thirty."

His cell phone abruptly rang, and Gage clenched his jaw. He didn't want anything to interrupt his plans with Aubrey tonight. Setting the ice chest back down, he checked the caller ID before answering. His pulse jumped when he recognized the number.

"Raintree."

"Gage. It's Larry Newcombe."

"Yes, sir."

"Sorry to bother you so late in the day. We were in meetings all afternoon, and we just now got out."

"That's quite all right." Gage told himself not to leap to conclusions, but it was hard not to. There were only a handful of reasons why a commanding officer called a Hotshot and it wasn't to report for duty.

"I didn't think you'd mind. Not when you heard what I had to say. Congratulations, son. Your promotion to crew leader came through."

Excitement and elation surged through Gage. It was a minor miracle he was able to maintain a level voice. "Thank you, sir." He looked over at his mother and grinned from ear to ear.

Her expression changed from curiosity to happiness, and she mouthed, "Did you get the promotion?"

He nodded, simultaneously listening to Commander Newcombe outline the responsibilities of his new position, which he pretty much knew thanks to Marty.

"Be proud of yourself," Commander Newcombe finished up. "There were a lot of qualified candidates to choose from, and we picked you."

"I'm very proud. And thank you again, sir."

After Gage disconnected, he gave his mother a bear hug, kissed her soundly on the cheek and swung her around the kitchen.

"Stop it," she squealed, laughing all the while.

Gage swung her around once more for good measure. Damn, but he felt good. He'd been waiting a long time for this promotion and had worked hard for it.

"I'm so happy for you, sweetheart," Susan said once she caught her breath.

"That makes two of us."

"I know Aubrey will be happy, too."

Gage's grin went slack. Not ten minutes ago he'd been seriously contemplating returning with her to Tucson. Then his promotion had come through.

His mother must have sensed the direction of his thoughts for she asked, "What are you going to do? Stay or go?"

"I don't know." He hefted the ice chest onto his hip. "Guess I'll talk to Aubrey tonight."

And say what?

Did it really matter?

She'd made it clear from the start her return to Blue Ridge was temporary. Which meant he either stayed here, or declined his promotion, let one of those other qualified candidates have it and went to Tucson with Aubrey.

Hell of a choice.

Just as he reached the back door, Biscuit began barking. "Are you expecting anyone?" he asked.

"No." His mother followed him out onto the back porch.

Biscuit stood at full attention near the edge of the yard, lifting her head every few seconds to sound another alarm. Not a vehicle was in sight.

"That's funny," Susan mused aloud.

Gage heard it then, the loud clatter of galloping hoofbeats. As he and his mother stared, his father's big buckskin gelding came charging up the side road for all he was worth, reins flapping and stirrups bouncing. Panic shot through Gage.

Where was his dad?

He dropped the ice chest and ran. The exhausted animal had reached the gate and stood there, sides heaving and nostrils flaring. Shoving open the gate, Gage gathered the reins and gave the horse a quick once-over, but there were no clues as to his father's whereabouts.

His mother came rushing toward him. She'd evidently gone back into the house because in her hand she held a walkie-talkie. As she approached, he could hear her frantic attempts to raise his father.

"Joseph, are you there? Can you hear me? Come in."

Her only reply was empty air.

Stopping in her tracks, she gazed at Gage, clearly on the verge of tears.

"Don't worry, Mom. I'll find him." He took the walkie-talkie from her and pressed the reins into her hands. "You unsaddle Comanche while I bring the ATV around. Call over to the Double S Ranch when you're done. See if one of their guys can drive the road to Neglian Creek crossing. I'll take the west trail and meet up with him there. One of us will find Dad."

"What if you don't?"

"Then we call the sheriff."

"Maybe we shouldn't wait."

Gage glanced at the sun dipping low toward the distant mountains. Not much daylight remained. "Put a call into the volunteer fire department, too." He bent and kissed her cheek. "Dad's going to be mad as hell at us for having half the county out looking for him."

His mom's breath hitched. "I'll take my chances."

Ten minutes later Gage crested the rise a half mile from their house. While the ATV idled, he had a look around. The trail to Neglian Creek was more than a path but less than a road, too narrow for a full-sized vehicle. Some spots were wide open, others thick with clusters of trees and brush.

His dad could be anywhere. Walking along the shaded creek bank. Resting on a fallen log. Lying hurt somewhere, unconscious from a fall.

Guilt ate a gigantic hole in Gage's middle. His dad really was in no shape to run the ranch alone. But then, maybe he didn't have to. With Gage's promotion coming through, him leaving with Aubrey had been reduced from a distinct possibility to a mere option.

It wasn't until he revved the engine that he remembered his date with her. Pulling the walkie-talkie from his pocket, he depressed the button on the side and raised his mother almost immediately.

"Do me a favor, Mom. Call Aubrey and postpone our date."

"All right." She updated him on her conversation with the Double S Ranch then signed off so she could call the sheriff.

Gage hit the gas and flew down the slope, dust and pebbles shooting out from behind the ATV. If they didn't find his dad soon, chances were they'd have to call off the search until morning.

A lot could happen to a person alone in the hills and on foot during the hours between nightfall and sunrise. Gage slowed to take a sharp turn and tried not to dwell on the many grave possibilities.

Aubrey clicked the "submit order" icon on her laptop computer screen. A second later, a confirmation page appeared. She reviewed the list of items carefully. Satisfied everything was there, she clicked on the "proceed to payment" icon.

"Here you are." Grandma Rose teetered into the kitchen, a cane in each hand. She'd been doing well with her rehabilitation but still suffered periodic bouts of unsteadiness. "What are you up to?"

"I just finished placing your first grocery order." Aubrey sat at the table, her laptop hooked up to the kitchen phone. "It'll arrive in three days."

"I don't like the idea of buying my groceries with a computer," Grandma Rose complained. She eyed the laptop as if it were an alien contraption. "I enjoy picking out my food."

"I know. And you'll be able to do your own shopping when Mrs. Payne or someone else takes you into Pineville with them on their errands. This is for times they can't. If you run out of something before the regular order is scheduled, call me and I can take care of it from any computer no matter where I am."

Grandma Rose's grumble had a resigned tone to it. She pulled out the chair next to Aubrey and sat down, struggling slightly with her canes. Aubrey resisted the urge to jump up and help. Her grandmother had to learn to do things by herself if she was going to live independently.

"I've also ordered you a Guardian Angel. It's supposed to arrive tomorrow by overnight mail."

"What's a Guardian Angel?"

"It's a small device you wear around your neck. If you fall or need help for any reason, you push a button. It automatically transmits a signal to Mrs. Payne, the emergency dispatcher in Pineville and the Blue Ridge Volunteer Fire Department."

"Sounds like a lot of fuss to me."

"I really hope you'll wear it. If not for yourself, for Mom. She worries about you being alone."

More importantly, should anything happen, Gage or one of his crew would arrive at the house in a matter of minutes. Aubrey took considerable comfort knowing he'd be there for her grandmother in the weeks and months to come.

Unlike her.

Aubrey put thoughts of leaving from her mind, something she'd been doing with increasing frequency of late. Gage was due to arrive any minute, and they were going on an evening picnic. She didn't know where, he'd made all the arrangements and refused to impart any specifics when she'd asked.

She really wanted the date to go well. They had so little time left together. True to his promise, he'd not once asked her to stay, but she felt pretty confident the thought had occurred to him. It had certainly occurred to her. Often. How could it not? She cared for Gage and their recent time together had been wonderful. It didn't take much effort for her to picture herself living on the Raintree ranch with him again—though not in the motor home—and volunteering at the clinic.

Would that be enough to keep her happy? More than anything, Aubrey missed her job. Part of her dreaded returning, afraid she hadn't conquered her crisis in confidence. The larger part of her, however, couldn't wait to walk into the hospital and experience that familiar rush of adrenaline coursing through her veins.

Dispensing antibiotics and taking blood pressure readings at the clinic, while enjoyable, couldn't compare to a busy E.R.

"Shouldn't Gage be here by now?" Grandma Rose squinted at the clock on the wall.

"He's running a little late, I guess." Aubrey unplugged the phone line from her computer. Selfishly, she hoped he hadn't been called to a fire. "You'll be all right while I'm gone?"

Grandma Rose dismissed Aubrey's concerns with a snort.

"Call me on my cell phone if you need anything." When her grandmother didn't answer, Aubrey touched her arm. "You okay?"

Grandma Rose sniffled and rubbed her nose. "Silly, I suppose. It's just that I've gotten kind of used to your bossiness. Going to miss it. Going to miss you, too."

"I'll be back. First long weekend I have off work."

"How does Gage feel about you leaving?"

Aubrey tensed. She wasn't ready to discuss her and Gage's future relationship or potential lack of it. A classic case of avoidance, without question. Recognizing a behavior pattern, however, didn't change it.

Fortunately, a ringing in another part of the house relieved her of answering the question. She went over to the counter and plugged in the phone she'd unplugged for her computer.

"Hello."

"Aubrey? Is that you?"

"Susan?"

"Yes. Thank goodness I reached you. The line's been busy for ages."

"What's wrong?" Aubrey frowned. Her former mother-in-law sounded upset.

"Gage asked me to call. He's going to have to postpone your date."

Her shoulders slumped. She'd been afraid of this. "A fire?"

"No. Joseph's missing. Gage went looking for him."

"Oh, my gosh!" Aubrey instantly straightened and glanced at her grandmother, who was watching her with concerned interest. "What happened?"

"We don't know for sure," Susan said. "He was feeling good today and rode over to the Double S Ranch to talk with the owner about sharing some water rights. Then an hour ago, his horse came home without him. I've called the sheriff. They sent a couple men out but don't think there's much they can do until morning. Gage and the foreman from the Double S are driving the trails to Neglian Creek crossing looking for Joseph."

Aubrey's heart went out to Susan. "Would you like me to come over and stay with you?"

Susan's voice cracked with emotion. "You wouldn't mind?"

"Of course not."

"I've been trying to reach Hannah. She's out with some friends tonight and not picking up her cell phone."

"I'll be right there."

Aubrey quickly filled her grandmother in on the situation with Joseph and then left for the Raintree Ranch. When no one answered her knock on the front door, she went inside.

She found Susan in the kitchen, sitting on the floor with her back against the refrigerator, a walkie-talkie in her hand, and sobbing as if her world were falling apart.

Chapter 12

"Mom! Come in, Mom!" Gage tossed the walkie-talkie on the seat of the borrowed Jeep and stomped on the gas. "She's crying and won't answer." He shot his passenger an exasperated scowl before turning his attention back to the road.

"Your mother always did have an emotional streak a mile wide."

"Goddamn it, Dad. She loves you."

Joseph swore far more colorfully than his son when they hit a pothole, and he came six inches off the seat. "Take it easy, will you? I'm not made of stone."

Gage slowed, but only because his mother would never forgive him if he didn't deliver his father in one piece.

"Hello. Gage, are you there?" A scratchy version of Aubrey's voice floated up from the seat beside him.

He grabbed the walkie-talkie and put it to his mouth. "Aubrey? Is that you?"

"Yes. I'm here with your mother."

Gage's anger and frustration instantly lessened. Aubrey was there. Waiting for him. "Glad to hear it."

"How's your father?"

"A bit bruised, but ornery as ever. We should be home in a few minutes."

"See you then. Oh, wait! We can meet you at the clinic if your dad needs medical attention."

Joseph leaned sideways and spoke into the walkie-talkie. "The only thing I need is a hot shower and a couple of aspirin." He then glowered at Gage. "No way is your ex-wife examining me. You understand?"

"She's a nurse, Dad."

"I don't care if she was the only medical help for five hundred miles and I was bleeding to death. She'd not examining me."

Gage shook his head, amazed yet again at the depths of his father's stubborn and utterly useless pride. "Why didn't you call in? Could have saved Mom a whole lot of grief and the rest of us a whole lot of bother."

"I figured on making it back to the Double S."

"Five miles on *your* ankle? I don't think so."

"I could've done it."

"And been laid up for weeks afterward. Have you no consideration whatsoever for the rest of us?"

"That's enough out of you," Joseph snapped.

Gage shut up only because arguing with his father was an exercise in futility.

Joseph had been anything but a fountain of knowledge since being picked up. Nonetheless, Gage had been able to piece together most of what happened thanks to the Double S foreman.

His father, upon reaching Neglian Creek crossing, decided a short break was in order and dismounted. Comanche evidently spooked at who knew what and bolted, leaving Joseph stranded. Given Comanche's placid disposition and proven dependability, Gage suspected there was more to the story. If so, his father wasn't telling.

With the Double S Ranch being half as far as the Raintree Ranch, Joseph opted to head back the way he'd come. The Double S foreman found him on the road and contacted Gage. They met up at a halfway point between the neighboring ranches. The foreman generously offered Gage the use of his Jeep and took the ATV, agreeing to swap vehicles sometime tomorrow.

No big deal.

And yet it had been a big deal, all because his father had refused to report in.

Why?

Gage pulled to a stop in front of the main gate and shoved the Jeep into Park. "Your ankle gave out, didn't it?"

"What are you talking about?" Joseph made no effort to get out and open the gate.

"Your ankle gave out while you were mounting Comanche and you fell. Or maybe you got bucked off and landed face-first in the creek."

Several seconds passed. Finally, Joseph leaned his head back and stared at the darkening sky.

"I wouldn't mind so much if it had been my face." He grimaced and gingerly rubbed his backside. "Get me home, will you, and out of this dad-gum torture contraption."

Gage was tempted to laugh at the ironic justice fate had seen fit to dispense. The flash of genuine pain in his father's expression stopped him.

"What if I weren't here to bail you out? What would you have done then?" As soon as the words left his mouth, he realized he was asking himself the questions and not just his father.

"If you quit firefighting, it wouldn't be a problem," Joseph grumbled.

"I meant not here in Blue Ridge."

"Gone?" His father's brow knitted in confusion. "Since when?" Understanding apparently dawned on him as he let out a grunt. "It's Aubrey. You're thinking of going with her to Tucson."

"Before we get into another argument, let me clarify something. I'm only considering going with her."

"You can't leave the ranch," Joseph said firmly.

"The hell I can't." Gage hit the steering wheel with his fist. "I'm thirty years old, Dad. I'll do whatever I damn well please." His voice rose. "Leave Blue Ridge or stay. Be a firefighter or not."

His father stared at him, not with anger or hostility but amusement.

"What?" Gage barked.

Joseph leaned his head back and chuckled.

"Glad one of us finds the situation funny," Gage said.

"It's just for a minute there, you sounded a lot like me."

Gage frowned. He'd thought the same thing the other day and hadn't liked it.

"I remember telling my father off," Joseph said, his tone reflective. "He didn't much cotton to my choices, either."

"You always wanted to go into ranching."

"True."

"So what choice could you have possibly made he didn't like?"

"I married your mother."

Gage's jaw went momentarily slack.

"She wasn't from Blue Ridge," Joseph went on. "And she wasn't from a ranching family. Your grandpa was dead certain she'd corrupt me. Lure me away from the ranch."

"What are you talking about? Grandpa adored Mom."

"Eventually. But not at first."

"Aubrey's not going to lure me away, Dad."

"I don't suppose she is. How could she? Firefighting did that a long time ago."

"No, it didn't." Gage came to a stop at the intersection leading to town and stared his father straight in the face. "It's probably the only thing that's kept me in Blue Ridge these past years."

Joseph returned Gage's stare. "I think I'm only just now starting to realize that."

* * *

"Let's go." Gage extended his hand to Aubrey and pulled her to her feet.

"Where?"

"On our picnic."

"You sure?"

They'd been sitting on the family room couch, watching a sitcom neither of them found funny, and waiting for Gage's mother to finish tending to his father. Aubrey had assumed their date was cancelled, so Gage's sudden announcement caught her off guard.

"Yeah, I'm sure. Dad insists he's fine, Mom doesn't need us and Hannah's on her way home. No reason we can't stick to the original plan."

Considering the tense mood both Gage and his dad were in, vacating the house for a couple of hours seemed like a good idea.

"Okay. Let's go." Aubrey grabbed her purse and shut off the TV while Gage went to inform his parents of their plans.

It soon became apparent where Gage was taking her. Bouncing down the dirt road in his truck, Aubrey had to grin. His choice of a picnic location was perfect and, she supposed, fitting. Ten minutes later they parked and climbed out.

The zigzagging beam of Gage's flashlight guided them through the darkness and along the slippery, winding trail. Low-hanging tree limbs blocked their path and required periodic swatting, as did a hungry mosquito or two. The potent smell of damp earth invaded Aubrey's nostrils, triggering a wave of nostalgia. The gurgle of rushing creek water combined with the chirp and buzz of nocturnal animal life inspired still more memories.

Their secret spot.

Why, she wondered, had Gage brought her here? To remember? Or did he hope to create new memories, ones to see them through the coming separation?

"Wait a sec." Gage bent down, swept aside a curtain of dangling willow tree branches and disappeared inside the secluded shelter. Placing the ice chest on a semi-level patch of ground, he stuck a hand out to her. "Pass me the sleeping bag and pillows."

She did, then parted the branches and joined him.

Their secret spot had lost none of its magic. Seeing moonlight shimmering off the water's glassy surface through a veil of leafy willow tree branches elicited a wistful sigh from Aubrey.

"Nice, huh?" Gage asked.

"*Very* nice."

The temperature inside the shelter was several degrees cooler than outside and felt good on her bare arms as they arranged their small camp to their liking.

Sitting beside her on the sleeping bag, Gage opened the ice chest and rummaged around inside. He removed two long-stemmed wineglasses and a bottle of Chardonnay, pouring them each a generous portion. Before taking a sip, Gage lifted his glass to Aubrey's cheek and rubbed the rim along her jawline.

"Here's to you," he murmured.

The sensation of smooth, chilled glass against her skin sent silken ribbons of pleasure spiraling through her.

They clinked glasses, shared a lingering stare ripe with promise, then sipped the tart, heady wine. While Aubrey lit three stubby candles and set them on a broad, flat rock, Gage served the food, which was nothing like Aubrey expected.

"Pâté and toast triangles?"

"You don't like pâté?" Gage's expression was crestfallen.

"No, I love it." She couldn't stop the laugh bubbling up from her throat. "I just didn't think you did."

He relaxed and resumed removing sealed plastic storage containers from the ice chest and spreading them out on the sleeping bag. "I've never tried it."

"What if you hate the taste?"

"There aren't many foods I can't choke down."

Having witnessed his ravenous hunger on multiple occasions, Aubrey couldn't agree more.

The next half hour flew by with Gage and Aubrey enjoying a veritable smorgasbord of delicacies—everything from miniature roasted potatoes to mango and kiwi salad to pickled herring.

"Now, this I like." Gage took another bite of baklava and chewed contentedly.

"It's Greek," Aubrey said, licking remnants of the sinfully rich pastry from her fingers.

"Let me do that."

He snatched her hand in midair and, before she could stop him, began nibbling.

"Quit it." She giggled and squirmed and then went utterly limp when his tongue probed her sensitive fingertips.

"Don't ever let anyone tell you that fingers aren't an erogenous zone," he murmured between licks.

Above the swaying treetops, a zillion and one stars twinkled in a blue-black velvet sky. Aubrey laid her head on Gage's lap, taking in the magnificent view. "Did you know the human body has something like a hundred erogenous zones?"

"You don't say?"

"It's true."

"I not only believe you, I'm willing to test each and every one of them." He lowered his head to her ear and gently tugged on the lobe with his teeth.

Her heart gave a small—make that a large—pitter-patter. "You're impossible."

His lips were sticky with honey from the baklava and incredibly delicious. They were also remarkably proficient in shutting her up when molded firmly to her own lips.

Drunk on desire more than wine, she curled an arm around his neck. Pulling him closer, she took control of the kiss despite her lower position. Her advantage didn't last long. Gage slipped out from under her and in a swift move Casanova would admire, pinned her beneath him on the sleeping bag.

What remained of their picnic dinner was instantly forgotten.

He nuzzled the fine hair at her temple. "Tell me. Is this one of your hundred erogenous zones?"

"Mmm. Maybe."

"And this?" He nudged her head back and pressed his mouth to the side of her throat where her pulse beat.

"How'd you guess?"

His hand breached the hem of her T-shirt and snuck up her rib cage.

"What about—"

"Enough talk." She silenced him with a provocative kiss calculated to tease and entice.

Gage evidently agreed. Finding far more interesting things to do with his mouth than converse, he said nothing more for several incredibly sensual minutes while he removed her clothes. Wherever his hands touched her body, his mouth followed. She watched unabashedly as he drew a nipple into his mouth, licking and suckling the taut tip. She continued watching, even when he moved lower. Small sounds of delight escaped when his tongue dipped into her belly button.

"When's it my turn?" she asked after yet another breathless shudder.

"Not yet."

Gage parted her thighs, cupped her bottom and lifted her hips. Aubrey waited in torturous, glorious anticipation. He took too damn long, tracing moist circles with his tongue on the insides of her thighs rather than concentrating on the areas that would do the most good. When his mouth finally found her center, she nearly cried out. Within minutes, he had her in a state of near frenzy. She might have teetered on the edge a bit longer but his tongue probed deeper, found her most responsive erogenous zone yet, and sent her flying skyward to float among the zillion and one stars.

Upon her return to Earth, she found Gage hovering over her. "That was a pretty neat trick," she said.

"You liked it?" His smile smacked of sheepishness.

"Mmm." She wriggled beneath him and reached for the zipper of his jeans. "Can I try?"

"Fair's fair, I suppose."

Once he lay naked beside her, she took his full and heavy arousal into her hands and then into her mouth. If the ragged groans emanating from his chest were any indication, she then took him on one incredible ride.

"Come here." He tugged on her arm, pulling her on top of him.

"I wasn't finished," she complained, though not seriously.

"Trust me, you're hardly finished."

He pulled a condom from what appeared to be thin air. She discovered one or two more of his erogenous zones while he covered himself, distracting him as much as possible. When he finished, she straddled his hips and guided him inside her.

"This is better," she crooned, rocking back and forth in a seductive rhythm.

"Not quite."

"No?"

He framed her face with his hands and gathered her to him. When their lips were within kissing distance, Aubrey unfurled her legs and stretched out.

"Now, this is what I had in mind." Gage wrapped his arms around her and anchored her to him.

Every inch of her body from breast to toe melded to every inch of his, leaving only enough space remaining for a few molecules of air.

He moved slowly, withdrawing from her and then plunging back inside, quickly bringing Aubrey to the verge of another shattering climax. She'd never felt so close to Gage. So joined in every way. Physically, emotionally, and spiritually.

"Eyes," he said, his voice ragged, "are an erogenous zone, too."

"How so?" she managed in a strained whisper. He was so hard, so very deep inside her. Aubrey gasped and bucked slightly.

"Watching yours while I make you climax is a giant turn-on for me."

His words reached her through a sensual haze as she gave herself over to an array of exquisite sensations.

"Open your eyes, sweetheart. Look at me."

She did and knew exactly what he'd been talking about. His dark eyes, staring hotly into hers, were incredibly arousing. Aubrey quit fighting and promptly lost it. Again.

Gage followed by a few seconds. Her limbs like liquid, she rolled off him, utterly exhausted and, at the same time, deliriously content. Hands clasped, they stared at the leafy ceiling of their shelter, rewarding themselves with a well-earned rest.

She couldn't help but recall their last visit to this place. Gage had lain beside her as he did now and asked her to marry him. Aubrey certainly didn't expect history to repeat itself, yet she suffered a tiny pang of disappointment when the moment passed without him proposing.

Loathe to separate, they snuggled and chatted about nothing in particular. Eventually, the moon sank beneath the far-off mountain peaks and the temperature dropped several degrees, turning the pleasantly cool air to downright chilly. Two of the candles had burned out, leaving hard wax puddles on the rock. By the light of the remaining candle they dressed and packed the ice chest. Content to stroll arm in arm, they said little on the return walk to Gage's truck.

Halfway home, Gage broke the silence.

"I got some good news earlier today."

"You did?" She smiled in expectation. "What?"

"I've been promoted to crew leader."

"That's wonderful! Why didn't you say something when you were opening the wine? We could have made a toast."

"Stay in Blue Ridge." Gage found her hand on the truck seat and brought it to his lap. "Live with me. Don't go back to Tucson."

"Wow." Aubrey hadn't seen that coming. Then again,

wasn't she hoping for a similar declaration not forty-five minutes earlier?

"Damn." He grimaced. "That didn't come out right. But I'm not sorry I asked."

"We talked about this already." She chose her words carefully. The last thing she wanted was to end their truly lovely evening with an argument.

"There's no rule saying we can't talk about it again." He didn't look at her. The single-lane, tree-lined road was pitch-black and required his total concentration. "We deserve more time together, a chance to see where our relationship is going."

"I need to return to my job. I explained all that to you and thought you understood."

"You'd only have to give up your job until Hannah graduates." A hairpin turn loomed ahead. Gage swung the truck hard to the right. Ghostly limbs of overgrown pine trees slapped the passenger door causing Aubrey to flinch. "After that, I'd move to Tucson," Gage said when they exited the turn.

"You'd move?"

"Actually, I talked to Mom about it this afternoon. We were thinking Kenny Junior might be willing to work on the ranch in exchange for room and board."

"Really?"

It surprised Aubrey to learn that Gage would willingly leave his family and home so they could be together. Surprised *and* pleased.

"Your dad's gout will probably worsen over time, not

improve. You sure you'd feel comfortable leaving, even after Hannah graduates?"

"She can handle the ranch, no problem. And besides, Dad listens to her more than he does Mom and me. If Kenny Junior's there, so much the better."

"What about my father?" Aubrey asked.

"What about him?"

"You and he aren't exactly buddies."

"We get along fine."

"You've seen him once in the last ten years. At my grandfather's funeral. And you spoke to each other only when necessary."

"So he and I aren't the best of pals. It's you I'd be living with, not him."

And wouldn't her father be tickled pink about that arrangement? She decided to lay that obstacle to rest and tackle another.

"If I were to stay in Blue Ridge and move in with you, and that's a big if, where would we live?"

"On the ranch."

"Not in the motor home. Please."

"God, no." He laughed. "We'd fix up the old bunkhouse. Later on, after we left for Tucson, Kenny Junior could move in if he was so inclined."

The notion of residing on the Raintree ranch did appeal to Aubrey. She'd loved that aspect of her and Gage's brief marriage. Still, it wasn't that simple. Country life was and had always been a summer vacation for her. A temporary break from the mad rush of the city. Could she survive peace and quiet on a long-term basis?

"What about income? Your family can't afford to feed and clothe another person, not one who isn't earning their keep. And let's face it, I'm no cowhand."

"I bet the town would hire you on at the clinic, part-time at least. The folks here are crazy about you. Just look at how many patients swarm the place on the days you work."

"I do enjoy working at the clinic." And on the plus side, she'd be nearby should her grandmother require anything. "But I miss my job. You and I are a lot alike when it comes to work, you know. We're both adrenaline junkies. You get your fix from fighting fires, I get mine from the E.R."

"Maybe there's something else you can do to take the place of the E.R."

"Like what?"

"Go back to college."

"College?"

"Why not?"

"I didn't realize Pineville College had a master's program for nursing."

Gage paid her sarcasm no mind. "They probably don't. Of course, you *could* change your studies to ranching."

"Ah…right."

Houses came into view as they reached the outskirts of town. Cutter's Market had four parked cars out front, evidence they were doing a booming late-night business by Blue Ridge standards.

"I'm only trying to explore some possibilities," he snapped.

"Which is good." Aubrey leaned over and kissed Gage's cheek. He was trying to compromise, and she was resisting his every suggestion. The reason, she hated to admit, had more to do with her and less to do with them.

"The thing is, I still have my freezing-up problem to contend with. If I don't return to the E.R., I'll never know for sure if I've conquered my fears." And it would be too easy after a year-and-a-half absence to stay away indefinitely.

"You don't think you'll have an opportunity to test yourself at the clinic?"

Aubrey recalled the day of her grandfather's first heart attack when she'd sat with her grandmother in the clinic. "I might."

"I hate to sound like a broken record, but become a medic with the Hotshots. I know the Sierra Nevada captain's been after you to do just that."

She rolled her eyes. "Your father would have a fit."

"What you do is none of his business."

"It's his business if I'm living on his ranch," she reiterated with a determined head shake. "I won't be the cause of more discord between the two of you."

They pulled into her grandmother's driveway, and Gage parked the truck near the front porch. There were more lights on in the house than Aubrey would have anticipated given the lateness of the hour, but she didn't pay much heed. Her mind was too preoccupied with Gage and their conversation.

He met her at the passenger door and enveloped her in a warm embrace. "Think about staying. That's all I ask."

Leaning down, he brushed her cheek with his. The slight scratch of his five o'clock shadow reminded her of the many intimate pieces she'd felt that scratch during their recent lovemaking.

"We have a little time," he said. "You're not leaving for another two days." His voice was low and coaxing, the hand stroking her back soothing.

"Okay," she murmured.

"I'm serious, Aubrey. The situation's not perfect. But it's not permanent, either. Open yourself up to the possibilities before you say no. Surely there's a solution we can both agree on."

"I will think about it. I swear."

Like him, she wasn't ready to end their relationship. Truthfully, the only thing holding her back from accepting his proposition to move in with him was her reluctance to quit her job. That, more than the logistics of her staying, was what she needed to contemplate over the next two days.

"Will I see you tomorrow?" she asked.

"I'll call you sometime around lunch when I get a break."

At the front door, Gage drew her close. His tongue traced the outline of her lips before delving deep inside her mouth and sampling every corner. She stood on her toes, linked her arms around his neck and moaned with contentment. All these years, she still hadn't grown tired of his kisses.

Dim voices floated to her from inside the house. Her grandmother must have fallen asleep in front of the TV.

Gage gave her yet another lingering goodbye kiss. At the rate they were going, he'd never make it back in his truck.

All at once, the porch light came on and the front door opened. A tall, dark figure appeared behind the screen door.

"Aubrey? Is that you?"

She and Gage sprung apart. Momentarily disoriented, Aubrey didn't recognize the man at first. Then she did and her heart, already beating fast from kissing Gage, skipped erratically.

"Dad!"

"Don't act so shocked to see me."

"Well…I…" How could she not act shocked when he was the last person she'd expected to see tonight?

"Hello, Gage. Nice to see you again."

"Good evening, Dr. Stuart."

"How's your family?"

"Fine, thanks."

Neither man's demeanor held any discernable warmth, which did nothing to calm Aubrey's jangled nerves.

"What are you doing here, Dad?" Instantly self-conscious, she smoothed her hair. She vaguely pondered why she hadn't noticed her parents' Lexus and figured they must have parked it behind her SUV.

"Your mother and I came up to check on your grand-mother."

"Oh. Okay."

He opened the screen door and gestured her and Gage inside. "And to drive with you back to Tucson."

Chapter 13

"I've missed you."

Aubrey went through the front door and into her father's arms. "I've missed you, too."

Gage followed her inside, ignoring the laserlike glare searing into the back of his head.

Dr. Alexander Stuart hadn't exactly rejoiced when he learned about Aubrey's and Gage's elopement ten years ago. He'd wanted her to finish medical school before settling down. And while Gage never truly believed he'd intentionally sabotaged his and Aubrey's fledgling marriage—not consciously, anyway—he was relatively sure Dr. Stuart had breathed a very big sigh of relief when the divorce came through.

"Darling. You're back. Mother told us you went on a picnic. How nice." Carol May Stuart floated up from the couch with the grace and elegance of a swan taking flight.

Watching her, Gage found it hard to believe they shared the same humble beginnings. Not that he disliked his former mother-in-law. Far from it. While Carol May hadn't exactly welcomed him into the family fold, she hadn't opposed his and Aubrey's marriage, either.

"Hi, Mom." Aubrey met her mother in the center of the living room, and the two hugged fondly.

"Small-town living must suit you," Carol May gushed. "You look wonderful. Doesn't she look wonderful, Alex?" Holding Aubrey's hand, she stepped back and beamed.

"She does indeed." Dr. Stuart's glance darted from Aubrey to Gage, and he shifted uncomfortably. Finding his ex-son-in-law on the front porch with his tongue halfway down his daughter's throat was probably just as awkward for him as it was for Gage.

Carol May tugged Aubrey toward the couch, where they both sat. "I can't believe how well Mother is doing." She cast a fond glance at Rose, who sat across from them in her favorite recliner.

"Aubrey's to be commended," Rose said. "She's a top-notch nurse."

Dr. Stuart moved to stand at the end of the couch beside Aubrey. A sentinel guarding the treasure, thought Gage. She'd told him her father hadn't wanted her to leave her job for six weeks and come to Blue Ridge. Was he afraid Gage might try and talk her into staying?

Well, hadn't he done exactly that? So, maybe Dr. Stuart did have a legit reason to worry.

"I can't take all the credit. Grandma is an easy patient."

"That's not what you told me last week," Rose complained with good-natured humor. "Or the week before."

Aubrey's posture relaxed for the first time since the porch light came on unexpectedly during her and Gage's kiss. "Well, there were days…"

"Gage, it's wonderful to see you again." Carol May aimed her radiant smile at him. "I hear you've become a wilderness firefighter."

"Yes, ma'am."

"He was promoted to crew leader today," Aubrey chimed in.

"Congratulations." Carol May appeared impressed.

Her husband less so. "That's a very dangerous occupation," Dr. Stuart said. "How does your mother feel about it?"

"She's pretty supportive, really." Gage studied the dynamics of the room and chose to stand by the side table near the entry, specifically because it put him opposite Dr. Stuart.

"And your father? Is he pretty supportive, too?"

"He's coming around." Gage would rip his fingernails out one by one with a pair of rusty pliers before discussing his family situation with Dr. Stuart.

"Hannah's attending Pineville College." Aubrey perched on the edge of her couch cushion. "She's taking over management of the ranch when she graduates."

Her efforts to diffuse the tension in the room were wasted. The invisible daggers shooting from one man to the other would fell anyone accidentally crossing the line of fire.

"Good for Hannah," Carol May said.

Small talk continued for the next twenty minutes, though Carol May, Aubrey and Rose dominated the conversation. When he wasn't being asked a question, Gage studied the Stuarts, Aubrey and her father in particular.

She loved him, that much was undeniable. And respected him. She also craved his approval, though if asked, she might deny it. But Gage knew Aubrey about as well as anyone did, and he'd witnessed her relationship with her father firsthand over the years. The once insecure little girl had grown into a woman who wanted to pick her own path, regardless of how her father felt or what, in his opinion, was best for her.

The trouble was, Dr. Stuart hadn't quite learned to let go.

Then again, Gage asked himself, was his relationship with his own father any different?

Not much.

When he and Aubrey eloped ten years ago, they should have stayed in Las Vegas and away from their dads. Maybe they'd still be married.

"Dolores Garcia announced she's retiring in two months," Dr. Stuart said abruptly.

"She is?" Aubrey swivelled on her cushion to stare up at her father with undisguised excitement.

"Really, Alex?" Carol May arched her delicately penciled eyebrows. "You didn't mention that on the ride up here."

"Who's Dolores Garcia?" Rose asked.

That's what Gage wanted to know, and why Aubrey seemed so fired up about her retirement.

"She's the nursing supervisor in the E.R." Dr. Stuart answered Rose, but it was Aubrey he looked at. "Been at Tucson General for twenty-something years."

"She's my boss," Aubrey clarified. She swung back around to face the room, though her attention was clearly elsewhere.

"I see." Gage's attention was also wandering, and he didn't like the direction it had taken.

"You need to put in your application right away." Dr. Stuart squeezed Aubrey's shoulder. "Your first day back at work. It's this Tuesday, right?"

Gage's head shot up. He waited for Aubrey to tell her father she was contemplating staying in Blue Ridge.

"Dad, I'm not qualified to be nursing supervisor. They won't give me the job."

She'd avoided the question, supporting Gage's bad feeling that more was happening than met the eye.

"No," Dr. Stuart concurred. "As head nurses, Clair Rittenbacher or Karen Karpinski will probably be recruited to replace her. But you *are* qualified for either of their positions," he added.

All at once the puzzle pieces clicked into place. Dr. Stuart hadn't made the trip to Blue Ridge solely to check on Rose. He had a second agenda, which was to facilitate Aubrey's return to her job so she could take that next important step up the career ladder.

Not altogether different from the night he'd shown up at the motor home, suggesting she return to school and switch her major to nursing, and he'd then provided her with the means to do it.

Gage's anger mounted. Aubrey talked by phone regularly with her family. Had Dr. Stuart noticed a recent change in his daughter's attitude? Or had he gotten wind from Carol May's conversations with Rose?

She fidgeted beneath Gage's scrutiny, unable or unwilling to offer a comment. And while it wasn't his place to speak for her, he was just mad enough at her father to overstep his boundaries.

"As it turns out," Gage said, "Aubrey might not be returning to Tucson. She's considering moving in with me."

"What!"

If Gage had been hoping to throw his former father-in-law for a loop, his plan was a rousing success.

"Is this true?" Dr. Stuart came around the corner of the couch to face Aubrey.

Seeking to restore the balance of power, Gage advanced several steps toward Aubrey.

"Why, that's wonderful," Rose exclaimed, the only person in the room besides Gage tickled at Aubrey's potential change of residence.

Aubrey certainly wasn't tickled. The frown she shot Gage shouted in no uncertain terms that she didn't appreciate his interference. Three seconds later he understood why.

"What the hell is wrong with you?" her father demanded.

"Dad—"

"You can't be seriously thinking of abandoning a promising career to live in this backwater town with him."

"Now, wait a minute, Alex." Carol May stiffened. "I was raised in this same backwater town."

"And fled the day you turned eighteen. Wisely, I might add." He ignored Rose's softly uttered protest.

Carol May didn't. "Was that necessary?"

"Whether I stay here or return to Tucson is my decision to make." Aubrey stood, her movements deliberate. "And I'll ask you to leave me to it."

Gage smiled. The Aubrey he'd known ten years ago didn't have the gumption to stand up to her father. Proud of her courage and maturity, he silently cheered her on.

Dr. Stuart, however, wasn't someone who relented easily and proceeded to make his case. "Head nurse would put you in a nice position for future promotions. Who knows when another opportunity like this one will come along?"

"You're right." Aubrey settled back on her heels. "Which is why I'll be returning to Tucson in two days. Not because it's what you want," she added, cutting off her father when he would have said more.

The smile on Gage's lips died. "What do you mean,

returning to Tucson? Not thirty minutes ago you agreed to think seriously about staying in Blue Ridge."

"And I will." Conviction and determination were decidedly lacking in her voice.

Hope for a future with Aubrey seeped slowly out of Gage. He'd been a fool to believe he could counter Dr. Stuart's powers of persuasion. "It sounds to me like you've already decided."

She hesitated too long before answering. "Not...entirely."

Who was she kidding?

Who was *he* kidding? Aubrey might have toyed with the idea of moving in with him, but she was never serious about it. Not like him.

"I'm glad to see you're being sensible." Dr. Stuart visibly relaxed.

And why not? He'd won. Again.

Yet it was Aubrey and not her father Gage directed his anger at. She'd strung him along these past weeks, and, like an eager-to-please puppy, he'd obliged her. Fresh resentment mingled with a decade-old sense of betrayal.

"Have you ever seen a commitment through to the end?" he bit out. "Just once?"

She drew herself up in mild shock. "Excuse me?"

"You quit school when you were a freshman because you couldn't cope with the pressure and came running here. We get married and after six short weeks, you hightailed it back home the second Daddy came around and crooked his little finger."

"That's not true." Fists planted firmly on her hips, she stared at him with incredulity.

"How else would you describe it?"

"We were miserable."

"We were newlyweds. Adjusting to the change. And we weren't miserable every second." He could tell from the slight widening of her eyes she'd caught his meaning. "Then, two months ago, we have what amounts to the same scenario. Only instead of college, it's your job you can't handle. So, just like before, you leave Tucson and head here. Surprise, surprise, Daddy shows up, and he convinces you it's in your best interest to go back with him. Tell me I'm wrong."

"Can't handle your job? What's he talking about, Aubrey?" Carol May demanded. Clearly she hadn't been included in the loop regarding Aubrey's career crisis.

"My grandmother needed me," Aubrey said, addressing Gage, not her mother.

"Your grandmother needed a nurse. Not necessarily you." Somewhere in the back of his mind Gage realized he should shut up, but once started, he couldn't— or wouldn't—stop. His pain ran too deep, he hurt too much. "Face it, Aubrey, you grabbed the first available excuse to bail on another commitment. Just like you're doing tonight."

"You're…wrong."

"Is having a relationship with me really that scary?"

"Of course not."

"Why don't I believe you?"

She pushed an unruly lock of hair back from her face

with unnecessary impatience. "You know how important my career is to me and how few job options there are for nurses in Blue Ridge."

"You couldn't wait eighteen months? I said I'd move to Tucson when Hannah graduated."

"The emergency department at Tucson General isn't all that big," Dr. Stuart interjected. "There may not be another head nurse position open for years. If you care about her, you won't hold her back."

"He's pressuring you into leaving, Aubrey," Gage said. "Can't you see it?"

"He's not the only one," she snapped. "*You're* pressuring me into staying."

"Like I pressured you into marriage? Like your father pressured you to go back to school and is doing essentially the same thing now with your job? Can't you ever make up your own mind about anything?"

"I…" Her face crumbled, proof his accusations stung.

Gage sighed. He'd made his point, but the victory was hollow. "All I asked you for was two days. Two days to consider the possibilities. You didn't last an hour."

Carol May rose from the couch. "Why don't we retire to the kitchen and give Aubrey and Gage some privacy." Over her shoulder she said, "Alex?"

He didn't budge.

"Don't bother." Gage whirled around and headed for the front door. Privacy wasn't going to help resolve the problems between him and Aubrey. At this point, nothing would.

She followed him to the door. "Gage. Wait…"

He stopped and stared down at her. "Give me one reason to."

She was so pretty. And vulnerable. He could see she hated the fact they were arguing, and it tore him up inside. Yet as mad as he was, if she gave even the tiniest indication she'd stay, he'd sweep her in his arms, kiss her soundly and forget their fight ever happened.

She wasn't about to do any such thing. He could see that, too.

"You're being stubborn." She sniffed, blinked back tears.

"Yeah, I am. You know why? Because I want all of you. Not just the part your dad isn't controlling."

"What about your dad? He controls you."

"He sure as hell tries to. But the difference between you and me is I recognize it, admit it, and am doing my dead level best to fight it." He pushed open the screen door and hit the porch.

"My dad is right about some things," she called after him.

Gage stopped at the bottom step but didn't turn around.

"Becoming a nurse was a good career choice me," she said to his back. "And we weren't ready for marriage."

He rubbed his neck, which was stiff and sore. "Doesn't appear like we're any more ready now."

She opened the screen door and stepped out onto the porch. "I'm sorry."

Before he could respond, his radio went off. He listened to the dispatch, then reached for his cell phone.

"Gage?"

"I have to go," he said and jogged to his truck.

For the first time since running into Aubrey two months ago at the convenience store in Pineville, he was glad to be called to a fire.

On impulse, Aubrey pulled the twin bed she'd been sleeping in the past two months away from the wall. With one hand on the windowsill, she bent and peered into the narrow space she'd created between the wall and the wooden headboard. What she saw brought a smile to her lips and bittersweet sadness to her heart.

There, lined up in a not quite straight row, were fourteen *X*s carved into the back of the headboard. One for each summer she and Annie had stayed with their grandparents. It had been a tradition for the girls to carve a new *X* on the matching twin headboards their last day there before starting the drive home.

Since the marks weren't rubbed out or painted over, Grandma Rose must not have found them. That, or she treasured them with the same sentimentality as Aubrey.

She was tempted to carve another *X*, one for this summer, then chided herself for her silliness. She wasn't a kid anymore. And Annie wasn't with her to make a game of the ritual.

Besides, marking the headboard would be admitting she was really and truly leaving Blue Ridge…and Gage.

Aubrey and her parents were scheduled to depart in less than an hour, and she still wasn't fully convinced she was doing the right thing.

Everyone she ran into yesterday asked her why she

was leaving and wished her good luck in a singsong voice suggesting she'd need it where she was going.

Did they know something she didn't?

"Aubrey?" Grandma Rose tapped lightly on the door.

"Yeah. Just a minute." Aubrey climbed awkwardly to her feet. Butting her legs against the footboard, she pushed the small bed back into place and winced guiltily at the loud scraping noise. "Hey," she said, flinging the door open. "What's up?"

"Everything all right?" Grandma Rose studied Aubrey's face.

"Fine."

"You look flushed."

"Oh." Aubrey dismissed her grandmother with what she hoped passed for a nonchalant laugh and gestured her into the bedroom. "I was crawling around behind the bed looking for any forgotten items."

And she'd found some. Fourteen *X*s.

"Is this a bad time?" Grandma Rose asked.

"No, not at all." Aubrey smiled. She'd been smiling a lot the last day or so, and it had yet to feel natural.

Grandma Rose perched on the edge of the bed. "I have something for you."

"What's that?" Aubrey sat down beside her.

Souvenirs were another farewell tradition. Grandma Rose would present Aubrey and her sister with a token gift their last morning in Blue Ridge. It was never much. Just a little memento to remind them of the summer.

"Here." Grandma Rose reached into the pocket of

her floral smock and withdrew a small object. "I've been waiting for the right moment to give this to you."

The gift was hardly token and not what Aubrey expected. Her grandmother placed it in her hands, prompting a protest.

"I can't accept this."

"Why not?"

"It's too special." Emotion caused her throat to close.

Housed inside the antique sterling-silver frame was a black-and-white photograph of Grandma Rose and Grandpa Glen taken more than fifty years earlier on their honeymoon in San Francisco. Arms linked and dressed smartly in the fashion of the day, they stood on a grassy knoll. Behind them, stretching endlessly, was a magnificent view of Golden Gate Bridge. And yet, they had eyes only for each other.

The photograph had occupied a corner of her Grandma Rose's dresser since shortly after it was taken, and Aubrey knew her grandmother cherished the keepsake.

"Which is why I want you to have it," Grandma Rose insisted. "I'm getting older and there's too much stuff in this house for me to take care of. With my bum hip, I need to lighten my housework."

Aubrey couldn't imagine how much extra housework one little framed photograph could cause. She mentally placed her and Gage in the picture, calculating how old they would be if their marriage had lasted fifty years. But then, they didn't have a photograph from their honeymoon, mostly because they'd never gone on one. Not a real honeymoon, leastwise. Unless an overnight stay in a cheap Las Vegas hotel counted.

It seemed to Aubrey that the cosmos was forever conspiring against them. Each time they came close to making a life together, something intervened.

Something? Or *someone?*

"Grandma," she said, "do you think I let Dad control me?"

"Well…" Her grandmother pursed her lips thoughtfully. "I'm not sure I'd put it that way."

Half annoyed and half intrigued, Aubrey asked, "What way would you put it?"

"You're very bright and talented. Always have been. People like you are expected to do well. Be incredibly successful. Problem is, parents of bright and talented children can do them a disservice. They see the potential, are proud of it and push their offspring too hard."

"Like Dad?"

"He can be a force to be reckoned with when he wants to."

"Which is most of the time." Aubrey thought back on her relationship with her father, attempting to look at it from a different angle. "You think I'm afraid of failing?"

"And of letting your father down."

"Sounds like classic first-born syndrome to me."

"It does."

Aubrey had intended to be funny but her grandmother obviously took her seriously, which sobered Aubrey.

"Oh, I'm not saying you haven't ever rebelled,"

Grandma Rose continued. "You did that just recently by coming here when he wanted to hire someone."

"But I haven't exactly cut the apron strings, either," Aubrey said glumly.

She traced a finger back and forth across the photograph of her grandparents, thinking more of her love for Gage than her somewhat dysfunctional relationship with her father.

The pink-and-turquoise Barbie phone on the small desk started ringing. Grandma Rose creaked to a standing position and went to answer it. When Aubrey first arrived two months ago, she'd been surprised and amused that the once adored possession still functioned.

"Hello. Oh, hi, Eleanor." Grandma Rose nodded at Aubrey. "She's still here. Do you want to talk to—" Deep creases formed in her grandmother's brow. "What's that?"

Several seconds passed during which her grandmother's concern visibly increased. Aubrey set the photograph on the nightstand and went to stand near her.

"Thank you for calling, Eleanor. I appreciate it." Grandma Rose hung up the phone and turned to Aubrey. "The fire changed direction during the night. It's fifteen miles east of Blue Ridge and heading this way."

"What!" Aubrey struggled to digest the unexpected news. "It was thirty miles away and headed in the opposite direction when we went to bed last night."

"Apparently the wind changed course around midnight."

"Oh, my God."

Shock set in as Aubrey realized the seriousness of the situation. She ran to the window behind her bed and pushed aside the curtain. Smoke filled the distant sky, hanging low over the hilltops and shining an eerie incandescent silver in the early morning light. Fear seizing her, she stumbled away from the bed.

"I have to go tell Mom and Dad. No way are we leaving now. Did Eleanor recommend you evacuate?"

"Not yet. She said she'd keep everyone advised of the fire's status."

"Still, I think we should prepare for the possibility. Fifteen miles isn't that far."

How was Gage doing, she wondered, and what was he feeling having to fight a fire so close to his hometown? Something her grandmother said about the direction of the fire suddenly penetrated her brain and triggered a rush of alarm.

"The Raintree ranch is east of Blue Ridge. At the rate the fire's traveling, it could reach there in a matter of hours!"

"Dear heaven."

"I think I'll call Susan. Ask if she needs any help."

Before Aubrey could pick up the phone, it rang again. Grandma Rose answered it.

"Hello. Yes, just a moment." She passed the phone to Aubrey, her eyes solemn. "It's someone named Larry Newcombe. Says he's a commander with the wilderness firefighters."

A dozen questions raced through Aubrey's mind in the three seconds it took her to place the phone to her ear, most of them centering on Gage and whether or not he was safe and unharmed.

"This is Aubrey Stuart," she said in a tight voice.

Commander Newcombe didn't waste time with a greeting. "I hope you don't mind me contacting you at home, Ms. Stuart. We were in contact with the local authorities and they gave us your name and number." He cleared his throat. "We need your help."

"My help? How?"

"We're short medics and injuries have been heavier than usual. The BLM and Forest Service are flying some more in, but they won't arrive until this afternoon."

"I see."

"Is there any chance you can come?"

Weeks of resistance to the idea of volunteering with the Hotshots vanished in a flash. "Of course, I'll be there as quickly as I can."

"Thank you, ma'am. We sure appreciate it."

She gave the commander her cell phone number, then opened the desk drawer and removed a pad of paper and pen. "I'll need directions."

"Fire camp is on Verde Road, about four miles south of where it junctions with the highway. Look for the markers. Once you arrive in camp, we'll transport you to the front line."

Front line? The term sounded scarily like warfare to Aubrey. "How close will I be to the fire?"

"A mile or two."

Aubrey swallowed.

"I take it you've been recruited," Grandma Rose said when Aubrey disconnected with the commander.

"Appears so." Folding the paper with the directions and stuffing it in her pocket, Aubrey filled her grandmother in on the details as best she knew them.

"How long will you be away?"

"I don't know." Aubrey shrugged. "As long as they need me, I suppose."

"You be careful."

"You, too. And call Susan for me if you don't mind." Together they left the bedroom and went in search of her parents. "The folks will evacuate you if it comes to that. And speaking of the folks…"

Aubrey sighed. She didn't figure her parents would be happy with the news or the least bit understanding. Her father especially.

To her utter and complete astonishment, she was wrong.

"Naturally, you must go," her mother said when Aubrey finished explaining to her parents about Commander Newcombe's phone call. "I'll contact the hospital for you, explain your delay."

Aubrey's mother been doing laundry most of the morning, catching it up for Grandma Rose before they left. Clean clothing and linens were folded and stacked in neat piles on the kitchen table, filling every available space.

"Thanks, Mom." Aubrey gathered her purse and a few personal necessities she thought she might need. Spying the clean laundry, she decided a change of clothing was in order. And sturdier shoes. Turning in a half circle, she made a beeline back to her bedroom, where she'd left her packed suitcases.

A few minutes later, her father met her on the porch and walked her to her SUV. "You say the Hotshots are understaffed?"

"That's what I'm told." Aubrey opened the driver's side door and tossed her tote bag onto the passenger seat.

Admittedly, she'd been a little cool to her father since the other night, though she couldn't blame him entirely for what had happened. He might have been the catalyst for her and Gage's argument but not the cause of it, in spite of what Gage claimed.

She had only herself to blame for that fiasco.

"Wait a minute, Aubrey," he said when she would have escaped into the SUV.

Expecting a lecture, she cut him short. Her father was *not* going to talk her out of helping the Hotshots. "Dad, I need to leave. Now." In the short time it had taken her to get ready to leave, the columns of smoke had doubled in size.

"Do you..." Her father hesitated, something he rarely did. "Do you think the Hotshots could use a doctor, as well as a nurse?"

"What?" She was tempted to glance at the sky and see if it had fallen. Surely she'd heard wrong.

"If they're short of medical help, they could probably—"

"Are you serious?"

"Well...yes. I've already spoken to your mother.

She'll drive your grandmother to a motel in Pineville if the authorities recommend evacuating Blue Ridge."

Stupefied, Aubrey stared. Her father, the great Alexander Stuart, heart surgeon *extraordinaire,* had just offered to help treat firefighters under conditions that were bound to be harsh and with equipment that, compared to the ultramodern operating room he was accustomed to, could only be called primitive.

"Wow." She blinked and when he didn't disappear, she smiled.

"Is that a yes?"

"An unequivocal yes!" Leaping into his arms, she hugged him fiercely. "Thank you, Daddy." Abruptly, she pushed away from him and frowned. "Do you still remember basic triage?"

"Get in the car," he said gruffly, giving her a playful shove. "And quit picking on your old man." He went around to the passenger door. "I'll have you know I could outsuture you with one hand tied behind my back."

"Just checking." Laughing, she started the engine and passed him the paper with the scribbled directions. "Here. You be navigator."

Their camaraderie lasted for several miles. Aubrey had never worked with her father before and discovered she eagerly anticipated the opportunity. Or was it practicing emergency nursing again after a too-long absence that had her blood pumping and her nerves tingling? Except for when she and Gage were making love, she hadn't felt this alive, this excited, since leaving Tucson. In hindsight, she'd been wrong not to accept Captain

Greenough's invitation and become a volunteer medic when he first asked her.

Could this be the happy medium she and Gage were searching for the other night?

The question and its possibly significant answer were instantly forgotten as Aubrey and her father rounded a bend and reached a large clearing.

The entire mountainside glowed a fiery orange. Smoke rose from the tops of the flames in giant, fluffy white columns that seemed to tower as high as the clouds themselves. In the wake of the flames lay acres upon acres of scorched landscape.

Aubrey hit the brakes and parked the SUV. For several moments, she and her father stared in stunned silence.

"Good Lord," she said, her voice scratchy from having been temporarily silent.

Her father grunted and cleared his throat. "If there really is a hell on Earth, I do believe we're looking at it."

His sentiment matched her feelings exactly. She pressed the accelerator and resumed driving, thinking not of herself and her father, but of the perils Gage and all the Hotshots faced while fighting this unholy monster.

Chapter 14

"Ready?"

"Almost." In response to her father's cue, Aubrey lowered herself to the ground in front of the injured firefighter.

The man, a burly ten-year veteran who looked strong enough to bench-press a tree trunk, lay in one of two cots set up in the medical tent. He'd been brought in about an hour earlier with a dislocated pinky. The affected finger stuck out from his hand at a ninety-degree angle and probably hurt like the dickens—or had hurt until the Novocain her father administered took effect a few minutes ago.

"You hanging in there?" Aubrey asked. Draping an arm over the upper half of his body, she leaned close.

"I think so." The man grinned and the dirt caking his

face cracked in several places. "Could be worse. You're a lot prettier than the last medic who patched me up."

He smelled of smoke and sweat, though it was hardly noticeable over the acrid odor of burning wilderness. The smoke was inescapable, even at a distance of two miles from the fire. It permeated the air, causing Aubrey's eyes to sting and her lungs to burn.

Blinking back tears, she unbuttoned the man's yellow fire-retardant shirt in order to ease his breathing. Earlier she'd removed his hard hat, setting it on the ground next to his equipment pack.

"Should I bite down on a stick or something?" the man asked.

Aubrey returned his grin. "Only if you want to."

"You think I'm kidding, don't you?" His laugh deteriorated into a hacking cough.

Since their arrival sometime around nine, she and her father had worked nonstop. When Aubrey last checked her watch, it was almost four. Lunch, consisting of a protein drink, was gulped down between two bee-sting victims and a severe case of friction blisters.

Some of the firefighters, like the one suffering dehydration, had received rudimentary first aid from a medic on the line before being transported to their medical tent, a short fifteen-minute drive from the blaze. The more seriously afflicted firefighters, and Aubrey understood from snatches of various conversations she overheard there'd been a few, were flown directly to the hospital in Pineville or, if need be, as far as Phoenix.

The noise was relentless. People shouting, trucks roaring, the wind whistling and aircraft buzzing.

She'd witnessed the helicopters, zipping back and forth like giant insects, pouring water on the fire, air-lifting firefighters to and from the fire, and transporting cargo. Planes—tankers she'd been told—also flew overhead, dropping brightly colored fire retardant from compartments in their bellies and missing the helicopters by mere inches.

The fire had started three days ago, the result of a lightning strike. While it had claimed nearly a thousand acres of land, lives and property were thus far spared. Talk among the firefighters was that could change—and possibly soon would—if the Smokejumpers, Hotshots, Helitack and Engine crews weren't able to stop the blaze from heading into Blue Ridge. The Hotshots and other ground crews were on a race against the clock, attempting to cut a line around the perimeter of the fire that, God willing, would hold and save the town.

Wind, the same one that had caused the fire to change course during the night, presented the greatest danger. It had picked up speed, with gusts reaching forty-five miles per hour. Sparks and flying debris were starting new fires so fast, the firefighters weren't able keep pace. Aubrey didn't understand all the terms and jargon being bantered about, but she picked up enough to ascertain the people in charge were worried.

That worry was contagious.

Every second Aubrey's mind wasn't focused on a patient, she was thinking of Gage and praying for his well-being. She would have liked to check in with her mother, but her cell phone didn't work, not that she'd found a spare second to place a call.

Her father rose to a half-standing position, braced their patient's hand in his lap and, using his weight, popped the pinky back into its socket.

"Is it over?" The man looked questioningly at Aubrey, who'd positioned herself to block his view of the procedure. Sweat beaded his upper lip, more likely the result of nervousness than pain.

"Not quite." She patted his shoulder and stood. "But the hard part's over. You just take it easy while I get you some ibuprofen."

No sooner did she turn than the wind blew so hard, the nylon tent rattled and shook, the entry flaps snapping like flags mounted to a parade vehicle. The gust didn't let up and continued to pummel the tent with blasts of hot, stale air.

Icy chills danced up Aubrey's spine. An overwhelming sense of dread accompanied the chill, and Aubrey shivered.

Gage!

She couldn't explain how she knew, but something was wrong. Terribly, frighteningly, wrong. Her feet cemented to the ground, she went from shivering to shaking. The background noise grew in volume, becoming unbearable. She covered her ears, remembering the night her Uncle Jesse and Aunt Maureen were brought into the E.R.

"Aubrey, sweetheart. Are you okay?" Her father came up behind her.

"Dad…" She let him hold her, but it didn't quell her shaking.

"Hey," the injured man called from the cot. "What's going on?"

At that moment, the tent flaps were shoved aside and a grim-faced firefighter entered. "Wanted to give you folks a heads-up. We just received an alert from command post. There's a dry cold front moving in. Could mean trouble of the big variety. Prepare for incoming, just in case." As quickly as he arrived, he left.

"Incoming?" Aubrey asked. "Like in injuries and casualties?"

"Yeah," her father answered, as serious as the firefighter had been. "We'd better hop to it."

Aubrey's last thoughts before sprinting into action were of Gage and how she wished their last words hadn't been angry ones.

"This isn't the place I would've picked to make a stand." Gage straightened, ignored the arrows of pain shooting up both sides of his back, and stabbed the axe end of his Pulaski into the ground.

"Yeah, well, sometimes we don't get to pick." Marty reattached his radio to the front of his jacket. "The fire does it for us."

The Hotshots had been hard at it, cutting a fire line since sunup. On the hill opposite them, across a narrow ravine, flames devoured everything in their path, impervious to the war being waged against them. Starved for water after a dry summer, the brittle vegetation supplied the perfect fuel.

Low-flying tankers dropped retardant, covering the untouched landscape with a blanket of red chemical powder. While bulldozers toppled trees and brush, lumberjacks wielded chainsaws, providing a solid second line of defense. Ground crews, Gage's among them, provided the first—a backfire they'd set hours earlier in the hopes of halting the fire by forcing a convection column.

If their cumulative efforts failed, the results could prove to be the most disastrous wild land fire in the state's history.

Command post had just called, warning them of the approaching cold front and accompanying high winds. Of all the news they could have received, it was without a doubt the worst. Gage's bones, already weary well past the point of exhaustion, tingled with a sense of foreboding.

For ten straight hours, he and his crew had been pounding the ground, with only periodic ten-minute breaks—and that was just today. Yesterday, they were at it for fourteen straight hours. The day before was a blur, beginning around 11:00 p.m. when he left Aubrey standing on the porch of her grandmother's house and ending some twenty-four hours later when he and his crew lay down to sleep in the dirt of the fire line they'd just dug.

Six hours later, they were up and at it again, cutting trees, scraping earth and burning safety zones. Somewhere or other, there'd been a second short snooze, Gage couldn't remember when.

The fire had started out small. Didn't they all? And until this morning they'd foolishly believed it would be quickly contained.

They were wrong.

By midmorning, what had been a gentle breeze progressed into a strong wind. That was when all hell started to break loose. The cold front, however, would make the wind look like a sneeze in comparison.

The firefighters, over a hundred in all counting three Hotshots squads, Smokejumpers, one Navajo crew and one inmate crew, had been ordered to take a stand. A different location, one less susceptible, would have been preferred. Time and the weather denied them the luxury of choosing.

They either stopped the fire at this steep, rocky slope or the flames would roar right over them, pushed by the relentless wind. The first privately owned land the fire would reach belonged to Gage's family. The town of Blue Ridge lay eight miles beyond that.

He hoped to hell his father and Hannah had moved the herds to the west pasture. The cows would move themselves when confronted with a fire and likely scatter. They could get stuck in a gully or run into a fence. Either situation spelled the end to both their lives and the Raintree finances.

Had Aubrey left for Tucson yet? Gage wondered. Was it even today she was supposed to leave? He'd lost track of the date, measuring the passage of time by the Hotshots' progress, not hours or minutes.

God, he was tired

"Call the crew together." Marty's order shattered Gage's momentary lapse of concentration.

The Blue Ridge Hotshots took a short reprieve from their labors to discuss strategy and determine the fastest escape route to their safety zone. Should there be a blowup, a very real possibility with the wind acting like the inside of a blender on high speed, Gage wanted every one of them to make it out in one piece.

Their weariness forgotten, the crew returned to work with renewed gusto. Arms resembling the pistons of a finely tuned machine, axes, shovels, and Pulaskis hit the ground in rapid fire succession. Foot by foot, they cut a line, trying their damnedest to reach the Navajo crew on the lower end of the slope and close the gap before the fire crossed the ravine.

Sweat dripped from every pore, soaking their grime-encrusted clothing. What were, in reality, forty-pound equipment packs felt as if they weighed a hundred and forty. Smoke, thick and foul, breeched their protective equipment, seeping into their lungs. Breathing became sheer agony.

Still, the Hotshots kept digging. Nothing would stop them, not when the enemy continued to advance.

So much was at risk—so much depended on them—and the Hotshots took the responsibility personally. Gage more than the others. This wasn't just any town, any people. Blue Ridge was his home, the lives in jeopardy those of his friends and family.

All at once, the Navajo crew members were practically beside them. Positioned at the end of the Blue Ridge line, Gage signaled with a raised hand. The Navajo crew member nearest to him pointed. Gage looked up, and his superheated blood instantly froze.

The fire had vaulted across the narrow ravine, propelled by the strong, oxygen-rich wind. Before his eyes, the fire caught and grew to an amazing size. Like a giant emerging from the entrance to hell, it funneled up the hill toward them. In its wake lay a wide path of burning trees and brush.

Gage hollered a warning to his crew, who simultaneously raised their heads. Until that moment, they'd had their noses to the grindstone, focused exclusively on digging the line. Several of the men shielded their faces with their forearms and stepped back. One crossed himself.

Suddenly, the fire exploded into a tower of flames a hundred feet tall. Bits of fiery debris rained down, igniting small fires every place they landed. If the Hotshots didn't get the hell out of there, they'd be dead.

"Run!" Gage shouted. He didn't have to give the order twice.

Breaking formation, his crew dropped their tools and scrambled up the slope toward the safety zone on top. The Navajo crew had the same idea and were one step ahead of the Blue Ridge Hotshots.

Gage knew he should follow. There was nothing in

his training or his past experiences that didn't scream at him to run for his life. But ten feet of ground remained open. It could be insignificant—it could also be the gate through which the fire passed.

Remote as that possibility was, he couldn't take the chance.

His Pulaski slammed into the ground again and again until his chest ached and his arms trembled. He didn't realize for some seconds he had company. Marty worked beside him.

"You're an idiot," Gage screamed at him.

"Takes one to know one."

Another minute flew by. They closed the gap to five feet. Two. Then it happened. An invisible wave of heat blasted them, throwing them backward. Gage glanced up and stared into a mammoth wall of fire—what some called the mouth of the dragon.

"Shit!"

His knees buckled, his insides clenched. He wasn't ashamed to admit he'd been scared plenty during his career as a firefighter. All those times rolled into one didn't match the terror gripping him now.

Twisting sideways, he shoved Marty. Hard. "Move!"

They sprinted up the slope, the fire chasing them. Flames blistered their backsides, licked their clothing. Whether they dropped their equipment packs or the fire burned through the straps, Gage wasn't sure. The lack of extra weight proved a blessing.

"Go, go, go!"

Fingers clawing at any available handhold, feet grappling for traction, they half ran, half crawled. And still, the fire kept coming. Fast. So fast. Through watery eyes, Gage saw the top of the slope where his crew waited. He and Marty were almost there. Incredibly, they'd gained a few yards on the fire.

Then, without warning, the earth beneath them collapsed. Marty stumbled and bowled into Gage, knocking his legs out from under him. Gage pitched forward and landed on his face. He began to slide. Whatever air his lungs held whooshed out. Dirt filled his mouth. His vision blurred. Dimmed. Pain seized his limbs, immobilizing them.

He lay there, unable to do more than breathe the dragon's poisonous fumes, absorb its searing heat.

Aubrey's face appeared before him, first in a younger incarnation, then as she looked today.

Gage grunted. He wasn't ready to die, not by a long shot. But unlike the movies, the revelation didn't miraculously empower him with the strength to rise and stagger that last little bit to safety.

It did, however, fill him with the determination to hang on, something someone was yelling at him to do if his cotton-plugged ears were hearing right.

Yeah, hang on. If only to see Aubrey again and apologize for their stupid fight. Afterward, he'd drop to his knees and tell her he loved her. Tell her he didn't give a rat's ass about her father or his father or his job or anything else getting between them and a lifetime of happiness together. He'd move with her to Tucson. Hell, he'd move with her to the dark side of the moon if that's where she wanted to live.

For twenty-four years, since the day he met her in Sunday school, she'd been the only one for him. The love of his life. A ten-year separation hadn't lessened his feelings for her. Nothing would. Certainly not this fire.

A hand clamped around his right wrist and pulled. Another hand grabbed his left wrist. Still another hand grabbed him by his shirt collar. Gage was dragged over dirt and rocks and small sticks poking up from the ground. He thought his stomach and the side of his face might be permanently scraped off, though he didn't complain. Had he been able to speak, he would have thanked his buddies for coming to his rescue.

God willing, they had Marty, too. He figured they did. Any firefighter worth their salt would cut off their arm before leaving one of their crew behind.

Gage tried to move but someone placed a restraining hand on him.

"Christ, Raintree. You and Paxton scared the crap out of us."

The voice belonged to Freddy Gomez, a rookie Gage thought showed real promise. If the kid returned next summer after surviving this fire, they'd know for sure he was crazy like the rest of them.

"Get 'em some water," someone hollered.

In the next instant, a canteen was placed to Gage's mouth. He tried to drink. Most of the water spilled down his chin and neck and into his shirt, which, considering how hot he was, didn't feel half bad. Hands fumbled with the buttons of his shirt and breathing became a little easier. Fingers pushed a tablet into his mouth and the taste of salt exploded on his tongue. His headgear was removed, and a cold pack was placed on his forehead. Gage wanted to whimper with gratitude.

"Let's go."

Go where? Gage vaguely wondered. Thinking coherently had become a real nuisance, so he stop trying.

There was a rush of movement and he was suddenly suspended in midair. For an instant he panicked until he realized his men were carrying him. He tried to open his eyes but they were sealed shut. Swollen, he hoped, not burned. Had he lost his goggles? He couldn't recall. His ears appeared to function well enough, though what was being said sounded garbled.

"Radio in for a helicopter."

"Screw the copter. Not enough time. There's an engine on top. Let's load 'em in that. Road 128 is clear."

"Where's the closest medic station?"

"I'll find out."

Gage relaxed. Marty was alive, too, or the guys wouldn't be in such a rush to transport the two of them to help.

His peace of mind didn't last. Constant jostling took a toll on him in the form of nausea and a throbbing headache. He fought the urge to vomit by biting down on the insides of his cheeks. When he felt himself being loaded into the back of the engine, the nausea eased but not the dizziness. The engine roared to life and in the next minute, he was riding the world's fastest merry-go-round with no pole on which to cling.

Someone laid a damp cloth over his face to block the sun. Gage sighed and let go, drifting into a state halfway between consciousness and unconsciousness. His last lucid thought was of the line they'd dug and whether or not it would hold.

Chapter 15

Onlookers stared as the bright yellow Forest Service engine barreled down the gravel road, kicking up a mini-whirlwind of dust and pebbles. Aubrey clamped her teeth together and grimaced when the driver took the last curve at a speed far exceeding what any sane person would deem safe.

"Here they come," her father said. Picking up one of the lightweight stretchers, he began walking.

Aubrey grabbed the second stretcher and hurried after him. They knew only that two injured firefighters were being brought in, victims of a blowup.

Injured, she reminded herself. *Not dead. Not yet.*

And not if she could help it.

Keep it together, Aubrey. Don't freeze.

Since receiving the radio alert advising them of the

injured firefighters, she'd been battling anxiety, acutely aware of her father's presence. Embarrassment at freezing up was a minor concern. Failing a patient was an altogether different matter.

She was an E.R. nurse, good at what she did. Better than good. At least that much was true until the night her Uncle Jesse and Aunt Maureen died. The past two months had been a cakewalk for Aubrey. Working in the clinic, helping at the community center, hadn't exactly put her competency in a crisis to the test.

Not like today.

Her nerves stretched tighter with each step she took as visions of charred flesh filled her mind. She willed the grisly images away.

Should the firefighters be suffering from third degree burns, they'd need every ounce of her skill. This was not the time to fall to pieces.

You can do it, Aubrey.

Amid a cacophony of grinding gears and squealing brakes, the engine skidded to a stop beside two other vehicles. Men piled out from inside the cab, scrambled down from on top and leapt off from the sides where they'd been hanging.

"Medic!" one of them shouted.

Aubrey and her father broke into awkward trots, hampered by the portable stretchers.

Two men remained on top while the rest gathered at the back of the engine. They were sweaty and filthy, barely discernable as human. One of the guys on the ground turned sideways, then another.

Aubrey's steps faltered. So did her heart.

"You all right?" Her father spared her a quick glance over his shoulder.

"Fine."

But she wasn't fine. She recognized the name printed on the men's helmets. Her eyes went straight to their face. She recognized them, too. In the three weeks she and Gage dated, she'd met most of the Blue Ridge Hotshots.

More familiar faces appeared as equipment and protective clothing were discarded.

Where was Gage?

Trotting faster, Aubrey scanned the group, her concern escalating to fear as she studied and dismissed each firefighter in turn.

No Gage.

Where the hell was he?

Don't jump to conclusions, she cautioned herself and promptly refused to heed her own advice.

Her father reached the engine ahead of her. A firefighter offered to take the stretcher from her and she let him, reminding herself that the injured men would have been flown to the nearest hospital if their condition was critical.

Relax. Keep moving.

Why wasn't Gage with his crew?

The firefighters crowded in around Aubrey and her father. Voices merged, and she had trouble deciphering them. An icy sensation formed in her middle and radiated outward, pooling in her fingers and toes. Her movements slowed, became sluggish, hampered by her lead-weighted limbs.

It was the night her Uncle Jesse and Aunt Maureen died all over again.

Not now. Please!

"Give us some room," her father shouted.

He was instantly obeyed, and a hole opened. Four firefighters stood ready with the stretchers.

"Stand by." Her father climbed on the back of the engine and motioned with his hand. "Lower them down."

Aubrey held her breath and stared as the first casualty was gingerly placed on a waiting stretcher and strapped in.

Marty! She recognized him immediately. And he was all right! Talking, in fact.

Fists balled at her sides and feet rooted to the ground, she watched them load the second man onto the remaining stretcher. A cloth covered his face, preventing her from identifying him. Her father hopped off the engine and bent over the man, removing the cloth.

The entire right side of his face was scraped and bleeding. So were his hands, she noticed. Sweat had matted his hair to his head, and his eyes were swollen shut. Beneath numerous layers of dirt, his exposed skin shone bright red.

He didn't move, not even when one of the firefighters accidentally bumped the stretcher. Not even when her father spoke into his ear.

Aubrey, however, did move. Like lightning.

"Let me through!"

Plowing into the small crowd, she pushed and shoved her way to his side.

"Is he alive?"

Dear Lord, she never dreamed there'd be a day when she'd have to ask that question about Gage.

"Yeah, he's alive," a young man Aubrey thought was called Freddy answered. He carried the front end of Gage's stretcher. "Just got the shit banged out of him. Marty, too."

She could see that for herself.

Picking up one of Gage's battered hands, she clasped it in hers. His flesh was warm. Gloriously, wonderfully warm.

Then again, maybe too warm. He must be burning up inside.

Her father offered a more detailed medical assessment than Freddy's as they walked the stretchers toward the tent. Aubrey let her gaze wander over Gage, mentally concurring.

"What happened?"

She suppressed a shudder as the tale of the unexpected blowup was recounted along with Gage and Marty's valiant efforts to close the line. They were damn lucky to get out of there, damn lucky to have a crew willing to risk their lives to rescue them.

"Put them on the cots," her father ordered once they entered the tent. "And easy does it. Aubrey, I'll get the IVs started. You prep the patients."

Hydrating Gage and Marty and lowering their body temperatures were the number-one priorities. Lacking a pole, Aubrey's father handed the IV bags to the two closest firefighters, one being Freddy.

"Keep these well above their heads at all times."

Using a pair of scissors, Aubrey cut off Marty's shirt and then Gage's, leaving them both bare to the waist.

Given the events immediately preceding the blowup, they were probably suffering from smoke inhalation and heat exhaustion. Possibly heatstroke. Their exact prognosis wouldn't be fully determined until she and her father had finished conducting thorough examinations.

Marty was awake and alert, correctly answering the questions put to him. She wished Gage would rouse. He'd mumbled incoherently when she hooked him up to the portable oxygen supply, but not since. She thought she heard him mutter her name, then admonished herself for grasping at straws.

"What medical steps were taken in the field?" her father asked, inserting IV needles into the backs of each man's hand.

Freddy told them.

Slamming two Insta-Cold packs on top of a cooler to activate them, Aubrey laid one on Gage's forehead and the other on Marty's, who kept refusing to lie still.

She passed him some water and instructed, "Sips only. I mean it." Using a sports bottle with a spout, she dribbled water into Gage's mouth.

He licked his lips and croaked a raspy, "Thank you."

Though she knew he was hardly out of the woods, her hopes nonetheless flared.

While her father saw to Marty, Aubrey took Gage's

temperature, which was elevated, and tended to his many abrasions. Later, when he was more responsive, she'd check his eyes and flush them with saline solution if necessary. For now, she gently sponged them with cool water.

He talked in broken sentences, mostly about the fire. He made more sense than earlier but far from perfect sense. Bit by bit his body temperature decreased, and bit by bit his mind cleared.

When she was done, she sponged his chest with a washcloth and mild cleanser. Beginning at his neck, she made small circles, frequently rewetting the washcloth in a basin of water and squeezing on a fresh dab of cleanser.

Aubrey didn't hurry. She knew every inch of Gage's torso—having explored it on numerous occasions with her hands and mouth—and treated it to a thorough bathing. His arms and hands received the same careful attention.

Medicine wasn't the only method of treating the sick and injured. A loving touch also healed. With each stroke and caress, she willed Gage to recover, her fingertips communicating more effectively than any spoken word.

Lost in her task and oblivious of her surroundings, she leaned down and dropped a kiss on his chest, right over the place where his heart beat, strong and steady.

When she lifted her head and looked at his face, she nearly came unglued.

Through puffy eyelids, he watched her, his gaze focused and the corners of his mouth curling in a crooked grin. "You're here," he said in a gravelly whisper. "I thought I was dreaming."

She gave a small gasp.

His grin drooped. "Do I look that bad?"

"You look awful," she wailed and wrapped her arms around his neck, pressing her cheek to his.

Hissing, he flinched.

Aubrey immediately drew back, realizing she'd mistakenly irritated his abraded cheek. "Oh, gosh. I di—"

"S'all right. His grin returned, still crooked and impossibly sexy. "My mouth doesn't hurt."

"Good." She kissed him soundly, careful to cup only the left side of his face.

He reeked of smoke, sweat and gasoline, but he tasted like heaven on Earth and felt like forever and ever.

His arm came up and encircled her waist. Held her. Cherished her. When they separated, Aubrey was crying.

"Do you have any stomach cramps?" she blubbered.

"No." He chuckled. "Is that why you're crying?"

She shook her head and sniffed. "I'm crying because I said some terrible things to you the other night, and I'm sorry. So, so sorry."

"Shh, baby." He lifted his hand and rubbed his knuckle along her jawline. "Don't apologize."

"I was wrong."

"We were both wrong. And both right." He stared at her with undisguised hope. "Since you're still hanging around, maybe we can talk later."

"We're going to do a lot more than talk."

"Oh, yeah?" His tone was low and suggestive. "Like what?"

She guessed he was thinking of his old motor home and how they might go there and "talk" like the day he'd burned his hand. Little did he know she had something far different in store for them.

When precisely she'd made up her mind, Aubrey wasn't sure. It might have been when she saw Gage being lowered from the engine, or when he carried her sick grandmother into the house. For all she knew, it was the day they ran into each other at the convenience store, and this moment had been coming for the last six weeks. Pinpointing the exact second her life changed was irrelevant. Aubrey loved Gage and couldn't—*wouldn't*—leave him. Ever.

She sat up straight, steeled her resolve and blurted, "Like get married."

"Are you proposing?" He shot up, or tried to shoot up, and got only as far as leveraging an elbow on the cot before Aubrey placed a restraining hand on him.

"Yeah, I am." Brushing aside the last of her tears, she busied herself by checking his IV, intensely cognizant of everyone else in the tent watching them. "Any headache? Dizziness?"

"No and no. Aubrey, I—"

"Nausea?"

"Damn it, Aubrey!"

Freddy, who was still standing at the head of Gage's cot holding the IV bag, didn't bother to hide his amusement. Aubrey ignored him, along with the three other people sharing the tent who were also enjoying the show.

"Stop fussing for one lousy minute, will you?" Gage snapped.

She did stop fussing, and their gazes connected. So, it seemed to Aubrey, did their souls.

"You sure you want to marry me?" he asked. "Really sure? No running back to Tucson this time. Once you're wearing that ring, you're stuck with me for good." As if to emphasize his point, he found her hand and folded it inside his.

"I'm sure." She could hear the absolute certainty in her voice, and it pleased her. Bending down to kiss him again, she discovered yet another manner in which touch healed.

"I love you," she murmured against his lips. "I have since I was four years old. And for the record, I don't want to date long distance, and I don't want to just live together."

"Me, either."

"Not so fast." She placed a finger on his lips when he would have sealed their engagement with another kiss. "I expect the whole nine yards this time."

"Meaning?"

"Diamond ring, long white dress and a romantic honeymoon in some fabulous, far-off locale." She sighed, remembering the photograph of her grandparents. "San Francisco."

Gage angled his head and said to Freddy, "Is it just me, or is she being bossy again?"

"Take my advice, *amigo*. Agree with whatever she says. You'll stay married a lot longer this time." When his buddies broke into raucous laughter, Freddy made a face. "What? Am I wrong?"

"Men." Aubrey harrumphed and took Gage's temperature, glad to see it was nearly normal.

Suddenly serious, Gage asked, "What about your job? And the promotion?"

"I'm considering a career change."

"Since when? And to what?"

"Since I started working with my dad." She turned toward her father and beamed. "I'm going back to school to become a physician's assistant."

"That's great," Gage said.

"Yeah, it is great."

Her father winked at her, and Aubrey sensed the many pieces of her life coming together.

Leaving Marty's side, her father came over to stand beside her. He stroked her hair, the gesture a familiar one that harkened back to when she was a little girl. "I'd ask how our patient's faring, but it appears to me like you have everything under control." He extended his hand to Gage. "I guess congratulations are in order."

Gage didn't hesitate and returned the handshake.

"You're a fine man, Gage. What you did today took courage. Your family will be very proud of you."

"Thank you, sir."

Her father nodded before releasing Gage's hand. "Don't you think it's time you called me Alex, considering you're about to become my son-in-law? Again."

"Past time, Alex."

Kissing the top of Aubrey's head, he commented, "Your mother will be overjoyed. She's been planning your and Annie's weddings for years."

Aubrey rolled her eyes, imagining the commotion her mother would soon be generating. "I'd forgotten about that."

Every head turned when the tent flaps opened, and a tall, authoritative man squeezed into the tent.

The firefighters holding the IVs snapped to attention. Gage attempted to rise.

Before Aubrey could restrain him, the man said, "Relax, Raintree." He approached the cot, his hand extended. "Ms. Stuart?"

"Yes?" She stood and accepted his handshake.

"I'm Commander Newcombe. Thank you for coming."

"Happy to, sir. And this is my father, Dr. Alexander Stuart. He came with me."

"I heard we had a famous heart surgeon on board." Commander Newcombe went over to the other cot and shook Aubrey's father's hand. "We're honored and grateful for your help, as well. How are our patients?" His glance traveled from Marty to Gage.

"They're going to be fine," Aubrey answered.

"I'll be back on the line as soon as I can stand." Digging his heels into the cot, Gage tried to rise. He didn't get far.

"You're not going anywhere for the next twenty-four

hours, except to the infirmary at Fire Camp," Aubrey interjected.

"You listen to the young lady," the commander warned. "She knows what she's talking about."

"Hey, I've been telling him the same thing," Freddy chimed in.

Gage grumbled. "The fire will spread to our ranch if it's not stopped."

"One of the tankers radioed in a few minutes ago," the commander said. "The backfire your men set and the line you dug is holding."

Gage didn't look convinced, but neither did he defy doctor's orders, rip out his IV and make a run for it.

"You're to be commended, Captain," the commander told Marty. "You and your crew leader." He turned to Gage. "You have a real future ahead of you, Raintree. Have you ever considered making firefighting a full-time career?"

"I have. Often."

"Excellent. We can always use good instructors and administrators. Come see me when you're ready."

"Yes, sir."

"Oh, I almost forgot. I have a message from your family. We've been in contact with them because of the fire's proximity to your ranch."

"A message?"

"Your mother sends her love and says not to worry about them. Take care of yourself."

Gage smiled, and Aubrey thought it was just like Susan to put her son's safety ahead of her own.

"And your father wishes you well."

"My father?"

"Yes." The commander quirked one eyebrow. "I believe his exact words were 'good luck'."

"Well, I'll be damned." Gage shook his head.

Aubrey reached down and put a hand on his shoulder. She didn't want to read too much into the two words, but maybe—hopefully—Joseph Raintree was beginning to come around.

She walked the commander to the tent flap. "Do you suppose the fire will be contained soon?"

"Hard to say. But my guess is the worst is behind us."

Aubrey pulled the tent flap aside and peered out. Flames could be seen sprouting from the tops of distant trees, and smoke climbed in billowy columns to the sky.

"May I inquire how long you're going be in Blue Ridge?"

She grinned broadly. "A while."

Another year and a half, at least. Once she and Hannah both finished school, then Aubrey and Gage would move to Pineville. Or not. She could always run the clinic.

"Can we count on your help during the next fire?" Commander Newcombe asked.

"You can." Wherever she and Gage lived, she'd continue working part-time as a wilderness medic for the Forest Service.

He saluted her, then ducked and went outside. Aubrey returned to tend to her patients. Happiness filled her at the sight of Gage and her father, the two men she cared most about in the world, talking amiably and no longer at odds.

The whine of a distant siren sounded. Faint at first, it increased in volume.

"Gentlemen," Aubrey's father announced, "your limo has arrived."

Aubrey grabbed one of the portable stretchers.

"No!" Gage's objection halted her in midstep. "I may have been carried in here but I'm walking out."

"You're too sick and weak." Her protest had no effect on Gage, especially since Marty, with the help of her father, was already standing.

"Fine." She huffed. "Then let me help you."

Gage relented with a shrug. "If it involves your arms around me, then okay."

She and Freddy managed to hoist Gage to his feet but it was a struggle. They shuffled across the tent with Freddy on one side of Gage, holding the IV, and Aubrey on the other, holding the portable oxygen tank.

"Do I get to come to your wedding?" Freddy asked.

"Sure." Gage grunted. "You can even be one of my groomsmen."

"All right!"

Maneuvering the tent opening required considerable effort. Gage was out of breath and sweating profusely when they finally emerged on the other side where the EMTs waited.

"Ride with me?" Gage asked Aubrey.

"I…should…probably stay. In case there are more

injured." She wanted desperately to accompany him in the ambulance but duty called.

"Go," her father said. "I'll hold down the fort and drive your car home later."

"Really?"

"Yes, really. And don't forget to call your mother."

She blew him a kiss before crawling into the back of the ambulance after the EMTs had loaded Gage. The last thing she saw through the rear window of the ambulance as it pulled away was her father clapping Freddy on the back.

Then, looking down at Gage, she saw the rest of her life stretched out before her.

"You know where I want to go when this is over?" he mumbled as the EMTs took his and Marty's vitals.

"The motor home?"

"There, too." He had trouble keeping his eyes open. "I was thinking of the creek. We can celebrate."

Aubrey smoothed a damp lock of hair from his face. After ten years, she had everything she wanted—could have *always* had, only she'd been too stubborn and too afraid to realize what really mattered in life. Not where she lived or what job she held, but being with Gage.

"I'd like that," she murmured and pressed a kiss to his forehead.

After all, they had a lot to celebrate, and their secret spot was the ideal place.

* * * * *

REQUEST YOUR FREE BOOKS!

2 FREE NOVELS
FROM THE ROMANCE COLLECTION
PLUS 2 FREE GIFTS!

YES! Please send me 2 FREE novels from the Romance Collection and my 2 FREE gifts (gifts are worth about $10). After receiving them, if I don't wish to receive any more books, I can return the shipping statement marked "cancel." If I don't cancel, I will receive 4 brand-new novels every month and be billed just $5.99 per book in the U.S. or $6.49 per book in Canada. That's a savings of at least 25% off the cover price. It's quite a bargain! Shipping and handling is just 50¢ per book in the U.S. and 75¢ per book in Canada.* I understand that accepting the 2 free books and gifts places me under no obligation to buy anything. I can always return a shipment and cancel at any time. Even if I never buy another book, the two free books and gifts are mine to keep forever.

194/394 MDN FVU7

Name _____ (PLEASE PRINT) _____

Address _____ Apt. # _____

City _____ State/Prov. _____ Zip/Postal Code _____

Signature (if under 18, a parent or guardian must sign) _____

Mail to the Harlequin® Reader Service:
IN U.S.A.: P.O. Box 1867, Buffalo, NY 14240-1867
IN CANADA: P.O. Box 609, Fort Erie, Ontario L2A 5X3

Want to try two free books from another line?
Call 1-800-873-8635 or visit www.ReaderService.com.

* Terms and prices subject to change without notice. Prices do not include applicable taxes. Sales tax applicable in N.Y. Canadian residents will be charged applicable taxes. Offer not valid in Quebec. This offer is limited to one order per household. Not valid for current subscribers to the Romance Collection or the Romance/Suspense Collection. All orders subject to credit approval. Credit or debit balances in a customer's account(s) may be offset by any other outstanding balance owed by or to the customer. Please allow 4 to 6 weeks for delivery. Offer available while quantities last.

Your Privacy—The Harlequin® Reader Service is committed to protecting your privacy. Our Privacy Policy is available online at www.ReaderService.com or upon request from the Harlequin Reader Service.

We make a portion of our mailing list available to reputable third parties that offer products we believe may interest you. If you prefer that we not exchange your name with third parties, or if you wish to clarify or modify your communication preferences, please visit us at www.ReaderService.com/consumerschoice or write to us at Harlequin Reader Service Preference Service, P.O. Box 9062, Buffalo, NY 14269. Include your complete name and address.

We hope you enjoyed reading

JUST KATE by #1 *New York Times*
bestselling author LINDA LAEL MILLER and
HIS ONLY WIFE
by acclaimed author CATHY McDAVID!

Both were originally
Harlequin® series stories!

Discover more heartwarming contemporary tales
of everyday women finding love and becoming
part of a family or community from the Harlequin®
American Romance® series. Featuring small-
town settings and irresistible cowboys, Harlequin®
American Romance® stories are must reads.

HARLEQUIN®

American ★ Romance®

Romance the all-American way!

Look for four new romances every month
from Harlequin American Romance!

Available wherever books are sold.

Enjoy a sneak-peek excerpt from Cathy McDavid's upcoming Harlequin® American Romance® story, COWBOY FOR KEEPS.

Conner Durham has gone from flashy executive to simple cowboy seemingly overnight. At least Dallas Sorrenson has appeared back in his life—and she's apparently single!

* * *

The laughter, light and music, struck a too-familiar chord. His steps faltered, and then stopped altogether. It couldn't be her! He must be mistaken.

Conner's hands involuntarily clenched. Gavin wouldn't blindside him like this. He'd assured Conner weeks ago that Dallas Sorrenson had declined their request to work on the book about Prince due to a schedule conflict. Her wedding, Conner had assumed.

And, yet, there was no mistaking that laughter, which drifted again through the closed office door.

With an arm that suddenly weighed a hundred pounds, he grasped the knob, pushed the door open and entered the office.

Dallas turned immediately and greeted him with a huge smile. The kind of bright, sexy smile that had most men—Conner included—angling for the chance to get near her.

Except, she was married, or soon to be married. He couldn't remember the date.

And her husband, or husband-to-be, was Conner's former coworker and pal. The man whose life remained perfect, while Conner's took a nosedive.

"It's so good to see you again!" Dallas came toward him. He reached out his hand to shake hers. "Hey, Dallas."

With an easy grace, she ignored his hand and wound her arms loosely around his neck for a friendly hug. Against his better judgment, Conner folded her in his embrace and drew her close. She smelled like spring flowers and felt like every man's fantasy. Then again, she always had.

"How have you been?"

Rather than state the obvious, that he was still looking for a job and just managing to survive, he answered, "Fine. How 'bout yourself?"

"Great."

She looked as happy as she sounded. Married life obviously agreed with her. "And how is Richard?"

"Actually, I wouldn't know." An indefinable emotion flickered in her eyes. "As of two months ago, we're no longer engaged."

It took several seconds for her words to register, longer for their implication to sink in.

Dallas Sorrenson was not just single, she was available.

* * *

*Look for COWBOY FOR KEEPS by Cathy McDavid, available March 5, 2013 from Harlequin®
American Romance®!*

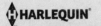